W9-CQN-355

RESOLUTE

THE LOST FLEET ◇ OUTLANDS

RESOLUTE

THE LOST FLEET ◆ OUTLANDS

JACK CAMPBELL

ACE

New York

ACE
Published by Berkley
An imprint of Penguin Random House LLC
penguinrandomhouse.com

Library of Congress Cataloging-in-Publication Data

Names: Campbell, Jack (Naval officer), author.
Title: Resolute / Jack Campbell.
Description: New York: Ace, [2022] | Series: The lost fleet: outlands
Identifiers: LCCN 2021046821 (print) | LCCN 2021046822 (ebook) |
ISBN 9780593198995 (hardcover) | ISBN 9780593199015 (ebook)
Subjects: LCGFT: Novels.
Classification: LCC PS3553.A4637 R47 2022 (print) |
LCC PS3553.A4637 (ebook) | DDC 813/.54—dc23
LC record available at https://lccn.loc.gov/2021046821
LC ebook record available at https://lccn.loc.gov/2021046822

Printed in the United States of America
1st Printing

Book design by Laura K. Corless

To Constance A. Warner, who walks her own road, always striving, always seeing the best in herself and others, always seeking not just knowledge but understanding.

For S., as always.

THE FIRST FLEET OF THE ALLIANCE

ADMIRAL JOHN GEARY, COMMANDING

FIRST BATTLESHIP DIVISION
Gallant
Indomitable
Glorious
Magnificent

SECOND BATTLESHIP DIVISION
Dreadnaught
Fearless
Dependable
Conqueror

THIRD BATTLESHIP DIVISION
Warspite
Vengeance
Resolution
Guardian

FOURTH BATTLESHIP DIVISION
Colossus
Encroach
Redoubtable
Spartan

FIFTH BATTLESHIP DIVISION
Relentless
Reprisal
Superb
Splendid

FIRST BATTLE CRUISER DIVISION
Inspire
Formidable
Dragon
Steadfast

SECOND BATTLE CRUISER DIVISION
Dauntless
Daring
Victorious
Intemperate

THIRD BATTLE CRUISER DIVISION
Illustrious
Incredible
Valiant

FIFTH ASSAULT TRANSPORT DIVISION
Tsunami
Typhoon
Mistral
Haboob

FIRST AUXILIARIES DIVISION
Titan
Tanuki
Kupua
Domovoi

SECOND AUXILIARIES DIVISION
Witch
Jinn
Alchemist
Cyclops

TWENTY-SIX HEAVY CRUISERS IN FIVE DIVISIONS
First Heavy Cruiser Division
Fourth Heavy Cruiser Division
Eighth Heavy Cruiser Division

Third Heavy Cruiser Division
Fifth Heavy Cruiser Division

FIFTY-ONE LIGHT CRUISERS IN TEN SQUADRONS
First Light Cruiser Squadron
Third Light Cruiser Squadron
Sixth Light Cruiser Squadron
Ninth Light Cruiser Squadron
Eleventh Light Cruiser Squadron

Second Light Cruiser Squadron
Fifth Light Cruiser Squadron
Eighth Light Cruiser Squadron
Tenth Light Cruiser Squadron
Fourteenth Light Cruiser Squadron

ONE HUNDRED FORTY-ONE DESTROYERS IN EIGHTEEN SQUADRONS
First Destroyer Squadron
Third Destroyer Squadron
Sixth Destroyer Squadron
Ninth Destroyer Squadron
Twelfth Destroyer Squadron
Sixteenth Destroyer Squadron
Twentieth Destroyer Squadron
Twenty-third Destroyer Squadron
Twenty-eighth Destroyer Squadron

Second Destroyer Squadron
Fourth Destroyer Squadron
Seventh Destroyer Squadron
Tenth Destroyer Squadron
Fourteenth Destroyer Squadron
Seventeenth Destroyer Squadron
Twenty-first Destroyer Squadron
Twenty-seventh Destroyer Squadron
Thirty-second Destroyer Squadron

FIRST FLEET MARINE FORCE
Major General Carabali, commanding

3,000 Marines on assault transports and divided into detachments on battle cruisers and battleships

ONE

THE blare of an urgent call alert shattered the quiet of "night" routine in the admiral's stateroom aboard the Alliance battle cruiser *Dauntless*. John "Black Jack" Geary, out of his bunk within seconds of the alarm beginning to sound, yanked on his uniform at the same time as his stateroom's display lit up. "Admiral, a ship has arrived at the jump point from Pele."

Usually, the arrival of a ship from another star wouldn't trigger an urgent alert. Especially when that ship had arrived at an area one light hour, or roughly one billion kilometers, from where *Dauntless* and the rest of the Alliance ships were orbiting. But the Alliance fleet was very far from home, orbiting the star named Midway on the very edge of human expansion into the galaxy. And Pele, where that ship had come from, was controlled by the mysterious enigma race that had launched repeated attacks on humanity.

"Just one ship?" Geary demanded. "It's an enigma?" The aliens had been known to send ships to Midway just long enough to take a look at things in the star system before jumping back to Pele.

"No, sir," the bridge watch stander replied. "It's human design. A heavy cruiser. It's not transmitting any identification. We just got a tentative ID from the fleet's sensors that it's the *Passguard*."

"The *Passguard*," Geary repeated, feeling an emptiness inside. The *Passguard* had been the flagship of an attempt by the Rift Federation to independently contact the alien Dancers who were (apparently) well-disposed toward humans. When last seen, the *Passguard* had been in the company of six other ships, two of them light cruisers and the other four destroyers. But getting to the Dancers required crossing through space controlled by the enigmas, and the enigmas had earned their name because of their fanatical attempts to hide all information about themselves from humanity. "Alone?"

"Yes, Admiral. No other ships have come out of jump. If that is *Passguard*, she's displaying serious external damage. We're not detecting any indications of active systems aboard her."

A dead ship? But dead ships didn't exit jump space. That required a working jump drive and either a human or a still-functioning navigation system to trigger it. "I'm on my way to the bridge," Geary said, moving quickly into the passageway outside his stateroom. The passageway was nearly empty at this time of the ship's night, only a couple of sailors some distance away who were running checks on equipment. They looked his way as Geary left his stateroom, their expressions too far off to see clearly, but probably worried about anything that brought the admiral rushing out of his stateroom.

They'd been in this orbit for over a week, waiting for proof that the project to entangle the hypernet gate at Midway with the Alliance hypernet had succeeded. A strangely monotonous week, given that they were so far from the Alliance and so close to the danger posed by the enigmas. Time on a warship was a strange thing, even when not considering the changes to the way time flowed when a ship accelerated to a tenth or two-tenths of the speed of light. The days could fly by in a blur of duties and watches to be stood and necessary things to be done. But those same days could drag, the duties and the watches and the necessary things pretty much the same from one day to the next. Even the hardest work could get boring when it didn't change, and that created another unchanging problem, because there were few things in the universe as dangerous as sailors or Marines who were bored and liable to come up with something that "seemed like a good idea at the time."

So Geary found himself both worried by this newly arrived ship, and relieved that something had happened to cause a break in the routine.

Getting to the bridge took only a minute, but he wasn't surprised to see that he hadn't beaten *Dauntless*'s commanding officer getting there.

Captain Tanya Desjani, in her ship's command seat next to his, was eyeing her display. "*Passguard*, if that is *Passguard*, hasn't maneuvered since leaving jump. Our sensors aren't picking up any indications of active systems operating aboard her." Desjani shook her head. "If that ship hadn't just left jump I'd assess it as completely dead, a derelict. But they must still have a working jump drive."

"Maybe it is dead," Geary said, "except for the jump drive."

"That's kind of hard to believe, Admiral, that the crew got wiped out and everything else got knocked out but the jump drive, and the jump drive's automated control also survived as well as emergency power for it." She shook her head again. "I think there are still people alive on that wreck, if *Passguard* managed to fight back to the jump point at Pele at the cost of the other ships with her. But it's also possible that *Passguard* was captured, and the enigmas rigged it to show up here as an apparent derelict to be used for a sneak attack."

Geary frowned. "If the wreck is rigged to explode, it could only take out whatever shuttle or ship came close to examine it. Maybe the enigmas sent it back as an object lesson? This is what happens to human ships that come to Pele?"

"Maybe," Desjani said. "There's only one way to get an answer, and if there are any humans still alive on that thing they probably need help as fast as possible."

Space offered few obstacles to a clear view of objects far more distant than *Passguard* was at the moment. Geary studied the external damage his fleet's sensors were evaluating on the heavy cruiser, wincing inside as he imagined the beating *Passguard* must have taken. He'd once been on the losing side of a fight with his own cruiser, the *Merlon*, the ugly memories of having his ship pounded until it was helpless flooding his mind.

He fought down the images of the past, knowing that Desjani was right, and if anyone remained alive aboard *Passguard* they were probably in desperate need of help.

But help would take a while to get to them. In human terms, space was almost unimaginably huge. One light hour, a billion kilometers, was nothing compared to a light year that equaled ten trillion kilometers. But to humans it was very far indeed. Even pouring on all the acceleration the latest warships could manage it would still take several hours to cover a light hour's distance and brake to match *Passguard*'s own vector. And that was on top of the hour that had already passed while the light from the heavy cruiser's arrival was traveling from the jump point to where *Dauntless* was orbiting. "If there are still crew aboard, it's amazing anyone survived the jump."

"They were luckier than the ships with them," Desjani said, not trying to hide her bitter feelings. "A lot of good sailors must've died proving how stupid it was for the Rift Federation to try to get to Dancer space all on their own."

He couldn't argue the point because he felt the same way. The small force the Rift Federation sent had been able to bluff its way across human space, but hadn't stood a chance against the enigmas.

He knew what he needed to do: detach some of his ships to intercept *Passguard* and either assist any survivors or destroy any enigma traps on the ship. Geary began to run through the necessary steps in his mind before suddenly halting himself.

For a long time he'd been in command of a fleet operating on its own, making his own decisions on what needed to be done and then doing it. He'd fallen out of the habit of requesting permission before acting.

Geary touched his communication controls. "*Boundless*, this is Admiral Geary. I need to talk to Ambassador Rycerz as quickly as possible."

"We need permission?" Captain Desjani grumbled in a low voice so the others on the bridge couldn't hear. "Isn't this an emergency?"

"It's not that kind of emergency," Geary said. "Ambassador Rycerz is the highest-ranking civilian authority representing the Alliance here, and that means I request permission before I act on this."

Desjani looked annoyed but didn't try to argue. She knew how he felt about the importance of deferring to civilian authority, and showing others that he did so. A century of war had badly frayed ties between the fleet and the government, ties that Geary was determined to repair. His recent experiences on the Alliance capital world, Unity, had only reinforced that resolve. A more rational person probably would've been discouraged or deterred by assassination attempts aimed at him, as well as the betrayal of Alliance laws and principles by parts of the Senate, but then again a more rational person would've given up long ago.

A virtual window popped up on Geary's display, showing Ambassador Rycerz in her office aboard *Boundless*. She'd obviously also been awakened recently. "Admiral. Is this about that ship from Pele?"

"Yes," Geary said. "Our sensors have identified it as the *Passguard*, the cruiser that was leading the Rift Federation force trying to reach Dancer space. It's very badly damaged. Request permission to coordinate with Midway's authorities to send some of my ships to rescue any survivors."

Rycerz's eyes searched his own. "You think someone might still be alive on that ship?"

"It's possible. If so, they might be on their last legs."

"Then we have to do whatever we can." The ambassador paused, thinking, her expression somber. "Do you think the enigmas destroyed the other Rift Federation ships?"

"Yes," Geary said, not trying to cushion the blow of his assessment.

"The enigmas have been utterly ruthless when it comes to dealing with humanity."

"Why?" Rycerz ran one hand through her hair. "Did the Syndics handle their contacts with the enigmas that badly?"

"When we went through enigma space, the civilian experts with us debated that question," Geary said. "We simply don't know enough about how the enigmas think, and they've refused to go beyond threats when dealing with us. The best guess our experts came up with is that the enigmas are so obsessed with protecting everything about themselves from any outsiders that they'll do anything to stop anyone who might learn anything. They've apparently had the same attitude toward the Dancers."

"You couldn't find any factions willing to speak with us? Are the enigmas that uniform a culture?"

"They're not united," Geary said. "We saw clear signs of heavily defended borders within enigma space. But when it comes to dealing with outsiders, they are apparently of one mind."

Rycerz made a face, looking to one side. "I've been reading all of the reports on the enigmas, including those by the civilian experts with you last time, and there's nothing in any of them that contradicts you. Murderously paranoid, by human standards."

"And probably perfectly rational by their standards," Geary said. "Not that that's much consolation for the humans that run afoul of the enigmas. Believe me, we tried to find ways to negotiate with the enigmas, to even just talk meaningfully with them. All they'd do was use human avatars to threaten us."

"Diplomacy requires some willingness on the other side to actually talk," Rycerz said. "Didn't the Rift Federation know about your experiences with the enigmas?"

"They did. Their senior officer on that cruiser, the *Passguard*, is Captain Kapelka, who was with us when we went through enigma space. She knew what she was heading into."

"And now we have a wreck returned to us," Rycerz said sadly. "Go ahead, Admiral. See if there's anyone left to save. Let me know if you run into any problems with Midway's people. If you do, I'll try a direct appeal to President Iceni."

"Thank you," Geary said, hoping it wouldn't come to that. Communications with the planet Iceni was on would require hours for light-speed communications to make the round trip.

He switched to a different circuit, the one used to communicate with the local authorities at Midway. Not part of the Alliance to which Geary's fleet belonged, Midway had once been part of the Syndicate Worlds empire. But the leaders of Midway had rebelled as the corporate empire of the Syndicate Worlds crumbled in the wake of the century-long war against the Alliance. And as they were sort-of friends and partners, he couldn't ignore their sovereignty over this star system.

Midway's small fleet was also orbiting, only about ten light minutes from Geary's fleet. Their heaviest warship, a single battleship, was too ponderous for quickly chasing down *Passguard*. And Midway's sole battle cruiser was near the primary inhabited world, another two light hours distant. But Midway also had a handful of cruisers and smaller Hunter-Killers if it decided to deal with *Passguard* and keep the Alliance warships out of the matter.

He tapped the control to send a message to the commander of Midway's flotilla. "Kommodor Marphissa, this is Admiral Geary. My fleet has identified the warship newly arrived from Pele as the Rift Federation cruiser *Passguard*. If any of the crew are still alive, they need assistance. I'm preparing to send a task force to intercept *Passguard*. Please advise if you have any objection to my dealing with this matter. Geary, out." *Boundless* had been close enough for real-time conversation, but the Midway flotilla was ten light minutes away, meaning every back-and-forth would take twenty minutes.

Desjani sat back, frowning. "I recommend one battle cruiser and a couple of heavy cruisers. The Marine detachment aboard *Dauntless* should be large enough to deal with anything aboard *Passguard* unless that wreck is crammed with enigmas. And if it is, we'd be smarter to stand off and blow it apart rather than engage in a hand-to-hand fight."

"Two battle cruisers," Geary said. "And four heavy cruisers. Just in case the enigmas have rigged a trap. I want enough force on hand to deal with any surprises."

"What if Kommodor Marphissa says no?" Desjani asked. "Midway is worried about the Alliance trying to take over here so they might want to demonstrate that they don't need us."

"They can also say that *Passguard* should be our problem, not theirs, and be glad to hand the whole problem over to us," Geary said. "We'll take *Dauntless* and *Daring*, along with the Fifth Heavy Cruiser Division. I'll have General Carabali scramble some reinforcements for the Marine detachments so we'll have some more muscle on hand if a boarding action is required."

"Lieutenant Castries," Desjani said to one of the bridge watch standers. "Notify *Daring* and the Fifth Heavy Cruiser Division that we're going after *Passguard*, then work out the intercept vector."

Geary himself called General Carabali, who promptly offered to come along in the assault transport *Tsunami*. "That'll give us plenty of Marines and the hospital facilities aboard this ship," she pointed out.

Geary glanced at Desjani, who rubbed her chin as she thought. "If *Tsunami* pushes her acceleration for all she's worth, and we limit our own acceleration a bit, she can keep up," Desjani said. "*Dauntless* has a good sick bay, but it can't match the capabilities aboard an assault transport. Having those medical resources along might be worth the slightly longer time to reach *Passguard*."

He nodded to Desjani. "Good idea," Geary said to Carabali. "We'll do that."

"Lieutenant Castries," Desjani said. "Notify *Tsunami* that she's coming along, and to be prepared for extended maximum acceleration. Then modify your intercept of *Passguard* to include *Tsunami*'s acceleration limits."

"Aye, aye, Captain," Lieutenant Castries said, working quickly at her watch station.

Twenty minutes went by in a flash as they worked on the preparations, the report from the communications watch coming as a surprise. "Admiral, there's an incoming message for you from the Midway Kommodor."

Geary tapped accept, seeing an image of Marphissa appear. Young for her responsibilities, Midway's senior fleet commander had gained her job when the former Syndicate Worlds commanders in this star system all came to untimely ends during the revolt. From what could be seen around Marphissa, the Kommodor was aboard a shuttle rather than the battleship.

"Admiral Geary, this is Kommodor Marphissa of the free and independent Midway Star System," she said. "Midway accepts your offer of assistance in dealing with a former Alliance warship. I am transferring to the cruiser *Manticore* which will accompany whatever force you send to intercept *Passguard*. Provide more information to me as soon as possible. For the people, Marphissa, out."

Desjani rolled her head back with a sigh. "Lieutenant Castries, we will also be accompanied by Midway's cruiser *Manticore*."

"Aye, aye, Captain." To her credit, Lieutenant Castries flinched only slightly as she began reworking the intercept for a third time.

DIFFERENT warships had different abilities. Battleships, massive, heavily protected, and heavily armed, were also cumbersome compared to other warships. Battle cruisers sacrificed a lot of that protection and some of that armament to reduce mass and add more propulsion units, making them the most agile warships despite their size. In a situation like this, when time mattered, the ability of battle cruisers to reach *Passguard* as quickly as possible was a perfect match to the requirements.

Along with the four heavy cruisers and the assault transport *Tsu-*

nami the Alliance ships accelerated away from their former orbit and the rest of the Alliance fleet, their path through space a long curve that would intercept the path of *Passguard*. Along the way, Midway's heavy cruiser *Manticore* slid in from below to join up with the Alliance ships. A few months ago the idea of a Syndicate Worlds–designed cruiser operating with Alliance warships would've felt very strange, and even now it seemed a bit odd. But the fact that Midway's warships were operated by partners of the Alliance made the weird pairing workable.

Aided by inertial dampers that kept the forces of acceleration from squashing frail humans and tearing apart their stronger but still vulnerable ships, the fastest warships known to humanity would still require a bit more than six hours to accelerate, cover the billion kilometers, and brake their velocity again to match that of the badly damaged *Passguard*. While the ability to cross such distances in such a short time was a huge tribute to human ingenuity, it still felt woefully inadequate. Six hours could be a very long time when racing to help people who could be barely hanging on to life.

That this was a rescue mission rather than a threat or a now-dead ship became more probable more than two hours after the ships started out.

"Captain," Lieutenant Yuon said, "sensors have spotted a light flashing from the *Passguard*. Visible light, repeating a pattern. Three quick flashes, three long flashes, and another three short flashes. Then a pause, and the pattern repeats."

Desjani glanced at Geary. "I'm not more than a century old like some people, but that sounds like the ancient SOS distress signal to me."

"Me, too." He didn't respond to her gibe about how long ago he'd been born as he hunched forward, gazing at his display. "How powerful is that light, Lieutenant?"

"Sensors estimate it's a hand light, Admiral. Probably an emergency spotlight. Sensors are spotting enough slight variation in the timing of the flashes to estimate they're being triggered by a human and not an automated control," Yuon added.

"So, someone is still alive on that ship."

THEY had time to spare before the intercept with *Passguard*, so Geary called a virtual conference to hash out any problems before then. The conference compartment aboard *Dauntless* could virtually expand to appear to accommodate hundreds of people, but it required no adjustment this time to fit the number of those present. Geary himself and Tanya Desjani were actually here, while the virtual presences of Captain Vitali from *Daring*, General Carabali aboard *Tsunami*, Captain Adam Ochs (who also commanded the Fifth Heavy Cruiser Division) on the cruiser *Tenshu*, and Kommodor Marphissa aboard *Manticore* were also "seated" around the table.

"We have apparent confirmation that there are survivors aboard *Passguard*," Geary began. "Any guesses why they haven't been able to repair any comm systems at least?"

Captain Ochs shook his head. "*Passguard* is about ten years old. Lucky to survive that long, but that means her systems are old and unreliable. Before she was recalled to the Rift Federation the joke in the heavy cruiser community was that every resupply for *Passguard* included plenty of bubble gum and duct tape to keep the ship in one piece. With heavy damage on top of that, it wouldn't be surprising if nothing is working aboard that ship."

"We know the jump drive is still working," Captain Vitali said. "Otherwise they couldn't have left jump space. What the hell was the Rift Federation thinking sending a ship like that through enigma space?"

"*Passguard* was their flagship," Geary said. "That's why it was sent. As far as what they were thinking, I have no idea. We never expected to see any of those Rift Federation ships again."

Desjani grimaced. "I'm a little concerned that they waited to flash that distress signal until we were well on our way."

"That part makes sense," Captain Vitali said. "I was in a similar situation once."

Nobody asked him to elaborate on that situation. Most of the officers and sailors in the fleet had survived at least one ship being shot out from under them during the bloody and once seemingly endless war with the Syndics.

"If whoever is still alive on *Passguard* is dependent on survival suit sensors," Vitali continued, "then they couldn't have spotted our ships while we were orbiting that far from them. But, once we accelerated, even the limited sensors on the suits could've spotted the energy our propulsion units were putting out, and that would've given them a general direction to aim their light toward."

"It's also the perfect lure for a trap," General Carabali cautioned. "I recommend when we reach that ship we first send a single shuttle in to check on it and see if there really are human survivors."

"That'll take extra time," Vitali pointed out. "Every minute could count."

"I realize that," Carabali said. "Nonetheless, I believe it's the only proper course of action."

Everyone looked at Geary, because he'd have to decide this.

"Who'll be on the shuttle?" Geary asked.

"Marines," Carabali said. "An entry team to get through any barriers, a couple of corpsmen to conduct immediate medical assessments, and some muscle in case they run into trouble. They'll all be volunteers," she added.

Captain Vitali aimed a twisted smile at Geary, while Captain Desjani snorted in derision. He knew why. "Volunteer" was one of those words that meant something different to Marines than it did to the rest of humanity. In the Marines, "volunteering" consisted of a senior enlisted or an officer informing various Marines that they'd been chosen for the job.

But he couldn't argue with Carabali's logic. Risking a single shuttle and a squad of Marines made a lot more sense than sending a warship close to what could be a massive bomb. "Very well," Geary said, a heaviness inside him as he spoke the words that might mean more deaths of those he was responsible for. "That's what we'll do. Now I want recommendations from everyone about whether we should try taking *Passguard* in tow for salvage."

Captain Ochs shook his head again, looking worried. "Admiral, from the damage we can see, that ship is torn up bad. *Passguard* was a candidate for scrap before she was shot up. Even if we can take her under tow without the ship breaking in two, there's unlikely to be anything aboard worth salvaging."

"You don't think we should even plan for a tow attempt?"

Ochs waved one hand slightly. "No, sir. That is, there's no harm in planning. It'll be good practice. But I don't think we should expect *Passguard* will be in any shape to tow, or that she'll be worth the effort."

Kommodor Marphissa spoke up for the first time. "Midway does not want the wreck of a heavy cruiser sailing through our star system as a hazard."

"The wreck's not moving very fast," Desjani pointed out. "And within a few months it'll leave this star system and head into the big dark."

"Nonetheless," Marphissa said. "Its current track will take the wreck closer to our primary inhabited world than I am comfortable with."

"If we can't tow it," Geary said, "we'll make every effort to nudge it onto a vector up or down out of your star system so it'll be clear of your own space traffic."

"Thank you, Admiral."

The Kommodor's easy acceptance of his assurance earned Geary another sidelong look from Desjani. The people of Midway, raised under the duplicitous and everyone-for-themselves environment of the

Syndicate Worlds, and conditioned by the long war to automatically distrust anyone from the Alliance as well, nonetheless had decided that Black Jack Geary was "for the people" and could be trusted to keep his word. Anyone else would've been pressed for guarantees. But not Black Jack.

"Our ships will assume positions far enough from the wreck that our shields can handle the explosion if *Passguard*'s power core blows," Geary said. This part was easy, making decisions based on physical capabilities and limitations. "I want the battle cruisers to have their weapons locked on *Passguard*," Geary said. "Captain Ochs, I want all of your cruisers to be watching for anything coming off of *Passguard*, and ready to engage. If the enigmas have planted anything mobile and dangerous on that ship, I want it taken out fast."

"And *Manticore*?" Kommodor Marphissa asked.

"Are you willing to, um . . ." What was the most diplomatic way to put it? "Stand off and allow us to deal with any threats that develop?"

Marphissa glanced around the table as she considered the question. Finally, she nodded. "I saw your ships in action at Kane. *Manticore* will stand off and only engage if something hazardous gets past you." Marphissa gave a thin smile to Desjani. "I doubt that will happen."

Desjani returned the smile. "Nothing will get past us."

THREE hours later, the main propulsion units and thrusters on all of the warships ceased firing as the ships slid into position around *Passguard*, their vectors perfectly matched to that of the crippled cruiser so that the entire group of ships was moving through space as one. The two battle cruisers were closest, but still fifty kilometers away from the wreck, the assault transport *Tsunami* above and slightly to one side of *Dauntless*. The Alliance heavy cruisers were all one hundred kilometers out from the wreck, spaced around *Passguard* to catch anything that might launch from it. Midway's cruiser *Manticore* was one hundred and fifty kilometers away, positioned to intercept anything that got past the heavy cruisers and headed farther in toward the star.

This close, the light still blinking an SOS from *Passguard* could have been dimly made out by the naked eye. The sensors on the warships had no trouble pinpointing its exact location. "It's at a secondary access hatch forward of amidships," Geary told General Carabali. "We can see two figures in survival suits who seem to be operating it. Launch your bird as soon as possible and find out if they're for real."

Carabali nodded. "They're on their way, Admiral."

"The enigmas like to generate images of virtual humans for visual communications," Captain Desjani said, her eyes on her display where every hole in the ravaged hull of *Passguard* could be clearly seen. "Have they ever faked humans in survival suits or armor?"

"Using robots?" Geary asked. "Not according to the Kommodor. She sent a query on that to Colonel Rogero, since his forces engaged the enigmas at Iwa, but we haven't received a reply yet."

"Light speed is slow," Desjani said in a resigned voice. "Look at that mess," she added, nodding toward the image of the wreck.

"It's amazing they were able to jump out of Pele," Geary said. How had any of the crew survived? His suspicion that this might be an enigma trap designed to lure in human rescuers flared back to life.

The Marine shuttle swooped over *Dauntless*, zooming toward the wreck.

Geary called up a view from the shuttle as it closed on *Passguard*. The two figures in survival suits were still at the hatch, waving as the shuttle drew closer. Were they truly living survivors? Or puppets set to lure in would-be rescuers?

The outer access hatch that had once been part of *Passguard*'s hull was mostly gone, only a shattered fragment still hanging on to the inner hinge. Inside, the edges of torn and broken alloy marked the former air lock, the inner hatch barely visible wedged to one side. Aside from the two figures, no other sign of life could be seen even this close.

The shuttle matched vector to *Passguard*, hanging less than a dozen meters from where the two figures waited.

"Send in the reconnaissance team," General Carabali ordered.

Four Marines left the shuttle, individual maneuvering packs on the backs of their battle armor pushing them swiftly across the small remaining gap.

TWO

GEARY linked his display to one of the Marine scouts, seeing what the scout was seeing as she reached the side of *Passguard*. The two figures in survival suits certainly looked human from this close. Their faceplates were partially fogged by condensation, a sign of a suit with its life support on its last legs. But what could be seen were clearly human faces.

Static interspersed with words came over the circuit. ". . . need . . . all . . . fail . . ."

"Their suits' power must be nearly dead," the scout reported.

"They're beckoning us to follow inside the ship."

Geary waited. This was General Carabali's call, unless she asked him for guidance or approval.

"Wait," Carabali ordered. "Captain O'Bannon," she said to the senior officer on the shuttle, "this looks real. Don't waste time going in slow. Take your whole team in now."

"Understood," O'Bannon said. "Move it," he told the other Marines on the shuttle. "This is still a potential threat environment until we see what's inside. Stay frosty. Everyone stay together once we're inside."

As the remaining Marines jumped across the gap, Geary glanced at his display, where a prominent control pulsed red—his control over the weapons on the battle cruisers and heavy cruisers. Right now, they couldn't fire, but could if he touched that control and shifted it to green. Should he have the warships stand down their weapons?

Not yet.

The last of the Marines reached the wreck, seizing onto the edge of a broken bulkhead. "Rodriguez, Udayar," Captain O'Bannon ordered two of the scouts. "Remain here to relay communications and guard our exit point. Everyone else, follow me."

As O'Bannon gestured to them, the two sailors from the *Passguard* nodded wordlessly before turning to lead the way inside the ship. Geary, now viewing events through the perspective of O'Bannon's battle armor, saw a nightmarish tangle of wreckage that had once been passageways and compartments in the cruiser. Everyone moved carefully to avoid jagged edges even though the Marine battle armor would have protected them. Geary shivered as symbols popped up on O'Bannon's face shield to mark lifeless bodies scattered among the broken shards of the ship.

Finally reaching an intact hatch, the sailors wrestled with it until O'Bannon ordered some of his Marines to help. Inside was a compartment that had been jury-rigged into an air lock. Instead of being brightly lit, it was gloomy, with only a dim glow from emergency lighting that was on the verge of giving out. Once the hatch was again closed, everyone waited as pressure built in the compartment. "That's a slow pressure build," Captain Ochs commented. He was in on the link, of course, but knew to remain silent unless he had something important to contribute. "Their pumps aren't in good shape, or their power is really low."

Cracking another hatch, the sailors from *Passguard* yanked open their survival suits, gasping for breath, sweat streaking their faces. Both were women, and both looked ready to collapse. But they stood watching the Marines, waiting for them to open their faceplates to talk.

Geary, seeing the red warning signs on the Marines' faceplates, wasn't surprised by Captain O'Bannon's next words. "The air in here is pretty bad. Can I get a safety call on this?"

A doctor monitoring them from aboard *Tsunami* replied. "The atmosphere has a lot of volatized chemical compounds, the carbon dioxide level is higher than it should be, and the oxygen level is barely adequate. Nothing immediately hazardous, though. It's okay to breathe for short periods, but no more than half an hour, tops."

"Okay," Captain O'Bannon said. "I'm unsealing."

Geary heard O'Bannon cough in a way that sounded like he was gagging. "Volatized chemical compounds," O'Bannon said. "Doc, next time just tell us it stinks in here." He looked at the sailors, both of whom did their best to straighten to attention as they saluted.

"We ur . . . urgently," one of the sailors said as if she was having trouble getting words out. "Need assistance. Life support is . . . nearly gone."

"What's working on this ship?" O'Bannon asked.

"Life support," the other sailor said. "We've . . . shut down . . . jump drive. Backup power . . . almost exhausted. Using . . . for life support."

"Every . . . thing else . . . gone," the first sailor said.

The doctor on *Tsunami* called in again. "Remote readings of those two indicate severe dehydration. They look like they haven't had much to eat for a while as well. We need to get them to medical as fast as possible."

"Understood, Doc," Captain O'Bannon said before addressing the two sailors again. "Who's in command?"

"Lieutenant Velez. He put us . . . on watch. These are . . . last working suits. Told us . . . stay out . . . flash distress . . . until someone came."

"Smart move," O'Bannon said. "Can you take me to him?"

Both sailors nodded and, stumbling, led the way deeper into the ship. The amount of emergency lighting still glowing varied by compartment, creating a strange tableau of shifting levels of light and shade as the Marines followed. Geary saw other survivors sprawled about the compartments, trying to conserve energy but attempting to rise as they saw the Marines. He realized that his right fist was clenched very tightly as he saw how bad those sailors looked. "General Carabali," he called. "I've seen enough to be sure this isn't a trap. Get the rest of *Tsunami*'s birds scrambled along with the mobile medical teams. I want to evacuate the surviving crew as fast as we can safely do it."

"Understood, Admiral," Carabali said.

Captain O'Bannon had reached a compartment that had once been an office, but now held haphazard piles of expired emergency gear and a single officer slumped at the desk.

"Lieutenant?" one of the sailors called. "Lieutenant, we've got help."

"You're in charge, Lieutenant?" Captain O'Bannon asked, his voice firm but not sharp.

The lieutenant jerked himself erect, staring as if unsure whether this was really happening. His eyes grew a little more alert as he struggled to his feet. "I . . . yes. I'm in command." He paused, wavering slightly on his feet. "Lieutenant Velez."

"How many of you are left, Lieutenant Velez?"

"I . . ."

"How many of your crew are left, Lieutenant?"

"Seven . . . seventy . . . three," Velez said. "Request . . . aid."

"You've got it. More is on the way. But we need to know something, Lieutenant. Did the enigmas ever board your ship? Could they have placed anything, any device, on your ship?"

Velez appeared confused for a long moment, then shook his head several times. "No. They never . . . never boarded us. They just . . . wanted to kill us. Destroy . . . the ship."

"Thank you, Lieutenant." Captain O'Bannon turned to his Marines. "Lopez, Tanaka," he ordered the corpsmen, "start triaging so the medical teams coming from *Tsunami* know who to start with."

"They should search the whole ship," Desjani said to Geary. "Both to ensure the enigmas didn't plant any surprises and to get ID data from every body they can find. They can also make sure no one else is alive in some separate portion of the ship."

He nodded. "General, get some more Marines over there and search that ship from bow to stern. Assume there may be enigma devices present until we absolutely know there aren't. We want to get DNA from all bodies and ensure there are no other survivors."

"Yes, Admiral," Carabali said. "I assume I should still prioritize shuttle runs for medical evacuations."

"Yes," Geary said. "Also have your people download any data that survives on the systems aboard the wreck. Every bit of existing data from every system, whether it's knocked out or not. We're going to need that for reconstructing what happened to that ship." He reached over to his controls, shutting off the weapons release command. "All units, stand down weapons," he ordered. "Captain Desjani, assemble a damage control team and send them over to the wreck with everything needed to rig a temporary new air lock on *Passguard*'s hull and connect it to the spaces that still have atmosphere."

"Aye, aye, sir," Desjani said. "Lieutenant Castries, notify Master Chief Gioninni that he's to lead that team. I want them over there and setting up that temporary air lock so fast even the Marines will be impressed."

Geary, frustrated and wanting to do more, but having done all he could, watched more shuttles launching from *Tsunami*, leaping outward on their way to the wreck that had once been the heavy cruiser *Passguard*.

"Do we have an estimated arrival time for medical teams?" Captain O'Bannon called. "I'm worried some of these space squids might not make it even a few more minutes. The air in here is horrible and from the looks of things they ran out of food and water a while back."

"Five minutes, Captain O'Bannon," General Carabali replied. "We've got wonder water and portable life support gear coming as well," she added, using the Marine slang for emergency hydration fluid. "Tell those squids to hang on."

"Will do, General."

Geary sat back, closing his eyes to block out the views from the Marines already inside *Passguard*. "Seventy-three survivors. Out of what? Four hundred?"

"If the Rift Federation brought the crew up to full strength while they were home," Desjani said. She glared angrily at her own display where the same images were visible. "We should make sure this footage is sent back to the Rift Federation, to the people who sent that ship out on a suicide mission. Let them see what happened to the ones who followed their orders."

"Yeah," Geary said. "We should definitely do that."

The other shuttles were coming close to the wreck, disgorging more Marines hauling equipment, all of them moving with as much haste as possible under these conditions.

"Master Chief Gioninni reports he's launching," Lieutenant Castries said. "He estimates twenty minutes to get the temporary air lock rigged."

"Tell him if he can do it in less than twenty I'll give him a chance to fix the ship's liquor inventory before I check it again."

Geary gave Desjani a questioning look. "Gioninni has been skimming the official liquor supply?"

"Of course he has," she replied. "But he'll get that air lock rigged faster than anyone else could. Which may save some lives hanging in the balance."

One thing the long war had done was perfect the fleet's ability to provide emergency medical support. Geary just had to sit and watch while the medical teams boarded *Passguard* and went to work with skills and procedures honed over a century of dealing with wounded comrades. The Marine combat engineers were just as efficient with rigging up portable life support that began clearing the nearly toxic atmosphere inside the still-pressurized area inside the wreck. Nonetheless, Geary felt the common urge to issue an unnecessary order just for the sake of appearing to contribute something to the situation. But he fought it down, remembering similar "helpful" interventions by his own superiors in the past. "It's funny how hard it is to not interfere with well-trained people who are doing their jobs well," he commented to Desjani.

She nodded. "Everyone wants to feel important at a time like this. You already made the important decisions, Admiral."

But after watching most of the survivors from *Passguard* evacuated to *Tsunami* it turned out he was still needed.

"Admiral? We have a problem." General Carabali looked as if she wasn't sure whether to be angry or not. "There's only one survivor left aboard. Lieutenant Velez. He won't leave the wreck."

"Give me a relay to talk to him," Geary said, guessing what was keeping Velez from leaving.

The link came through Captain O'Bannon's battle armor. Geary could see Lieutenant Velez, more alert after receiving some emergency care and rations, standing stubbornly inside the temporary air lock. "This is Admiral Geary," he said, trying to sound as if this were a routine situation. "What's the problem, Lieutenant?"

Velez looked toward O'Bannon, his eyes wide, his mouth twitching. "I am acting commanding officer of the Rift Federation warship *Passguard*," he said, the words coming out slowly but forcefully. "I will not abandon my ship."

Geary sighed, understanding the lieutenant. Ground forces soldiers wouldn't have. They didn't have any equivalent to the powerful symbolism of a captain leaving his or her ship. But the Marines spent enough time around the fleet to know how strong the compulsion was for a captain not to leave their ship, and so had called for help rather than force Velez off the wreck. "Lieutenant Velez, it is the duty of a commanding officer to decide when it is appropriate and necessary to abandon a crippled vessel. You know the state of your ship. *Passguard* has been destroyed. There is no duty, no obligation, to remain aboard a ship that is no longer livable or capable of any action."

"My duty is to remain with my ship," Velez said, his voice stubborn even though it wavered because of his physical state.

"Your ship is dead. Your duty," Geary said, "is to your surviving crew. If you stay aboard what remains of *Passguard*, who will look after your crew? Those sailors need you, Lieutenant. You can do nothing for that ship. But your crew needs you. You've brought them this far. Don't abandon them now."

Velez blinked in confusion, shaking. Finally, he nodded. "Yes. I . . . I need to see to the crew."

The medical personnel near Velez, sensing their moment, gently guided him through the air lock.

"That's the last of them," Captain O'Bannon said as Velez left.

"Stay in place for now," General Carabali ordered. "Have your people record everything they can. No one has spotted any enigma souvenirs, but stay alert. Medical is sending over survey bots to go over the entire structure of the wreck looking for DNA fragments. We want to account for as many of the crew as possible."

A half hour later, Dr. Nasr, *Dauntless*'s chief medical officer, called Geary. "Admiral, I've been able to get an update," he said, his voice heavy. "Five of those aboard *Passguard* were already dead when our medical teams reached them. That leaves sixty-eight survivors. The doctors aboard *Tsunami* are confident they won't lose any more."

"How long had those five been dead?" Geary asked, dreading to hear it might have been a matter of hours or even minutes.

"Three had died more than a day ago," Nasr said. "The other two perhaps half a day. Dehydration, malnutrition, foul air, and in the case of four of them injuries sustained during combat against the enigmas. We could not have gotten to any of the five in time to save them."

"Thank you, Doctor," Geary said. Was Dr. Nasr telling him the truth, or telling him things that would spare his feelings? Either way, those sailors had died before their ship could arrive at Midway and before help could reach them.

He went back to his stateroom, wanting to be alone for a little while, so he could be without everyone looking to him for guidance and example. Slumping back in his seat, he rubbed his eyes as if that would help calm his thoughts. Why did some live and others die? Why couldn't he have saved those five? But he hadn't even had a chance to do that. They'd been doomed before they escaped from the enigmas.

At least he'd saved the other sixty-eight.

His door alarm sounded, creating an answering burst of irritation in him. Couldn't he have five minutes to himself? But he knew whoever had come must have an important reason, and so pressed the entry approval.

Captain Desjani came in. She left the door open behind her, as she always did when visiting his stateroom. "How are you doing, Admiral?"

"I've been worse." He looked away from her and found his gaze on an image of the battered interior of *Passguard*, which did nothing for his mood. He realized that one fist was tightly clenched, as if ready to throw a punch, but at what he didn't know. "What's up?"

"We need to discuss something. I know we had agreed to alter the vector of *Passguard* so it'd leave the star system, but you can't send that wreck into the big dark," Desjani said. "There are a lot of remains of her crew aboard, even if some of those remains might be only a patch of dead cells. They need a proper burial."

"I don't—" Geary rubbed his face with both hands, wondering why her words rattled him so badly. Why this whole thing was rattling him the way it was. He'd seen so many ships destroyed in the last few years. It still hurt, but it was a hurt he'd grown miserably accustomed to.

Hadn't he? "What's wrong with me?"

She sighed. "I think you know, but won't consciously think about it. It's an anniversary."

"Anniversary?" He glared at her, wondering why she'd bring up something personal between them at this time. "We didn't get married on this date. And even if we did we're not supposed to even think about that while aboard ship and on duty."

"No, Admiral," Desjani said, her use of his rank emphasizing that this wasn't a personal matter. "It's an anniversary for *you*. One hundred and two years ago today you ordered the crew of *Merlon* to abandon ship in Grendel Star System. You know that inside, but you're not allowing yourself to realize it."

He inhaled sharply, those events coming into painfully clear focus. His cruiser *Merlon* had been escorting a convoy, as a training exercise rather than out of any belief that there was danger, but while passing through Grendel had encountered a Syndic flotilla on its way to launch a surprise attack on the Alliance. He'd ordered the convoy to run for safety and warn of the incoming attack, and had been forced to sacrifice his ship in a desperate rearguard action to give them time to get away. The last one off his ship after he ordered the surviving crew to abandon it, he'd been left with only a damaged escape pod that had frozen him into survival sleep. Everyone had thought him dead.

The Alliance, reeling from the surprise Syndic attacks, had declared him a great hero. For nearly a century afterwards as the unwinnable war dragged on, the Alliance had kept inflating his reputation, using the example of Black Jack to inspire its people. And when he'd finally been found after nearly a hundred years and awakened aboard this same ship *Dauntless*, his first sight that of Captain Tanya Desjani, he'd discovered that everyone thought he was someone he'd never been. Everyone he'd ever known was dead, and everyone now alive thought he was the hero who could save them.

They'd needed him, so he'd done his best to be that person. Even as he discovered a century of war had warped the people of the Alliance in some ways their ancestors would've been appalled by. He'd also done his best to show them that the things they were doing because they were "necessary to win" had not only not resulted in victory, but had tarnished and set back their own cause.

"Admiral?" Tanya said, her voice unusually gentle, but still fully professional. "Are you okay?"

"Yes." He took another deep breath, more slowly. The latest meds could dull the pain of the past, but not wipe it away. "I knew it subconsciously, but didn't want to consciously acknowledge it."

"Did you have another nightmare recently?"

"Yes." Geary shut his eyes for a moment, which was a mistake since it let the images from last night stand out more strongly. "The usual one. Stumbling through the wreck of my cruiser, seeing my dead crew members all around, wondering why I was still alive. Why I had any right to be alive." He paused. "I even see people like Cara Decala, my executive officer, lying dead. She got off the ship. I know that. She died years later, in another battle, while I was frozen in survival sleep. But I see her dead then."

"Survivor guilt is hard to handle," Desjani said. It might have sounded glib, except that he knew how well she understood what she'd said. Tanya had also lost a lot of friends. "But keeping it inside doesn't make it better. You need to talk to the doc, or to me or Duellos, and get more meds if you need them. Don't try to fight this battle on your own."

He nodded, trying to focus on here and now. "You're right."

"I always am."

And somehow she had once again managed to rally his spirit when the burdens seemed too heavy to bear. "You actually keep track of that date?"

"The whole fleet does," she said, smiling a bit as he flinched. "There used to be commemoration ceremonies every year on the anniversary of Black Jack's Last Stand."

"Ancestors save me," Geary said, glad that he'd never had to witness any of those ceremonies. "Why haven't—"

"When you came back, it didn't seem right to keep celebrating your heroic death. During the ceremonies we all took an oath to follow your brave and epic example," Tanya added.

"All right. You've successfully distracted me. Please don't recite that oath to me." Now that he understood the source of his distress, he could master it as he took a few moments to think while Tanya waited patiently. "The dead crew members of that ship do deserve proper burials. What happens if we instead alter Passguard's track to send the wreck into the sun?" He knew she would have already worked that out.

"We can do it so it poses no real threat to navigation," she said.

"Two of the heavy cruisers and some portable maneuvering units attached to the wreck can gradually swing it onto a vector that's safe."

"Completely safe?"

"Mostly safe."

"Okay." Another pause to think. Finally, Geary touched his display to activate the comms on it. "Kommodor Marphissa, this is Admiral Geary. I know we'd agreed to divert the track of *Passguard*'s wreck into the dark between stars, but we've discovered many dead aboard. We have to give those dead an honorable burial. Will Midway agree to allow us to alter the track of the wreck so it ends in Midway's star? I am assured we can do so without unduly hazarding navigation within your star system, but I recognize your right to have the final say in this. To the honor of our ancestors, Geary, out."

With *Manticore* so close, Marphissa replied within minutes, her eyes searching Geary. "Admiral, I do not entirely understand your request. Why is it necessary for the wreck to be consumed by our star?"

"It's our belief," Geary explained. "Everyone, and everything, came from the furnaces of the stars. Eventually, we all return to the stars, to someday be reborn. A proper burial in space is always aimed at sending the deceased into the nearest star to rest until the day they return."

Midway's Kommodor eyed Geary. "It's religion, then. You understand, the Syndicate outlawed such beliefs. The Syndicate didn't want any rival for control of the people. It couldn't stamp out such things, but what . . . metaphysical belief systems existed had to remain hidden and thus are very fragmented. Are you saying the Alliance has just one such belief?"

"No," Geary said. "There's one broad consensus of belief, but within that are numerous shadings, from fairly rigid interpretations with strict rules to simple spiritual feelings that lack any structure. And of course there are those who don't believe in such things at all. Military burials are designed to be acceptable to as wide a range of beliefs as possible, because we have all too often had to conduct mass burials."

"And this proper burial matters greatly to you?"

"It does," Geary said.

Marphissa nodded. "Then out of respect for you, at least, I will give conditional approval. But this is something I must ask President Iceni to give final approval on. I will contact her and let her know this is a matter of importance to you."

"Thank you, Kommodor," Geary said.

"It is only a small thing." Marphissa paused. "Those of us raised in the Syndicate tend to believe in nothing because all we were taught to believe in was false."

"I'm sorry," Geary said. "What you believe should be your choice. It's unfortunate that you weren't given any choice."

Marphissa smiled slightly. "But now I have a choice. I believe in President Iceni and in what she seeks to do. I chose that. And the Syndicate has not been able to stop me. I will contact you as soon as I receive a reply from President Iceni."

THE mood in the conference room aboard *Dauntless* usually varied depending on the topic. This time it felt as somber as a funeral home. The virtual presence of Lieutenant Velez sat at the table, his eyes clear but haunted. Geary sat opposite him, Tanya Desjani to his right. Dr. Nasr was seated next to and watching Lieutenant Velez, even though doctors aboard *Tsunami* were monitoring his health. Lieutenant Iger, the intelligence officer aboard *Dauntless*, was also present, though maintaining a low profile.

Kommodor Marphissa's virtual presence sat at the table as well, a matter that had occasioned some debate on whether a representative of a foreign power should be present. But since this matter intimately involved the enigmas, Geary had decided she should be here.

"How are you doing, Lieutenant?" Geary asked.

Velez made a small shrug, his face working. Even though he'd received emergency care, the bones on his face still stood out against skin drawn tight by days of stress and lack of food. "I am . . . well." He looked up as if suddenly remembering something, his eyes on Geary. "Thank you. Thank you, Admiral, for your aid. For ensuring no more lives were lost."

"I'm only sorry we couldn't save more. Can you tell us what happened?"

Lieutenant Velez rubbed his face, his hand moving with quick, jerky twitches. "I do not know if that is . . . authorized."

Desjani leaned forward a bit. "Lieutenant, you and your ship fought alongside us in a lot of battles. We haven't forgotten that. We're not asking for Rift Federation secrets. But we are supposed to proceed through enigma space soon. Anything you can tell us might help us avoid the fate of *Passguard*."

Velez flinched, then nodded. "We reached Pele Star System. There were enigma picket ships posted at the jump points for Hua and Hina."

"Hua has been renamed," Geary said. "Apparently the name too closely resembled that of a notorious and dead Syndic CEO, so Midway has changed the name of that star to Lalotai. I told them we'd respect that even though we don't have to."

Velez squinted at Geary as if having a little trouble absorbing the new name. "La-lo-tai?"

"What does that mean?" Desjani asked Geary.

"It's an Old Earth culture's name for the underworld, or the place where monsters dwell," he replied.

Captain Desjani smiled briefly. "Then it's a perfect name for an enigma-owned star."

Velez waited a moment longer before he began speaking again. "Enigma picket ships at the jump points for . . . Lalotai and Hina. Captain Kapelka took us along the quickest vector to the jump point for Hina Star System."

"What? Hina?" Even though Geary had promised himself he wouldn't interrupt Velez again, he burst out with the words. "Captain Kapelka knew she had to jump to Hu—to Lalotai in order to reach Dancer space."

Velez nodded, looking distressed. "We weren't told the reason, but talk among the officers was that we wanted to trick the enigmas. We knew Hua, I mean Lalotai, was an enigma defensive outpost against the Dancers. Even though Captain Kapelka didn't explain why we were apparently going to Hina, we thought it was a plan to mislead the enigmas into gathering their forces at Hina, which would mean stripping warships from . . . Lalotai."

Captain Desjani nodded. "We know the enigmas have some form of faster-than-light communications, so Kapelka figured the picket ships would send messages to both Lalotai and Hina. Once their ships at Lalotai used the hypernet gate there to head for Hina, they'd be out of communication until they arrived, which could've given your force a small window to get through Lalotai before the enigma ships could return."

Lieutenant Velez nodded as well, the movements jerky with tension. "That's what we guessed the plan was. It . . . it wasn't a bad plan, was it?"

It was Geary's turn to nod. "It's probably the best plan Captain Kapelka could've come up with." It also required the enigmas to react just right and just like humans would, which was why he would never have risked his ships on such a plan unless he had absolutely no choice. Kapelka had likely felt she didn't have any choice.

"We kept waiting for the picket ship at the jump point to Hina to jump to confirm when we'd be there," Velez said. He paused, looking puzzled. "But it didn't. We were only five light minutes from the jump point for Hina when Captain Kapelka ordered us to shift vector and accelerate toward the jump point for . . . Lalotai."

"Kapelka still didn't explain what she was doing at that point?"

"No, Admiral."

"Did the enigma ship waiting at the jump point for Lalotai enter jump before you reached it?" Kommodor Marphissa asked.

"No," Lieutenant Velez said, shaking his head once with a sharp motion. "It accelerated away from the jump point. Chasing it would've only delayed us so we jumped for Lalotai." He squinted at Marphissa, finally taking in her uniform. "You're . . . uh . . ."

"A local expert," Geary said in a matter-of-fact way that implied Marphissa's presence was a given, the sort of thing no one would have any cause to question.

"Did you see any new enigma ships arrive at the jump point for Hina before you jumped for Lalotai?" Geary asked.

Velez blinked before shaking his head again. "No, sir."

"What was your position aboard *Passguard*?" Captain Desjani asked.

"Weapons Officer," Velez said. "I didn't have much to do at Pele since there were no enigmas near us. Not that I minded that."

"Wasn't anybody worried?" Kommodor Marphissa exploded in frustration. "You knew how fast the enigma warships are and how much they hate having humans in one of their star systems."

"Everyone was scared," Lieutenant Velez said, staring at Marphissa. "We weren't supposed to talk about it. Yuki—I'm sorry, Lieutenant Franzen, our medical officer, told me she was passing out calming meds like candy. But she wasn't supposed to tell anyone. Captain Kapelka didn't want people talking about it."

"Lieutenant Franzen isn't among the survivors," Geary said.

"No." Velez breathed deeply in and out, his face working with emotion. "She . . . died . . . too."

Hating to see how reliving this was hurting the lieutenant, but knowing he needed this information, Geary tried redirecting the conversation, keeping his tone professional and dispassionate. They were all doing that, he realized, speaking with their best official voices to soothe Velez with the sound of business as usual. "You were expecting trouble when you arrived at Lalotai?"

"Yes. Yes, Admiral. Full combat alert, all weapons ready to fire." Velez had his gaze fixed on the table. "We were at full combat readiness when we left jump at . . . at Lalotai," he repeated as if trying to refute charges of negligence that no one had made. "And . . . they were there. Waiting near the jump point. I don't know how many. Too many."

He took another long, slow breath, his eyes seemingly fixed on sights he wanted to forget and could not. "The destroyers were in the lead. They were gone in seconds. I think *Machete* went first. Exploded. Then *Scythe*. Torn to pieces. Then *Soedoek* and *Katar*, so fast, I don't know how they died. *Octave* and *Tierce*, the light cruisers, were behind the destroyers. I think *Tierce* blew up. *Octave* took so many hits, she came apart. They never . . . had a chance," Velez said, his voice breaking.

He paused for a few seconds to recover before continuing. "*Passguard* was at the rear. Because we had the delegation aboard. We were supposed to be at the back of the formation to protect the delegation," he repeated, as if trying to justify why the heavy cruiser had survived. "The destroyers and light cruisers absorbed most of the initial enemy attacks, but then the enigmas shifted to us, and we were taking hits. Bad hits. All of my weapons were shooting back. I . . . I think we hurt one of their ships," Velez said, his eyes haunted. "My gunners, they got one of the enigmas. They were dying, weapons being knocked out, but they fought until the end."

"Of course they did," Geary said, knowing that Velez had to believe that the sacrifices of his sailors had been worth something. "No one has ever questioned the bravery and the skills of Rift Federation sailors."

Lieutenant Velez stared at Geary, momentarily silent, before nodding quickly. "Yes, Admiral. We were outnumbered so badly, though. Courage and skill, their sacrifices, weren't enough. Captain Kapelka ordered us to turn about, accelerate back to the jump point. The enigmas were all over us, but we kept shooting and we made it." He paused. "We thought maybe the enigmas hadn't expected us to fall back. But my gunners kept them off us for long enough. We were able to jump back for Pele."

Lieutenant Velez grimaced, as if his memories physically hurt him. "In jump space we had time to make some repairs and . . . and deal with our casualties. We had nearly a hundred dead and wounded. Half of my weapons were out of commission, but we were able to repair the rest."

"What was Captain Kapelka's plan at that point?" Geary asked.

"Had she abandoned the attempt to reach Dancer space and was just trying to get back to Midway?"

"I think so." Velez shook his head. "She, Captain Kapelka, didn't say. Those days in jump, she spent a lot of time in her stateroom. Didn't talk much. Maybe we were all like that, expecting to die when we came out of jump at Pele. But we didn't die right off, because when we left jump, there weren't any enigma warships waiting at the jump point."

Lieutenant Velez sighed, his head bent down toward the table, sounding as if he was fighting back tears. "They were at the jump point for Midway. Three light hours from us. Thirty-three of them. Waiting. We had no choice. We assumed the enigma warships from Lalotai would have jumped after us and they'd come through jump behind us soon. We had to head for the jump point for Midway at the best acceleration we could manage and try to fight our way through the enigmas at the jump point. It was the only chance we had."

Velez looked puzzled. "The ships from Lalotai didn't come out of jump until we'd been at Pele for four hours. No one could figure out why they'd waited so long to jump after us."

"That is odd," Geary said, running possible explanations through his mind, explanations that kept coming back to some different enigma way of thinking.

But Kommodor Marphissa made an intrigued noise, causing everyone to look at her. "Jump drives," she said. "Every ship travels at the same velocity in jump space, no matter how fast or slow it's going in real space. We don't even question that anymore. It just is. But all we know is every human ship, using human jump drives all designed from the first prototype on Old Earth."

Geary stared at her, surprised as he realized the implications. "And maybe jump drives invented by someone else, such as the enigmas, might differ enough to produce a different speed in jump space?"

Marphissa spread her hands. "Maybe."

"We have no way of measuring velocity in jump space," Desjani said, gazing at Marphissa. "Maybe a fundamental difference in jump drive design would produce a few hours' difference in travel time."

"Couldn't we just do the math?" Lieutenant Iger asked. "This much distance over this much time should give us velocity."

"No," Desjani said. "We have no idea how big jump space is. Every theory assumes it's a lot smaller than real space. But we can't measure distance in there any more than we can velocity, so all we know is time along with two unknowns of velocity and distance."

"It didn't matter," Lieutenant Velez said abruptly. "They weren't far enough behind us. They accelerated hard, harder than we could have even if *Passguard* had been undamaged. All we could do was watch them closing the distance while we charged at the jump point for Midway. The ones behind us got within range while we were still an hour from reaching the jump point and started sniping at us."

"Did your rear shields hold?" Geary asked.

"We had to divert power," Velez said. "Captain Kapelka told me not to shoot back because they needed the power for the shields."

"That went on for an hour?"

"Yes, Admiral." Emotions of shame and rage flitted across Lieutenant Velez's face. "All we could do was take hits. We couldn't even shoot back. And the ones behind kept getting closer, while the ones ahead just waited. As we closed on the jump point, the enigma warships guarding the jump point came at us. Captain Kapelka said we had to blow through them, get to the jump point. But my hell lances had no charges. Everything was going into the shields. We had no missiles left, just grapeshot." He fell silent.

The others waited.

"It's hard to remember," Lieutenant Velez said after a long moment, blinking, his expression a map of awful events still raw in his mind. "We came into contact with the force ahead of us, and . . . I don't know. So many hits. Everything happening at once. We tried to engage a couple of the enigma ships. We got some grapeshot hits in. A few. Before nearly all my gunners died. Then our shields collapsed. Enigma hell lances came through the bridge. Most of those on the bridge died. I don't know why I didn't. I don't know why the ship survived, held together. I wasn't even sure where we were, where the enemy was. Almost all of our systems were dead. All weapons gone. But the jump drive lit up. We'd reached the jump point. I activated it, and we went into jump."

Lieutenant Velez shuddered, drawing in a deep breath. "Captain Kapelka was dead. A lot of others. But the jump drive hadn't been knocked out."

Velez had to pause again. No one else said anything, their minds on the terrible ordeal the crew of the *Passguard* had endured.

"The power core had started an automated shutdown due to damage just as we jumped," Velez finally continued. "Our surviving engineers said a safe restart would be impossible. We'd lost everything except those backup power sources that hadn't been destroyed. Almost all of the other officers were dead, all except Ensign Potexi. I . . . I was in command. I prioritized life support, though we had to maintain power to the jump drive, too. Just those two things. I decided we had to abandon parts of the ship that we didn't need. We had to conserve our survival suits and everything else. I ordered everyone still alive into parts of the ship that we could pressurize. I had to keep them busy. I remembered that. Don't give them time to think. To be scared.

"We had to search the ship, look for people who might be trapped elsewhere. It . . ." Velez swallowed, looking ill. "A lot of dead. Everywhere. We found a few still alive, and got them back with the rest of us." He stopped speaking, frowning. "Nguyen. He was one of the wounded we found. I don't remember seeing him with the rest of the crew on this ship."

Dr. Nasr spoke up, his voice respectful. "Petty Officer Nguyen died, probably half a day before you left jump space."

"Oh." Lieutenant Velez blinked, his mouth twisting. "I thought . . . we'd saved him."

"You did save the rest," Nasr said.

Velez stared at the table before speaking again abruptly. "We just . . . tried to keep going. Sealing off leaks where we were, trying to keep the remaining life support systems going, conserving survival suit oxygen. There were so many holes in the ship." He turned eyes once more haunted on Geary. "Admiral. We could look right out at it. Jump space. We could see it directly through the holes in the ship. It's . . . Don't. Don't ever look at it. Not with the naked eye."

"How'd you get out of jump when you reached Midway?" Captain Desjani asked, breaking the pained silence. "That requires extra power."

"We took the remaining life support off-line, rigged all of our remaining backup power to the jump drive, and hoped that'd be enough," Lieutenant Velez said. "That . . . was all we could do. We hoped someone would see us, would come help us. But we didn't know, couldn't know, until your Marines arrived." He fell silent, staring at the table.

"You did an impressive job," Geary said. "Setting your priorities, maintaining discipline, getting that ship back, and saving the rest of your crew. I'm amazed."

"The rest of your crew owe their lives to you," Captain Desjani added. "You did everything possible, Lieutenant, and you got them here."

Lieutenant Velez nodded silently, his eyes still on the table, his expression filled with pain.

"Do you think there were any survivors from the other ships?" Captain Desjani asked. "The ones lost at Lalotai?"

"I don't know," Velez said, looking miserable. "Maybe a few. Our systems reported some escape pods being launched. I don't know if they got clear."

Kommodor Marphissa shook her head with grim finality. "The enigmas rarely take human prisoners. Usually they just wipe out a defeated force."

Velez stared at Marphissa. "We couldn't . . ."

"No," she said. "You couldn't have saved them. *Passguard* barely escaped being destroyed there as well. There was nothing more you could've done."

Lieutenant Velez nodded again without saying anything. Looking at him, Geary knew Velez would spend the rest of his life vainly wishing there had been something more he could've done.

"I need to get my ship home," Lieutenant Velez suddenly said, looking up and around at the others. "My crew and my ship."

Geary exhaled heavily. "Lieutenant, we've conducted an extensive survey of the wreck." He used the word "wreck" deliberately, to emphasize the condition of the *Passguard*. "Your ship cannot be repaired. It would have to be totally rebuilt. It would require a major shipyard job to even get it into shape to be towed without the ship breaking apart. There is no possible way to get it back to the Rift Federation without extensive work. Do you understand?"

Lieutenant Velez shook his head in denial. "No. I have to bring my ship home."

"That is not possible, Lieutenant," Geary said, keeping his voice unyielding. "The Alliance will get you and your crew home, because we still honor the contribution of the Rift Federation and its citizens to defeating the Syndicate Worlds. But nothing short of a miracle from the living stars themselves could get *Passguard* back home again.

"What we can do," Geary added as Lieutenant Velez stared at him, "is offer your ship and the dead aboard it an honorable burial in the fires of Midway's star. We can alter the vector of *Passguard* to bring it into the star. Midway's rulers have agreed to allow that."

Velez shook his head again, blinking rapidly. "No. I must . . . bring everyone home. Get my ship home."

"Admiral," Dr. Nasr cautioned, frowning at information displayed before him. "Lieutenant Velez is not emotionally or physically stable. He requires rest."

"Thank you, Lieutenant," Geary said. "We'll speak again later."

Velez's image vanished as the doctors aboard *Tsunami* went to work on him.

"Well, that didn't go as well as it could have," Desjani said. "But no matter how Velez feels about it, his ship is junk. Hallowed ground because of those who died aboard it, but it's junk."

"Lieutenant Iger," Geary said, "how does what he said match with the records we recovered from *Passguard*?"

Iger made a vague motion. "Most of what we recovered were housekeeping files and routine records. None of Captain Kapelka's files seem to have survived, or anything else operational."

"That's sort of odd, isn't it?" Desjani asked.

"Yes, Captain," Iger said. "It is odd. There were places where backups should've survived. But nothing remained intact." He hesitated, glancing at Kommodor Marphissa.

"Go ahead, Lieutenant," Geary said. Marphissa had noticed, and it wouldn't do for her to think important information was being kept from Midway's rulers.

"Admiral," Iger said, speaking slowly, "we can't be certain, but it appears likely that at least some of those files were destroyed subsequent to the fights with the enigmas."

"Lieutenant Velez and the other survivors deliberately wiped any surviving operational files?" Geary asked.

"I think they did," Lieutenant Iger said. "They may have had orders to do that. It's hard to believe that Captain Kapelka didn't issue any orders for what they should do if she didn't survive the attempt to jump for Midway."

"So, Lieutenant Velez is holding back on us?" Desjani said.

Dr. Nasr was the one who nodded, however. "Captain, I believe the physical reactions I was seeing reflected just that. Much of his stress was consistent with trying not to reveal information."

"All right." Geary sat back, trying not to let anger color his decisions. "He's still doing his best to follow orders. We can respect that, and we have to consider Lieutenant Velez's wishes, but we are not legally bound to follow them. *Passguard* is a wreck, a navigational hazard. As such, Midway can decide what to do with it, or defer to us on that decision."

"President Iceni has already agreed to let you decide that," Kommodor Marphissa said. "Unless you wish to change your plans."

"No," Geary said. "We will conduct a formal funeral service, to which the survivors from *Passguard* will be invited. Then two of Captain Ochs's heavy cruisers will nudge the wreck onto a new vector, assisted by portable maneuvering units we'll attach to the wreck. Captain Ochs has run the maneuvers through his systems and says it'll take three days of gentle nudging to get the wreck on the right vector for the portable units to handle the rest of it. As soon as the funeral service is complete, the battle cruisers will escort *Tsunami* back to the rest of the fleet. The heavy cruisers will rejoin us when their task is done. I'll inform Ambassador Rycerz of my intentions in case she has any concerns. Any questions?"

Before anyone could respond, both Kommodor Marphissa and Captain Desjani checked their personal comm pads in response to alerts unheard by the others.

"A ship has arrived at the hypernet gate," Marphissa said.

"She's broadcasting her identity as the Alliance assault transport *Chinook*," Desjani added. "Fleet systems have confirmed the ship is *Chinook*."

"That's the test ship, Kommodor," Geary told Marphissa. "It traveled here directly from Alliance space. That confirms Midway now has a link straight to the Alliance."

Marphissa nodded, smiling. "That will please President Iceni. You understand, Admiral, if it had not been you behind this move, we would never have agreed to give the Alliance a nonstop path to our doorstep. But our new ability to send merchant ships to deal directly with markets in the Alliance will greatly increase the value and revenues from our hypernet gate, and boost trade throughout this entire region of space. The Syndicate will not be happy. I should inform my leaders immediately of the significance of this ship's arrival."

As soon as Kommodor Marphissa's virtual self had vanished, Lieutenant Iger held up his hand. "Admiral, there's something else."

Geary halted his move to stand up, dropping back into his seat. "Now what?"

"Sir, the diplomatic delegation aboard the *Passguard* was not wiped out."

THREE

"WHAT?" Geary looked at the others, seeing the same surprise with the notable exception of Dr. Nasr. "You're saying one of the Rift Federation's diplomats who were aboard *Passguard* is still alive?"

"Yes, sir. One of the supposed crew members rescued from the wreck did not match the data in the fleet's files from when *Passguard* was assigned to the Alliance fleet," Iger explained. "I conferred with Dr. Nasr and he did his own checking. The person identified as Petty Officer Second Class Masurin is not Masurin."

Startled, Geary again looked to Dr. Nasr.

The doctor spread his hands, looking unhappy. "The physical description is not too far off, but the DNA absolutely does not match. It does not match anyone known to have been among the crew of *Passguard*."

"Couldn't it be a different Masurin?" Geary asked. "A new crew member with the same name?"

"During intake processing Masurin claimed to have been among the crew for years," Lieutenant Iger said. "Combine that with the destruction of operational files, and it seems even as the survivors of *Pass-*

guard's crew were doing their best to live, they were also taking time to conceal as much of their mission as possible from whoever rescued them. That's understandable if they thought they'd be rescued by the people who run Midway. But why they'd continue the deception with us is puzzling."

"Do they know about it?" Geary asked, feeling foolish for bringing up a possibility that seemed more like space opera than reality. "What if this Masurin was an enigma agent? And the enigmas . . ."

"Somehow manipulated the rest of the crew into not seeing the switch?" Dr. Nasr finished, having apparently seen the same sort of shows that Geary had.

Lieutenant Iger hesitated longer than usual before replying as he clearly tried to frame his reply in respectful terms. "Sir, that . . . um . . . uh . . . the one posing as Masurin definitely has one hundred percent human DNA."

"Could he be a human captured by enigmas and brainwashed?" Desjani asked.

Geary wasn't sure if she was serious until she winked one eye at him. Trust Desjani to have fun with this.

Iger paused again, finally shaking his head. "That's . . . not *impossible*, Captain, but there'd still be the matter of changing the memories of the survivors from *Passguard* to accept this person in place of Masurin. If the enigmas could do that, I don't know why they wouldn't have already taken over human space and wiped us out as a species."

"This is true," Dr. Nasr said, apparently a bit disappointed in the alien spy scenario having to be ruled out.

"Which means Masurin must have been one of the Rift Federation diplomats," Geary said. "There's no other source on *Passguard* for Masurin to have come from."

"We could call them on it," Captain Desjani said. "Bring this Masurin in for a talk with Lieutenant Iger."

The idea was tempting, but Geary shook his head. "No. I'll bounce this one up to the ambassador. Whatever game the Rift Federation is playing doesn't pose a threat to our ships. Keep an eye on Masurin, Lieutenant Iger, but don't be obvious about it."

This time everyone else did leave the conference room, until only Geary and Desjani were left. She cocked an inquisitive eye his way. "You don't seem terribly worked up about that Rift diplomat hiding among *Passguard*'s survivors. Aren't you worried about whatever the Rift is trying so hard to keep us from finding out?"

"Of course I am," Geary said with a shrug. "But it's not my problem. I get to punt it to the ambassador, so she can deal with it."

"And if Ambassador Rycerz screws it up?" Desjani sighed. "I admit, anything the Rift Federation is planning shouldn't pose any threat to us. But I'd like to know what they were going to offer the Dancers that they thought was so important that they threw away seven warships and the lives of nearly everyone aboard them."

He only nodded in reply, thinking that she was right, that it would be nice to know what the Rift Federation's leaders had been planning. But the odds of that information being critically important to the fleet's mission seemed too small to worry about compared to the threat posed by the enigmas.

THE burial ceremony was held aboard *Dauntless*, with virtual links to all of the other ships. *Dauntless* had closed to within a few hundred meters of *Passguard*, one bulkhead of the shuttle hangar projecting a view into space centered on the wreck. In addition to Alliance sailors and Marines standing in ranks to honor the dead, those survivors of *Passguard*'s crew who were able to handle the physical strain also stood in their own formation.

Geary read the service, not wanting to risk missing a word even though he already knew it almost by heart after so many other services, wondering how many more such burials he might have to preside over. Like the other Alliance personnel, he wore the burial armband that consisted of a gold stripe, a black stripe, and another gold stripe.

"The dark is only an interval," Tanya said, as she always did. "They'll come back to the light."

He never debated whether that was true. Not with her. She needed to believe it. If he was honest, he had to believe it, too. Otherwise the already terrible human cost would too quickly become unbearable.

Geary occasionally glanced toward Lieutenant Velez, who had continued vigorously opposing abandoning the wreck of his former ship and had formally protested the Alliance's actions. Velez had threatened to boycott the funeral service, until it became clear that it was going forward regardless of whether he attended.

"To the honor of our ancestors," Geary called, ending the service. As he did so, thrusters lit off on the two Alliance heavy cruisers with towlines attached to the sturdiest remaining portions of the wreck. So did the thrusters on portable maneuvering units. Together, they began altering *Passguard*'s vector gradually enough to avoid tearing the wreck apart.

Boundless had left the rest of the fleet to join with the ships near the wreck of *Passguard* so that Ambassador Rycerz could attend the service in person. She stood to one side, attended only by Colonel Webb and a couple of his special forces soldiers who eyed the nearby sailors and Marines as if every one were a potential assassin.

"Thank you for coming," Geary said to her.

"It was the least I could do," Rycerz said, her eyes on the displays where the images of the dead were still visible. "It's clear that the fleet still regards those Rift Federation sailors as . . . what's the word . . . shipmates? So I felt on behalf of the Alliance I should honor them as if they were our own."

"It was an important gesture, coming in person," Geary said. "Not many are openly saying it, but I can tell they were impressed that you made that effort."

"I hope you don't think I did it just for show," Ambassador Rycerz said. It was hard to tell just how she felt about that.

Geary barely avoided shrugging in reply. "One of the lessons I've learned is that everything we do might as well be for show. It gets judged that way regardless of our motives."

"You would know that as well as anyone, wouldn't you?" Rycerz looked to one side, where the ranks of fleet personnel still stood, waiting to be dismissed. "I want to personally thank those Marines as well."

"Which Marines do you mean?"

"The ones who went aboard the *Passguard* first." Rycerz paused, plainly trying to find the right words. "They're trained to kill, to risk their lives to defeat an enemy," she finally said. "But that same training, those same skills and equipment, could also be used to get help as fast as possible to men and women who desperately needed it. Even though those Marines thought they were risking their lives to do that. That's right, isn't it? They thought it might be a trap?"

"They did," Geary said. "They went in ready for anything."

"Risking their lives to save others." Rycerz sighed, shaking her head. "That ship, *Passguard*, almost embodies the contradictions of humanity. Built to wage war against other humans, callously sent on a mission facing impossible odds, and yet when everything went wrong the survivors hung together to save each other, and our own weapons and humans intended for war raced to save them. We should build more monuments to moments like that, Admiral, and fewer to battles."

"It was like that before the war," Geary said. At times like this, he was forcefully reminded that he was the only one present who actually remembered what things had been like before the war with the Syndicate Worlds began. "Hopefully it can be that way again." He led the ambassador over to the ranks of the Marines. Rycerz gave a short speech thanking them for their dedication and skills, saying they were the best ambassadors for what the Alliance aspired to be.

Afterwards, as the neat formations of sailors and Marines dissolved into a mass of personnel all heading somewhere else, Rycerz beckoned Geary to an unoccupied corner of the hangar. "I dropped in on Lieutenant Velez yesterday," she said. "He complained again about how we were disposing of *Passguard*."

"I hope you said 'you're welcome,'" Geary replied.

"Not as bluntly as that," Rycerz said. "I visited all of the survivors, including 'Petty Officer Masurin.' I have a diplomatic database on *Boundless*. Masurin's appearance matches that of a middle-level Rift diplomat named Carine Jolovetz. There's not a lot of information on her, except for a note that she is fervently devoted to Rift Federation independence and will object to anything she thinks impinges on it. Needless to say, she didn't break in any way from her imposture as Masurin."

Geary shook his head, feeling a mix of anger and resignation. "When the war ended, parts of the Alliance went looking for a new enemy because that was all they knew, fighting against someone. It looks like the Rift Federation has done the same, but the new enemy they're looking at is us. I admit it'll be a relief when we send the survivors back aboard *Chinook*. Did *Chinook* bring any updates I should know about?"

Rycerz paused, gazing at him. "Perhaps I should summarize rather than go through them one by one. Every government or association in human-occupied space, including private companies and foundations, is trying to learn as much as possible about the Dancers. Some are making open requests, many are employing espionage. What they seek includes the exact routes you took to reach the Dancers and return to human space."

The implications of that were easy to see. "They all want to contact the Dancers directly instead of letting the Alliance be the only ones able to speak with the aliens. The Rift Federation expedition wasn't an isolated case. It's the first of many. And we've just established a direct link with Midway so they don't need to cross Syndic space to get a lot closer to the Dancers." Another thought hit on the heels of the first. "Are they trying to learn about the enigmas as well?"

"Yes . . . and no."

He got that, too. "They want to know the route through enigma space, but not anything about the danger?"

Ambassador Rycerz shook her head, gazing into infinity. "Those who have made open requests have been clear in their belief that the hostilities with the enigmas are due to either the Syndicate Worlds invading their space or to the Alliance fleet under a certain famous officer invading their space, or both. They are certain a properly peaceful approach will produce better results."

"I thought our reports, including those from the civilian experts on nonhuman intelligence who were with us, made it clear that we tried a peaceful approach."

"No one wants to hear that a nonhuman intelligent species doesn't want anything to do with us," Rycerz said. "If they're hostile and attack us? We can understand that."

"But they have attacked us," Geary said.

"Have they?" Her expression made it clear she was asking him to think outside his own experience.

He took a moment to do that. "They've attacked the Syndics. And the former Syndics at Midway. And the Alliance fleet, when we entered their own space."

Rycerz nodded, her mouth twisting. "They've attacked other humans, but they haven't attacked the Alliance, except when we sent the fleet into their territory. And you just know the Syndics provoked the attacks, right? This isn't just coming from part of the public. Parts of the Alliance government have expressed those sentiments, though if you try to quote me I'll deny telling you that."

"The Syndics may well have provoked attacks," Geary admitted. "Still, I'm surprised that the idea the enigmas don't want to coexist with us is so hard to grasp. Especially after the enigmas appear to have leaked hypernet technology to us in the hopes humanity would discover that hypernet gates could be used as weapons capable of destroying entire star systems, and use that against ourselves."

"That's speculation," Rycerz said with a sigh. "We don't have proof."

"And the possibility that the enigmas tricked the Syndicate Worlds into starting the war with the Alliance in the first place—"

"What?" Ambassador Rycerz gave him a wide-eyed look of surprise.

He gazed back at her, puzzled by the reaction. "I put it in my reports. Some of the things we learned about the Syndics, and the enigmas, led us to wonder if the Syndics hadn't been counting on enigma support in their initial attacks on the Alliance. As bad as those attacks were, they couldn't have knocked out the Alliance, and they missed some very important potential targets."

Rycerz frowned in thought, one hand going to her chin. Finally, she looked back at Geary, surprising him with a tight smile. "If that's true, it's a good thing."

"How is that a good thing?" he asked, baffled.

"It means the Syndics were able to talk to the enigmas about something the enigmas wanted. To discuss matters enough to at least develop a joint plan. That's a lot more than we've seen with the enigmas elsewhere, right?"

"A lot more," Geary agreed.

"We just have to find a thing, or things, that the enigmas want badly enough," Ambassador Rycerz added. "If we can get them talking, maybe we can start actually communicating with them."

"The only thing they seem to want that badly is us being wiped out."

Rycerz nodded slowly. "And be sure that there will be some segments of humanity willing to promise that, assuming they can use the enigmas against their human enemies and somehow avoid themselves becoming victims. That must be what the Syndic leaders intended, and they got betrayed straight off. We'd have to be very careful what lies we told." She noticed Geary staring at her last words and laughed. "A very old book named *The Devil's Dictionary* defined 'diplomacy' as 'the patriotic art of lying for one's country.' It's what we do, Admiral. But if it's not done well, it can cause more harm than good. You've given me something important to think about. Thank you."

"I'm glad that I could help." He gestured toward the image of *Passguard*'s wreck. "Once the cruisers finish their work here they can rejoin the rest of the fleet. In three days we should be able to break our orbit and head to the jump point for Pele."

"Make it five days. Or six," Ambassador Rycerz said. "We're going to have to take *Boundless* and *Dauntless* to near orbit about Midway's main planet again. Do you enjoy formal diplomatic receptions, Admiral?"

"Not really," Geary said.

"Then I regret to inform you that we're going to have one. Both President Iceni and General Drakon will attend in person. As will you and I and diverse others, of course."

"Of course." At least dreading the upcoming diplomatic reception would for a few days give him some respite from dreading the trip through enigma space.

"RELAX," Desjani advised as she ran a critical eye over his uniform, making a minor adjustment to something that hadn't seemed perfect to her.

Geary sighed. "I never liked diplomatic receptions when I was a junior officer. I always felt awkward."

"If you're going to command a fleet, you need to get used to this sort of thing," she said as the shuttle came to rest in *Boundless*'s spacious dock. "If things get too rough just give me the sign and I'll pretend I got a high-priority message about something you have to return to *Dauntless* to deal with."

The walk through *Boundless* from the shuttle dock to the ballroom gave them a chance to check out the security along the route. Colonel Webb's "honor guard" special forces had been augmented with an impressive number of Marines in dress uniforms.

Inside the ballroom, Geary stopped for a moment as he saw that one entire wall was projecting an image of being open to space, the globe of Midway's primary world an arc of mostly blue and white across the bottom half. The view was awesome, dramatic, and profoundly disturbing to anyone with much experience in space.

"Why do civilians like this?" Tanya grumbled, distrustful eyes fixed on the view. "Being exposed to open space? They do realize how deadly that is, right?"

"But until it kills you, you get one hell of a view," someone said.

Geary and Desjani turned to see General Drakon eyeing them with a crooked smile. Drakon's uniform betrayed only a few signs of its Syndicate Worlds origin, and bore on the left breast only a small cluster of campaign ribbons. Drakon apparently wasn't the sort to show off rafts of medals and ribbons. Surprised to see the co-ruler of Midway apparently alone, Geary glanced around, spotting men and women who had that particular bodyguard look about them ranged nearby, covering every approach toward Drakon.

"You've spent time in space, General?" Desjani asked.

"Sure." Drakon gestured toward the view of Midway as if he were ordering a unit to charge it. "The Syndicate doesn't believe in specialized space infantry like the Alliance Marines. Ground forces fight everywhere. It's more efficient that way," he added dryly.

"Have you given any thought to specialized space infantry?" Geary asked, thinking he should try to learn anything he could while speaking directly to Drakon.

"A bit." Drakon smiled again, this time looking slightly predatory. "Colonel Rogero's brigade has been getting a lot of space combat training. We can't call them Marines, of course." He glanced around the ballroom. "Is your Marine commander here? Carabali?"

"She's helping coordinate security," Geary said.

"I was wondering if we'd faced off at Wotan," Drakon said. "Tough fight."

"I'll ask her to call you," Geary said, not surprised that General Drakon had been briefed on the backgrounds of the senior Alliance officers.

Drakon gazed at the planet below them a moment longer before glancing at Desjani. "Choosing aim points for orbital bombardment?"

Captain Desjani gave a guilty start. "To be honest, yes. Not seriously, though."

"Force of habit," Drakon said. "It's how you and me view the universe, right? We've spent so many years doing it that now we do it without even thinking." He paused, frowning. "That's what worries me about all of these aliens. We don't really know how they view things. What do *they* see when they look down at a planet? I understand that's a big part of this Alliance mission. To learn more about how they think."

"That's right," Geary said. He realized that Drakon's bodyguards had set up a tighter perimeter surrounding the three of them, maintaining their privacy. "They've helped humanity, but a lot of people would like to have a better handle on why they've done that."

"I'm one of those people," Drakon said. "I want to discuss a deal."

"A deal?"

The general turned his back on the view of Midway, facing outward toward the star Pele. "You want our continued cooperation. You want Midway as a forward base. Don't deny it," he added before Geary could speak. "You're a good commander. You think about things like that, right? It's what we do. But we also have to keep the people happy. I want my people to know we're not giving away anything to your people."

Drakon paused, waiting for Geary's reply.

"I understand," Geary said, not wanting to say more before he knew what Drakon was driving at.

"President Iceni and I want to send two representatives along with you to Dancer space," Drakon said. "So we can say we're participating in this mission, and so we can say we're watching you. You're Black Jack, so our people believe you're for them, but you've got a lot of people working for you that don't get that benefit of the doubt."

"Who do you want to send?" Geary asked, trying his best to keep his tone of voice as neutral as possible.

Drakon took a drink from the glass in one hand before replying. "Colonel Rogero for one. His loyalty to me is unquestioned, and he's operated independently before. The other will be Kommodor Bradamont."

"Bradamont?" Desjani blurted out in surprise.

Drakon smiled again. "Right. See, Bradamont's devotion to Rogero couldn't be clearer. She's going to support him. President Iceni considers her to be reliable. But Bradamont is also one of your people, and you've already established that you consider her valuable enough to have represented you here. If she sees anything wrong, she'll be able to get to you. We can both be sure she'll respect our interests. Win-win, right?"

"I thought you'd want to send those two colonels we met on a previous visit to Midway," Geary said.

"Two colonels?" Drakon paused, his expression closing down, his eyes hooded. "Malin and Morgan. They're both . . . no longer available."

"I see." Whatever had happened to Malin and Morgan, it hadn't been something that Drakon enjoyed recalling. Geary realized that Desjani was giving him a look warning him to be careful with his words. He thought for a moment before nodding. "So, Rogero and Bradamont. I don't see why we can't make that happen." That was a neutral statement, not a commitment, right?

Drakon nodded as well. "Good." He glanced at Midway again. "How'd your officers like Midway?"

Lieutenant Iger and Lieutenant Jamenson had spent a few days of "honeymoon" on the planet. Fleet intelligence had wanted Iger to report on actual conditions there, but Geary had warned Iger not to do or say anything that would mark him as collecting intelligence. "They enjoyed it," Geary answered truthfully. "Lieutenant Iger says it's a really beautiful planet."

"It is," Drakon agreed. His eyes took on a brooding quality again as he looked at the planet below them. "Beautiful planets don't always survive the attention we give them. Gwen Iceni and I are both tired of planets being trashed. You've seen Kane, what the revolt and then the Syndicate retaliation has done there. I've spent my life destroying things." His gaze shifted to Desjani.

She nodded in reply to the unspoken question. "I have, too. But then, some things needed to be destroyed."

"Yeah." Drakon grinned, not taking offense. "Like that buried enigma base at Iwa. We couldn't get to it on the ground. We think the enigmas may be a generation ahead of us on ground combat capabilities. So we pulled our people off the planet and dropped a thirty-kilometer-wide rock on the base."

Desjani's eyes lit up. "A thirty-kilometer-wide rock?"

"Yeah," Drakon said. "Cracked the planetary crust. The planet used to be marginally inhabitable by humans, but not anymore. I wasn't there, but the videos are something. I'll send you some."

"Thank you, General," Tanya Desjani said, looking like she'd just found a big present for her hidden in a closet.

"We had to send a message," Drakon told Geary. "Let the enigmas know that if they stuck a foot into human space and wiped out any more settlements we'd tear that foot off and ram it down their throats. Maybe it won't deter more attacks. But they know what we'll do if they try again. We had a ship pop into Pele and broadcast that video to the enigma sentry ships there." He rubbed his chin with one hand. "And we told them we don't want more war with the enigmas. Leave us alone and we'll leave them alone. What we want is to build something here. Something that lasts. We're trying, anyway. Gwen is talking to your ambassador right now about sending some of our representatives along with that ship back to Alliance space. They want to talk deals, but they also want to learn how things work there." His eyes went to Geary. "This voting. And elected government. The workers here seem happy with it, but it feels unstable. I keep wondering what would happen if something happened to Gwen."

"It is unstable," Geary said. "Democracies can be destroyed in all kinds of ways. It's a constant vigilance problem."

"I've heard rumors that the Alliance is having some problems dealing with how things are after the war with the Syndicate formally ended," Drakon added.

"They're true," Geary said. "Nothing like the problems the Syndicate Worlds has faced, of course." Should he mention the disastrous dark ship program and the way some members of the Alliance Senate had secretly taken actions against Alliance law? No, not unless Drakon asked about it and showed he already knew. "We're trying to fix them."

"Hmmm." Drakon looked down at the drink in his hand. "I've got a daughter," he said abruptly. "I worry about her. Someday I'd like her to see the Alliance in person."

Surprised at the sudden change in topic, Geary glanced at Desjani, who was maintaining a poker face. "I don't see why she couldn't," he said.

"Would you personally host her?"

Desjani's eyebrows went up. After a moment, she nodded to Geary.

"We'd be happy to," Geary said. "When . . . ?"

"Not for a long time," Drakon said. "The kid is still in diapers. But someday, you know? Good talking with you, Admiral. You, too, Captain. I'd better link up with Gwen."

"Good talking to you, General," Geary said.

As Drakon moved off, still surrounded by his guards, Geary rubbed the back of his neck. "Did we know that they had a daughter?" he asked Desjani.

"He said *he* had a daughter," she pointed out. "Not that they had a daughter. Drakon never said 'we' as in him and Iceni when he talked about the daughter."

"Why would Iceni tolerate that? It sounds like the kid was born not too long ago."

Desjani shrugged. "The mother could be someone who died a decade ago and left some eggs frozen. If I read Iceni right, I think you can assume whoever she was, the mother is dead."

"He's worried about her," Geary said.

Desjani laughed, surprising him. "Oh, yeah. Didn't you catch all of that? Yes, he's worried *about* her, but he's also worried about *her*."

He tried running that through his brain twice and still couldn't figure it out. "What?"

"He's worried about what'll happen to her," she explained, "but he's also worried about what she'll do. Usually daughters have to be a bit older before their fathers worry about both of those things. I wonder what her mother was like. Oh, by the way." Desjani pulled back one sleeve of her dress uniform to reveal the bracelet she'd been left by Victoria Rione. "This thing was going crazy with alerts while General Drakon was near us. That uniform of his is laced with enough hidden defensive and offensive equipment to take on a destroyer single-handed."

"I guess in some ways Drakon still thinks like a Syndic. Or still has to cope with the problems created by the Syndic system." Geary looked around them, realizing that even though Drakon had left there was still a bubble around him and Desjani, as if the others present were reluctant to approach them. "I guess if we want to talk to anyone else we'll have to make the first move."

"There's a bunch of uncomfortable-looking scientists over there," Desjani said, pointing to a corner near a refreshment table.

"I see Dr. Bron and Dr. Rajput," Geary said. "Since that group is going back on *Chinook*, we should wish them a safe journey."

"And Dr. Cresida," Desjani said, her voice flat. "If she wasn't Jaylen Cresida's sister I'd be happy to kick her butt hard enough to help her on her way back to the Alliance."

"She saved our butts from what Dr. Kottur planned," Geary reminded her. He led the way to the scientists, who seemed happy to see a familiar face. "Thanks for the great work you guys did. We're sorry to see you go."

Dr. Bron looked at his companions. "Uh, about that, Admiral. Uh, we're trying to get approval to stay."

"Stay? At Midway?"

"No, with this fleet," Dr. Rajput said. "We talked about the chance to interact directly with the Dancers and learn firsthand about their technology. We want to try that."

"Is someone objecting to that idea?" Geary asked.

"Security officials on the ambassador's staff," Dr. Bron said. "They're worried about our best scientists being, um . . ."

"Within the grasp of horrible alien claws," Dr. Cresida said, her voice and expression both deadpan. "What if they suck out our brains and learn all of humanity's secrets?"

"We already gave them duct tape," Geary said.

The scientists looked uneasy, only Jasmine Cresida speaking what was on their minds. "Which we've been informed was a mistake not to be repeated."

"What?"

"Giving away human technology—" Dr. Bron began in a tone that made it clear he wasn't happy.

"Duct tape?" Desjani said.

"Was stupid," Dr. Cresida finished for Dr. Bron. "Or so we're told."

Dr. Rajput made a face. "It's like they expect the Dancers to hand us all of their tech while we hold on to every bit of ours like dragons protecting their gold."

"Who is 'they'?" Geary asked in what he thought was a reasonable tone. From the way everyone's eyes went to him, though, he must have sounded at least a bit as upset as he felt. "Whose policy is this?"

"The tech transfer people on the ambassador's staff," Dr. Cresida said.

"This doesn't technically fall under your responsibilities," Desjani cautioned him.

"No, it doesn't," Geary said. "But I do have a stake in the success of this mission. Why did the Alliance send along so many people who seem set on sabotaging it?"

An uncomfortable silence followed his statement, one that was finally broken by Dr. Cresida, who was watching him in that speculative way she had, as if trying to fit him into some sort of grand unified theory of human oddities. "You ask interesting questions, Admiral," she said. It was hard to tell what Dr. Cresida meant by that.

"I'll speak to the ambassador," Geary promised them.

He and Desjani headed toward Ambassador Rycerz, resplendent in official Alliance diplomatic black tie, but saw her engaged in conversation with General Drakon and President Iceni, the small group isolated by the combined forces of both Iceni's and Drakon's bodyguards, who were mingling in a visibly uncomfortable way with some of Colonel Webb's special forces soldiers protecting the ambassador. Rycerz, looking about for a moment, spotted Geary and very subtly shook her head to indicate he shouldn't barge in. Whatever this was didn't involve the military side of this mission.

Frustrated, Geary led Desjani to one side of the ballroom, the side opposite the virtual window on space, to where an autobar waited for customers. "You know the trick with these, right?" Desjani said. She entered a rapid series of commands that resulted in a new menu popping up. "And now instead of being limited to the cheap stuff, we have access to the VIP drinks. Want a single malt?"

"Sure. Neat." He took a look at the new menu. "Did Master Chief Gioninni show you that trick?"

"I knew that trick before Gioninni reported aboard," Desjani said. She looked over as a man in an obviously new suit came walking up and stared uncertainly at the autobar. "Need some help?"

"This is a different drink menu, isn't it?" the man asked.

"No," Desjani said. "It isn't. What's your poison?"

"Um . . . that." The man touched the command, waiting as the bar produced the drink.

Seeing that Rycerz was still engaged with Iceni and Drakon, Geary nodded to the man. "Hi. What brings you to Midway?"

After a long pause while the man appeared to be trying to remember the answer to the question, he nodded quickly. "Senn. My name's John Senn. I'm an historian."

"An historian?"

Senn nodded wearily, his posture that of a man expecting to hear jokes he'd already heard countless times. "And why do they need an historian, right? It's hard to get people interested in even what happened a hundred years ago, let alone much longer ago than that."

"As it happens," Geary said, "I'm pretty knowledgeable about what happened a hundred years ago. So why are you here?"

"Because I studied something everyone else thought was garbage," John Senn said, his stance stiffening as if he expected a challenge. "Visits by aliens to Earth, prior to humanity expanding into the universe. And then evidence of sentient alien species in star systems we've explored and occupied since then. Which made me either a fool or a huckster in the eyes of other historians. The idea was always regarded as somewhat fringe and off the wall, something populated by gullible conspiracy theorists. And once we started traveling to other stars, and finding no other intelligent species, the possibility that Earth might've been visited by such species was totally discounted. We should've at least found ruins marking the presence of aliens on other worlds, right? As a result the idea of studying evidence of alien visitations to Earth became regarded as fit for scholars of folklore or popular superstition, not an actual historical specialty."

"Why'd you do it, then?" Geary asked.

John Senn paused, thinking. "I guess because everyone told me it wasn't worth looking at. It made me wonder how many people had seriously looked. Or if they'd discounted any possible real evidence because it was tainted by all of the nonsense peddled by true believers. My decision was . . . not welcomed by other historians. I've been sidelined. I could never get a doctorate because my attempts at dissertations were all dismissed as nonsense. But then that admiral found some intelligent alien species. Is he here?"

"Right here," Desjani said, pointing at Geary.

"Oh! I'm sorry! I—!"

"It's all right," Geary said. "So, suddenly you weren't a fraud?"

John Senn grinned. "Suddenly I was the only expert on plausible evidence of alien presence in human-occupied space. Because I was always rigorous, you see? I just tried to look at things with clear eyes instead of already knowing what they were before I looked. Like those ruins the Dancers say they left in Durnan Star System? Those had been dismissed as natural phenomenon even though they looked remarkably regular. But if you went in thinking, 'It can't be aliens,' then you're going to conclude it can't be aliens."

"That's very—" Geary began, halting when he saw Desjani look past him with sudden concern. He turned, seeing General Drakon moving toward them very quickly, his surrounding screen of bodyguards trying to keep up.

As Drakon got within a couple of meters of them he said one word. "Duck."

Desjani stared at him. "How did you hear about the duck?"

"What?" Geary said, though he wasn't sure if he was addressing Drakon or Desjani.

"Duck!" Drakon repeated, his hands reaching to grab Geary and Desjani and drag them down.

Glimpsing Senn the historian looking on with a baffled expression, Geary swung one hand out as he fell, snagging a grip on Senn's new suit and pulling him down with them.

As they all hit the deck, the autobar exploded.

FOUR

THE blast reverberated through the ballroom, followed by a moment of shocked silence, which quickly dissolved into shouts. Geary saw the military and bodyguards present dropping to the deck in case the first explosion was followed by others, while the civilians mostly stood frozen in shock.

A half-dozen Marines rushing to Geary nearly ended up in a fight with Drakon's bodyguards before he and Drakon told both sets of protectors to stand down.

Reaction teams spread through the ballroom, scanning for more threats and ushering guests toward the exits.

John Senn the historian began slowly, shakily coming to his feet, only to freeze when several weapons held by bodyguards and Marines lined up on him. "I'm not dangerous," he said. "I'm an historian."

The Marines lowered their weapons, but Drakon's bodyguards did not.

Drakon gestured to them. "Stand down, I said." Looking at Senn, he studied him. "In the Syndicate, historians are people who change

records of the past to match whatever the current policy is or whatever
the current leaders want. That's why 'lie' and 'history' mean the same
thing in the Syndicate. What kind of historian does the Alliance use?"

Senn stared at Drakon in disbelief. "A different kind. A good historian tries to learn what really happened, even if that offends people."

"Interesting idea," Drakon said. "How is it you're still alive?"

"Sometimes I wonder." Senn looked at the remains of the autobar.

A Marine major ran up to Geary. "Sir, if you will follow me—"

"Hold on," Geary said, watching Drakon glance around with a sort
of weary fatalism before walking over to the remains of the autobar.

"Looks like they used a shotgun frag pattern," Drakon commented
to Geary. "Look at the upward angles of the exit holes. This was aimed
at whoever was standing in front of the menu. That's why no one else
got hurt. The frag went over their heads." He gave Geary a twisted
smile. "Lay you odds there was a biometric fuse to trigger it. You never
touched the menu, did you?"

"No," Geary said.

"If you had, it probably would've gone off instantly and we'd all be
mourning your untimely end. But you were close enough for the fuse
to go active. My, um, scanners picked that up."

"Why didn't our security spot this?" Ambassador Rycerz demanded
as she reached them, gazing in shock at the wreck of the autobar.

"Maybe you ought to ask them about that," Drakon said with a
smile that exposed his teeth. "I guess President Iceni and I should call
it a night. Thanks for the entertainment."

"I deeply apologize for—" Rycerz began.

Drakon waved off her words. "There's a saying in the Syndicate. The
party hasn't started until the first assassination attempt."

President Iceni, her eyes taking in every detail of the scene, nodded,
her composure cool and controlled. "You should have a talk with your
security workers, Admiral. They may be in need of some motivation."

"Yes," Geary said. He nodded to Drakon. "Thank you, General."

Drakon grinned. "Now you owe me one."

"I do. Gearys honor our debts."

"So do I, Admiral." He waved a farewell and followed Iceni as she walked away, her movements casual and unworried in a way that was clearly designed to convey confidence and strength. Iceni must have had to put on such displays many times.

A Marine colonel had shown up to reinforce the major. "Admiral, we should clear the area."

Geary watched Drakon and Iceni almost strolling out of the ballroom on their way to the shuttle dock. "Okay. But we walk at my pace." Being rushed out of here would not only create the wrong image of him, it might also spread fear among those remaining. The leaders of Midway knew that.

Colonel Webb had also shown up from the command post where he'd been overseeing security. Webb looked ready to spit fire, but he kept his voice steady and calm. "I will find out what happened," he promised Rycerz and Geary.

"You might want to check the rest of the autobars first off," Desjani suggested. "It was just chance that we went to this one."

Surrounded by Marines who had brushed off offers of support from Webb's special forces, Geary walked slowly out of the ballroom, aware of all the eyes that were on him. Like Iceni, he acted totally unconcerned on the outside, even though on the inside his guts were churning in belated reaction to the assassination attempt.

ONCE he and Desjani were in *Dauntless*'s shuttle, away from the eyes of others, Geary finally relaxed, letting a slow shudder roll through him. "Damn," he muttered.

"Whoever did that had better hope I don't catch them," Desjani said, a low tremor of fury in her voice. "How the hell did something like that get past security?"

"I have a feeling that Colonel Webb will be intensely focused on that," Geary said, leaning back in his seat as he tried to calm himself.

"Did you see him? People like Webb take a lot of pride in being able to do their jobs well, and that pride just took a major hit amidships."

"Good," Desjani retorted. "It's a good thing Drakon told us to duck."

Which reminded him of something. "Why did you say that? When Drakon said 'duck' you said something about how did he know?"

Desjani grimaced. "And so it begins. Okay. I've been keeping something from you."

"What is it?" Geary asked, eyeing her with worry.

Desjani gave him a flat look. "We have a duck aboard the ship."

"What?"

"There's a duck aboard *Dauntless*. You know, feathers, quack. A duck. I found out yesterday."

"A duck." Geary paused to try to make sense of that. "How—?"

"The Marine detachment," Captain Desjani said. "They somehow smuggled it aboard at Varandal, and have kept it undetected until now."

"That's . . . both disturbing and impressive," Geary said, trying to imagine how the Marines had kept the ship's interior sensors from spotting a duck. "What with that and what just happened to us, it looks like our security sensors have some unexpected blind spots."

"You might say that."

"Why did the Marines smuggle a duck aboard the ship?"

Desjani sighed. "Booze was involved, to the surprise of absolutely no one looking into it. Drunk Marines returning from liberty came across a duck and decided to bring it back with them. Gunnery Sergeant Orvis claims he knew nothing of the duck. I'm going to give him the benefit of the doubt on that."

"What were they feeding it?"

"Fruits, vegetables, ration bars, beef jerky—"

"Beef jerky? They fed a duck beef jerky?"

"They're Marines," Desjani said. "Apparently the duck didn't really like the jerky, but it loves fish cakes. And the occasional beer."

"Where were they getting the occasional beer?" Geary asked.

"Another good question," Desjani said. "Fortunately, Master Chief Gioninni noticed the occasional beers disappearing from ship's inventory and went looking for the answer."

Geary nodded, happy that something finally made sense. "Because Gioninni was unhappy with someone else misappropriating beers?"

"You got it." Captain Desjani sighed again. "Anyway, we've got a duck."

"What are you going to do with it?"

She raised an eyebrow at him. "I could bump that question up to the admiral, since *Dauntless* is your flagship."

"But you won't," Geary said, hoping that was the case. None of the options he could think of would bode well for the duck, and inflicting a bad fate on the creature would likely hurt the morale of a lot of sailors and Marines around the fleet. It felt odd to worry about that in the immediate aftermath of someone trying to kill him, but he did. "Maybe Midway—"

"I am not leaving an Alliance duck at the mercy of the former Syndics in this star system!"

"Any number of commanding officers turn a blind eye when it comes to a ship's mascot," Geary suggested, remembering ships that had unofficially carried a dog, or a cat, or some more exotic creature. "It's always been that way."

Captain Desjani shook her head, frowning. "Fleet regulations prohibit mascots. I don't turn a blind eye to regulations. But I won't make the duck suffer for the dumb actions of those Marines. Therefore, I'm informing you that the duck is officially a member of the crew."

He hadn't expected to hear that, either. "Officially? Don't members of the crew have to be human?"

"You'd think that'd be the case, wouldn't you?" Desjani said. "But, in fact, the regulations are written broadly enough to include anyone, which means they also, broadly interpreted, can include a duck."

"So, it's not a mascot, it's a member of the crew." Geary shrugged. "Okay."

"You'll have to confirm the duck's rank as an ensign under battle-field promotion regulations," she added.

"Why an ensign?"

"So the Marines will have to salute the duck."

"Okay," Geary said again. Trust Tanya Desjani to find a way to make discipline and punishment as effective as possible. "What else are you doing to the Marines?"

Captain Desjani frowned. "Since my Marine detachment appears to have way too much free time on their hands, Gunny Orvis and I are going to work their butts off. In addition to them now officially having primary care responsibility for the duck."

"Is that a good idea? Beef jerky. And beer."

"They're Marines."

Which really did explain everything.

EARLY the next morning, Geary and Desjani sat in a secure conference room aboard *Dauntless*. Also present in person was Lieutenant Iger. Opposite them sat the virtual presences of both Ambassador Rycerz and Colonel Webb. Webb, never the most open or happy of people, was even more closed off and somber than usual.

"As Captain Desjani suggested," Webb said, "every other autobar had the same booby trap installed, designed to discharge fragmentation into Admiral Geary as he touched the drink menu."

"How did those things pass undetected?" Geary asked.

Webb's jaw tightened. "They were very precisely designed. Every aspect of them was configured to avoid detection by the latest Alliance security systems. Which meant whoever designed them and installed them knew everything there is to know about our latest security systems."

Ambassador Rycerz let out a loud sigh. "Which means in turn that this was an inside job."

"Yes, Ambassador," Webb said, looking as if those words were being physically pulled out of him by painful hooks. "I cannot rule out any of my own personnel as possibly being involved, because all of them were capable of it."

"How did General Drakon's detection devices spot the danger?" Rycerz asked.

"Syndic gear, and their stuff is still basically Syndic even though they've been modifying the hell out of it, isn't exactly like ours. Tiny differences in operating parameters and sensitivity and things like that. Those differences were enough that something working on Syndic standards was able to spot indications of something designed specifically to defeat Alliance sensors."

Geary nodded. "Maybe we should consider trying to get access to more of the latest Syndic gear so we can piggyback their capabilities on top of our own."

Webb frowned at him, then nodded. "That's certainly worth looking at, Admiral."

"Where do we go from here?" Rycerz asked.

Colonel Webb's frown deepened. "I admit that I paid insufficient attention in the past to the possibility that one of my own soldiers might be involved in illegal activity. I assure you that won't happen again. Everyone has heard about the attack. We need to give them something, so I propose leaking word that we suspect Drakon—"

"Bad idea," Geary said. "That could seriously poison the well, especially after he saved my life."

"Rogue elements at Midway?" Rycerz suggested. "Someone opposed to both Drakon and Admiral Geary?"

"That could work," Webb said. "What I want to do is give whoever was behind this a false sense of confidence that we're hunting up the wrong trees. That's the best way to get them to make a mistake." He paused. "I also recommend that Admiral Geary avoid if possible any further visits to *Boundless*. That's where maximum danger seems to exist for him."

"I agree," Rycerz said. "And I like your proposal. I'll find a way to let President Iceni know what we're doing so she won't feel we're lobbing false allegations to protect our own reputations. Colonel, you and your soldiers were handpicked for this mission because you are all exceptionally capable. Unfortunately, that's turned into a two-sided coin. I'm counting on you to prevent any further attacks."

"Yes, Ambassador," Colonel Webb said. "I *will* find out who's doing this."

"In the meantime, I'm going to make sure anybody and anything that has any physical contact with *Boundless* gets gone over with a fine-tooth comb," Tanya Desjani said.

"Lieutenant Iger," Geary said, "cooperate fully with Captain Desjani on this, and let us know if you hear anything that might bear on it, no matter how trivial it may seem."

After Iger had left and Webb's virtual presence had vanished, Ambassador Rycerz visibly sagged, the tension she'd been carrying inside finally allowed to show. "Can we trust Colonel Webb?"

Geary weighed the question. "I don't know," he finally said. "But he's going to assume we're watching him regardless. Why wasn't he inside the ballroom last night, shadowing you?"

Ambassador Rycerz made a face. "We jointly decided it would be best for Colonel Webb to monitor the reception from a nearby location. He was maintaining a low profile aboard *Boundless* because a couple of days ago he was needed at an odd hour, and instead of asking one of his soldiers to wake him, *Boundless*'s duty officer sent a junior ship's officer. That young fool tried to wake Webb by shaking his shoulder."

"Ancestors save us," Desjani said. "Waking a special forces combat veteran that way? Is the junior officer dead?"

"The junior officer suffered some broken bones but fortunately avoided dying." Rycerz grimaced. "I'd heard it was a bad idea to try to wake combat veterans in that manner, but I half thought it was just some sort of military in-joke."

"No," Geary said. "Ground forces and Marines in particular can be dangerous to wake. Their instinct when 'attacked' in their sleep is to defend themselves. General Carabali court-martialed one of her corporals for thinking it would be funny to send a newly arrived recruit in to wake her like that."

"I take it the recruit survived," Rycerz said.

"With a number of bruises," Geary said. "All right. I understand Webb's reasons for not being at the reception in person. You might ask President Iceni for some tips on staying alive when some of your own people might be trying to kill you."

Rycerz's laugh was short and bitter. "They already think the Alliance is as deep a snake pit as the Syndicate Worlds. I'm beginning to wonder why I got chosen for this mission. Am I really an exception to those who seem to have been selected for their ability to sabotage what we're supposed to do?"

"I think so," Geary said. "But your instructions, like that throwdown you did with me at Atalia, might've been slanted to create problems. That way, if you did your job as directed, you'd create even more trouble. Speaking of problems, the physicists who linked the hypernet gate here to the Alliance want to stay with you and see what they can learn from the Dancers."

"Why is that a problem?" Rycerz asked. "I think it's a great opportunity."

"They've been stonewalled by the tech transfer people on your staff."

Ambassador Rycerz didn't say anything for several seconds, her face hardening. "I'll take care of that," she finally said in a carefully controlled voice. "We don't have much time, do we? *Chinook* is heading for the hypernet gate tomorrow?"

"That's correct," Geary said. "They'll probably be happy to have fewer passengers since they've already gained the survivors from the *Passguard* as well as the former prisoners of war we picked up at Kane."

Rycerz nodded, her expression shadowed. "What do you think is going to happen to Lieutenant Velez? He saved everyone who survived aboard *Passguard*. He got them to safety. But . . ."

"But the mission was a disaster," Geary said. "And a majority of the Rift Federation fleet was wiped out."

"They might recognize his heroism," Desjani said. "Play up the survival, the impressive achievement of getting *Passguard* to safety despite all of the damage done to her. Or they might make Velez a scapegoat, him and the other survivors. If the people who ordered those ships on that suicidal mission want to avoid accepting any responsibility, they might try to pin the failure on Lieutenant Velez. He's low ranking, he's an emotional wreck after holding his crew together long enough to get them here so he'll have a hard time defending himself, and he's convenient."

"You have a very low opinion of politicians, don't you, Captain?" the ambassador said.

"Politicians and admirals," Desjani replied. "Present company excepted. When things go bad and there's a choice between letting the chips fall where they may or protecting an admiral's backside, the choice is almost always to protect that admiral."

"Or that politician," Rycerz said. "I won't debate you on that. All right, let me see what else I need to fix. Please don't die, Admiral."

CHINOOK returning to Alliance space meant all of the prisoners of war recovered at Kane would go back with it. Including one former POW in particular.

Geary stood up as his grandnephew Michael entered the admiral's cabin. He ought to be used to this after spending so much time around his grandniece Jane, but it still felt very odd to realize that in terms of age he was about the same as they were. "I'm glad you could stop by."

"I'm glad you could take time to see me," Michael said, acting both subdued and polite. "And that you're still alive."

"I've had more than my share of luck." Geary waved him to a seat before sitting down himself. "You and I haven't had much time together. Jane has talked about you, of course, but I still hate to see you go."

Michael nodded, his eyes on the deck. "I wanted you to know all of the former prisoners from my camp are going back. They appreciate the offer to join your ships, but they have people to see and lives to restart."

"Understood. Are you okay?"

"All in all considered? I'm great." Michael paused. "I know our first encounters weren't, um, happy reunions."

Geary smiled in the hope of relaxing Michael, wondering what he was having trouble saying. "You had your reasons."

"Yeah." Michael blew out a long breath, still avoiding Geary's gaze. "I needed to talk to you. About what happened at Kane. During the engagement with the Syndics."

Why would Michael be worried about that? "I've said it before. You did a great job maneuvering your ship in that fight. Even Tanya said she couldn't have done better."

"Thanks. Coming from her that really means something." Michael gazed at one bulkhead, his eyes growing distant, as if they were looking through it. "There's something that's not in my report. Something very important."

"What's that?"

"I froze." His eyes regained their focus, coming back to gaze at his great-uncle. "For a few seconds I couldn't move, couldn't talk, couldn't think. Paralyzed with indecision. Maybe fear, too." Michael ran one hand through his hair, grimacing. "It wasn't just the loss of *Repulse*. I've lost ships before that. We all have. I don't know what it was. Maybe just one battle too many. Maybe the stress of being in that Syndic prison for so long. I managed to snap out of it, but I'm not sure how, and I'm not sure if I could snap out of it again." He sighed. "I'm not safe in command, not anymore. That's the truth. I honestly think I would freeze, maybe for a long time. Even at Kane my seconds of paralysis might have been fatal if they'd come at a different time."

What should he say? Geary tried to find the right words. "The war was hard on a lot of people. There are medications—"

"Yeah, I know. Happy pills. The docs could fix me up. Maybe." Michael made another face. "Admiral—"

"For the love of our ancestors, Michael, this is a personal visit. Call me John."

"Okay, Great-Uncle John, here's the truth." Michael inhaled deeply before speaking. "I don't want to be fixed. I don't want any more lives riding on my orders. I don't want another command. I've done my time, I've served honorably, and I'm done." As the last words left him he sagged in his seat like someone who'd just overcome a mighty obstacle.

Geary nodded. So that was it. He should have been expecting this. "Jane told me you two never wanted to join the fleet."

"We didn't have any choice," Michael said with a shrug. "The Geary curse, as we called it. Maybe if Dad had lived he would've let me take another path. Mom believed wholeheartedly in the Geary thing, though. She'd never have wanted us to let down Black Jack. Sorry for using that nickname." His face saddened, creased with old pain. "When Mom and Dad died . . . I was twelve, Jane was ten. Uncle Deake and Aunt Diana were already gone, and Diana's husband died the next year."

Michael looked up again. "Mom and Dad were on different ships. Did Jane tell you that? They died the same week, in battles at stars fifty light years distant from each other. It's hard to believe in the benevolence of the living stars when that happens."

"I'm very sorry," Geary said. "I remember Deake. He was . . . just a baby the last time I saw him."

"I don't remember much about him, either," Michael said. "He was gone a lot. Fighting. The only time I saw my dad break down was when we got the notice that he was missing and presumed dead." Another sigh. "So, it was me and Jane. I had to be the example. The eldest Geary of the last two left. And every step was measured in relation to you. No," Michael added. "Not you. That myth they made of you. Black Jack. No one could've lived up to that."

"I sure as hell can't," Geary said.

"From what I hear, you've made a good try of it." Michael sat back, looking as if he'd shed a burden. "I did my best. For Jane's sake, and Mom and Dad, and Uncle Deake and Aunt Diana. I got good at it. But I never loved it. And I admit I wasn't a model officer. Tanya probably told you I had a mouth on me. Hell, you experienced that yourself before *Repulse* was destroyed. Now . . ."

"You're going to leave the fleet," Geary said. "If that's what you want, go for it. You've done your time and served with honor. The fleet, the Alliance, has no right to demand more of you." He felt a wave of sadness, thinking of how many of his relatives had died during the last century because of his supposed example, but kept it inside. His great-nephew didn't need to be consoling him at a moment when Michael was finally confessing his true feelings.

Michael nodded in reply to the words Geary spoke, then unexpectedly smiled. "I needed to hear that. I needed to hear that from *you*. I don't know why. It's like only you could give me permission. Release me from my fate. Like some old fairy tale, where I'd been cursed and only one thing could lift the curse."

"I'm sorry," Geary said again, feeling inadequate to be hearing these things, and still feeling guilt at the way his supposed example had warped the lives of his relatives. "What do you want to do after you leave the fleet?"

"I don't know." Michael laughed. "I never thought about it. Why bother? I was a Geary. I had to go into the fleet."

"Go home," Geary urged him. "To Glenlyon. Go to the bunker and talk to Lyn."

Michael's smile turned into a grin. "Did you do that, too? Go down there and try to trigger the AI so you could talk about things you couldn't say to anyone else?"

"Yeah, I did that," Geary admitted. "I've dealt with a lot of AIs, but whatever Lyn did all those years ago is still the closest I've encountered to feeling like the real person is there. That woman was a genius."

"Did you show Tanya that secret room?" Michael asked.

"Yes," Geary said, laughing himself this time. "She signed her name on the wall alongside my old signature."

"What about the Room?" Michael asked. "Your old room? I was allowed to look in when I was kid, even take a couple of steps inside, but not touch anything."

"We stayed in, uh, the room," Geary said. "Stuff was touched."

Michael's face softened. "Good. I always felt as if . . . the way that room was kept unchanged . . . kept other things from changing. Like time and life were frozen in there. It felt wrong."

"It certainly weirded me out," Geary said. "Put in your resignation, Michael. You've earned it. How about Jane? She hasn't said anything about leaving the fleet, but I thought that was because we were looking for you."

"Jane." Michael shook his head. "Funny thing. She was just as unhappy as I was to be forced to serve by the Black Jack thing. But she not only got good at it, she learned to love it. Space is in her blood now. She is a Geary, after all, and that seems to be a family curse, too. A lot of us love space more than we do home. She'll serve as long as the fleet wants her. But I can't resign yet. I've got one mission left. I need to go back with those guys, the other survivors from *Repulse*, the others who were prisoners with me, and make sure they all get taken care of."

Geary nodded again. "Feel free to throw around the Geary name if you aren't getting results. Admiral Timbale is in charge at Varandal. He'll be happy to see you."

Michael made a face. "Timbale and I had words once . . . I was a jerk. Maybe if I apologize he won't hold it against me."

Feeling a little awkward, Geary remembered something. "I was forwarded a message by General Drakon yesterday. One of Midway's warships came back from Kane and carried a situation report from Colonel Aragon."

"Colonel Aragon?" Michael asked, raising his eyebrows. "Do you mean Executive Aragon?"

"Midway's people use normal military ranks," Geary said. "While we were still at Kane, Colonel Rogero told Aragon to start calling herself colonel instead of executive."

"How's she doing?"

"Not great," Geary said. "The locals are just barely abiding by their agreement not to attack Aragon's soldiers or the civilians they're guarding until Midway's transports get back there to lift them all off-planet. But there've been frequent attempts to provoke Aragon's soldiers into firing, probably to provide an excuse for an all-out attack to massacre the civilians."

Michael made a face. "War brings out the beast in a lot of people, doesn't it? Destina ran a tight ship, though. If anyone can keep those soldiers from overreacting, it's her."

"You seem to admire her."

"I do," Michael said, smiling again. "Can you believe I'm saying that about a Syndic executive? But you know I owe her my life. All of us who were prisoners in that orbital facility owe our lives to her." He gave Geary a speculative look. "Did I ever mention that? One of the things that tipped Destina off that the internal security agents, the ones the Syndics call snakes, were planning something bad was that stockpiles on the facility were all being drawn down. Like, at a certain point there'd be no more food. That's what made her dig to discover her unit would be getting orders to go fight Drakon's people. She's pretty certain that if she hadn't led her unit in a revolt and freed us, once that Syndic battle cruiser showed up it would have taken on all the snakes at the facility as well as Destina's unit. Then they would've set the facility's power core to overload and sailed off."

"Leaving you all to be blown to dust?" Geary said, shocked. "But . . . you at least were a great bargaining chip."

"Or a tremendous liability," Michael said. "Bring me out into the open and all the Syndic promises to free the Alliance POWs they were holding would be shown to be lies. I'm not surprised they decided to just get rid of the evidence."

"Damn." They talked a bit more, but the gap between their shared experiences was so great that they kept going back to the war, which was at least a form of bonding.

"I should be going," Michael finally said, checking the time. "It's nice of Tanya to put one of *Dauntless*'s shuttles at my disposal, but believe it or not I never wanted special treatment." He stood up, extending one hand. "I'm glad I got to know the real you. To finally understand."

Geary got up, gripping Michael's hand. "Me, too. Go have the life you always wanted."

"I hope there's still time for that." Michael Geary smiled slightly and walked to the door, but paused before opening it. He looked back with a rueful expression. "I just had a thought. What if the life I lived, the life I was forced into, kicking and screaming every step of the way, what if it turns out that was the life I really wanted? And I wouldn't admit it to anyone, even myself? Do you think the living stars would mess with someone that way?"

"You're asking me what the living stars might do to someone? The guy who drifted frozen in survival sleep for a century while everyone he knew grew old and died?"

"Yeah," Michael said. "I guess they would. I guess it's up to us how we deal with what the living stars send us." He hesitated, frowning. "I see Pelleas is still in command of *Gallant*. And Burdock is still captain of *Encroach*."

"That's right," Geary said, wondering why Michael had brought up those two battleship captains. "Pelleas distinguished himself during our last transit through Indras."

"Good." Michael shrugged. "Before . . . you were in command, they kept trying to get me to vocally support Admiral Bloch. Of course, they weren't alone in that back then."

"No," Geary said, remembering those days, and incidents like the Captain Falco mutiny. "Burdock and Pelleas haven't caused those kinds of problems for me. Why did you bring it up now?"

"Jinani Burdock sought me out yesterday," Michael said. "She wanted to talk about things back home. Politics. Saying the Alliance still needed a Geary to lead it. I told her the same thing I'd said when Bloch was in command of the fleet, that I wasn't that Geary." Michael turned a twisted smile toward Geary. "It was like she was waiting for me to take charge of the conversation. She and Pelleas are like that. Perfect Alliance battleship commanders. Steady and predictable to a fault, but not much in the way of initiative."

"Don't let Jane hear you say that," Geary commented, wondering what Captain Burdock had wanted Michael to say or do.

"Ha! Jane's heard it a lot. But the only reason she was given a battleship instead of a battle cruiser was to rebuke her for refusing to act like Black Jack supposedly did." Michael snorted in what seemed like self-mockery. "Anyone like Burdock or Pelleas looking for that in me is still going to be disappointed as well. See you on Glenlyon."

"Make sure you say goodbye to Tanya before you go!" For just a moment, he wasn't an admiral. He was a great-uncle saying goodbye to the grandnephew he barely knew, and trying to end this conversation on a high note. What would it have been like if he'd met great-grandnephews on Glenlyon?

The thought caused a long-buried memory to suddenly resurface. "Michael, do you have children? Jane said something about that to me once, but there wasn't anything in the family home about them."

The face Michael turned to him this time was rigidly controlled, as fixed as the visage of a statue. "I don't have any children waiting for me," he said, his voice also oddly emotionless.

"Is there something . . . ?" Geary asked, startled and worried by Michael's reaction to the question.

"No. It's just . . . a difficult topic." With an obvious effort, Michael smoothed out his expression and his voice. "It'll be nice to see Glenlyon again. I hope to see you there. May our ancestors guide you safely home."

And then he was gone before Geary could say anything else.

Geary kept his eyes on the closed door for a moment, wondering if he'd see Michael again, but knowing there was more than a small chance he wouldn't. Especially after what had happened at the diplomatic reception.

Which made him realize something else.

Michael had already left, but he could send him a message, warning him to be careful. Geary sat down, also quickly tapping out new orders for Admiral Timbale and the captain of *Chinook* as well as some requests. *Chinook* would carry Timbale's orders back to Varandal, delivering them well before the ship arrived at Umbaru Station.

The people who were trying to kill him might also target Michael. Because he was a Geary. He'd need protection.

Damn.

Maybe there was a Geary curse.

EARLY the next day, *Chinook*'s thrusters fired, followed by her main propulsion, accelerating the assault transport toward Midway's hypernet gate for the trip back to Alliance space. On the bridge of *Dauntless*, Geary watched *Chinook* for a moment, marveling that the long and dangerous journey through Syndic and former Syndic space once required to reach Midway had now been reduced to a single hypernet leap. "Sometimes I feel like we're just treading water," he said to Desjani. "Not getting anywhere. But that new hypernet link might really change things for the better."

She tossed him a skeptical glance. "One of these days, Admiral, that optimism of yours will lead you into trouble."

"It might. How's the shuttle bringing Colonel Rogero and Kommodor Bradamont doing?"

"Two minutes out. Then two minutes to secure it for acceleration. We can head out in four minutes."

"Good." As much as he was dreading what the enigmas might do, he was extremely tired of waiting here with little to do but worry. He took another look at his display, the armada of Alliance warships arrayed in orbit about the distant star of Midway. Over two hundred and sixty warships, all told. Michael Geary had looked at them with eyes that had looked on too many battles and commented that the fleet had sometimes lost nearly that many in one fight, Alliance and Syndic warships slamming at each other until one side finally crumbled, tens of thousands dead on both sides. And then the immense resources of the Alliance and of the Syndicate Worlds, scores of star systems with many planets, churned out new ships and found new sailors to replace those who'd died. And so it had gone, year after year, for nearly a century.

Michael had been stunned to learn that Geary's ships now represented the majority of the Alliance fleet. Stunned, and hopeful that the people and the resources once fed into the endless maw of the war were being put to better use.

But . . . "The gate."

"Hmmm?" Desjani said.

"Midway's hypernet gate," Geary said. "Now that it's linked to the Alliance hypernet, we're on the front lines of the defense against the enigmas. It's no longer a far-distant fight. The defense of human space is at our front door."

That had changed, too.

He'd already arrayed the fleet for the transit to Pele, and arrival there. Maybe the enigma ships that had nearly destroyed *Passguard* were gone. Maybe they'd been reinforced, and were waiting to hit the next human ships to come out of jump at Pele. Either way, the fleet would be ready. The twenty battleships under Geary's command, massive, heavily armed and armored, were formed in a three-dimensional defensive lattice at the front of the formation along with numerous heavy cruisers and destroyers. In the center were the assault transports, the auxiliaries vital to the fleet's long-term survival, and *Boundless* with its scientific and diplomatic embassies, surrounded by more destroyers and light cruisers. Behind them was another lattice made up by the eleven battle cruisers that were all that remained in Geary's fleet.

Able to react most quickly, the battle cruisers would intercept anything trying to attack from other angles.

If the enigmas were waiting at Pele, they'd be in for a nasty surprise.

"*Dauntless*'s shuttle is secure," Lieutenant Yuon reported from his bridge watch station.

"Good," Geary said. "Let's go." He tapped the command already prepared on his display.

On more than two hundred and sixty warships, thrusters and main propulsion lit off, accelerating the Alliance fleet toward the jump point for Pele and whatever waited there.

FIVE

JUMP space was notorious not only for the way it wore on human nerves with increasing force as the days went on, but also for the inability to do anything outside of the ship. Technically, bots or humans could work on the outside of the hull while in jump space, but if they lost physical contact with the ship for even a moment they'd be instantly and forever lost in the gray nothingness. Any task worthy of that level of risk was extremely rare. But even looking outside the ship brought no relief from the shut-in feeling, since no stars were visible, only the endless gray of jump space. Occasionally, at unpredictable intervals, bright lights with no known origin would suddenly flare in jump space. But those were too infrequent to watch for, and if seen could be just as likely to induce feelings of dread as of wonder. The resulting enforced inward focus while in jump space usually left too much time for worrying about things that couldn't be changed by worrying.

It did at least give Geary time to formally welcome Midway's representatives aboard *Dauntless*. Although even that felt odd, to have a formal dinner in the admiral's stateroom while thinking about what the enigmas might have waiting at Pele.

At least his dress uniform wasn't too uncomfortable. And Tanya looked outstanding in her uniform. "Captain Desjani, why are you fussing so much more than usual with my uniform?" Geary asked her.

"Just checking the modifications," she said, peering intently at one lapel.

"Modifications? I thought it went out for cleaning."

"As long as we had it, Senior Chief Tarrani and I decided to see about adding a few enhancements," Desjani said. "It's probably stuff a Syndic CEO would laugh at, but you'll be better protected next time we have to attend a diplomatic reception."

"What did you do to my uniform?" Geary demanded.

"Relax. Nothing is armed yet."

"'Armed'? Are there weapons built into this outfit?"

"Just a few. We're adding stuff to your working uniform, too."

"Tanya—"

"Oh, look, your guests are here."

It still felt strange to see Honore Bradamont wearing not the uniform of the Alliance fleet but that of Midway.

"Admiral Geary," Bradamont said, "I have the honor to present my husband, Colonel Donal Hideki Rogero of the ground forces of the free and independent Midway Star System."

"It's nice to see both of you again, this time in person," Geary said. The expandable table in the admiral's stateroom could have handled larger parties than the four of them, but Geary liked it this way. Four people, one on each side of the table. Each place was already set with plates and utensils, the plates automatically keeping the food on them at the right temperatures. Though they looked like fine china and crystal, the settings were made of materials strong enough to stop anything short of a hell lance. Sailors joked that the only thing tougher than the fleet's plates were the steaks sometimes served on special occasions.

As they gathered, before sitting, Geary reached for the wineglass at his seat. So did the others. "To absent friends," Geary said, raising his glass in the ancient toast to those dead in battle.

Rogero matched the movements of the Alliance veterans while saying nothing. "The Syndicate banned that toast," he explained. "They claimed it harmed morale by emphasizing those who'd died. As a result, we always do the toast silently, saying the words inside ourselves."

The toast over, everyone sat down, Geary moving with particular care despite Tanya's assurances that nothing had yet been armed.

"What delicious meal has the fleet prepared for the admiral tonight?" Bradamont asked.

"See if you can guess," Desjani said.

Bradamont speared a piece of meat from her plate and chewed thoughtfully for a moment. "It tastes like chicken. Which means it's not chicken."

"Right." Tanya raised her fork. "It's Ganymede rock lobster. Vat grown, of course, since Ganymede is a bit far to go for a lobster dinner."

"It's not bad," Rogero said. "Is this a traditional recipe?"

"My cooks said it's called thermidor," Desjani said. "I considered having them serve some of the vat-grown steaks that taste like chicken, but we had the lobsters on ice, and you know that old warning about leaving Ganymede rock lobsters in the fridge for too long."

"I thought that was just a legend," Bradamont said.

"So was he," Desjani said, pointing at Geary. "Welcome aboard to both of you, by the way."

"Thank you," Colonel Rogero said. "Admiral, I've never had the chance to thank you for your orders to Honore Bradamont, making her your representative at Midway. Neither of us believed we could ever see each other again. You made that happen."

Geary waved away the words. "I owe more than that to an officer like her. To be honest, it was Victoria Rione's idea."

"Rione?" Bradamont asked in disbelief. "That bi—"

"Hey," Tanya Desjani interrupted. "Hero of Unity Alternate. Dead battle sister." She raised her wineglass again. "Honor her memory."

"She was still a rhymes-with-witch," Bradamont grumbled after the toast.

"Yeah, she was," Tanya said. "But she died with honor. And she did give the admiral the idea of stationing you at Midway."

"Then I for one consider her to be a paragon of human virtue," Colonel Rogero said, smiling.

"How are you both doing?" Desjani asked in a not-too-subtle change of topic. "Your uniforms aren't Syndic, but they aren't Alliance. Have you run into any problems aboard because you're wearing them?"

"I can fight my own battles, Tanya," Bradamont replied with a half smile to remove any sting from the words.

Desjani took another drink, setting the glass down as she shook her head. "Anywhere else, that's true. But *Dauntless* is my ship. Which means any battles aboard *Dauntless* are my battles."

"I'll concede that," Bradamont said. She looked to one side, a slight frown forming. "Nothing much in the way of problems. Most of the crew are interested, and treat me as if I was still an Alliance fleet captain. There are a few, all junior sailors, who seem hostile. I don't know what's going on there, but when one of them tried to dis me I took him apart. Verbally," Bradamont added with another smile.

"I wish I'd been there to help dice that sailor into smaller pieces," Desjani said. "Verbally." She glanced at Geary. "The new recruits."

"What does that mean?" Bradamont asked.

"There's a percentage, we don't know how large, of our new recruits who joined to defend the Alliance against the aliens and other foreign threats," Geary explained. "Not just the Syndics. Any external, um, danger as they define danger."

"Oh, great," Bradamont said, stabbing a piece of "lobster" on her plate with extra force. "Now that the war is over the patriots are crawling out of the woodwork to save the Alliance."

"Something similar is happening in the regions still controlled by the Syndicate," Colonel Rogero said. "We've heard there's been an increase in volunteers to be snakes."

"The Syndicate's Internal Security Service," Bradamont explained. "The nice people who arrest, torture, and murder anyone suspected of being insufficiently loyal to the Syndicate. Can you believe that people volunteer to do that?"

"I've met a few on the Alliance side who would probably do it if they thought they could get away with it," Desjani said.

"Too many people see what they know crumbling," Geary said. "And are willing to do anything to prevent that."

Rogero gave a somber nod, chewing as if not tasting his food. "Back on Midway, and in the surrounding star systems, we were happy to see the Syndicate crumble. There's been a price to pay for our freedom, though." He grimaced. "I hope the people of Kane can overcome the traumas they've endured. The ones I spoke with when we were there were too eager for the blood of their enemies."

"I emphasized to President Wake at Kane that I owed a personal debt to Colonel Aragon, and would be very unhappy if she or any of her people were harmed," Geary said. "What about this new leader in the region? Imallye?"

Bradamont and Rogero exchanged glances. "Dangerous," Rogero said. "Not insanely so, but ruthless. She played the Syndicate well enough to get her own little empire set up, which is impressive as well as worrisome. Her long-term goals are uncertain."

"She hates President Iceni," Bradamont added. "Some old grudge related to Imallye's father. She claims that won't drive her actions, but . . . let's say we're going to keep an eye out toward Iwa."

"That was a tough fight there against the enigmas and the Syndics, wasn't it?" Desjani asked.

"Yeah. A four-way fight between the enigmas, Midway's flotilla, a Syndic flotilla, and Imallye's flotilla," Bradamont said, looking grumpy. "I missed it because I was defending Midway. Did you hear how they took out the buried enigma base?"

Tanya Desjani nodded, smiling. "A thirty-kilometer-wide rock dropped from space. General Drakon sent me videos of the impact."

"I was so mad I missed that. If I'd been there, we would've used a sixty-kilometer-wide rock."

"Only sixty? I'd have dropped a one-hundred-kilometer-wide rock from orbit," Tanya said. "Just break the whole planet into asteroids."

"It's the only way to be sure," Honore Bradamont agreed. "When you really want to destroy something, there's nothing like a woman's touch."

Tanya grinned. "Hey, that reminds me. Do you know anything about General Drakon's daughter?"

Even Geary picked up on the chill that rose on the other side of the table after Desjani's question.

"Why do you ask?" Colonel Rogero said in a suddenly formal and unrevealing tone of voice.

"Because at the diplomatic reception the general asked the admiral and me to personally sponsor his daughter when she visits the Alliance someday. I gather that's not going to happen for at least several years yet, but we were . . . a bit curious about his daughter."

"I see. He asked that of you." Rogero rubbed his lower face, thoughts running behind his eyes. "And you want to know who the mother is."

"Only if that is important," Geary said as Desjani nodded in agreement.

"The mother can't be separated from the child, even though the mother is . . . hopefully . . . dead."

"They buried her," Bradamont said.

"That means less with Roh Morgan than it does with most people," Rogero said. "You met Colonel Morgan during one of your visits to Midway Star System, didn't you, Admiral?"

"Yes," Geary said.

"How did she strike you?"

He paused to think, knowing that Tanya Desjani was giving him an arch look. "Beautiful and dangerous."

Rogero nodded. "You need to add one word. Psychotic."

"Seriously?"

"Someone faked her initial psych screening, and thereafter Morgan learned how to break into the system on her own and gundeck her psych evals. Whatever else you could say about her, Morgan was a brilliant hacker and assassin." Rogero's face twisted. "Everyone knew that she was fanatically loyal to General Drakon. We didn't know she was literally insanely loyal. And since she kept faking her psych evals she never got any treatments."

"Why did General Drakon—?" Desjani began, staring at Rogero.

"I don't know," Rogero said. "He doesn't talk about it. I gather it was a matter of shame for him. General Drakon never followed Syndicate practices that winked at sexual coercion. He didn't sleep with subordinates. I don't know how Morgan managed it, but I know it wasn't something he did frequently. I'd be surprised if it had happened more than once."

"She's dead now?" Geary said.

"Yes. Morgan and two others, during the general's wedding to the president."

"When you say 'during the wedding,'" Desjani asked, "do you mean 'during' in the sense of 'in that same time frame,' or 'during' in the sense of 'blood on the wedding garments'?"

"The latter."

"Maybe," Geary said, looking at Desjani, "if she heard that, your mother would stop complaining about our wedding."

"In your dreams. I'm never going to be forgiven for not having a full state wedding with at least half the Kosatkan royal family in attendance. So, this Colonel Morgan wanted General Drakon's child out of some distorted sense of hyper-loyalty?"

"Only partly," Rogero said. "General Drakon only spoke of this to me once, but if you're going to host his daughter someday you should know of it. Morgan's plan was to raise their daughter to be an unbeatable warlord who would conquer all of human space and become empress of humanity."

After several seconds of silence, Tanya shook her head. "And to think I accused my mother of having exaggerated ambitions for me. Is that why General Drakon is worried about his daughter? Because her mother had a second home in cloud cuckoo land?"

"Yes," Colonel Rogero said. "He's determined to save her."

"Huh." Tanya Desjani nodded with grudging admiration. "I wouldn't have tagged the general as a loving daddy type, but I have to respect that he intends fighting for his daughter."

Rogero shrugged, his fork lightly touching his food. "General Drakon is both extremely loyal to his people and very stubborn. He doesn't give up. Even when Roh Morgan was completely unraveling he was trying to save her. It doesn't surprise me at all that he will do all he can to save his own daughter."

"Can't everything be fixed these days?" Geary asked. "Mental and emotional problems like that?"

"Yes and no," Bradamont said. "There's still that thing called personality. Someone like Morgan can be technically mentally and emotionally sound, yet still be a total shipwreck. If you removed everything that could make someone irrational, overly emotional, obsessive, and impulsive in the wrong ways, what was left wouldn't be human. It'd be a machine."

Desjani grinned. "Like that one guy you dated when you were an ensign?"

"We do not speak of that," Bradamont said.

The conversation wandered into safer ground for the rest of the meal, Bradamont offering reassuring stories of her acceptance by those at Midway, and she and Desjani telling stories about each other.

But as the meal was winding up, Rogero adopted a formal tone again. "Admiral, I want to inform you that I have in my possession combat records of the encounter on the ground at Iwa. General Drakon authorized me to share those with you."

"Just with me?" Geary asked.

"I asked if anyone else could see them and the general said yes. He wants your experts to see them."

"So you'd be willing to present your information to our Marines?"

Rogero nodded. "We have a common foe. If we're going to defeat them, it's going to need everything we've both got."

"We've got three thousand Marines," Desjani said.

"That's not enough. Ten times that number wouldn't be enough." He paused, eyes hooded in thought. "Since Iwa, I've been thinking about what my soldiers and I experienced. We know the enigmas are obsessed with their privacy. You've told us that when you passed through enigma space they had clear internal borders. Like humans, the enigmas have apparently fought each other. So, imagine if you're a being obsessed with hiding everything about yourself. What kind of ground combat systems do you develop?"

Geary frowned as he realized the implications. "Something that hides me, and can see the enemy despite their efforts to hide."

"And that's your first priority!" Rogero said. "For all of their history of combat against each other. Not killing the enemy. Remaining hidden, and being able to kill them before they spot you. That's what we encountered on the ground at Iwa. Nothing we had could survive to get a single look at the enigmas. But they seemed to see us as if we were in a fishbowl."

"What about scouts in stealth suits?" Desjani asked.

"The snakes sent some Viper scouts in before my people landed," Rogero said. "The latest and best stealth available to the Syndicate. They all died within seconds."

"Couldn't you fire blind?" Geary said. "Keep the enigmas' heads down and score hits by chance?"

"We had to, out of desperation," Rogero said. "But put yourself in the situation. Every time one of our weapons fired, it produced a signature giving away its exact location to the enigmas, who could then target it. We were firing blindly, and every shot from us told them exactly where we were. But their own shots often had no signature we could detect to pinpoint their origin. You know where that kind of thing would end. We were firing and moving immediately, but it was still a losing game."

"But you managed to get almost all of your people off the planet," Bradamont said, leaping to Rogero's defense. "As well as the surrendered Syndicate workers and their families."

"I wasn't dropped on that planet to conduct a successful retreat," Rogero said, frowning down at his plate. "But it was fortunate we were able to get so many off the planet."

Geary shook his head. "What you're describing, hiding and hitting the enemy before that enemy even sees you, is what the Syndics, and we, initially faced thanks to the quantum-coded worms in our fleet software. The enigmas actually found a way to completely blind all of our sensors to them by sabotaging our sensor software. They'd been able to wipe out Syndic warships with impunity thanks to that."

"We checked out our own ground combat systems repeatedly," Rogero said. "They had been infected by those worms at one time, before your people warned us about them, but showed no signs of the worms at Iwa. The enigmas might be doing some things humanity literally hasn't even thought of yet."

"Like quantum-coded worms," Geary said. "We have some nonmilitary scientists with us, on *Boundless*. Do you have any objection to my sharing your records with them?"

"General Drakon said anyone."

"Good."

"That reminds me," Desjani said to Bradamont. "There've been some upgrades to the fire control systems that I think you'd be interested in. The admiral already said I could show you all of it."

"Cool. Tomorrow?"

"Sure. I've got some inspections lined up in the morning. Say thirteen hundred, meet at my stateroom?"

"I'll be there," Bradamont promised as she and Rogero stood to leave. "You had me at 'fire control systems upgrades.'"

Immediately after Bradamont and Rogero had left, Geary stood gazing at the door to his stateroom.

"That went well," Desjani said. "What's got you suddenly looking depressed?"

He looked over at her, not trying to conceal his feelings. "The enigmas. They won't talk to us. They keep attacking us. They're so obsessed with their privacy that they commit mass suicide rather than surrender. We can't even go in on the ground with overwhelming force to try to capture most of them alive. Everything we learn about them, every experience we have with the enigmas, seems to be pushing us toward one single solution."

"Genocide," Desjani said. "Coexistence is impossible, so we have to wipe them out."

He was struggling with the answer to that when she said something else.

"But we're not going to do that." It wasn't a question. She'd made a firm statement, and now smiled for a moment at his surprised reaction. "You didn't expect to hear that from me? Someone who once bombarded Syndic cities? Let me tell you something you probably haven't figured out yet. Yes, I thought we had to bombard cities, kill civilians indiscriminately, in order to win that war. But I hated it. I thought we'd been forced into doing that by the actions of the Syndics, and that's one of the reasons why I hated *them*. After you came back and reminded us of certain things, I made a private vow that I would never be forced into any course of action again. I can make choices, and I will make choices."

"But if there is only one choice—"

"Jack, I can think of three times this fleet was doomed. No way out. We were all going to die. And then someone saw another choice that no one else had. In two cases that was you. At Unity Alternate, it was Victoria Rione. Just because we can't see another choice with the enigmas right now doesn't mean another choice doesn't exist or won't exist. Maybe the entire universe is pushing us to commit genocide of the enigmas. I don't like being pushed. I will *not* make that choice, and I know *you* won't make it. Am I right?"

He smiled. "You're always right."

"Hey, you're learning. So, are we good?"

"Yes." Relieved, something else slipped out right after that. "I love you."

"We're on duty, Admiral," Tanya Desjani said, waving an admonitory finger at him. But she smiled as she said it before turning to leave his stateroom.

The conversation about Drakon's daughter had reminded Geary of something else, though. "Did Michael have children?"

Desjani looked back at him, her smile gone. "That's something you need to ask Jane about."

"Do you know?" he asked, aggravated that no one would answer what should be a simple question.

"I'm not getting in the middle of that," she said. "It's between you and Jane. Ask her."

And since he couldn't ask Jane while the fleet was in jump space, that's where he had to leave it.

AND so they came to Pele.

The enigmas had been recently stirred up by the ill-fated Rift Federation expedition, and had been in this star system in force to try to ensure that *Passguard* never made it home. There was no way of knowing how many of those enigma warships might still be here, poised to hit any retaliatory attack sent by humans.

The Alliance fleet dropped out of jump with the usual mental jolt that left human minds fuzzy for a few critical seconds. But, even through that mental fog, Geary noticed the lack of alarms that would have indicated nearby enigma warships, and the lack of alerts that automated weapons systems on the human warships were firing in self-defense.

"Only two enigma warships detected in the star system," Lieutenant Yuon announced as soon as he could form words. "One near the jump point for Hina, and the other at the jump point for Lalotai."

"It's just like when the Rift ships got here," Desjani said, sounding highly mistrustful of that.

"It worked for them last time," Geary muttered, gazing at his display. He magnified images of the enigma warships, each of them more than three billion kilometers from the newly arrived human fleet. Space offered no real barrier to seeing every detail of the squat, turtle-like shapes of the enigma ships, which were about the same mass and volume as human destroyers. Even though these images were more than three hours old because of the time required for light to cross that distance in space, there was no reason to think the enigmas had maneuvered significantly since then.

Relieved to have avoided a fight here, but also worried about what the enigmas might be planning, he gave the order for the entire fleet to head for the jump point for Lalotai. He held the fleet's velocity at point one light speed so as not to stress the auxiliaries or *Boundless*. "Thirty point two hours to the jump point for Lalotai on this vector," Lieutenant Castries called as the fleet steadied out.

"They'll be waiting at Lalotai," Desjani said.

"I know," Geary said.

OUT of jump and once more able to communicate freely with other ships, Geary put in a call to *Boundless*.

Ambassador Rycerz had the look of someone who hadn't been sleeping well. "Is this new problems or old problems, Admiral?"

"Mostly old, I guess. We've got more than a day to transit to the jump point for Lalotai. It'll take five days in jump space to reach Lalotai. Once at Lalotai we'll head for the jump point for a Dancer-owned star system. I fully expect our transit through Lalotai to be opposed."

"You mean we'll have to fight our way through."

"I assume so. There's always the chance the enigmas will decide we're too tough a bone to chew and will just shadow us once they see we're heading for the Dancer star."

"What are the chances of that?" Rycerz asked, studying him.

"I really can't judge," Geary said. "No one knows enough about the enigmas to know when they'll make a fight to the death and when they'll avoid that. But we're going to make it clear we're heading for that jump point, not for any enigma-occupied world or orbital facility, so they shouldn't think we're intending to attack them or trying to learn more about them."

Rycerz made a face, but nodded. "*Boundless* is broadcasting a message to the two enigma ships that are in this star system. Requests to talk, promises to abide by a mutual agreement to leave each other alone, that sort of thing."

"Don't hold your breath waiting for an answer that goes beyond 'go away or we'll kill you,'" Geary said.

"Even Pandora held on to hope, Admiral," Rycerz said, smiling slightly. "How are those Midway representatives behaving?"

"They've been very forthcoming," Geary said. "Colonel Rogero is sharing some detailed combat records that should be invaluable to our Marines."

"Invaluable." Rycerz seemed to be tasting the word to see if she liked it. "And they've asked for nothing in return?"

"Kommodor Bradamont explained that the leaders of Midway are very pragmatic," Geary said. "Does or does not something benefit them? In the case of the enigmas, anything that makes us more effective against the enigmas automatically benefits Midway, though I expect General Drakon is hoping we'll share any insights with him."

"We don't want a war with the enigmas," the ambassador said. "I know we have one, but we don't want it."

"I understand and I agree," Geary said. "I think we may have to prove to the enigmas that we can beat them whenever and however they attack, but will not use that to attack them. Maybe then they'll be willing to talk about some way of coexisting. Is there anything happening on *Boundless* that I should know about?"

"Frustratingly little," Rycerz said, immediately changing the subject. "Admiral, my instructions for interacting with the enigmas are . . . very limiting. However, they fail to limit what *you* can communicate to them. I may or may not ask you to send a message while we're at Lalotai."

"I'll be waiting for it," Geary said, wishing for a moment that he had his own spy aboard *Boundless* to assure him that everything was under control there. The ambassador's avoidance of discussing that wasn't exactly reassuring.

The call ended, he checked the display in his stateroom. The two enigma warships had by now seen the arrival of the Alliance fleet, but hadn't altered their orbits, hanging near the jump points that each were guarding. Silent, not responding to human pleas to talk. Smug, too, Geary thought, knowing he was attributing human emotions to them based only on his own gut feelings. The enigmas knew they'd annihilated the Rift Federation ships. They were surely planning to take out this human fleet, too.

They wouldn't. He was sure of that. But he hated to think of the potential damage the enigmas might inflict on his ships and sailors at Lalotai.

If only they knew more about the enigmas. About what they could do.

Which reminded him of something.

He put in another call to *Boundless*, asking to speak to the physicists who Ambassador Rycerz had ensured had accompanied the fleet as they wished.

His call was answered by Dr. Jasmine Cresida, who gazed at him silently.

"I wanted to speak with one of the physicists," Geary began.

"I have responsibility for answering calls during this time period," Dr. Cresida said. "Lucky you."

Yeah. Lucky me, Geary thought. Dr. Cresida didn't seem like someone who was warm to anybody, but in his case she had never hidden the fact that she blamed him for her sister's death. "There's something

I need to bounce off someone with more knowledge of physics than I have."

"I'm fairly certain that I meet that requirement," Dr. Cresida said, her voice and expression both flat.

Geary took a moment to calm himself before continuing. "You may not be aware of the details of what happened to the cruiser *Passguard* when it was in enigma space."

"No."

"Something odd occurred during that time." He explained about the four-hour delay in the enigmas from Lalotai reaching Pele as they pursued *Passguard*. "We've never noticed that kind of delay before. In fact, the enigmas always seem to try to destroy any human ships as quickly as possible. Someone suggested that the four-hour delay might be caused by the enigmas' using a fundamentally different kind of jump drive that produced a slightly different velocity in jump space."

Jasmine Cresida watched Geary for several seconds before replying. "That's . . . an intriguing idea."

"Really?"

"Did you expect me to laugh scornfully when you suggested it?"

"To be honest," Geary said, "yes."

"I'd hate to disappoint you, Admiral. Ha. Ha. Ha."

He had to admit each "ha" contained an impressive level of scorn. "But you think there might actually be merit in the idea?"

"I think . . ." Dr. Cresida began. "I think it would be a mistake to discount the idea. All human jump drives use basically the same principles to work. We know extremely little about jump space. Therefore I think the concept is worth looking into. Prematurely discarding ideas just because it's not how we've done things is, I think, almost always a mistake." She paused. "Does it surprise you that I said that?"

"No," Geary said. "Your sister, Jaylen, had the same philosophy. That's how she found the quantum-coded worms in our software."

Dr. Cresida looked away for a moment. "What are our chances of getting access to an enigma jump drive?"

"I'd say there's no chance at all. All of our previous experience with the enigmas is that they self-destruct their badly damaged ships to avoid anyone learning anything from them."

"What if the entire enigma crew was dead?"

"From what we've seen, we assume they have a dead-man switch capability built into their systems," Geary said. "So even if the entire crew is dead, or incapacitated, the ship will still self-destruct."

Jasmine Cresida closed her eyes. "I don't understand."

"A dead-man switch is what we call—"

"I know what a dead-man switch is," she interrupted, opening her eyes to gaze at him. "I don't understand why anyone would use one. What if there were badly injured enigmas still alive on the ship?"

Geary made a face, rubbing the back of his neck. "I can't claim to fully understand it, either. But their privacy, protecting everything about themselves, seems to be the first priority for the enigmas. And it's not like humans have never followed such priorities. There have been societies in humanity's past in which soldiers would suicide rather than surrender."

"Really?" Dr. Cresida shook her head. "So we know nothing about enigma jump drives."

"We know they were recently able to jump from a star in enigma-controlled space to Iwa in what used to be Syndic space. Our jump drives couldn't handle a jump that far."

"But we have no idea how the enigmas 'handled that.' All right. How about the Dancers, Admiral? Would they give us one of their jump drives to examine?"

He hesitated, startled by the question. "I honestly don't know. I don't think we've ever asked for access to a particular piece of technology."

"Can you make such a request? Dr. Macadams is refusing to interact with us."

Geary made a sympathetic grimace. Dr. Macadams, head of the team on *Boundless* responsible for learning more about the Dancers, was one of those Alliance officials who seemed to have been chosen specifically to sabotage the mission. "I can make the request through my own channels to the Dancers. I regard anything about the capabilities of their equipment as impacting my responsibilities to protect the Alliance mission."

"Dr. Macadams is unlikely to agree."

"I don't spend a lot of time worrying about whether Dr. Macadams will like what I'm doing," Geary said.

"We may actually have something in common, Admiral," Cresida said. "Who was it who suggested that idea about the enigma jump drives?"

"Kommodor Marphissa."

"A Syndic."

"Former Syndic." He gave Dr. Cresida a curious look. "Do you think a Syndic education gave her a better perspective on things?"

"A different perspective," Jasmine Cresida said. "From what I've been able to learn, those subjected to formal Syndicate Worlds educations tend to be skeptical of everything because so much of what they were taught were lies. The math and the engineering were probably fairly accurate, but everything else was tainted. Someone who's learned to distrust what they were told is more likely to discount the common 'everyone knows' attitude that so hobbles advances. Of course they also distrust things that are true, which hobbles them. I'm not surprised that this Kommodor thought of something that Alliance-educated people did not. You have reasons to believe what you're told. They do not."

"That's very interesting," Geary said.

"I'm so glad you're entertained. Is there anything else?"

"Yes," he said, deciding not to let her words get under his skin. "Colonel Rogero from Midway has combat systems records from the ground fighting at Iwa against the enigmas. I was wondering if any of you would want to see them."

"Why?" Jasmine Cresida seemed genuinely baffled.

"The enigmas appear to be using technology for ground combat that may be a generation ahead of ours, using things we haven't developed or even conceived of yet."

"Oh." Dr. Cresida shook her head as if disappointed that the request made sense after all. "It's not something I'd want to look at, but I will let Dr. Bron and Dr. Rajput know in case they're interested."

"Thank you, Doctor."

"Are we done now?"

"Yes, we're done."

Dr. Cresida reached for her comm controls but hesitated for a moment. "Goodbye."

TWELVE hours later, General Carabali called. "I wanted to give you a rundown on Colonel Rogero's presentation to Marine officers about the ground battle at Iwa."

"And?"

Carabali made a face. "About what you'd expect at the start. Polite silence on the main coordination link, because I made it clear anything else would result in serious consequences. On the back channel, lots of trash talk about how Syndics couldn't do the job. But then Rogero activated the combat records. We could experience the fight from the perspective of being inside the battle armor of Rogero's officers. Everything got real quiet at that point."

"I know how Rogero evaluated the battle," Geary said. "What do you think?"

"I think he did everything right. But they were seriously outmatched. I have no idea what numbers they faced, but . . ." Carabali shook her head. "They were outmatched."

"What would happen if we sent every Marine we had against a similar objective?"

This time Carabali shrugged. "Massive losses in the first wave, subsequent waves pinned down, unable to advance, eventual withdrawal under fire. The same thing that happened to Rogero's troops, and to the Syndic ground forces that led the first attack. I think he's right that the enigmas have pursued different primary priorities in ground combat than humans have. Sir, I do not recommend engaging in ground combat with the enigmas. Not unless we spot a tiny force that is clearly isolated."

"If a tiny force couldn't handle us," Geary said, "they'd suicide. Blow up our objective."

"And any Marines close enough to them," Carabali agreed. "We need a whole lot better idea of the enigmas' capabilities. Until we do, and work up some countermeasures, offensive ground action is just suicide by another name. On defense we might stand a chance, if they have to come at us. But I would advise against even that at this point."

"I won't commit the Marines against the enigmas unless there's absolutely no alternative." He felt that with everything he learned alternatives were growing fewer and fewer. But that wouldn't stop him from continuing to look.

A long walk through the passageways of *Dauntless* sometimes cleared his mind, or at least distracted it. Geary went through passageway after passageway, stopping by watch stations to chat with the sailors there, letting them know he valued them and their work. But no matter how far he walked, he still felt trapped.

They had to go to Lalotai. The enigmas would very likely be waiting there, having been alerted by their picket ships here using the enigmas' rudimentary faster-than-light communications capability, and having set a trap best suited to dealing with the Alliance fleet. And he'd be in among them within minutes of the fleet coming out of jump, too late to react in time to whatever was waiting.

Tired, but still restless, he headed for the worship spaces. If he didn't find inspiration there, perhaps he'd at least find comfort. As he reached them, he saw Gunnery Sergeant Orvis already waiting for one of the small rooms. "How are you doing, Gunny?"

"I've been worse, Admiral." Orvis grinned. "See these teeth? I lost nearly all the originals when my jaw got shot off. I tried to tell the docs when they regrew it all to give me a better chin, but they said that was up to my own DNA. Helluva thing when you can't even get a new chin."

"I'm pretty sure they could build you a new chin," Geary said.

"Sure, but it's the principle of the thing. I'm not vain! No way I'm going to choose to get my chin redone. But if it was gone and they had to regrow it, I wouldn't have minded having a better one. Excuse me, sir," Orvis added as a room came free.

A moment later another room opened, giving Geary a spot. He went inside the small compartment, just large enough for up to two people. A bench was set into one wall, opposite it a candle that had already burnt down a ways. Geary shut the privacy door and sat down, activated the lighter, and set a flame to the candle. "I haven't talked to you enough lately," he said to his ancestors. "My apologies. I feel like there's something just out of my sight, and you might help me see it, so I ask your aid once again. There are so many lives riding on my decisions. Please help me make the right choices." He paused, wondering why his words seemed to echo something else. A drop of melted wax ran off the top of the candle, rolling down the side until the wax solidified partway down, earlier than he'd expected. Why was that? He'd watched the drop form, saw it start down, why couldn't he know where it would stop?

It should be predictable. To a fault? Why did that . . . ? What Michael had said about battleship captains. Captain Pelleas and Captain Burdock in particular. Funny he should think about them at this moment when he was trying to get hints for how to handle problems.

The behavior of battleship commanders aside, there was so much he couldn't predict. What did they call that? Chaos something. Some things you could be certain of. Like Gunny Orvis, stuck with the same chin because his DNA that made the original was going to make the same thing again. Or the enigmas, knowing the Alliance fleet would come out of jump in the same formation in which it had entered jump.

He watched another molten drop of wax form, knowing it would soon roll down the side of the candle, but not able to predict what would happen as it rolled.

Oh.

"I get it. Thank you," Geary said to his ancestors, reaching to pinch out the flame.

By the time he reached his stateroom, he had mentally sketched out an idea. Calling the bridge, he spoke to the comms watch. "Notify all ships that there will be a conference of all commanding officers three hours before we reach the jump point for Lalotai. Ask Captain Desjani and Lieutenant Jamenson to contact me. We have some work to do."

The enigmas thought they had all the cards, but he had one left to play.

SIX

HUMANITY still faced many challenges, problems it had trouble adequately addressing or fixing. But when it came to holding meetings, something few people enjoyed or wanted, humanity had some amazing tools at its disposal.

Geary stood at the head of the table in *Dauntless*'s primary conference room. Actually a compartment a few meters on each side with a two-meter-long, one-meter-wide table in the center, when paired with conferencing software the compartment (and the table) could virtually expand to include as many participants as desired. In this case, that meant Geary was looking down a table with hundreds of fleet and Marine officers seated on each side, the most senior officers closest to him. All of the officers could see and hear Geary as clearly as if they were seated close, while all he had to do was focus his gaze on any officer no matter how distant and they'd suddenly seem to be right next to him as well. It didn't make him like big meetings, but it did make them as painless to run as possible.

Every commanding officer of every ship in the fleet was here, even Captain Matson of the *Boundless*, who wasn't military.

He found himself gazing at Captain Adam Pelleas of *Gallant*, looking relaxed as he waited for Geary to speak. Next to Pelleas was the virtual presence of Captain Jinani Burdock of *Encroach*. That was a little odd since ship commanders tended to sit next to other commanders from the same division or squadron. *Gallant* was in the First Battleship Division while *Encroach* was in the Fourth. He probably wouldn't have noticed that, though, if not for Michael's parting statement about those two captains.

All of the nonsense surrounding Colonel Webb, and *Boundless*, and the attempt to kill him at the reception, and the sabotage that Dr. Kottur had attempted was making him paranoid. Understandable, but a distraction.

He centered his thoughts on the reason for this meeting. "You know the situation we're in," Geary told his officers. "The enigmas think they can safely plan for how to hit us most effectively when we reach Lalotai, because their picket ships here will tell them what our formation was like when we entered jump. The same thing they did to those Rift Federation ships. But we're going to give them a surprise. Every ship's maneuvering system will be preprogrammed to execute a special formation the moment we arrive at Pele."

"Won't the enigmas expect that sort of thing?" Captain Badaya asked.

"They might expect something," Geary said. He touched controls to bring a 3D image of the fleet in its current formation into view above the table. The formation was a neat ovoid, *Boundless*, the auxiliaries, and the troop transports in the center, twelve battleships arrayed along the front, eight battleships deployed along the rear, the eleven battle cruisers forming a belt about the middle, the twenty-six heavy cruisers, fifty-one light cruisers, and one hundred forty-one destroyers ranging alongside the heavier ships or forming outer layers of protection. "We're going into jump just as we are now, like this. I fully expect the enigmas to have set up an ambush to try to blow through the weaker areas in the defensive screen to hit the ships in the center."

"Changing the formation once we arrive will take time and disrupt our defenses," Captain Armus pointed out. "The enigmas will be able to hit us in mid–formation change."

"I don't think so," Geary said. "Here's how we're going to execute the formation change." He touched another command.

The neat array of Alliance ships dissolved into hundreds of individual ships all swinging onto individual vectors, not steadying out as they headed to their new station in the new formation but instead weaving through repeated vector changes. Instead of maneuvering by divisions or squadrons, each individual ship wove an individual path before eventually rejoining its fellows. Visually, it resembled nothing so much as an ant hill that had been kicked over.

But as each ship finally reached its new station, the Alliance fleet eventually steadied out into a fatter, shorter egg. Four battleships led the formation, four battleships stiffened the rear, while another eight were arrayed in groups of two around the center. In the center itself, where the most vulnerable ships once again clustered, the last four battleships were tucked in close. The rest of the units in the fleet were arrayed in clusters around that center to form the fat egg. At the same time, the vector of the overall formation had changed nearly ninety degrees "down" so the fleet was diving away from the jump point instead of proceeding straight out from it.

A prolonged silence followed Geary's display, a silence finally broken by Captain Armus speaking again. "I don't understand."

"What is that mess?" Captain Parr of the *Incredible* asked. "Admiral, ever since you returned to the fleet we've been about maneuvering quickly and efficiently. Am I wrong in saying that this represents the least efficient and most chaotic set of maneuvers possible to realign into a new formation?"

"That's exactly what it is," Geary said.

Captain Jane Geary's hand hit the table. "I get it. Admiral, please initiate the formation change simulation again. Parr, pick a target to engage."

Captain Parr frowned, his eyes jumping about as he tried to locate a useful target. "I can't. They keep making vector changes, and I can't tell what formation they're going to fall into, so there's no way to predict where— Ah. It creates an unpredictable mess of vectors that doesn't offer any clue to the final formation and only a general sense of what the formation's final vector will be. And if a ship's vector can't be predicted, fire control systems can't aim for where it'll be when it's time to shoot. Not ours, and not the enigmas'."

"Exactly," Geary said. "The enigmas know how we maneuver. Neatly and efficiently and smoothly, sliding in the most effective vectors from one formation to the next. Not this time. We're changing the game on them."

Captain Ochs from the heavy cruiser *Tenshu* was staring at the ant's nest of maneuvering ships. "Admiral, aren't a lot of those vectors bringing individual ships awfully close to other ships?"

Captain Desjani smiled. "This is exactly what our automated maneuvering systems excel at. None of the maneuvers goes outside their safety margins."

"It looks like they go damned close to going outside those safety margins," Ochs said.

"True. But they don't actually go outside."

Captain Vitali of the battle cruiser *Daring* shook his head. "With all the near misses that are going to happen, I'll be surprised if there's a dry pair of underwear left in the fleet when this goat rope is over. Tanya, is this your work?"

"Not me," Desjani said. "I helped refine a few maneuvers, that's all."

"I have access to someone with the necessary skill set to come out with the most complex way possible to change from one formation to the next," Geary said.

"You didn't find that person on Unity, did you?" Captain Duellos asked. "Fleet Headquarters seems to excel in people who unnecessarily complicate things."

Captain Badaya shook his head. "Fleet Headquarters are amateurs compared to whoever did this. You don't let that person near anything important, do you, Admiral?"

"No comment," Geary said. He'd already written a classified report giving full credit for the maneuvering plan to Lieutenant "Shamrock" Jamenson, the officer with the uncanny ability to confuse things to the maximum extent possible while also keeping them technically accurate and correct. She'd already been invaluable with manipulating fleet expenditures to allow legally proper but bureaucratically suspect payments for repairs and overhauls of ships, without the bureaucrats being able to understand exactly what was happening in time to stop it. But if Jamenson's skills became too widely known, her effectiveness would be greatly diminished.

Captain Matson of *Boundless*, as a civilian rather than a fleet officer, spoke up diffidently. "Admiral, I'm a little unsure about how much protection my ship will have while this, um, interesting maneuver is being carried out."

Geary gestured to the depiction of the formation. "During the change of formation, no other ship will be continuously staying tight with you for your protection. But, at any one time, major units will be passing close by. You will have strong protection at all times, but it will be in the form of ships trading off the role as they head toward and past you. That's true of the auxiliaries and the troop transports as well."

Captain Smythe, the senior engineer and commander of the ponderous auxiliaries, rested his chin on one fist as he gazed at the maneuver. "My elephants are going to be dancing, aren't they? Are you certain all of the auxiliaries can make those vector changes you're calling for?"

"As long as they're accurately reporting their current mass," Desjani said. The auxiliaries, with bunkers of raw materials to construct replacement parts, new fuel cells, and other necessary items, could see big shifts in their mass depending on how full those bunkers were.

"They're accurate," Smythe said. "My auxiliaries aren't exactly experienced at this level of intricate maneuvers, though."

"Your automated maneuvering systems can handle it. Just sit back and enjoy the show."

"The show?" Smythe made a face. "Do you mean the show where a fraction of a second's mistake in a single ship's maneuvers will result in a collision that vaporizes it and whichever ship it collides with?"

"I find myself paraphrasing an ancient commander," Captain Armus said. "I don't know what effect this plan will have on the enigmas, but it certainly scares me."

"It looks like fun," Captain Parr protested.

"To a battle cruiser captain!"

"I have confidence in you all," Geary said to shut down the debate. "The enigmas think they have us nailed. They think they know what we'll do in any given situation. We're going to show them how wrong they are. If they get worried enough about what we'll do next, they might decide negotiating is a better idea than fighting."

"I'm good with this plan," Captain Jane Geary said.

"I don't know if I'm good with it," Captain Badaya said, "but I really want to watch it happening."

"Me, too," Armus said. "From a safe distance. Say, ten light minutes. But I won't have it said the battleships held back."

"How about the assault transports?" Geary asked. "Any concerns?"

He wasn't surprised when Commander Young of *Tsunami* shook her head. "No problem, Admiral." Assault transport captains were famous for claiming they could take their ships anywhere Marines needed to be dropped off or picked up. "No drop zone too difficult" was their unofficial motto. "But we'll probably advise the Marines to keep their eyes closed during the first half hour or so after arriving at Lalotai."

"That's not a bad idea," General Carabali agreed in a dry voice.

"It might also be a good idea for those on *Boundless*!" Captain Badaya added with a laugh.

"I'm considering doing that myself," Captain Matson said.

"Do not brief your crews on this until after we've entered jump," Geary said. "You'll have the maneuvers loaded into your system, but I don't want any gossiping between ships about the plan. We think we've shut off all of the enigma penetrations of our sensors and comm systems, but we're not certain."

"One last question," Captain Parr said. "Are we going in weapons free?"

"Yes," Geary said. "We have enough experience with the enigmas to know that if they're waiting at the jump point in Lalotai it won't be for a peaceful welcome. Weapons will be set to automatically fire if any enigma ships are within engagement envelopes when we drop out of jump at Lalotai." He'd wondered whether Ambassador Rycerz might object to that, but apparently seeing what had happened to *Passguard* had silenced any qualms or instructions she might have had about going in ready to shoot.

The meeting over, the virtual aspect of the compartment shrank with dizzying speed as officers disappeared from their seats. Within a few seconds, the only people present in the room were Geary, Desjani, and the virtual presence of Captain Duellos as he spoke with her.

As the two finished their conversation, Duellos faced Geary, saluting with a slight smile. "Sorry to hold you up, Admiral."

"Not a problem. How are you?"

"I've been worse."

"So have I," Geary said. "So I'll ask again. How are you?"

Duellos paused. "Bearing up and moving forward."

Desjani nodded. "He seems to be okay."

"How's Arwen?" Geary asked.

At the mention of his daughter, Duellos gave a full smile. "Ensign Duellos claims to be enjoying her time as a junior officer aboard *Warspite*."

"They're so easy on ensigns these days," Desjani said. "Not like when we were ensigns."

"Back when it was tough," Duellos agreed.

"She's withdrawn her request to be transferred to a battle cruiser," Geary said.

"Has she?" Duellos nodded, still smiling. "Good. That means Arwen is feeling part of *Warspite*'s crew and taking pride in it. It also means she'll be protected behind the armor and shields of a battleship. I . . . don't want to lose her, too."

"And we don't want to lose you," Desjani said. "Hang in there."

"Of course." Duellos saluted, then his virtual image vanished.

"You do realize," Desjani said to Geary once they were alone, "that I won't just walk out on you. Not like Roberto's wife did."

"What if I did something horrible and unforgivable to you?" he asked.

"Then I'd probably maim you and possibly kill you," she said. "But I wouldn't just walk out."

"That's about what I thought."

As they turned to leave the conference room Geary's pad chimed with an urgent request. "I need to take this." Desjani didn't hesitate, nodding to acknowledge his words and closing the door behind her as she left.

General Carabali's virtual presence reappeared as Geary accepted her request. "Admiral, I want to brief you privately on information I've received from sources aboard *Boundless*."

"Sources?" He frowned, not liking the idea of parts of the fleet spying on other parts.

"Former Marines," Carabali explained. "I'm just exploiting personal networking to get impressions. They say *Boundless* is not a happy ship."

"I'd already gathered that," Geary said. "Do you have specifics?"

"Colonel Webb is running what amounts to a Spanish Inquisition to try to find out who made and planted those bombs aimed at you. His own soldiers are terrified of him. Their morale is in tatters. At this point their effectiveness can be questioned."

"Great." Geary covered his face with one hand to hide his angry, frustrated expression before smoothing it out and looking at Carabali again. "Anything else?"

"The scientists are openly feuding. There seem to be at least a half-dozen camps vying against each other. Dr. Macadams keeps issuing heavy-handed directives to them which only aggravates the problems."

"Do your sources know if Ambassador Rycerz has tried to rein in either Webb or Macadams?"

"No, sir," Carabali said, shaking her head. "They say she's clearly unhappy, though. If I may speak frankly, Admiral, I'm gaining the impression of someone who was given insufficient authority over her own staff."

"She was set up to fail, too," Geary muttered. "The members of the Senate who authorized this mission got blindsided by their opponents."

"I'm not sure I understand the reasons for the opponents doing that, Admiral."

He exhaled slowly while thinking about his words. "I think, General, that there are elements in the Senate who want to discredit the rest of the Senate in order to protect themselves. And having this mission be a spectacular failure, perhaps creating new external enemies of the Alliance in the process, would serve their purpose."

Carabali nodded, looking unhappy. "What do you intend to do, sir?"

"I intend to not fail," Geary said.

Carabali grinned. "I've got your back."

"Good. Let's show everyone the fleet and the Marines are nobody's fall guys."

GEARY sat in his command seat on the bridge of *Dauntless* as the fleet approached the jump point for Lalotai, his eyes on the virtual display before his seat. The enigma warship still orbiting near the jump point hadn't moved as the distance between it and the Alliance fleet shrank.

"They know they can accelerate faster than we can," Desjani remarked from her own command seat. "So he's waiting until the last moment, getting our hopes up that he'll stand his ground, before he heads off at maximum acceleration. Enigmas may be a lot different from us, but that sort of taunting is exactly what one human would do to another."

"It is, isn't it?" Geary filed that away in his mental drop box holding clues to how the enigmas thought.

"Five minutes until our leading elements are within range of the enigma ship," Lieutenant Yuon said.

Geary touched his comm controls. "All units in the Alliance fleet, this is Admiral Geary. No unit is to break formation to chase that enigma. That's what they want, to disrupt our formation right before we jump. But if any ship gets close enough to have a chance of a hit, you are authorized to fire."

"We've got a couple of light cruisers that might get a shot in," Desjani said, pointing to her display. "*Garnet* and *Passata*. They're arming missiles."

"Three minutes until the enigma ship is within range," Lieutenant Yuon said.

"Fifteen minutes until we reach the jump point on our current vector," Lieutenant Castries added.

Geary sat, watching his display, waiting.

"One minute until the enigma ship is within range of our nearest units to it," Lieutenant Yuon said.

"He wants us to waste missiles," Desjani said. "How close do you think he'll cut it?"

"I think," Geary said, "that if those two light cruisers hold off from firing at the first moment the enigma enters an engagement envelope, they might have a chance at a hit."

"You could call it," Desjani said, gesturing to his controls. "Decide when they fire."

"I won't," Geary said. "That's up to the commanding officers of those two light cruisers. They deserve the chance to make the call."

"The enigma ship is entering the extreme range firing envelope for *Passata*," Lieutenant Yuon said, following that a couple of seconds later with "The enigma is now within the extreme firing range for a missile from *Garnet*."

"He's probably really mad right now," Desjani said, her chin resting on one hand as she gazed at her display. "He wants us to start a futile chase, he wants us to waste weapons trying to hit him, and we're not playing along."

A few more seconds ticked by, the Alliance warships growing steadily closer to the enigma.

"*Passata* and *Garnet* have fired specter missiles," Lieutenant Yuon announced.

Geary watched missiles leap from the light cruisers, accelerating toward the enigma, which was pivoting in space and lighting off at full acceleration. Had that maneuver begun before or after the cruisers fired? He couldn't be sure, but the missile launch looked to have been timed very well. "What are the odds of hits?"

"Five percent and seven percent," Lieutenant Yuon reported.

"That's a lot better than zero," Desjani said.

There wasn't anything else to do, so everyone watched the enigma ship racing away, steadily building velocity, while the two specters closed the distance at a slowly decreasing rate.

"One of them is going to be really close," Desjani said.

"I think so," Geary said. The specters were nearly at their maximum acceleration range, their propellant almost exhausted. When their thrust cut off the missiles would continue on the same velocity, but the enigma would continue accelerating and walk away from them.

One specter detonated as its thrust cut off, followed a moment later by the second.

"He felt that!" Lieutenant Yuon said, his voice jubilant. "The fragmentation and gases of the shock wave should've hit him."

The enigma ship did stagger under the blow. Its shields weren't too badly impacted, though, and the ship suffered no damage.

"Hurt his pride, I bet," Desjani said with a grin.

Geary, smiling, tapped his comm controls. "*Garnet* and *Passata*, this is Admiral Geary. Damn good shooting, you two. When we get to Lalotai we'll probably encounter some targets that won't run away, and you'll get a chance at some kills. Keep up the good work."

"You just made the crews of two light cruisers very happy," Desjani observed.

"I make crews unhappy often enough," Geary said. "I might as well take advantage of any chance to balance that out."

Six minutes later they jumped for Lalotai.

FIVE long days spent worrying and preparing later, the fleet left jump at Lalotai.

Geary fought to clear the jump exit–induced fog from his brain, hearing alarms blaring that warned of nearby threats. He felt *Dauntless* twist under the push of her thrusters, her main propulsion kicking in to hurl her along a new vector as the automated maneuvering systems carried out the commands loaded into them earlier.

As his vision cleared, Geary heard *Dauntless*'s collision warning alarm uttering its high-pitched cries of danger. He'd barely focused on his display when the collision alarm sounded a second time as *Dauntless* pitched over again when her thrusters fired once more.

A heavy cruiser zipped by close enough for the collision alarm to scream a third time, there and gone again before Geary could even react, belated terror making him shudder in reaction as he heard Kommodor Bradamont in the observer seat at the back of the bridge gasp. "That's within safety parameters?" he demanded of Desjani.

"Yes!" she insisted. "This was your idea, Admiral! And it's working! Look!"

He managed to drag his gaze past the wild web of way-too-close vectors surrounding *Dauntless*, looking outside the hornet's nest that the Alliance fleet was mimicking. A swarm of enigma warships were clustered in three areas around the fleet, breaking off attack runs and pulling back in frustration.

"Seventy-seven enigma warships detected nearby," Lieutenant Castries called out, her voice higher pitched than usual.

"One of them's coming in!" Lieutenant Yuon added.

Geary stared as an enigma ship a little smaller than an Alliance heavy cruiser whipped toward the Alliance fleet and into the maze of ships. Even he had to admire how well the enigma maneuvered, somehow dancing a path between Alliance ships that themselves were often changing vectors. "He'll never make it to the center of the formation."

"No, but he will come close to us, I think," Desjani said, her hand poised over the controls to order *Dauntless*'s weapons to fire.

The enigma suddenly jogged left and up to avoid an Alliance destroyer at the same moment as *Dauntless* jogged down and right in accordance with the preplanned maneuvers.

For a moment, the enigma warship was close, *Dauntless*'s weapons locked on it.

"Tanya! No!"

Geary watched in disbelief as the enigma jogged away again, abandoning its attempt to penetrate the Alliance formation, now simply trying to get clear.

For her part, Desjani turned to glare at Bradamont. "Why the hell did you make me hesitate?" she demanded in a voice that would have frozen the blood of most people it was directed at.

But Bradamont returned the glare. "Because I realized just in time how stupid it would be to cripple the maneuvering capability of a ship that was barely managing to avoid collisions with Alliance ships!"

Geary suddenly got it. "It would have made at least one collision certain. Maybe multiple collisions."

"Ancestors save me," Desjani said, her tone shifting to dread. "I could have killed a half-dozen Alliance warships. Why the hell didn't you and I realize that and order our ships to avoid engaging the enigmas while this scramble is underway?"

"Good question," Geary said, quickly punching his own comm controls. "All units, do not fire at this time at any enigma warships among our own units. There's too great a threat of collision if we damage them." As if to emphasize his words the collision alarm wailed again while an Alliance battleship blundered past close enough to cause Lieutenant Yuon to gasp this time.

"Thanks," Desjani said to Bradamont before returning her entire focus to the situation.

"The three groups of enigma warships seem to be watching for openings," Lieutenant Castries said. "They're poised for attack runs."

"Our ships are already starting to steady out and assume their places in the formation," Geary said as much to himself as to anyone else. "There's going to be a gap between the time the high-value units in the center steady out and the time when the rest of the formation assumes their positions around the center."

But the defenders were taking up position. The assault transports with their close-in defenses formed a globe around *Boundless*, just outside of them the four battleships of the Third Battleship Division— *Warspite*, *Vengeance*, *Resolution*, and *Guardian*—spacing themselves around the globe. It was only as his gaze lingered on *Warspite* for a moment that Geary remembered Roberto Duellos's daughter was aboard her. He'd made the decision to assign *Warspite* to the final defense role solely because it fell out most easily in the maneuvers into this formation. But in so doing he'd placed Arwen Duellos in a dangerous position.

The auxiliaries were dropping into place ahead of and behind *Boundless*, while all around the chaotic movement of destroyers, light and heavy cruisers, battle cruisers, and battleships was resolving into the planned squat egg shape, the lighter units grouped together in threes or fours, while the heavier ones were in groups of two. The result was a three-dimensional lattice with paths between the groups of escorts, but anything trying to use those paths would get hit from multiple angles again and again.

The greatest danger was now, when the shape and vector of the formation were becoming apparent, but the escorts hadn't yet all assumed position.

"They're coming in," Lieutenant Castries said. "A group of twenty-nine enigmas above and off our port bow that's aiming for *Boundless*. Another group of thirty-one enigmas is off our stern and below, and seems to be aiming for the rearmost auxiliaries. Combat systems are estimating *Titan* and *Tanuki* will be their primary targets. The final group of seventeen is far off to starboard of us, and also heading in for *Boundless*."

Normally, space engagements happened incredibly quickly once the two sides closed to firing range. At combined velocities of up to nearly point two light speed, automated systems fired during the tiny fraction of a second when the opposing sides were close enough. Human reflexes couldn't begin to meet the reaction speed needed.

But this time the enigma plans had been completely thrown off by the Alliance anthill maneuver. They'd been forced to draw back and come around again, most of them chasing the Alliance ships so the relative velocities were low enough for humans to decide which target to engage and when. The slower engagement speed also meant the enigma ships would be running terrible gauntlets on their way into the human formation as they tried to hit *Boundless* and the auxiliaries.

Normally, also, anyone fighting in space used their force like the edge of a sword blade, the ships striking across a broad area. But with surprise lost, relative speeds low, and against the Alliance formation bristling with firepower, that would have simply resulted in rapid destruction of the attackers, so the enigmas had taken the only route that gave them a chance, lining up their ships in columns to strike like the points of daggers aiming for the center of the formation.

The group of twenty-nine wove its way between Alliance escorts, taking fire from hell lance particle beams and impacts from specter missiles. The enigma ships on the edges staggered under the blows, first one and then more breaking apart or exploding or simply spinning away, unable to control their movement after their thrusters and propulsion were knocked out.

But the enigma dagger kept on, led by a group of five massive warships. Clearly devoting most of their energy to keeping their shields up, the enigmas hurled some shots at the Alliance screening ships they were passing. The Alliance destroyer *Bolo*, unlucky enough to be within range of two of the big enigma warships as they passed, took enough hits for her shields to collapse and two particle beams to pass through the ship. Geary moved to order *Bolo* to pull back out of range, but the enigmas were already past the destroyer and could no longer target it.

"The leading ships are larger than any enigma warships we've encountered before," Lieutenant Yuon said. "Combat systems are estimating they carry heavy shields and armor forward, as well as heavy armament."

"The enigmas decided to make their own battleships," Desjani said, watching the attack. She was keeping her frustration mostly hidden as she watched other ships engage the enemy. "Not as big as ours, and more maneuverable, but same concept."

The large group of enigmas coming up the rear were overtaking the Alliance warships, and taking heavy fire as they came.

The smallest enigma group was trying to weave a path past the escorts, but had already lost two ships.

Geary took a long look at his display, getting a good feeling for the relative movement of the enigmas. He didn't have to let them maintain the initiative while the Alliance ships stayed on fixed vectors. He tabbed one large enigma group alpha, tabbed the second bravo, and the third and smallest delta, his designations immediately being shared across the fleet's sensor network.

Only then did he touch his comm controls. "This is Admiral Geary. First Battle Cruiser Division, break formation and intercept enigma group alpha. Second Battle Cruiser Division, break formation and intercept enigma group bravo. Third Battle Cruiser Division, break formation and intercept enigma group delta. Go get them. Geary, out."

Desjani let out a brief yelp of joy before she hit her own comm controls. "*Daring, Victorious*, and *Intemperate*, maneuver independently to nail these guys. Watch your safety margins around the friendly ships still holding formation." Her other hand went to her maneuvering controls. "I am assuming direct maneuvering control," Desjani announced to the bridge crew.

As Geary and the others on the bridge hastily rechecked their safety harnesses, *Dauntless* slewed over and down under Desjani's commands to her thrusters, her main propulsion lighting off with a jolt that hurled the battle cruiser toward an intercept with the enigma force that had started out with twenty-nine warships. Already down to twenty, the survivors were still forging onward, protected behind the moving wall formed by the five enigma battleships.

Waiting for them were the battleships of the Third Division.

Commander Plant, who came across as deceptively cheerful and easygoing, was renowned for the deadly ferocity with which she employed the vast armament carried by *Warspite*. "Make way for *Warspite*" was as much a warning as it was the ship's unofficial motto. She'd shifted *Warspite*'s position slightly to place her ship directly between the oncoming enigmas and *Boundless*, and pivoted the ship to face the enemy bow on. The battleship *Vengeance*, located "above" *Boundless*, swung out a bit to also better engage the enigmas, while the battleship *Resolution*, "beneath" *Boundless*, had taken up a similar position. Of the four battleships tasked with close defense of *Boundless*, only *Guardian* wasn't lining up to engage, because *Guardian* had to remain on the opposite side of *Boundless* to protect against the much smaller enigma force coming in from that side.

The edges of the enigma dagger formation were still being shredded by the interlacing fire of the Alliance ships they were having to race past, but the five new enigma "battleships" appeared unscathed, their shields flaring from hits but holding, their armor as yet untouched.

"*Daring*," Desjani sent. "Let's get the one closest to us. *Victorious* and *Intemperate*, take out the one on the opposite side. Let's see how these guys like null fields."

The four battle cruisers were diving almost straight "down" at the enigmas, their main propulsion cutting off as they reached the best firing vectors, thrusters firing along the sides to make minor adjustments, every weapon locked on. Alliance ships in the formation flashed by on all sides as the battle cruisers steadied on their firing run.

The charge of the battle cruisers only took a few seconds. Geary wondered if the enigmas noticed the battle cruisers coming down on them, if they had time to debate what to do, or if the enigmas were totally focused on trying to reach their target and determined to ignore anything that might distract them from that goal.

Dauntless flashed close by her target, specter missiles leaping out to hammer the enigma battleship's shields, followed by hell lances, and the solid ball bearings that were called grapeshot and were used only against the closest targets. Last of all, timed for the moment of closest approach, the even shorter-range null field projector created its deadly cloud. Within that cloud, atomic bonds failed, molecules coming apart. A massive gap appeared on the side of the enigma warship, as if an invisible monster had taken a huge bite out of it.

Dauntless shook as return fire from the enigmas slammed into her shields, then she was past the enemy and beginning to curve up and around for a second attack run.

An instant later, *Daring* went past the enigma as well, her null field tearing another enormous bite out of the enemy ship.

The enigma battleship reeled from the tremendous amount of damage it had suffered, unable to adjust course properly because of all the thrusters that had been destroyed where the null fields had struck. The battleship's forward and side shields collapsed, leaving it exposed to the barrage of Alliance fire from all sides. Veering out to one side and up, the battleship abruptly exploded.

On the other side of the enigma formation, *Victorious* and *Intemperate* had wreaked similar havoc on the enigma battleship there, which rolled out of control into the path of another enigma ship, both of them vanishing into dust from the force of the collision at the speeds they were going.

That left three enigma battleships racing toward *Boundless* as they led the enigma charge. With fewer primary targets to concentrate on, the Alliance fire tore at the enigma shields, finally creating spot failures just as the enigmas reached the final defense line where *Warspite* waited.

Warspite unleashed every weapon she had at the center enigma battleship, every weapon timed to hit at the same moment.

The enigma battleship disappeared in a blaze of energy as its shields collapsed and the mass of Alliance firepower tore through its armor.

At almost the same moment, the second surviving enigma battleship was hit by volleys from *Vengeance* and *Resolution* and was torn apart.

In a normal engagement, there wouldn't have been time for the Alliance battleships to fire a second volley, but with the enigmas overtaking the Alliance ships the relative velocity was slow enough to allow that, something that the Alliance battleships had planned on. All three unleashed their full fury on the last surviving enigma battleship.

As that enigma ship exploded, the following smaller enigma warships ran head-on into the expanding debris field of the three shattered battleships at the same time as every Alliance warship within range hurled shots at them. Unable to change vector in time to avoid the death trap, the remaining enigma ships in the column were annihilated in a matter of seconds.

Behind all of them, the other large enigma column was trying to climb up the rear of the Alliance formation to hit the large auxiliaries *Titan* and *Tanuki*. That group of enigmas was led by only three of their battleships. Using the same tactics as Desjani had used, *Inspire*, *Formidable*, *Dragon*, and *Steadfast* ripped sideways past the enigma warships, crippling the outer two battleships.

Already reeling from the firepower tearing into them, the twelve surviving enigma warships nonetheless held on, trying to complete what might well have been suicide runs against *Titan* and *Tanuki*.

But to get there they had to get past two more battleships screening the rear of the auxiliaries from that angle. *Dreadnaught* and *Fearless* pivoted as the enigmas passed beneath them, their bows following the enemy ships as the Alliance battleships hurled their massive armament into the tops and sides of the already battered enigma survivors.

None of the enigmas made it past the wall of fire.

On the far side of the formation, the smallest group of enigmas had started with only seventeen warships and was already down to eleven. Lacking a heavily protected enigma battleship and apparently less interested in dying valiantly and uselessly like their comrades, the surviving eleven broke off their attack run, instead each ship weaving frantically back out through the Alliance formation. The battle cruisers *Illustrious*, *Incredible*, and *Valiant*, aiming to hit the front of the enigma group as it tried to reach *Boundless*, found themselves out of position, unable to alter their tracks quickly enough to engage the fleeing enigmas.

It was one thing to target a ship on a predictable vector. It was another thing to try to hit a ship jinking unpredictably at high velocity. The same kind of erratic movements that had protected the Alliance ships from targeting when the fleet arrived at Lalotai were now protecting the retreating enigmas.

All eleven enigma ships made it out, bursting away from the death trap of the Alliance formation that had claimed their comrades.

Geary gave a grunt of frustration. "All battle cruisers, return to your positions in formation. Do not, repeat do not, attempt to pursue those surviving enigmas."

"Bob Parr isn't going to be happy," Desjani said, referring to the commanding officer of the *Incredible*.

"Neither will Badaya on *Illustrious*," Geary said. "They just got unlucky." Trying to chase the remaining enigmas would be a waste of fuel cells. The enigmas could outrace even human battle cruisers, and they had an eternity of space in which to run if they chose to.

Aside from the unfortunate *Bolo*, though, none of the human ships had taken serious damage. The enigmas had only been able to target individual human ships momentarily as they dove through the formation, and had been saving their heaviest throws to use against *Boundless* and the auxiliaries that they'd never reached.

Geary frowned as he saw an urgent message alert show up on his display. Why would a destroyer be calling him directly? "What is it, *Atlatl*?"

"Admiral, we've got one of them! We saw something fly off one of the big enigma ships after the null fields took bites out of them, so we diverted to intercept, and it was an enigma!"

Geary felt his breath catch. "You're saying you have an intact enigma body?"

"No, sir, we have a living enigma."

SEVEN

"SAY again, *Atlatl*. You have a *living* enigma?"

"Yes, sir. At least so far. They're either unconscious or pretending to be. I don't think it's an act. They were unprotected in vacuum for close to a minute. Our onboard medical specialist recommended we quarantine it by sealing it in a wound bag so that's what we did. It's still in the air lock. We're sure it needs medical help but—"

"Stand by, *Atlatl*." He switched to an internal circuit. "Dr. Nasr! One of our ships has a living, unconscious enigma in a wound bag. I need recommendations."

"Send it to *Mistral*," Nasr said immediately. "They have the best medical quarantine facilities in the fleet."

"Got it. Thank you. *Atlatl*, break formation and join with *Mistral* at your best speed. Transfer your . . . prisoner to the transport as quickly as possible. *Mistral*, *Atlatl* is bringing you a living enigma currently in a wound bag. I want the enigma isolated and treated."

It took only a moment before Geary heard another message. "*Atlatl*, this is Dr. Galen aboard *Mistral*. Is the enigma injured?"

"They were exposed to vacuum for nearly a minute without any protection beyond the outfit they're wearing," *Atlatl* replied. "As far as we can tell they haven't regained consciousness."

"Do they appear to be in physical distress?"

"Doc, we've got no idea. What's normal for one of these guys?"

Dr. Nasr had been linked into the calls, and now spoke to Geary. "Dr. Galen is exceptionally skilled. If anyone can save that enigma, it's her. But they'll have to follow strict quarantine procedures which will delay and inhibit some treatment."

"Understood," Geary said.

"We've got a living enigma?" Desjani asked after she returned maneuvering control to the bridge watch team.

"So far. Can I get a feed from *Mistral* when *Atlatl* comes alongside?"

"Yes, sir." Desjani gestured to her watch team.

"Admiral," Bradamont said, leaning forward in her seat, "may I—"

"Yes," Geary said. "You can also observe. Link her in, Tanya."

A moment later a virtual window popped up near his display, focused on one of *Mistral*'s main air locks, looking outward to space beyond where the slim shape of the destroyer *Atlatl* was gliding into position only a few meters from the assault transport. Figures in survival suits were gathered in the air lock, waiting as *Atlatl*'s main air lock opened and sailors in their own survival suits appeared, hauling a sealed wound bag. The wound bag, a roughly rectangular box that served as a survival suit for people who were too badly injured to be wrestled into a normal survival suit, held a vague shape lying inside.

The seconds required to transfer the bag seemed an eternity.

As soon as it was inside *Mistral*'s air lock, the waiting medical personnel clustered about the wound bag, checking the health readouts built into it.

Geary saw the eager figures pause, then slump in disappointment.

"They're dead," Dr. Galen reported. "No life signs. No brain activity."

The voice of *Atlatl's* commanding officer came on the circuit. "Doc, we did everything we could."

"I understand," Dr. Galen replied. "It's not your fault. We don't know what this person needed. We don't know what healthy is for them, or how they display a medical emergency. Even if they'd been human, saving them after that much exposure to vacuum would've been difficult. You did your best. Thank you."

"We had a living enigma," Geary said to Desjani. "Now we have a dead one."

"Admiral," Dr. Galen said, "request permission to undertake a full-scale examination of the remains. We'll do scans, an autopsy, genetic sampling, and everything else possible while maintaining full quarantine protocols."

He was about to tell Dr. Galen to go ahead when Dr. Nasr broke in. "Admiral, don't."

"Don't what?" Geary asked, startled and irritated by the interruption.

"Don't examine the dead enigma. Don't study it."

Dr. Galen sounded as frustrated as Geary at the disruption. "Every second we delay—"

"Admiral," Nasr said, his voice firm, "remember that place we went to on Old Earth. Kansas. Remember what the Dancers brought back there."

His anger dwindled as Geary recalled those moments when the humans had realized that the Dancers had brought home an ancient, dead human explorer. "The Dancers hadn't disturbed the body in any way that we could tell," he said.

"Exactly," Dr. Nasr said. "They had the body of a human, an alien to them, and they treated it with all of the respect as if it were one of their own. What impact did that have on all of us there? Admiral, what if we do *not* examine this enigma? What if we do *not* act in the manner the enigmas expect and fear?"

"Admiral!" Dr. Galen sounded disbelieving and determined in

equal measure. "We cannot pass up this opportunity! Time is critical for determining important data regarding this being as its biological systems shut down and begin deteriorating. I recommend in the strongest terms that we begin full examination of these remains immediately!"

"Wait," Geary said, trying to think. All of his own instincts argued for doing what Dr. Galen said. But . . .

It would be what the enigmas expected them to do, wouldn't it?

He took a deep breath. "I want that wound bag left undisturbed, and I want all personnel out of sight of that bag except for a couple of guards who are not to look directly at the bag. Make sure surveillance video is aimed so it only catches the edges of the bag."

"Admiral?" Dr. Galen questioned, her voice pleading.

"There are more critical factors we need to take into account, Doctor," Geary said. "Stand by."

Kommodor Bradamont, who'd been watching and listening, gave him a baffled look. "Admiral, what other factors matter? We've finally got an enigma."

"You heard Dr. Nasr," Geary said.

"I wasn't there on Old Earth."

"I was," Desjani said in a quiet voice. "I think you should listen to Dr. Nasr, Admiral."

That decided him. Taking another deep breath, he called Ambassador Rycerz.

Rycerz answered immediately, looked slightly depressed. "I know we won, Admiral. But I wish we hadn't had to."

"We have an intact enigma body," Geary said, drawing a look of shock from the ambassador. "The enigma was alive when one of my destroyers recovered them, but had been exposed to vacuum. We tried to save the enigma, but they died before we could get them to *Mistral*, one of my assault transports."

Rycerz nodded slowly. "So we can finally learn details about them."

"As one of my doctors pointed out, that's exactly what the enigmas expect, and fear, we'll do. Instead, I want to send the body back to the enigmas, without any examination or samples or scans."

The ambassador's expression shifted back to shock. "Why?"

"After we met the Dancers, they told us they wanted to send a ship to Old Earth," Geary explained. "They didn't or couldn't explain why. But when we got there, they brought out a sealed capsule containing the remains of a human pilot who'd been testing one of the first jump drive prototypes centuries ago. He must have been trapped in jump space until his ship finally came out in Dancer space. But the Dancers had not harmed the body in any way. There were no signs of autopsy or other invasive procedures. They'd respected those remains."

Rycerz watched him intently, thoughts moving behind her eyes. "I saw those reports. It was a profoundly important action by the Dancers. And now you think we have the chance to do the same thing for the enigmas? But should we? Isn't this our first real chance to get detailed knowledge about them?"

"Do we want detailed knowledge about them," Geary asked, "or do we want to take a chance at peace? If we show them that we had a perfect chance to violate their species' privacy, without them even knowing, and did not do that, maybe that will convince them we can be trusted. Not words. Actions. The enigmas know from interacting with Syndic leaders how little the word of humans can mean. The Kicks commit suicide if they're captured by us because they think they know what we'll do to them. I'm tired of aliens expecting humanity to fulfill their worst fears. This could be a major opportunity to address the enigmas' greatest fear of us with an unmistakable action."

"I see." Rycerz lowered her head in thought. "No matter what you and I decide, we're going to be attacked for it, aren't we?"

"I think so," Geary said. "So why not do what we think is right? Why not take a chance?"

"Why not?" Rycerz nodded again, looking at Geary once more. "Very well. I agree. Return the body, Admiral. Without any examination."

"Thank you."

"Which doctor was it who suggested this?"

"The head doctor aboard *Dauntless*. Dr. Nasr."

"Give him my thanks," Ambassador Rycerz said.

"I will." Geary called *Mistral* again. "Commander Young, I have orders for you."

DR. Galen was extremely unhappy. She wasn't alone. But Commander Young followed Geary's orders to the letter.

A burial detail wearing blindfolds went into the pressurized air lock, picking up the wound bag by feel and placing it inside a burial-in-space tube that had been lined with opaque material to prevent anyone seeing inside. Once the tube was sealed, the leader of the burial party recited the universal burial service before the tube was loaded into an ejection ramp.

As the tube was launched outward toward the star of Lalotai, Geary attached the video of the events to a message. "I want this broadcast to the enigmas," he told Desjani, whose comm watch had no trouble setting up the circuit.

"People of this star system," Geary said. "This is Admiral Geary of the Alliance. During the most recent combat between our ships and yours, we recovered one of your people who had been exposed to vacuum but was still alive. We regret that we were unable to save that person, who died of their injuries very soon after we recovered them. We gave that person an honorable burial service as we would have one of our own, and have placed their remains inside one of our burial-in-space containers and launched it outside of our formation. You will have no trouble intercepting it. I want to assure you that we did not conduct any examinations, studies, scans, or other information gathering on the remains. We have no samples. We have no pictures. We have, to the best of our ability, protected the privacy of that individual and of your species, because we know the importance you place on that. I repeat, we've learned nothing from the remains of this individual, and retained nothing about them. It is our wish to live in peace with our neighbors. It is our wish to avoid the loss of more lives. Please take this as a sign that we are sincere in our desire to avoid further conflict and negotiate terms by which we can transit star systems such as this without compromising your privacy. To the honor of our ancestors, Geary, out."

He slumped back once the message was ended, torn by doubts. "Do you think I did the right thing?" he asked Desjani.

She glanced at him. "Was it the easy thing?"

"Hell, no."

"Then it very likely was the right thing. You owe Dr. Nasr big-time for him having the guts to speak up when he did."

Geary felt a slight smile form. "I'm not sure I should thank him. Every scientist in human space is going to want a piece of me for this."

"Probably." She gave him another look. "The way that enigma fell into our hands. It was too convenient. I think it was a trap. Or a test, by something far bigger than humans or enigmas."

"Maybe you're right. I hope if the living stars tested us they think we passed." He finally looked back at Bradamont, who was watching him from the bridge observer seat with a carefully neutral expression. "I don't expect President Iceni or General Drakon to approve, though."

Bradamont shook her head. "I honestly have no idea how they'll react when they hear of it. But they are both certain that you are the most devious and farsighted individual in human space, so they'll probably conclude that you had a very good reason for doing it. A good reason for you, that is."

He caught the warning there. "Kommodor, I swear to you this action is intended to benefit both the Alliance and Midway. General Drakon said he wanted the enigmas to stop attacking. I'm trying to make that happen."

"If you succeed, Midway will owe you a huge debt."

"And if he doesn't?" Desjani asked, giving Bradamont a hard look.

"Then I'll lay out the truth as I see it," Bradamont replied. "That it was a long-shot attempt at breaking the stalemate between us and the enigmas that didn't pay off."

"Fair enough," Geary said.

The Alliance formation was still headed "down" relative to the jump point. It was time to get the fleet back on track. Space had no up or down, no right or left, but humans needed common references to orient their ships and movements. They'd long ago adopted a universal convention that made use of the few physical references offered in space. One was the star being orbited. Starboard or starward was toward the star, while port was away from it. Up was above the plane of the planets and other objects orbiting the star, and down was beneath it.

Geary brought the Alliance formation up and to port, aiming for the jump point for the Dancer star. That jump point was only one and three-quarters light hours away, so even at point one light speed the fleet could cover the distance in about eighteen hours.

He cast a worried eye on his display. The Alliance fleet, able to fall back on its enormous firepower advantage, had suffered little damage while nearly wiping out the attempted enigma ambush. He hated to think how much damage those enigma battleships might have caused if their initial planned attack runs hadn't been forced to abort by the confusing Alliance scramble when they first arrived at Lalotai. And, despite their losses, the enigmas hadn't cut and run. The eleven surviving enigma ships were together in a loose formation just outside of the range of Alliance weapons, pacing the human ships.

Most worrisome was the enigma hypernet gate, far off on the other side of the star system. If the enigmas made the choice to collapse that gate, sacrificing this star system and every enigma in it to destroy the Alliance fleet, there wouldn't be much he could do. But it seemed unlikely the enigmas would do that. This star system, facing off against the Dancers, must be regarded as particularly valuable.

He stood down the fleet from full combat readiness so the crews could rotate in sections for food and rest, but because of the nearby enigma warships had to have every warship maintain their weapons ready to fire. With some spare time finally available, he called the destroyer that had suffered two hits. "Lieutenant Laumer, I'm seeing you took a casualty."

"One of our chiefs lost a hand," *Bolo*'s commanding officer replied. "But he's not too upset because it isn't the hand he holds his coffee with."

"We'll get it regrown anyway," Geary said. "Two hull penetrations and that was your only casualty?"

"Our ancestors were looking out for us," Lieutenant Laumer said. "We did take serious equipment damage. My chief engineer recommends that *Bolo* pull alongside one of the auxiliaries to get the damage fixed properly."

"Good. Make sure Captain Smyth is aware of what you need. Tell your crew well done from me."

He stayed on the bridge a little while longer, making sure the fleet was properly in formation and on vector for the jump point, and worried that the remaining enigma warships might try something. Finally, exhausted, Geary went down to his stateroom to try to sleep. They had fifteen hours to go before they reached the next jump point, and it wouldn't help anything if he was strung out from lack of rest when they got there.

He managed to get in only six hours of sleep, though, before his stateroom alarm chimed urgently. "One of the enigma ships has altered vector, Admiral. It's left their formation but doesn't seem to be headed for us. Current estimates are that it will pass several light minutes astern of our formation." The watch stander paused. "We just got an update from the ship's systems, Admiral. They're estimating the enigma is aiming to intercept the burial tube we launched."

"How long?" Geary mumbled, trying to decide if he had to wake up right this minute.

"One hour to intercept, Admiral.

"Good. Thank you. Call me again in half an hour."

A good sailor never passed up the chance for another thirty minutes of sleep.

BY the time the enigma ship reached the vicinity of the burial tube, Geary was back on *Dauntless*'s bridge. By this time they were close to a light hour away from the enigma and the burial tube, so what they were seeing had happened nearly an hour ago, but that didn't really matter in this case.

The enigma closed on the burial tube, matching its vector but maintaining enough distance to be safe if the tube contained a booby trap. Keeping its distance, the enigma warship rolled over and completely around the burial tube.

"They're scanning it from all angles," Desjani commented.

He simply nodded, watching. Burial tubes were designed to be transparent to most sensors to ensure that no one would use them as weapons or to smuggle people or things. The material added to keep anyone from seeing the body inside wouldn't stop sensors operating in other spectra. The enigmas should be easily able to determine that there was nothing inside but the body of their fellow enigma and the wound bag still protecting it. They should also be able to tell that the body had retained all of its possessions and hadn't been compromised in any way by the Alliance.

After about twenty minutes of slow examination of the burial tube, the enigma warship suddenly accelerated past it. When it was about one hundred kilometers ahead of it, the enigma ship pivoted.

"He fired a bombardment projectile," Lieutenant Castries said, startled.

Detection of the firing and the impact of the projectile on the burial tube were nearly instantaneous. The burial tube and its contents vanished, blown into tiny dust fragments, while a few small pieces of the bombardment projectile continued on, tumbling through space.

"So much for the idea of respecting their dead," Desjani grumbled. But on the heels of her words, her face lit with sudden thought. "Unless that's their idea of a proper burial."

"What do you mean?" Geary asked.

"What do you mean what do I mean?" Desjani gestured to where the cloud of dust from the burial tube was dissipating to be lost among the debris of the universe. "Look at that. Think about it. The enigmas are obsessed with their privacy. Why would that end with their dead? Why would they bury Daddy in a hole somewhere where he could be dug up in ten years or a hundred years and someone could figure out he'd been left-handed? I will lay you odds that enigma burials since time immemorial have involved burning their dead to ashes and then grinding the ashes and then scattering the resulting dust."

"But . . ." He hesitated, thinking. "When we first fought the enigmas, at Midway, before they knew we'd cracked the quantum worms, before they knew we could fight back against them, they already had those self-destruct capabilities on their ships. Which means they weren't there just because of us. The enigma ships must have already had them."

"Exactly. Remember Colonel Rogero talking about the enigmas fighting each other on the ground? Why did we assume they aren't nearly as paranoid with each other as they are with us?"

"But how could their society function like that?" Geary protested. "We know they have cities. We know their ships have crews. Enigmas have to be able to work in groups."

Desjani shrugged. "Maybe it's a clan-based thing, or extended families. Something that lets them say the other enigmas in this clan or whatever can see me and talk to me and work with me. Because you're right, otherwise their society couldn't have evolved."

"They dispose of their dead by destroying them," Geary said. It made a terrible kind of sense. "Maybe by destroying their closest possessions, too? That would— Ancestors save me."

"What?" She gave him a look, puzzled by his sudden change of mood.

"Tanya, what's happened to the human settlements on planets the enigmas have taken over?"

"Destroyed without a trace," she said. A moment later her eyes widened. "That wasn't a spiteful act, erasing any sign of the human presence? Did the enigmas give our dead the same treatment they'd have given theirs?"

"I have no idea whether that's true or not," Geary said. "But if it is, if they're acting the same way they would with other enigmas, it could change a lot of things about the way we view them."

"Unless it also changes the way they keep trying to kill us it won't make much difference, though."

"True." With only a few hours left until they reached the jump point for Dancer space, he called the ambassador again.

It was morning on the ships. Rycerz was drinking coffee when he called, and nearly did a spit take when Geary explained the latest speculation aboard *Dauntless*. "You're saying the enigma destruction of human settlements on planets they capture is not necessarily malicious violence? That it could actually be a sign of respect?"

"I don't know that's true, Ambassador," Geary said. "It's a possibility, that's all. But we've been thinking about it in just one way. Maybe there are alternative explanations."

"Of course there are. But you do realize that claiming the enigmas are just misunderstood will be a little hard to sell as long as they keep killing every human that gets within their reach."

"Captain Desjani made the same point," Geary said.

"Good. In any event, it's up to the enigmas to decide what to do next. We've given them a gesture, what they should recognize as a large gesture. But they have to take the next step."

"I agree," Geary said. "We'll be jumping for Dancer-controlled space soon. Is there anything we need to discuss before we enter jump? Because our next stop should bring us face-to-face with the Dancers."

Rycerz hesitated, giving the impression of someone who had a great deal to say but for unknown reasons was remaining silent. Finally, she shook her head. "Not at this time. Do be sure to send your own greeting to the Dancers when we meet them. Tell them as much as you think they should know, and feel free to liberally interpret your orders to communicate directly with the Dancers on any issue impacting the security of this mission. We need to talk in more detail with each other after we arrive in Dancer space, Admiral. Talk in person, on your ship. I look forward to seeing you there."

After Ambassador Rycerz had ended the call, Geary gave Desjani a look. "Rycerz doesn't trust the security of our highest-encrypted comm system."

Desjani nodded, looking unsurprised. "Didn't Victoria Rione manage to break into every system no matter how encrypted? Mind you, I'm hoping our current opponents don't include anyone as viciously clever as Victoria Rione." She paused before giving him a glance. "I mean viciously clever in the nicest possible way, of course."

"Of course."

He sent out one more message, to every ship. "This is Admiral Geary. We've been on wartime status since leaving Varandal. When we arrive in Dancer space that changes. All ships are to be at peacetime readiness. Shields at standard strength, no weapons powered up, fire control systems inactive. We're already going to look aggressive just by showing up without an invitation. I want to ensure nothing we do or display creates an impression that we're there for anything but peaceful discussions. Remember, these are the people who helped us at Unity Alternate and at Midway. It's vitally important that this mission succeed. I expect everyone in the fleet to put their best efforts into making that happen. To the honor of our ancestors, Geary, out."

One hour and fifteen minutes later, the fleet jumped for the Dancer star.

IT should have been a calm few days in jump space. The dangers of Syndicate Worlds–controlled space and enigma-controlled space were past. Ahead lay the Dancers, who to the best of the fleet's knowledge had never attacked humanity and in fact had offered critical help more than once.

But *Boundless*, the hopeful embassy to the Dancers, was a snake pit in ways that resembled more attempts to sabotage the mission. And the reaction of the Dancers to the arrival of a human fleet in their space couldn't be predicted. They'd never displayed hostility toward humans, but it was entirely possible they'd respond to the arrival of the fleet by telling the humans to go home.

During the first day in jump, Dr. Nasr stopped by Geary's stateroom, nodding politely as he entered. "Admiral, I thought you should know that I spoke with Dr. Galen before we entered jump."

Geary leaned back in his seat, clenching his eyes shut. "Does she want to autopsy me?"

"At first," Dr. Nasr said. Geary opened his eyes to see Nasr grinning. "She was very unhappy with me as well. But I explained. I told her that if what you did succeeded, it might mean no more battles like the one we'd just fought at this star. That it might help us break the deadlock with the enigmas, and finally forge a peace agreement."

"I hope you didn't overpromise," Geary said. "That's my hope. I have no idea if it will work out that way."

"But it is a hope," Dr. Nasr said. "One that did not exist before. In light of that, Dr. Galen, reluctantly, agreed with your decision."

"Thank you," Geary said, his voice growing quieter. "But you deserve more credit than I do. If you hadn't spoken up and persisted I might never have thought of doing something other than what we'd automatically do."

"It was my responsibility, Admiral," Dr. Nasr said.

"Not everyone would have thought so." He nodded to Dr. Nasr. "If it works at all, maybe we'll have less fighting. I've given this fleet's doctors far too much work."

"You've given us far less to do than your predecessors, Admiral."

"Please sit down," Geary said. "How's everything going?"

"Mostly well," Dr. Nasr said, taking a seat opposite Geary. "These days, it's mostly stability work for officers and sailors dealing with the memories of actions and events that haunt all of us. If we could see the ghosts following this fleet it would form an armada that filled space."

"I wish you had something that would make the ghosts go away," Geary said. "Instead of just making them less painful and horrible."

"Do you truly wish that, Admiral? Would you truly want to forget?"

He thought about that, about forgetting the crew of *Merlon*, forgetting the people he'd known a century ago who had aged and died while he was frozen in survival sleep, about forgetting those he'd come to know in this difficult future but would never meet again in life. The memories brought a lot of pain, but also a lot more. "I guess not," Geary finally said. "I owe them remembrance."

"Yes," Dr. Nasr said. "I think so, too. The best we can do is to help people cope with the ghosts that follow them, so that the memories evoke a smile rather than tears or anger. It's not perfect. Perhaps it's not even right. But I think it's better than anything else anyone has tried or suggested." He paused, sighing. "I have some particular ghosts following me. Those Kicks we captured and tried to save."

Geary didn't have to refresh his memory of that. The Kicks, so named by the fleet's sailors as a shorthand for Krazy Kows, were cute, cuddly-looking herbivores who looked like crosses between cows and teddy bears. They also saw the universe as divided between their Herd and whatever the Herd needed, and everything and everybody else. To them, humans were just another species of meat-eating predators it made no sense to talk to. Meat-eating predators simply had to be wiped out before they ate any of the Herd.

"That was not your fault," Geary said. "No one could have saved them. Not when they could will themselves to death when they realized they'd been captured. In retrospect, we should have put them in an escape pod while they were unconscious and let them go." He grimaced. "That wouldn't have worked, though. We would have had to go back to that Kick-controlled star system to do that, and the fleet barely made it out intact the first time we went there."

"I could have pushed harder," Dr. Nasr said, frowning. "I could have tried harder to get those 'humanitarians' who insisted on awakening the Kicks to understand that would result in the deaths of the Kicks."

"Their refusal to listen to you does not reflect poorly on you," Geary said. "I know how hard you pushed. The deaths of those Kicks should not be on your conscience."

"Do you carry no deaths that should not be on your conscience, Admiral?"

"That's not a fair question," Geary said. "And as the doctor here you're supposed to help me feel better, not worse."

Nasr smiled. "Speaking of feeling better, you've read my reports on crew morale. It's surprisingly good."

"I'm getting similar reports from throughout the fleet," Geary said. Except for on *Boundless*. "I'm glad, though I'm not sure what I've done right."

"The one-sided victory at Lalotai didn't hurt," Dr. Nasr said. "But I think the main cause is a sense of purpose. Almost every sailor in the fleet feels that they are helping to accomplish important things. That's always big when it comes to morale. Is what I'm doing going to matter? And if it does matter, will that be for good or ill? Our crews believe they're part of something that will make a long-term difference, and one for the better."

"Not all of them," Geary said. "I know medical ethics constrain what you can tell me about what individual sailors tell you, but . . ."

"But medical confidentiality does not apply to matters that reasonably might involve danger to individuals or to the ship," Nasr said, quoting the relevant regulation. "Admiral, I've had some individuals express concerns, misgivings, about the intent of the Dancers. But, based on my experience and the medical readouts during examinations, I haven't heard anything that implies intent to take unauthorized actions."

"Good. Thanks." They talked a bit more, reminiscing about people and places. After Dr. Nasr left, Geary realized that he felt a whole lot better inside. *I need to give that doctor a medal.*

The next day, a pair of visitors showed up at his stateroom, Colonel Rogero and Kommodor Bradamont both acting formal in a way that broadcast this was not a social encounter. "Admiral," Bradamont said, "we'd like to clarify something before we reach Dancer space. Would you authorize a link so that Colonel Rogero and I can monitor conversations with the Dancers from this ship?"

"I can't do that," Geary said, holding up a hand to forestall Bradamont's objections. "I can't authorize any links to anywhere. Because our technicians are worried that establishing a link to that transmitter will allow the Dancer software to migrate across the link."

"You can't stop that?" Colonel Rogero asked, surprised. "There aren't any firewalls effective against the Dancer software?"

"We don't know," Geary said. "What we do know is that the Dancers sent us the software to allow us to use one of our transmitters as a communications device and a translator with them. We know the Dancer software, when loaded into an isolated transmitter, somehow adapted to our hardware. Every attempt to analyze the Dancer software has fizzled out. It's making our best code monkeys tear their hair out. We still don't know how that software works, or what all it can do. Which is why I can't authorize any links.

"But," he added, "I can authorize either one of you, or both of you, to be present in the compartment containing the transmitter. And I will do so. I know that's a lot less convenient. But it's the same rules anyone else in this fleet would have to live by, myself included."

"We can't ask for better than that, Admiral," Bradamont said, smiling with relief. "We do have a greetings message for the Dancers from President Iceni and General Drakon that we were hoping to be able to transmit."

"You need to get with General Charban and his people," Geary said. "Communications with the Dancers have to be . . . formatted properly. They can help you do that."

"Isn't one of those people Lieutenant Iger?" Bradamont asked.

"My intelligence officer," Geary said. "Yes. He was added to the team not to monitor things, but because he can help format the messages. He's a poet."

"A poet?"

"Not a great poet, but he's good at rendering words in haiku form." Geary paused. "Would you object to Ambassador Rycerz seeing your message to the Dancers?"

"That depends," Colonel Rogero said. "For information, we would have no objections. But if she would see it with an eye to approving it . . ."

"I understand you don't want that," Geary said. "I'll talk to the ambassador when we reach Dancer space."

"Is there a chance that she'd want our greeting sent from the transmitter on *Boundless*?" Bradamont asked.

Geary blew out a long, exasperated breath as he considered his words. "I'd say no. There may well be problems with the transmitter on *Boundless*."

"Hardware or software?"

"Bureaucratic."

After a pause, Colonel Rogero gave Geary a speculative look. "You understand, Admiral, that in the Syndicate, if a supervisor such as your ambassador was encountering problems with her subordinates, those subordinates would have a high chance of developing sudden, fatal, health problems."

"Health problems?" Geary said.

Bradamont shrugged. "You know the old joke about lead poisoning," she said, using one hand to mimic firing a slug-throwing weapon.

Rogero nodded. "Heart failure. Shock. Low blood pressure was a favorite official way of describing someone who died as a result of having their throat cut. Or low oxygen levels if they were strangled. Telling someone that they appeared to be at risk of sleep apnea was one way for a Syndicate supervisor to warn an individual that they might die in their sleep if they didn't shape up."

"You joked about that?" Geary said, appalled.

"Sir, you know how the fleet uses dark humor to get through tough times," Bradamont said. "So did the people stuck under the Syndicate."

Geary leaned back to better study Rogero. "You're not nostalgic for those times, are you?"

Rogero laughed at the idea. "No! Why would I be? It was justified in terms of efficiency, but it always had the opposite results. Those targeted were those who stuck their noses out trying to fix things. The mediocre kept their heads down and pretended everything was perfect, which the bosses loved because then they'd tell *their* bosses that everything was perfect." His brief burst of humor faded. "You never knew when you'd die or be arrested. Maybe because of what you did, maybe because of what it was suspected you did, maybe because somebody decided they didn't like you or needed to make their quota. Or you might get killed at any time by one of your own workers who'd decided they couldn't take it anymore. It's really surprising that more people didn't die in revenge killings when we overthrew the Syndicate on Midway."

"I thought President Iceni and General Drakon were able to keep a lid on things," Bradamont said.

"That's true. But it was very close. A lot more could've died. You've seen what can happen when Syndicate workers suddenly snap." Rogero nodded apologetically to Geary. "Forgive me a bit of melancholy at how close things were. Sometimes the past weighs on me." He paused. "And that was an exceptionally wrong thing to say to you of all people, wasn't it?"

"Don't worry about it," Geary said. "Go ahead and talk to Charban. Tell him I authorized full access for you two."

One day later, they came out of jump in Dancer space.

EIGHT

HE felt tense as the final seconds counted down. As tense as when arriving in Syndicate Worlds space, or in enigma space. Sure, the Dancers had always been friendly. But the Alliance fleet was doing the equivalent of bursting through the front door of a helpful but distant neighbor while brandishing a powerful weapon.

As Geary's head cleared of the mental fuzz created by leaving jump space, he noted first the lack of warning alarms.

When he was finally able to focus on his display, rapidly being updated by the fleet's sensors, he saw a reassuringly familiar set of Dancer installations and space traffic.

The closest Dancer ships were about ten light minutes from the jump point. Sixty of them, of various sizes, arranged in a breathtaking three-dimensional pinwheel. It tended to confirm earlier speculation that the Dancers made those gorgeous formations not to impress others but simply because they liked doing it.

And it made the neat human ship formation, which he'd earlier taken pride in, look like the work of toddlers. Enthusiastic, but unskilled.

He wasn't the only one who'd noticed that. All over the human formation, ships were making tiny adjustments to their positions, trying to be certain they were in exactly the right place relative to where *Boundless* was.

Something else should be happening right now. Geary checked for transmissions from *Boundless* and saw nothing. He tapped an internal communications control. "General Charban, have you heard anything being sent by the Dancer-modified transmitter aboard *Boundless*?"

"Not a thing, Admiral," Charban said.

Geary frowned in a way that made the lieutenants on the bridge exchange nervous glances. "Surely they know how impolite it is to show up in a star system and not immediately send greetings. When someone shows up in force like this and doesn't immediately communicate, it's outright threatening."

Charban shrugged. "I'm afraid that I have no idea what the bunch on *Boundless* may or may not know."

This was a security issue, ensuring that the Dancers knew the Alliance ships were here for peaceful purposes. "Go ahead and send our greetings to the Dancers, assuring them of our peaceful intent, and then the greeting from President Iceni and General Drakon. I'll call Ambassador Rycerz to let her know we're doing that."

Rycerz didn't answer, hopefully because she was busy trying to get the official greeting out from *Boundless*, so Geary left her a message.

He'd ordered the entire fleet to brake velocity, every ship turning to use its main propulsion to slow down rather than accelerate. Until he knew what the Dancers wanted, he didn't want to go charging deeper into their star system.

After about twenty minutes Charban called back. "Both greetings have been sent, Admiral. Ummm, I may have gotten us into trouble."

"How?"

"We were waiting for any indication that *Boundless* wanted to send, but we heard nothing. Once we finished the second message, though, *Boundless* started transmitting immediately, as if they'd been forced to wait on us. I think the transmitter aboard *Dauntless* and the one on *Boundless* may be linked somehow by the Dancer software, so that only one can transmit at a time. Which if true means the entire time we were transmitting, *Boundless* could not."

"Oh, hell." Geary bit back some stronger words. Charban looked genuinely regretful, and there really hadn't been any way to learn this beforehand. But aboard *Boundless* it would look very much as if the military had deliberately preempted the civilian communications with the Dancers. "I guess I'd better call Ambassador Rycerz again to apologize."

"Admiral, this one should be mine," Charban said. "I should own this."

"No," Geary said. "First, you were doing what I told you to do. And, second, if that idiot Macadams had been willing to test the transmitters jointly before we got here we would've learned about the problem. And, third, someone could've called us on normal comm channels and told us about the problem, which they didn't. I'm more than willing to stand up for that."

On the heels of those words, he called Ambassador Rycerz again, once more not getting through to her. After leaving a hopefully appropriately apologetic message, Geary got up from his command seat. "I'm going down to the room with the Dancer transmitter so I can hear their reply when it comes in as well as see the printed transcript."

Captain Desjani nodded to him. "Have fun. At the current rate of braking velocity, the fleet will achieve a stable orbit in . . . thirty-four minutes."

"Good. Then all we'll have to do is wait around to see what the Dancers decide to do with us."

The compartment holding the Dancer-modified transmitter felt more crowded than usual when Geary joined General Charban, Lieutenant Iger, and Lieutenant "Shamrock" Jamenson. Kommodor Bradamont and Colonel Rogero were also present, sitting back and watching. But there was still easily room for a dozen more people if needed. "How's it look?"

Charban sighed and shrugged. "The ball is in the Dancers' court. They might well be waiting for *Boundless* to finish transmitting, though."

"*Boundless* is still transmitting?"

Without saying anything else, Charban pushed some printouts at Geary.

Geary read, feeling a growing sense of puzzlement. The academics aboard *Boundless*, or at least Dr. Macadams, who ruled them with an iron fist, had refused to pay any heed to the hard-won lessons the fleet had gained on communicating with the Dancers. The rhythm and pacing of words mattered. Messages had to have an elegant structure, or the Dancers would treat them as if those speaking were infants.

The long message Macadams was still sending seemed to be mostly composed of simplistic sentence structures and words, as if aimed at a human toddler. But seeded in among that like boulders were references to what Geary assumed were academic theories. "What is . . . antispeciesmonoperspective exceptionalism?"

Everyone else shook their heads. As usual that made Lieutenant Jamenson's bright green hair stand out even before she replied. "It's probably against something. And I think whoever wrote this message is trying to tell the Dancers they're against it. Or maybe reassure the Dancers they're against it. Whatever . . . it is."

Anything that could confuse Jamenson must be a masterpiece of human double-talk. "Even you can't figure it out?"

"No, sir."

"It finally stopped," Lieutenant Iger said, staring at the transmitter. "There's no real sign-off. *Boundless*'s transmission just stopped."

The fleet's stable orbit was only about five light minutes from the Dancer formation nearest the jump point, so it wasn't surprising when a reply came in eleven minutes after *Boundless*'s transmission ended. The audio of the transmission carried the melodious flutelike tones of Dancer speech, followed by the translation in flatter human speech.

"Welcome, friend Geary,

"Surprised you are here many,

"Please wait, must learn plan."

"That's definitely for you," Charban said.

"And it's not exactly an enthusiastic greeting," Geary said. "But at least they called me friend."

Charban paused as he studied the transcript of the message. "I think the last line means they need to get instructions on what to do. If I'm right, in a few hours we should see one of the ships near their hypernet gate take off to report our arrival and get orders on what to do with us. Here's something else coming in. This is a reply to Midway's message, I think," Charban added, nodding toward where Rogero and Bradamont sat.

"Friends of friend, hear you,

"Your words of peace are welcome,

"Please wait, must learn plan."

Bradamont frowned slightly. "That's positive, isn't it?"

"It's not negative," Rogero said, his frown matching hers. "One of the things you learn in the Syndicate is to watch for what isn't said. In this case, they welcomed our words. But not us."

"They did call you friends of friend," Geary said.

"And they acknowledged your words," Charban said, tapping that part of the transcript. "They didn't simply ignore them. But, yes, it's clear that the Dancers are reserving judgment on you being here, just as they are with us. We all have to wait while they ask higher authority for the 'plan' to deal with us. There's nothing surprising about that."

"Here's something else," Lieutenant Jamenson said, reacting with surprise when the Dancer speech cut off almost as soon as it began.

"Hello, others."

After a moment of stunned silence, Charban laughed. "That's their reply to *Boundless*. Remember when they talked to us like that?"

"That's just your antispeciesmonoperspective exceptionalism talking," Geary said, unable to resist a smile at the thought of how Dr. Macadams must be reacting to that minimal reply.

"You might well be right," Charban said, grinning. "I have no idea."

The compartment's comm panel lit up. "Admiral, we've been advised that Ambassador Rycerz is on her way to *Dauntless*."

That was happening sooner than expected. "Thank you," Geary said. "Please ensure the ambassador receives a full security screening after she leaves her shuttle. She'll understand why. I'll meet her in the primary secure conference compartment."

He turned to see everybody else in the room trying not to look at him, all except General Charban, who stood up with a grim expression.

"If the ambassador is coming here this quickly to administer a personal chewing out regarding the transmitter issue—" Charban began.

Geary halted him with an open palm. "It's not that. I knew this was coming, though not so soon after our arrival." He paused, trying to decide what he could say. "There are some issues of concern that the ambassador and I need to discuss. But I want to emphasize that these issues are not anything between us. They concern . . . other actors and other issues."

Kommodor Bradamont stood up this time. "Admiral, if there are any concerns regarding Colonel Rogero and I—"

"No," Geary said. "I assure you not. I regard you both as reliable allies." He paused again. "Even though I'm not supposed to use that 'allies' word."

Bradamont smiled. "We'll let it pass this time, Admiral. If there is anything we can do, just say the word."

Geary nodded to her and Rogero, remembering General Drakon's advice. "Believe me, I will. But I have to talk to Ambassador Rycerz first."

RYCERZ was sitting in the conference room when Geary reached it. She waved a hand in greeting, staying silent until the hatch sealed and the lights above indicated the environment was totally secure. "Guess what your security screen found, Admiral."

"Another tick?" The tiny, mobile listening devices had been found twice already in places they should never have been.

"Right the first time." Rycerz sighed heavily, looking away. "I was supposedly fully screened before boarding the shuttle."

"Maybe the tick was on the shuttle and latched onto you during the journey?"

"The shuttle was also supposedly screened." Rycerz looked directly at him. "Admiral, here are my cards, laid on the table for you to see. I can't trust anyone aboard *Boundless*. I have to assume anything I say or do aboard that ship will be overheard and recorded." She paused for just a moment. "But I've decided that I can trust you."

"Why?" Geary said, genuinely surprised.

"Why?" Rycerz waved one hand. "I could say because your record is so ridiculously untarnished by actions or words aimed at personal advancement. I've had experts on the military check your career, with your own name removed, prior to Grendel one hundred years ago and they all informed me that you must be an idiot because you'd never make high rank by not focusing on your own advancement. But you are something far more dangerous than an idiot, Admiral. You are an honest man."

Geary sat back, watching her. "Was that a compliment? Or . . . ?"

Ambassador Rycerz tapped the table, her finger coming down hard with each tap. "At Atalia, we nearly had a fatal falling-out."

"You understand my reasons," Geary said.

"Yes. Now I do. But in my instructions, I was told to press the point, and that it would not generate any particular problems. I must be firm with you, to clearly establish your submission to civilian rule. But you would bend, because your ethics wouldn't allow you to risk your ships under anyone else's command."

He shook his head, wishing that he'd thought to bring some coffee to this meeting. "That's not how my ethics work."

"Clearly! My point is," Rycerz said, an angry gaze fixed on someone or something only she could see, "I was misled. And I had other so-called coordination issues I was supposed to press on you at Atalia. The more you resisted, the stronger I was to push. What would have happened, Admiral? Our working relationship would've been shattered."

"Who gave you those instructions?" Geary asked, knowing he looked as bewildered as he felt.

"That is a very, very good question," Ambassador Rycerz said. "Do you know what the highest levels of bureaucracies excel at? Hiding who was responsible for decisions. No fingerprints. No accountability. Accountability is for the little people. I went through my instructions, which bear every sign of having been fully vetted and authorized by all necessary parties. And there is not one name in them to identify their originators."

She slapped the desk angrily. "I should have spotted that right off the bat. Even before I left Unity aboard *Boundless*. But it was very well done, Admiral. And I had no reason to suspect those instructions." Rycerz went silent for a few seconds before looking at Geary again. "On your honor, Admiral, were you given secret instructions regarding me?"

He didn't have to hesitate. "No. On my word of honor, I received no secret instructions regarding you. Not even official hints that I should behave in certain ways."

"Because they knew you were an honest man, which meant they couldn't trust you."

"That statement is disturbing in so many ways," Geary said.

"I suppose it is," Rycerz said with a crooked smile. "I think it's clear that those who want this mission to fail did not want you and me working together. They wanted to sabotage that possibility as soon as they could."

He nodded. "Which would have left you totally isolated aboard *Boundless*."

"Isolated and effectively impotent," Rycerz said. "After studying my instructions I realized that I have no real authority over Dr. Macadams, and I cannot actually order Colonel Webb to do anything. Even Captain Matson has an escape clause in his orders allowing him to disregard my instructions if he feels they would hazard the safety of the ship or its crew."

That last seemed reasonable, Geary thought, but on top of the other things seemed just another limit on her authority. "What about your staff?"

"That's interesting." Rycerz paused to rub her eyes. "Admiral, I'm sorry, but is there any coffee available?"

"I was just thinking the same thing. Hold on." Geary cracked the security hatch, seeing the lights above it turn red. He wasn't surprised to see two Marines from *Dauntless*'s detachment standing sentry outside the hatch. "I'll be right back," he told them.

He knew there was a break room only about twenty steps away on this same passageway. The coffee dispenser was fleet standard, which for reasons known only to fleet supply was decorated with the usual depiction of happy cups of coffee marching off to be consumed by eager sailors. Geary had always found the image of coffee cups merrily marching to their deaths a bit disturbing.

He got two cups, along with a couple of cubes of also fleet-standard "creamsweetstuff," and hastened back to the secure room.

"That junk will keep you awake, Admiral," the Marine corporal advised with a grin.

"So I've heard," Geary said. "Have you noticed anyone taking an unusual interest in this compartment?"

Both Marines shook their heads. "Just the usual foot traffic, sir," the corporal said. "We've gotten a few looks for being posted here, that's all."

"Good." He went inside the room, set the hatch to seal again, and placed her coffee before the ambassador. "It's not fancy, but . . . it's coffee."

"I'll take it." The ambassador dumped the entire "stuff" cube in her coffee, waited for it to dissolve, then shuddered as she took a taste. "You're certain that it's coffee?"

"Fleet coffee has a certain reputation," Geary said, taking a drink of his own. "There are various stories about where it's sourced from. None of which you probably want to hear."

Rycerz smiled. "I'll take your word for it. Now, my staff. That's an interesting situation. They couldn't be fully insulated from my control, but when I dug into the fine print of their agreements to take part in this mission, I discovered that my ability to require them to do what I want is fairly limited. I have to avoid pushing them to the wall, because if I do, they'll discover they can just slide through the wall and be beyond my reach. I don't want to give the impression all of my staff are untrustworthy. I believe that most of them are. But with so little to do until the Dancers respond to our diplomatic outreach, my staff are . . . I suppose 'restless' is the right word."

"In the military," Geary said, "we're warned that nothing creates trouble faster than having too little meaningful work to do. Crews get restless."

"I can't just make up work," Rycerz said. "We already have dozens of contingency plans prepared to respond to anything the Dancers say or propose."

"What about the enigmas?" Geary asked. "Could I request help on the diplomatic side for dealing with them? That would give your people something worthwhile to do."

Rycerz set down her coffee and leaned forward, eyeing Geary. "Exactly what sort of help are you speaking of?"

"My ships have to return through enigma-controlled space. We've attempted a breakthrough with the enigmas by returning that body unexamined."

"But there's no telling how the enigmas will respond," Rycerz said. "Or how you should respond to different enigma proposals. Let's clarify this. You, as fleet commander, are requesting support from my staff in determining possible enigma responses to our outreach, and how you should reply to each of those possible responses."

"Yes," Geary said. "I really don't want to be responsible for figuring that out myself."

"Oh, this is excellent." Rycerz sat back, smiling again. "A formal request from the fleet for my staff's support. Meaningful work, and an acknowledgment that my staff has skills the military recognizes and needs. And, as a bonus, a clear signal that you and I are working together rather than being at each other's throats." She paused, taking a sip of coffee. "It will be interesting to see if that provokes any responses from those trying to ensure this mission doesn't succeed."

"Are you safe?" Geary asked.

"Me?" Rycerz laughed, though there didn't seem to be any humor in the sound. "I'm perhaps the safest person there is. As long as I'm alive, I can be blamed for the failure of the mission and punished accordingly. But, if I'm dead, they might have to look for other scapegoats to satisfy the demand for retribution, and that might overturn some rocks that our opponents don't want exposed to the light of day. Oh, no, Admiral, they want me alive when this mission fails."

"It's not going to fail," Geary said.

"Damn right." She raised her cup, they touched the rims together briefly, and then they both drank to affirm their vow.

AS Ambassador Rycerz was leaving, she passed a data disc to Geary before boarding her shuttle. "Colonel Webb asked if you'd run checks on these individuals aboard *Boundless*. I don't know how legitimate his concerns are, but I thought I should give him the benefit of the doubt."

"It doesn't hurt to check," Geary said. "Though I'm not sure we'd find anything that wasn't already available aboard *Boundless*."

Not much more than half an hour later, he was proven wrong when Lieutenant Iger showed up at Geary's stateroom. Iger stood in the center of the stateroom, looking about as uncomfortable as Geary had ever seen him. "Admiral, there's nothing in our files on any of these people."

"Something seems to be bothering you, though."

"Yes, sir." Iger displayed a picture of a man on his comm pad. "This individual. Lieutenant Joseph Paul in *Boundless*'s crew. I know him.

This is really Lieutenant Commander Christopher George, Fleet intelligence."

Geary rubbed his chin, trying not to show how unhappy he was. . "Fleet intelligence planted a mole among *Boundless*'s crew, without informing me or you?"

"Yes, sir," Iger said.

"How can you be certain that this man is Lieutenant Commander George?"

"Four years ago," Iger explained, "I was ordered to attend a training course. One of the other officers in that course was then Lieutenant George. We were assigned a room together in the transient officers quarters."

"For how long?" Geary asked.

"Three weeks, sir."

"Three weeks." Something about that didn't seem right. "Wouldn't whoever gave Lieutenant Commander George his orders have done a check to see if anyone like you in the fleet could recognize him?"

"They should have," Iger said. "But it's a minor item in our individual records, and there are a lot of intelligence officers. It wouldn't be too surprising if no one noticed I was on *Dauntless* and had also spent time around Lieutenant Commander George, especially if they were in a hurry." Iger frowned down at the picture. "Colonel Webb was concerned about the pattern of 'Lieutenant Paul's' personal records. I can see why. At first glance, they're unremarkable, but it's the very lack of anything that stands out which seems odd. Why would someone with such a total lack of experience with anything but the most routine of jobs, such a total lack of exceptional appraisals, have been hired to be part of the crew of *Boundless*?"

"Is there any way for you to contact Lieutenant Commander George without it being detected by anyone aboard *Boundless*?"

Iger shook his head. "No, sir. If I talked to him it would draw attention to him. If you *want* to expose him, that's what we should do, but I strongly recommend against that. We don't know that he's doing anything we'd disapprove of. He may simply be observing and recording events to ensure nothing is covered up."

"Whatever he's doing," Geary said, feeling anger growing inside despite his efforts to tamp it down, "if Colonel Webb doesn't know about it then Lieutenant Commander George is in a dangerous position. Right now Webb is looking for an assassin and a spy. George is already on his scans as a suspect. How do I keep Lieutenant Commander George from being put on the rack by Colonel Webb and his soldiers?"

"I don't know, Admiral," Lieutenant Iger said, his jaw tight with tension.

Victoria Rione would've known how to handle this, how to turn spy versus spy and keep anything from exploding. But he didn't have her anymore. He didn't have anyone with that kind of devious thinking or experience.

Or did he?

"Hold on, Lieutenant," Geary said. He made sure that Iger wasn't within the view of his display before making a call. "Colonel Rogero. I'm hoping for some advice."

He explained his dilemma, trying his best to hide who was involved where.

After he'd finished, Rogero nodded. "This isn't beyond my experience, Admiral. The danger to Captain X comes from the fact that Major Z does not know who Captain X is and what he is doing. The answer is fairly simple. Tell Major Z. Major Z will now believe he knows what needs to be known about Captain X. He will become a known quantity. Perhaps one to be enlisted in support of Major Z at some point. Captain X will continue carrying out his orders, which if not aimed at Major Z will simply confirm for Major Z that Captain X is not a threat."

"I see." Geary hesitated. "You have experience with that kind of situation?"

"Isn't that why you called me?" Rogero paused, his eyes going distant for a moment. "The snakes wanted us to suspect each other, to never know which of our co-workers was an informant. We gained a lot of experience with handling such situations. Either that, or we died fairly young."

Geary took a moment to reply. "I'm sorry."

Rogero shrugged. "If you ever wonder for a moment why snakes die quickly when the workers get the upper hand, that's one reason."

The call ended, Geary saw Lieutenant Iger giving him an alarmed look. "Are you going to follow that advice, Admiral? Compromise Lieutenant Commander George's identity to Colonel Webb?"

"You heard Colonel Rogero's reasoning," Geary said. "It's true, isn't it?"

"But . . ." Iger moved both hands as if trying to reach something that evaded his grasp. "Whatever mission Lieutenant Commander George is on is classified. We'll be compromising that mission."

"Lieutenant," Geary said, leaning back in his seat, "neither you nor I was told about George being aboard *Boundless*. We have no idea what his mission is. But I have no reason to believe that mission poses a danger to *Boundless* or anyone aboard that ship. Do you agree?"

"Yes, sir," Iger said. "Officers like George and I aren't special operators. We don't commit sabotage or try to hurt people. We just collect information."

"So we can tell Colonel Webb that Lieutenant Commander George poses no danger, that whatever his mission is, it is not anything contrary to Webb's own mission."

Lieutenant Iger hesitated before nodding again. "Yes, Admiral. That's true."

"Because I'll tell you honestly, Lieutenant," Geary added, "from what I hear of conditions aboard *Boundless*, we need to protect George from potentially becoming collateral damage in their attempts to find whoever tried to kill me."

Half an hour later, Geary was back in the secure conference room, along with Lieutenant Iger. The virtual presence of Colonel Webb sat across from them, listening. Webb, who had sat quietly during meetings in the past, this time seemed to be fighting off repeated twitches of his fingers. But when Geary and Iger were done briefing him, Webb smiled for a moment, like a wolf catching sight of prey.

"I get it," Webb said. "Fleet intel not trusting me, or you. Trying to have their own set of eyes secretly documenting everything. This might help a lot."

"How so?" Geary asked.

"If this Lieutenant Commander George has been spying on what's going on aboard *Boundless*, maybe he spotted something my own sources have missed. Or maybe he'll see something in the future. But I need to talk to him, Admiral. I need him to cooperate."

Geary looked at Iger, who seemed to be trying to avoid any expression that might imply his feelings about the matter. That left it up to him.

"I think you're right, Colonel," Geary said. "I hadn't thought that George might be able to help you. I merely wanted you to know he wasn't a danger."

"So you'll tell George to cooperate with me?"

Lieutenant Iger spoke carefully. "Sir, we don't know what Lieutenant Commander George's orders are. Or who they came from. Even if Admiral Geary tells him to cooperate, he may be bound by orders that take precedence over that."

"That wouldn't be a smart attitude for him to take," Colonel Webb said, two of the fingers on his right hand tapping rapidly.

"Colonel," Geary said in a low but forceful voice, "I don't want anything to happen to Lieutenant Commander George. If he does not cooperate and you feel his presence aboard *Boundless* hinders your own work, I will order him transferred to another ship. But I will first tell him that I expect his full cooperation with you on anything that might provide leads to the security issues you are pursuing. Let's see how he responds."

Colonel Webb inhaled slowly before nodding. "Understood, Admiral."

After Webb's virtual presence had vanished, Lieutenant Iger stared at the place where he'd been. "Admiral, thank you. I wasn't sure before but . . . Christopher George really might be in physical danger, isn't he?"

"I think so," Geary said. "Something Fleet intel apparently didn't think about before they came up with their brilliant plan." He punched in another call. "Let's have a talk with our friend the secret intel officer."

A few minutes later, another virtual presence appeared, wearing the civilian crew uniform of the *Boundless*. "Lieutenant Joseph Paul," he said, either doing an excellent job of feigning worry and confusion or actually feeling that way. "Why did you want a secure conference with me, Admiral?"

Geary gestured to one side. "You know Lieutenant Iger."

Paul shook his head. "Uh, no. I don't think I ever—"

"Chris," Iger broke in, "Admiral Geary knows who you are."

"Of course he does. My name's not Chris. I'm—"

Geary stopped him with a gesture. "Lieutenant Commander Christopher George, I am formally ordering you to reveal your true name and mission to Colonel Webb aboard *Boundless*, and cooperate with him to the best of your ability. Whatever orders you were given when you were sent on this mission have been overtaken by events. Do you understand?"

"No." Lieutenant Paul/Lieutenant Commander George looked from Iger to Geary like someone trapped in a nightmare and trying to find his way out. "I don't know what you're talking about. I'm employed by the Alliance as part of the crew of *Boundless* and not subject to your orders."

"Chris," Lieutenant Iger said, "why would Lieutenant Paul know he wasn't subject to Admiral Geary's orders?" As the other hesitated, Iger continued. "Your life is in danger. Colonel Webb suspected you of being involved in earlier assassination and spying attempts."

Paul/George shook his head. "I decline to abide by your orders, Admiral. I'm not whoever you think I am."

Geary shook his head in turn, his expression unyielding but not hostile. "I can't have loose cannons in this fleet. Your bosses should have coordinated with me, for your own protection. Now, you have two choices. Follow my orders to contact Colonel Webb and cooperate with him, or be transferred in prisoner status to my flagship, where you will occupy a bunk in the brig while Colonel Webb goes over your stateroom and everything you own, and my own personnel run a full DNA analysis on you. And don't bother asserting a right against DNA sampling. Out here, I can order it. Which is it going to be?"

Lieutenant Commander George stood silently for a moment, visibly trembling, his breath going in and out shakily. Finally he looked at Geary. "Sir, I have priority compartmented orders."

"From whom?"

"I can't divulge that, sir."

"I'm just supposed to take your word for it?" Geary asked. As George hesitated, plainly searching for an answer, Geary leaned closer. "Listen. You are not being asked to do anything that will harm the Alliance. That's what your oath is to, right? Just like mine. We're on the same side. And Colonel Webb needs your help. Which means I need your help."

"Sir . . ." George clasped his hands together tightly. "I have orders."

"Well, then you have a choice," Geary said. "Either you upset whoever issued those orders to you, or you upset me. And I already told you what's going to happen if you upset me. I am not ordering you to do anything which is in violation of your oath. I am, actually, trying to save your life, as Lieutenant Iger pointed out."

"Chris," Iger said, "you can trust the admiral. If you follow his orders, he will take responsibility."

"That's right," Geary said. "Anything you do under my orders is on my head. Do you want that on the record, Lieutenant Commander George?"

After another hesitation, George shook his head a final time. "No, sir. Your reputation is well-known. I will, under duress, comply with your orders."

Geary let himself smile slightly. Not in a gloating way. Just to signify approval. "Good. Here's one more order, though. If Colonel Webb orders you to do anything that you feel conflicts with my orders or your oath, I want you to contact Lieutenant Iger. Is there a stress word you can use that Colonel Webb wouldn't recognize?"

"Um . . . 'splice the main brace,'" George said. "The colonel will probably recognize that, but it's a common fleet term so he shouldn't be worried if he hears it."

"Good," Geary said. "If it gets bad, give Iger a call. He will let me know, and I will get you out of there."

George nodded, still worried. "Colonel Webb is, uh, pretty scary."

"I've got three thousand Marines with me," Geary said. "And I will use every single one of them if necessary to get you safely off *Boundless*. You're one of my people now. I take that responsibility seriously."

Lieutenant Commander George stared at Geary. "Th-Thank you, sir. I'll go speak with Colonel Webb."

As George's virtual presence vanished, Lieutenant Iger shook his head. "Will he be all right, sir?"

"He'll do his best," Geary said, "and we'll do our best." Which didn't really answer the question, but Iger seemed happy enough with it. "There's been something I've meant to ask General Charban. Have we been picking up any Dancer communications not intended for us?"

"No, sir," Iger said. "The general assumes the translation transmitter software is keeping us confined to a single frequency intended for that use. We've made some cautious explorations of the Dancer software controls and none of them allow any change in frequency or transmission type."

"Which means the Dancers are making sure we're not learning anything about them that they don't want us to know," Geary said. "Whatever the differences in thinking among different species, we all seem to want to keep other species from learning anything we don't want them to learn."

Lieutenant Iger frowned. "Admiral, we have strong cause to believe that the Dancers already know a great deal about humanity."

"Yeah. Our alien neighbors like the enigmas and the Dancers seem to have done a lot of research while humans were busy trying to kill each other." Geary rubbed his eyes, feeling unhappy about that and unable to do anything in particular about it. "And we're still working against ourselves. Half of the humans on this mission seem determined to undermine it."

The lieutenant's frown deepened. "Sir, we've been unable to spot any dangerous activity aboard *Dauntless*."

"And that doesn't make you happy?"

"No, sir." Lieutenant Iger hesitated before saying more. "We know from the assassination attempt against you at Midway that there are elements among us who want to kill you. Yet they either haven't tried to get at you on this ship, or . . ."

"Or they're up to something and we haven't spotted it," Geary said. "Kind of like that duck."

"Yes, sir, kind of like that duck," Iger agreed. "But we did eventually discover the duck."

"Only because the Marines hiding it did something stupid," Geary said. He clenched one fist, looking down at it. "One of the things I've learned is that it's very dangerous to make plans that assume your opponent will do something stupid. So far, whoever is behind a lot of this has been very smart."

"I don't think it's just one group," Lieutenant Iger said. "I think there are multiple efforts underway."

Geary gave him a questioning look. "Do you have some evidence of that?"

"More of a gut feeling," Iger confessed. "I've tried looking at everything we have as if I were a Dancer, looking for patterns. And I keep getting a feeling that there's more than one pattern, that the vague information we have so far doesn't all tie together."

"What does Lieutenant Jamenson think? If anyone can spot deceptive patterns, it'd be her."

"Lieutenant Jamenson doesn't have clearances necessary to see a lot of the information," Iger said. "But I have discussed it with her in general terms, and she warned me that people often try to present information that shows the pattern they want others to see. Deception, in other words."

"Or what Master Chief Gioninni calls misdirection," Geary said. "All right. Keep an eye on things, and let me know if Lieutenant Commander George contacts you."

He hoped that would be the last he had to deal with people and events on *Boundless* that day.

But a few hours later his stateroom door alert chimed. Dr. Nasr came in, looking as somber as Geary could recall him ever being. "What's the matter?"

"It's Colonel Webb," Nasr said in a heavy voice. "Something very serious."

NINE

DR. Nasr held out a data coin. "The report is on here. I did not think it wise to send it to you along normal channels."

Geary took the coin, handling it as carefully as if it were a bomb. From the way the doctor was acting, it might as well be explosive, and there was something uniquely worrisome about a doctor who looked so much as if he had bad news to impart. "What is it?"

"To summarize," Dr. Nasr said with a sigh, "Colonel Webb was scheduled for a mandatory psychiatric screening before we left Alliance space. Someone broke into the fleet's medical files and altered his record to delete that screening, so it was never conducted. Our code specialists found subtle but clear signs that someone was Colonel Webb himself."

Amid the thoughts tumbling through his mind as he looked at the data coin, Geary noticed one memory in particular: *Morgan learned how to break into the system on her own and gundeck her psych evals.* Colonel Rogero had told him that. He'd never suspected that he'd face the same situation.

But as his mind focused on that, Geary thought of something else.

According to Colonel Rogero, Morgan hadn't been caught doing that. Not until after she'd gone completely off the rails.

Someone with Webb's skills and experience had left subtle but clear signs of what he'd done?

Before they even left Alliance space?

That happened to surface now?

"How did this get spotted?" Geary asked.

Nasr gestured to the coin. "The technical explanation is in the report. The code monkeys summarized to me that the system software is always scanning for anomalies, and keyed on Webb's file."

"Recently?"

"Yesterday."

"Yesterday." Geary thought about that, not liking the feel of it. Thinking about what Lieutenant Iger had said, how Lieutenant Jamenson had warned against those trying to feed disinformation to others. About how so many things Ambassador Rycerz had told him about seemed to be focused on creating problems among those critical to the success of this mission. "Thank you, Doctor. I assume since you brought this to me that you're going to let me handle it?"

"Yes, Admiral," Dr. Nasr said. "That seemed the wisest course of action."

"Thank you," Geary said again. "I'll look this over and decide what to do."

After Nasr left, Geary read the report, trying to make it through the technical annexes as well that explained the precise means the fleet's code monkeys had used to reach their conclusions. It all seemed very damning when it came to Colonel Webb.

No longer entirely trusting the safety of discussions in the high-security conference room, he called *Dauntless*'s communications watch. "I want a maximum-security virtual call set up between me in my stateroom and Colonel Webb aboard *Boundless*."

It took about five minutes before the image of Colonel Webb appeared, standing in Geary's stateroom and looking both concerned and curious. "Has something happened, Admiral?"

"Yes," Geary said. "Do you recall a psych screening appointment prior to leaving Alliance space?"

Webb immediately nodded. "It was a couple of weeks before that. I was told I'd passed clean. Just the usual combat veteran issues. Has someone claimed otherwise?"

"You took that evaluation?"

"Yes, of course."

"Your medical record has been tampered with," Geary told him. "Someone made it look as if that screening never happened, that the appointment was deleted from your files, and that you did it."

Webb breathed in very slowly and very deeply, his eyes on the bulkhead behind Geary. "Do you believe that, sir?"

"I'm skeptical," Geary said. "And not just because of your immediate and frank acknowledgment of the screening. This is too easy," he added, hefting the data coin containing the report. "Evidence of gross misconduct on your part, illegal activity, just falling into our lap right after we reach Dancer space. Tell me, Colonel, if you had altered your medical record, what evidence would you leave of that?"

"None," Webb said. "I'm not boasting, Admiral. I'm simply stating that I know how to do it without leaving any tracks that could be traced to me."

"Do you have any proof that the screening was conducted as scheduled?"

Colonel Webb's lips widened in a wolf smile that displayed his canines. "Normally, officially, I shouldn't. But I keep a copy of my medical file."

Geary raised his eyebrows. "I didn't know that was possible."

"It's not . . . authorized, sir. But it is possible." Webb shook his head in anger. "I've had some issues in the past with official doctors, Admiral.

I download and keep a copy of my medical file to prevent a repeat of that."

"So, that *is* unauthorized," Geary said, making it a statement rather than a question.

"Yes, sir. I freely admit to having made multiple unauthorized accesses to my medical file to download copies. I've done nothing else," Colonel Webb added firmly.

Technically, unauthorized access to most systems was a minor offense. What could make it serious was what was done, such as "stealing" official files. Like most of those in the fleet, Geary had never understood how his medical file could belong to the government and not to him. But that was how the law read. "Colonel, I could rake you over the coals for what you just admitted doing."

"I'm aware of that, Admiral," Webb said, his tight posture somehow stiffening even more into a rigid stand at attention.

"But I won't." Geary dropped the data coin. "I'm far more concerned about who tried to set you up, and who is trying to create problems for this mission. You're not in my chain of command. But I'd like you to do two things for me. The first is to provide an unedited copy of your medical record to me that I can pass on to Dr. Nasr so he can fix your file in the system. The second is to help me find out who is doing all this."

Colonel Webb stared at Geary for a moment, before finally nodding and relaxing. "Thank you, sir. I assure you, I'm already trying to find who is trying to kill you, who I assume is the same as those who just tried to get me sidelined."

"They're not necessarily the same people," Geary said. "Lieutenant Iger thinks we have more than one set of saboteurs working on the inside. I suspect he's right. Will looking at the technical data for how your file was altered help you find any of them?"

"I doubt it," Webb said. "If they were good enough to get in and plant false tracks leading to me, they were good enough to conceal anything leading to them." He grimaced as if in pain. "It's something some of the people in my unit could've done. Maybe I'll see fingerprints I recognize."

Something about that didn't sound right. "Wouldn't your own people know you'd be able to spot their fingerprints in hacking?"

"They would assume I could," Webb admitted.

Geary leaned back. "Relax, Colonel. I've been thinking, which I know is a statement that alarms people when an admiral says it. The bit with Lieutenant Commander George. Maybe the people who put him on *Boundless* were careless, but he had markers that led you to suspect him and he could be recognized by my intelligence officer. Perhaps we were meant to spot him."

"Perhaps," Webb said, his voice cautious. "To sow mistrust?"

"Or to misdirect us," Geary said. "And now this bit with you. You've just acknowledged that there are members of your unit that have the necessary skill sets to do that. And to commit other acts, like an attempted assassination."

Webb's face twisted into an angry glare. "Yes. I am painfully aware of that, Admiral."

"And that's primarily where you've been looking."

The colonel brought his eyes back to meet Geary's, the glare shading into a puzzled frown. "Yes, sir. Of course."

"Colonel, Lieutenant Commander George may have been set up to be spotted. To create noise in the system that draws our attention. What about someone who wasn't?"

"Such as?"

"Do you know by sight every special forces soldier in your own particular skill set?"

"No, sir," Webb said without hesitating. "Our small units tended to be kept separate for security reasons. We'd get after-action reports from other units like ours, but they'd be scrubbed of any data that could identify the individuals. No one wanted one unit to be able to compromise another unit by accident." He paused. "You're suggesting that's our real opponent? Someone with the same skills and experience as my soldiers, but unknown to us?"

"Maybe," Geary said. "One of our opponents, anyway. Do you think it's plausible, or am I spooking at shadows?"

Colonel Webb didn't answer for several seconds, his head bent in thought. "It makes a lot of sense, Admiral. It makes one hell of a lot of sense." Webb slammed one fist into his open palm so hard that Geary expected to feel the impact vibrating through the deck even though the colonel was only here in virtual form. "How do you neutralize me and my people? How do you wreck our effectiveness as a unit? By destroying our trust in each other."

"If I'm right," Geary said, "and whoever planted this false evidence in your medical files doesn't see us react, they'll do something else that points back at you or someone in your unit."

Webb nodded, his eyes dark. "I don't like just waiting for something else like that, but it may be our only option." He hesitated, his gaze weighing Geary. "Admiral, maybe it's not another unit like mine. There's another level parallel to us. Even I'm not supposed to know they exist. But you hear things, you see things. You've wondered if my people were involved in any of that junk at Unity Alternate, haven't you? We weren't. As far as I know we were never targeted against any Alliance citizens unless they'd turned their coats and were actively aiding the Syndics. But we heard rumors there were others who would go after people who were only suspected of treason or other crimes."

"Too many damned secrets," Geary grumbled.

"Secrets are necessary," Webb countered.

"I know. But they make it too easy for people to hide things that shouldn't be happening." He paused, not wanting to go into a rant about the excesses of secrecy created by the war. "What's your suggestion, Colonel? How do we respond?"

Webb smiled slightly. "I act personally affronted, saying where others can hear that I've been unjustly accused and my denials blown off, but nothing is going to happen to me at this time. That'll lead our opponent to think their plan is working, and they might try another nudge to get you or the ambassador to get rid of me."

"In other words," Geary said, "encourage them to stage another incident that implicates you or other members of your unit."

"Exactly." Webb went silent for a long moment before speaking again. "What do they want? If we know that, we can better predict what they'll do."

"I can't be certain." Geary waved at the star field displayed on one wall of his stateroom. "Some, like Dr. Kottur, want to prevent us establishing closer ties to the Dancers. But things Ambassador Rycerz told me have caused me to wonder if others simply want to sabotage this mission so that other missions, representing other people or associations of star systems, will have a chance to move in and establish themselves as primary contacts with the Dancers."

"I have to tell you, Admiral," Colonel Webb said, "I don't like sitting and waiting for the other side to make a move. I understand why we have to, but I don't like it."

"I don't like it, either," Geary said.

As it turned out, though, he didn't have to wait very long at all.

GEARY was used to being awakened by alerts from his stateroom's comm panel. He was a lot less accustomed to being jolted from sleep by urgent tones from his door alert. Hastily pulling on a uniform, he opened the door.

Just outside stood a half-dozen irate Marines, a stone-faced Gunnery Sergeant Orvis, a furious Captain Tanya Desjani, and between the Marines a junior sailor with a defiant look on his face and fright in his eyes. "What happened?" Geary asked.

"We should discuss it inside," Desjani said, her tone of voice betraying none of her anger, only cold resolve.

That would have told him how serious this was even if the expressions on the Marines hadn't offered plenty of clues. Geary waved everyone into his stateroom, stepping back as they filed in. As the sailor moved it became obvious he had his hands secured behind his back, the nearest Marine on either side maneuvering him by holding on to his arms.

Only when the door was closed did Desjani speak again, her words as hard as steel. "Admiral, I must report an attempted assassination of Colonel Rogero and Kommodor Bradamont."

Geary's startled gaze went to the junior sailor, who licked his lips nervously but remained silent. "Are Rogero and Bradamont all right?"

"Yes, sir. Colonel Rogero had rigged a secondary alarm system on the door to his stateroom." Desjani made a face. "Force of habit from being in the Syndicate Worlds' armed forces, he said, where officers had to worry about out-of-control 'workers' and other officers who wanted to clear a path to promotion. That alerted Rogero when the door opened without an alert sounding. He and Bradamont confronted the sailor who entered, and restrained him just as the roving Marine sentry patrol came by."

"Captain Desjani, you said 'attempted assassination,'" Geary said, his own voice growing as formal and cold as Desjani's. "The sailor had a weapon?"

Gunnery Sergeant Orvis answered, holding out a sealed bag with a couple of tubes visible inside. "Chemicals, sir. For a binary gas weapon. When combined, the chemicals would have produced a nerve agent. Anyone in that compartment would've been dead within seconds."

"A nerve agent." Geary turned a disbelieving gaze on the sailor, who had still been trying his best to appear bold, but who visibly quailed when Geary's gaze fell on him. "You were willing to die to kill Colonel Rogero and Kommodor Bradamont?"

The sailor hesitated. "That . . . It wouldn't have been instant. I had two minutes to get clear."

Gunnery Sergeant Orvis snorted in contempt. "Is that what they told you? You stupid bootcamp. You would've died right along with them."

"Who gave you the chemicals?" Captain Desjani demanded.

"I . . . I don't know, Captain! We had drops set up. Code names."

Desjani turned her eyes to Geary. "I assume, Admiral, that you want this man fully interrogated before you have him shot."

The sailor jerked with shock. "You . . . you can't—"

His words broke off as Orvis turned a menacing look on him. "You should've paid attention when they taught you fleet regulations. Out here, the admiral can convict you based on just what we've told him, and order you executed by firing squad. And he won't have any trouble finding volunteers for that firing squad."

"Why?" Geary asked the sailor. "What's your name? Why did you try to murder Rogero and Bradamont?"

"Inglis. My name's Inglis." The sailor's voice quavered, his earlier defiance crumbling. "Because he's a Syndic! And she went over to them! Traitorous bi—!"

The sailor's voice cut off as the Marine on one side of him rammed an elbow into his gut. "Sorry, Gunny," the Marine said. "I guess I lost my balance for a moment."

"You joined the fleet after the war was over," Desjani said to Petty Officer Inglis, who was painfully trying to straighten up. One of Desjani's hands was twitching as if she were ready to fire a weapon.

"My father and my sister died fighting them!"

"Apparently," Geary said, "you forgot what they were fighting for when they died. Tell the interrogators everything you know and there's a chance I'll show you some mercy. Get him out of here."

"Put him in a maximum-security cell," Desjani ordered. "I want a sentry watching him constantly."

"Yes, Captain." Orvis gestured to a Marine corporal. "Get him there in one piece. I'll be along in a minute."

As the other Marines yanked Inglis out the door, Orvis shook his head at Desjani and Geary. "I believe him when he said he didn't know that stuff'd kill him, too. And that he doesn't know any names. I did some counterterrorist work. The planners always choose idiots who are just smart enough to pull a trigger or plant a bomb, but too stupid to ask questions or wonder why they're throwing away their lives while their bosses stay safe. We're probably not going to get anything useful out of him."

"See what we can find out," Geary said.

"Make sure your people know that *nobody* talks about this," Desjani ordered. "Not until we're ready to make an announcement."

"Aye, Captain." Orvis saluted and hustled after the others, leaving Desjani glowering at the door.

"You're not really going to show him mercy, are you?" she asked in a voice that trembled with her effort to control it. "He tried to murder people on my ship."

It was one thing to order someone to do something that might result in their death. It was another to act as judge, jury, and executioner. In this case, though, his own anger tempted him to instantly agree with her. That and knowing that almost every other sailor in the fleet would be unhappy if Inglis wasn't given the ultimate penalty after his actions stained the honor of all of them. "*If* he seems like he might be useful to us alive, maybe," Geary said. "But only then."

"What use could he be alive?" Desjani asked.

"Maybe someone will try to silence him. Giving us a chance to catch that someone."

"Hmmm." She nodded, calming herself. "*If* that seems possible, okay. But not for too long."

"No. Not for too long." Once, he couldn't have imagined himself saying that so calmly. But that had been a hundred years ago, when his universe had been a much simpler place.

HE didn't get much sleep the rest of the night, especially after he realized that fleet regulations required Inglis's execution to be broadcast to the fleet when it happened. That made it entirely too possible that the Dancers would be able to intercept and view it as well. How would the aliens respond?

After a grumpy breakfast of a ration bar and coffee, Geary called Ambassador Rycerz, once again getting only her message box. He left a bare-bones description of last night's events, then went looking for Rogero and Bradamont.

Rogero's nonchalance about the assassination attempt was almost as unnerving as the attempt itself. Despite everything, Geary had harbored a belief that the former Syndics were exaggerating the cutthroat nature of life in the Syndicate Worlds. But far from being rattled by this attack, Rogero took on the manner of a veteran dealing with a familiar danger.

Bradamont wasn't nearly as calm.

"Admiral, I assert my right to be part of the firing squad."

"Noted," Geary said. Because what else could he say? Fleet regulations written a score of years after his own supposed death during his "last stand" gave that right to the intended victims of capital crimes. And changes to attitudes wrought by a century-long war had made such victims often willing to assert their right to vengeance.

Seeking distraction, he headed for the compartment with the Dancer communications device. As he neared it, he was momentarily startled by the sight of a large duck waddling down the passageway, closely followed by a pair of Marines. "How is Ensign Duck doing?" Geary asked, feeling a little lightness amid his dark mood.

"Ensign Duck has breakfasted and is making his rounds," one of the Marines replied, her voice and face absolutely serious.

"Then carry on," Geary said. He watched the duck and the Marines head off down the passageway before going on and entering the Dancer transmitter compartment. Only General Charban was there at the moment, gazing glumly at the device.

"Anything new?" Geary asked, even though he knew Charban would've called him already if there were anything new to report.

"I'm afraid not," Charban said, leaning back a little farther. "Macadams and his bunch are sending another one of their long missives to the Dancers."

"Have they changed their approach?" Geary asked, dropping into a seat opposite Charban.

"Not really." Charban twisted his face in thought. "You know how when someone doesn't understand something, the person talking to them will sometimes try speaking louder, as if saying it at a higher volume will somehow make it more understandable? I think that's the best way to describe what Macadams and his brilliant cohorts are doing. They keep saying the same things, but they're trying to say them louder. Metaphorically speaking, that is."

"I'll bet the Dancers are impressed."

"They keep answering, 'Hello,' as if they're trying to hear someone who isn't coming across well," Charban said, a slow smile replacing his formerly gloomy expression. "Is there any way to get video and audio feeds of Macadams and his bunch as those Dancer replies come in?"

"I might try to get some," Geary said. "Speaking of Dancer replies, have they responded at all to our request for access to one of their jump drives?"

"Not a word." Charban spread his hands. "Maybe they need to bounce that question up their chain of command to see how they should reply. If so, we're probably going to be orbiting here for a while waiting on that. But I need to warn you again that the Dancers have sometimes simply avoided answering questions they don't want to answer. Rather than say no, they pretend we never asked the question."

"Are there certain kinds of questions more likely to be ignored?" Geary asked, casting a glance at the transmitter.

This time General Charban shrugged. "If there are, we've yet to be able to establish a pattern of which questions they won't answer. Maybe it's a vast cultural difference, where to them certain questions fall into a certain category even though to us they seem totally unrelated."

"Sort of like trying to talk to Dr. Macadams and his people," Geary said.

Charban grinned. "You said it, not me." He glanced at the transmitter as a low tone came out of it. "Ah. Macadams and company have finally finished." Another tone sounded. "That was a very quick response."

"What did the Dancers reply?"

Charban's smile widened. "Hello."

Geary smiled briefly, but his humor slipped away quickly. "Do you think the Dancers are annoyed by Macadams's attempts to communicate? I mean, replying that fast and that abruptly? Just one word?"

"Could be," Charban said with another shrug. "It does feel like a brush-off, doesn't it? But that's in human terms. The Dancers might think they're telling us, 'Go ahead, we're listening.'"

"I have enough trouble understanding other humans," Geary commented.

"Me, too." Charban cocked one eye at him. "I heard a rumor about an attempted murder aboard this ship. Is there any truth to it?"

Geary slapped one hand to his forehead. "Nobody was supposed to say anything."

"That's exactly when they do say something. So it's true?"

"Yes." He paused, wondering if he should even ask the question bothering him. "How do you think the Dancers would react if they became aware we'd executed one of our own sailors?"

Charban shook his head. "I honestly have no idea. For all we know the Dancers eat their own young. I don't really believe that but our knowledge of them is still very superficial."

The buzz of his comm pad cut off Geary's response. He checked it, feeling a heaviness fill him. "Never mind. They won't see an execution."

"Why not?"

"The sailor involved is dead."

"HOW the hell did this happen?"

Geary stood in one of *Dauntless*'s secure brig cells. Captain Desjani, Dr. Nasr, and Gunnery Sergeant Orvis stood nearby, the doctor and the gunny looking downcast and Desjani appearing more furious than Geary himself felt. The body of Inglis lay sprawled on the deck.

"He was given a full medical scan before being put in this cell," Dr. Nasr insisted. "Nothing untoward was detected. No implants, no suspicious blood content, no nanos, nothing."

"Then what killed him? And why couldn't he be revived?"

"His nervous system was fried," Desjani said, every word clipped off.

"Spontaneously?" Geary demanded.

"He was injected with the nerve agent by a dart," Dr. Nasr said. "I have not removed it."

"My Marines didn't allow anyone near this cell," Gunnery Sergeant Orvis insisted. "And the security system records back them up. No one was detected."

One word caught Geary's attention. "Detected."

"That's right, Admiral," Orvis said. "There's only one way this could've been done. Someone had to be wearing a stealth suit."

Desjani turned a sharp look on the Marine. "Are you saying one of the Marine scout stealth suits was used to do this? You're implicating another Marine in this?"

"No, Captain. High-security systems are keyed to spot tiny signs that a stealth suit is being used nearby, and since we know everything about the Marine suits, all the technical specs, the systems can spot them or at least alert that something isn't right." Gunnery Sergeant Orvis looked at Geary and Desjani with a stubborn and determined expression. "There's only one group with this fleet that might have a stealth suit even better than the ones the Marines use."

"Colonel Webb's people," Geary said.

"That's right, Admiral."

Desjani glared down at Inglis's body. "I want a full record of this site and the surrounding area and the body before it's moved, then a full medical examination. Make sure the masters-at-arms are fully engaged with this."

"Yes, Captain," Orvis and Dr. Nasr both said.

"Can we talk, Admiral?" Desjani added.

"Sure." Geary walked alongside Desjani, who remained silent until they reached his stateroom.

Once there, she stood, still angry. "Gunny Orvis has a point."

"He does," Geary said. "But we need to factor in a couple of other points."

"Such as?"

"The Marines don't like Colonel Webb's force. They think the Wendigos are special operator loose cannons."

"They have good reasons to think that," Desjani said.

"Granted." Geary didn't sit down, either, walking restlessly about the limited confines of his stateroom. "I was expecting another action aimed at implicating someone in Webb's unit, but I didn't expect it to happen so soon."

"Expecting?" Her voice was challenging. Desjani was still angry, but even when angry she never stopped thinking.

"If Webb's people wanted to silence Inglis," Geary said, "that would mean they're implicated in the attempt to murder Bradamont and Rogero."

"Yes."

"Why would they have used a throwaway like Inglis instead of doing it themselves? Why not kill Bradamont and Rogero the same way Inglis was killed?"

Desjani didn't answer, her brow furrowed with thought. "That still might have implicated them, but not as clearly as this does. Especially if they'd used that binary agent Inglis had instead of a dart under circumstances that required a stealth suit."

"That's right," Geary said. "Inglis's murder clearly implicates one of Webb's soldiers. If they did it, it means they were smart, capable, and effective enough to do something stupid that points directly at them even though Inglis himself couldn't have fingered them."

"Then why use Inglis in the first place?"

"Maybe they didn't. Maybe Inglis was part of some other problem, and whoever wants another finger pointed at Webb's soldiers took advantage of the opportunity."

She searched his eyes. "You've got other reasons to think someone is trying to set up Webb and his unit?"

"Yes." He met her gaze without flinching. "Which doesn't mean I'm not going to hit up Webb and contact Ambassador Rycerz about this. All indications are that we have an opponent with a means to go just about anywhere in the fleet without being detected."

"Why aren't you dead already?" Desjani asked, concern entering her gaze.

"Good question. Lieutenant Iger has a gut feeling that there are multiple players trying to sabotage this mission. I think he's right, and the player who just killed Inglis doesn't want to kill me the same way. But they do want to create problems for this mission."

"The attempt on your life at that reception at Midway could've, and probably would've, been blamed on the former Syndics," she said. "Maybe you need to die in a way that creates even more problems."

"That's certainly possible," Geary said, wondering why he was discussing this so calmly, why he wasn't as scared as he should be. Maybe because it didn't feel real to him. Maybe just because he was in denial. "People are trying to manipulate us, wreck this mission by turning us against each other. Not just against Webb and his unit, but distrust sown against our own sailors. Like you said a little while back, I don't like being pushed."

She nodded, arms crossed, looking just as angry but not at the same things. "You know, we really can't rule out the former Syndics at Midway having a hand in this. Maybe that's why they wanted Rogero on this ship. Even that assassination attempt at the reception could have been a setup designed to allow Drakon to save you. I like Bradamont, but she's bought into a system run by people who by their own admission have a lot of experience with dirty deeds done cheap."

He wanted to reject that idea, but couldn't. "I want to trust Drakon,

I want us to have friends out there, but you're right that I have to keep an eye on what they do."

"Rogero himself is under discreet but continuous watch," Desjani said. "I have to admit he hasn't done anything remotely suspicious yet. One other thought. Maybe some of those working against us will try to sow more distrust of the Dancers, or do something else to screw up our relations with them."

"Maybe." One more thing to worry about. "Though they'd have a hard time doing a better job of screwing up than Macadams and his team are."

His comm panel chose that moment to blare an alert. "Admiral! New ships have arrived in this star system!"

Desjani hit the reply. "This is the captain. Calm down, Lieutenant. Are these enigma ships?"

"No, Captain. They're not enigmas. They're not human or Dancer ships, either. Our systems can't identify them."

TEN

LESS than a minute later both Geary and Desjani were on the bridge, settling into their seats and staring at their displays.

"The new ships arrived at a jump point from what is probably another Dancer star system," Lieutenant Castries reported. "They don't match the designs of any known species."

Despite being about one and a half billion kilometers distant, the new spacecraft could be easily seen on the fleet's sensors. Geary looked closely at the images, trying to learn something from them. There were two, one much larger than the other. Physics and engineering dictated certain design features in spacecraft, so these weren't radically different from those of humans, enigmas, or Dancers. Main propulsion aft, and curved main hull to distribute stress on the structure. But these were both more rounded than human ships, as well as bearing other, smaller external design differences. "If these were human ships I'd guess the bigger one is a transport of some kind and the smaller is an escort. They're definitely not human design, though."

"They could be," Desjani said. "If they came from someplace isolated from the rest of humanity."

"I doubt it," Geary said. "Look at those hull fairings. Does any human-designed ship use those?"

She sat back, shaking her head. "None that I know of. Those definitely aren't enigmas or Kicks, and they're not Dancers. So who are they?"

"The Dancers don't seem to have reacted to their arrival," Geary said, looking at the ships closest to that jump point. The arrival had been close to an hour and a half ago, but no immediate movements in response could be seen among the nearest Dancer ships to that jump point. "It looks like these new guys proceeded in-system toward one of the planets. They must be known to the Dancers."

"They'll be seeing us, too, right about now," Desjani said. "Should we try to contact them?"

He almost answered immediately, but stopped as he thought about it. "That's a real good question. What's the etiquette when we're in a star system controlled by another species and yet another species shows up?"

"Sounds like a diplomatic question."

"It does." Geary punched his controls, making sure his message this time was marked as high priority.

Ambassador Rycerz replied this time, looking as if she'd been interrupted. "What is it, Admiral?"

"I'm requesting permission to attempt to directly contact the ships of what appears to be a new alien species that have recently arrived in this star system."

"A new species?" Rycerz closed her eyes. "What are they like?"

"We have no idea."

"Have the Dancers ever objected to any of our communications?"

"Objected?" Geary glanced at Desjani, who shook her head. "Not that we know of."

"Then I think we should definitely try to establish contact with these new ships so we can learn something about them," Rycerz said. "And if the Dancers object to our communications with the new ships, we'll have learned something new about the Dancers."

"Should it come from me, or from you?" Geary asked.

"Oh." Ambassador Rycerz nodded. "It ought to be from me. Using our normal communications, right?"

"Yes. *Boundless*'s regular transmitters." Those transmitters had been forcibly disabled during the Dr. Kottur incident, but having been rebuilt since were in fine shape. "Could you copy me on the message?"

"Certainly."

It took several minutes after Ambassador Rycerz signed off before Geary was alerted to a new message going out from *Boundless*. He made sure Desjani could also view it before accepting it.

"To the newly arrived spacecraft in this star system," Rycerz said, speaking slowly and clearly, "this is Ambassador Rycerz representing the Alliance of human-controlled star systems. We wish to establish contact with all other species so as to form peaceful and mutually beneficial relations. Please respond. To the honor of our ancestors, Rycerz, out."

"Not bad," Desjani conceded. "Do you think we'll get an answer?"

"I have no idea," Geary said. "But it'll take at least three hours for our message to reach them and any reply to get back to us, so we might as well relax."

"If the Dancers don't like us reaching out, we may hear something from them a lot sooner."

"Good point." He called General Charban to bring him up to date and warn him to be ready for a Dancer message concerning the new arrivals.

"Keep an eye on them," Desjani ordered her bridge team. "Let the admiral and I know immediately if anything changes."

Geary stood up, wishing he'd get some answers for once instead of more questions. But there were routine matters related to being in charge of a fleet that he'd been avoiding dealing with today. "I'll be in my stateroom for a while."

ONCE in his stateroom, and despite how little he wanted to handle administrative matters, Geary sat down and called up the messages wait-

ing for him to read and in some cases take action on. As he expected,
the vast majority were about routine matters that were nonetheless
necessary for him to see and comment on.

But one message from an unfamiliar source caught his eye. John
Senn? Aboard *Boundless*? Who was he?

Oh. The historian he and Tanya had met at the diplomatic reception.

Out of curiosity, and knowing he was avoiding other tasks, Geary
called up the message, seeing a haggard-appearing John Senn looking
at him. "Admiral Geary, I'm very sorry to bother you, and I hesitated
to take advantage of having met you in person at the reception, but I'm
pretty much at the end of my rope here. I've got nothing to do. Dr.
Macadams won't even meet with me, let alone listen to me or give me
any directions, the other doctorates working for him don't acknowledge me because I don't have one, and the ship's officers and crew are
nice enough but can't give me anything to do, either. And Colonel
Webb seems to think I'm extra suspicious because I was close by you
when that autobar exploded. I don't know what to do. I even tried talking to the physicists, and most of them ignored me, too. Except for Dr.
Cresida. She didn't sound nice, but she told me to try calling you because you're interested in unusual things. I think that was a compliment? I don't know. She's, um, a little hard to read. Anyway, can you
help me? I just want to do my job. Or have something useful to do. Um,
thanks."

The message ended.

It was a really minor matter. He had more important things to focus on.

But Senn had struck him as a decent, and interesting, person. And
at a time when his power as a fleet commander seemed unable to fix too
many other things, maybe he could fix this.

He put in a call to Senn, and given what the message had said wasn't
surprised when the historian answered immediately. "Admiral Geary!
Thank you for calling!"

"I'm willing to talk to the ambassador about you," Geary said, "but I need a better handle on what you want to do and why she should go to the mat for you."

"It wouldn't matter," Senn said, his body and attitude both drooping. "I need to talk to the Dancers, and there's no way Dr. Macadams will allow that."

"Dr. Macadams isn't the only person who can talk to the Dancers," Geary said, thinking about General Charban's group working overtime. "Maybe you can help me. I could use someone with a different perspective on issues."

Senn perked up. "I've often been accused of being different."

"Would you be willing to work at something that often wasn't directly related to your specialty?"

"Sure. No problem." Senn's eagerness to do something meaningful was clear enough to be painful. "I mean, I'm not just an historian. I've also dabbled in songwriting."

"Songwriting?" Geary asked, not believing that he'd heard right.

"Yes," John Senn said. "Back at Rosen Star System I've had a few songs recorded by professionals. I mean, I don't brag, but the songs did okay! Some even got a little popular in other star systems, and you know how hard it is to do that."

"Actually, I don't," Geary said. Songs were like poetry, weren't they? "If I can get you a bunk on *Dauntless*, will you shift to this ship and work with my team that's communicating with the Dancers? We should be able to work in some of your questions if you can help formulate all of our other messages."

"Would I—? I mean, yes! In a heartbeat! Just let me know!"

That call ended, Geary called Charban, who was yawning. "Sorry, Admiral," Charban said. "I was catching a nap after being on watch here most of the night, but Lieutenant Iger got called away about those new spacecraft arriving. So here I am again. What can I do for you?"

"Maybe I can do something for you. Could you use a professional songwriter?"

Charban froze for a moment. "I really hope this isn't a theoretical question," he finally said. "Yes. I could really use a songwriter. If we could figure out how to integrate music with our words I think we might achieve another breakthrough with the Dancers."

"Good. We've got one on *Boundless*. I'll have to get him transferred to *Dauntless*. He's technically an historian who has his own questions for the Dancers, but he says he's also written some songs that were popular within his star system."

"I'm tempted to ask for another miracle, but I'll accept this one," Charban said with a smile. "The sooner we get him the better."

"I take it the Dancers haven't contacted us yet about the new ships or our response to them?"

"Not a word, not a rhyme," Charban said.

If the newly arrived and apparently new species had sent a message as soon as they saw the human fleet, it would have arrived soon after the light announcing their arrival. If they responded to the greeting sent by Ambassador Rycerz, it should have arrived about three hours after the human message was sent.

Absorbed in the boring but necessary work that kept the fleet running, when Geary finally checked the time it had been four hours since Rycerz sent her message.

Switching his display to show the situation in space, he saw that the newly arrived ships had continued on a vector to intercept one of the Dancer-occupied planets in its orbit. There still hadn't been any apparent Dancer reaction in the form of their ships moving to meet the new ones.

"I asked the Dancers who their friends were," Charban reported soon afterwards. "No reply as of yet."

The only change by the next morning was that a shuttle brought John Senn from *Boundless*. Having arranged with Captain Desjani for Senn to be given a bunk in a shared junior officer stateroom, Geary didn't meet the shuttle, knowing that one of *Dauntless*'s junior officers would handle that task as well as familiarizing Senn with meal arrangements and the like.

But late in the morning, seeking a reason to talk to General Charban about the lack of Dancer responses, Geary collected John Senn to personally introduce him to the officers in the alien transmitter compartment. "You're going to try to find out if the Dancers or some other species they know ever visited Old Earth?" Geary asked as they walked through a passageway that was fairly crowded just before regular lunch hours.

"That's right," Senn said, looking around curiously at the fittings and the sailors. "This ship feels really different from *Boundless*. You can tell there are different legacies going into its design."

"Legacies?"

"Sort of like traditions," Senn explained. "Certain things are done in certain ways. Those can change. Fundamental concepts can evolve."

"Such as?" Geary asked, surprised by the realization that he was enjoying the conversation.

"Oh, well, to take a recent example, victory." Senn waved about him. "What constitutes victory? Different people, different cultures, have different interpretations. During some times and places, victory meant genocide of the losers. Other times and places it's been almost like a sporting event, with each side scoring what they consider meaningful goals against their opponent, until both sides decide the game is over. There's never been universal agreement among humans as to what victory means. But what about the Dancers, with a totally different history and mindset? How do they define victory?"

"I honestly couldn't tell you," Geary said. "I imagine it'd be related to the patterns they see. Completing such a pattern, for example."

"Patterns? Completing a pattern?" Senn grinned with delight. "That would be amazing. Somebody told me they think like engineers. They do? So it'd make sense if they defined victory in a concrete way like that. We've won when we've finished doing this tangible thing. And they'd probably go in knowing exactly what they want to do. Humans often don't. History is full of wars that got started by people who didn't really know exactly what they wanted to accomplish."

"Kind of like the Syndic leaders who started the last war," Geary said. "It was such a surprise when it started. No one had expected it because there didn't seem any reasonable goal that the Syndicate Worlds could achieve."

"There are varying historical schools regarding to what extent the initial Syndic attack was a surprise," Senn said carefully, eyeing Geary.

"It sure surprised me," Geary said.

"Some scholars think it wasn't a coincidence that you encountered that Syndic attack force at Grendel. That you were sent through there at that time in the expectation that you'd meet the Syndics."

"Really?" Geary surprised himself with a laugh. Thinking about Grendel rarely brought him any emotion but pain. But this . . . "All I can tell you is that nobody told me to expect anything like that."

"Seriously?" John Senn shook his head, smiling. "That news would cause an eruption among historians of the recent war. The ones who think the Alliance was secretly prepared for war, that is."

"We weren't," Geary said, remembering the confusion and chaos and frantic heroism by his crew as his heavy cruiser was pounded by superior Syndic forces. Something in his voice this time caused Senn's smile to vanish.

"I'm sorry," Senn said. "For me this is . . . academic. Events in the past. I can't imagine how it feels for you." He looked about at the sailors passing them. "Or for them."

"Did you lose anyone in the war?" Geary asked.

"Who hasn't? Most recently two uncles. A great-aunt. A cousin. My older sister was badly injured but survived. She came home, but she doesn't talk about it."

"Then you have some idea how it feels," Geary said. They'd reached the compartment and he led the way inside.

General Charban was slumped in a seat against the far bulkhead, his head back, his eyes closed, and his mouth open as he slept. Lieutenant Jamenson was sitting studying something on her comm pad, looking up when they entered. "Admiral," she said, getting quickly to her feet.

"At ease," Geary said, waving her to sit down again. "This is a new helper for you. He has questions of his own that we should try to work into the communications."

"John Senn," he said, nodding in greeting. "You're from Eire Star System?"

"Is it that obvious?" Jamenson asked with a smile, raising one hand to flick her bright green hair. At one point many of the inhabitants of Eire had had a genetic modification done to grant their descendants green hair, and that particular gene mod had proven durable over time.

"I'll let you two get acquainted," Geary said. "Lieutenant, let me know if General Charban isn't getting enough rest. All of you need to be able to function at your best if anything unexpected comes in."

"Yes, sir!"

As he walked toward the bridge, Geary couldn't stop thinking about what Senn had said. As he expected, he found Tanya Desjani in her captain's seat on the bridge, and sat down in the fleet command seat next to hers. "I had an interesting conversation with our new historian."

"Oh?" Desjani gave him a look that meant she knew he must be bringing this up for a reason.

"He thinks the Dancers, with their engineering skills and their interest in patterns, probably know exactly what outcome they want in any given situation."

She thought about that before nodding. "That makes sense. And that also means that everything the Dancers have said to us and done with us is aimed at achieving whatever that exact goal is."

"Yeah. They're not improvising. Charban mentioned to me that he couldn't figure out what connected the things the Dancers wouldn't answer questions on. Maybe that's the connection. Everything they tell us is aimed at moving us toward their exact outcome, and so is everything they *don't* tell us."

"That makes way too much sense for comfort," Desjani said. "I didn't think the Dancers were our friends. I always thought they were being driven by self-interest. That wasn't necessarily bad for us, like when they helped defeat the dark ships. But what if the Dancers' endgame is something they want and we really don't? If their every move is herding us without telling us why, it doesn't give me a warm and fuzzy." She gave him a sidelong look. "Sort of like Rione."

"I guess so." He had to admit that Victoria Rione had more than once pushed him in directions she wanted without his realizing it. "But Rione's end goals were pretty much the same as ours."

"So what can we do?"

He shrugged, unhappy but having to face reality. "What we're already doing. Keep moving forward but watch where every step is going to land so we don't step on a mine."

"Like mines in space, mines in the ground are usually hidden so you can't see them before you step on them," Desjani said.

ANOTHER day in orbit. Charban and his assistants, now with John Senn aiding them, had sent more questions out but had received either no answer or answers that were vaguely reassuring but lacking in specifics.

He'd expected things to happen once they were in Dancer space. Instead, they seemed to be simply waiting for something to happen, either another problem within the fleet or whatever the Dancers intended.

The request to call *Boundless* came as a welcome distraction. To his surprise, Dr. Cresida answered it. "You asked me to call?" Geary said.

"The universe is full of surprises, Admiral." Cresida looked down, then back at him. "I find myself in the difficult position of having to request a favor from you."

"A favor? Doctor, I already owe you. What do you need?"

"My colleagues and I came here in hopes of learning something of Dancer scientific discoveries, but that has proven impossible because the only transmitter aboard this vessel which is capable of communicating with the aliens is under the exclusive control of a megalomaniacal incompetent."

"You're speaking of Dr. Macadams," Geary said, trying not to smile.

"Obviously." Cresida paused again, as if bracing herself. "I am told that you have a similar transmitter on your ship."

"It's Captain Desjani's ship, my flagship, but yes. It's the original transmitter loaded with the software the Dancers sent us. Do you want to make use of it?"

"If possible." Dr. Cresida grimaced. "I know time on the device must be extremely valuable. I have nothing tangible to offer in exchange for asking for that time."

"Doctor," Geary said, "you're working on behalf of the Alliance. We're not going to, uh, charge you for using the transmitter. I do need to tell you that my people working directly with it are pretty tied up rendering messages into formats the Dancers will pay attention to, so I don't know how long it would take us to get your questions into the right formats to send out."

"Formats? What sort of formats?"

"The Dancers appear to equate certain forms of speech with, um, sophistication of the speaker. General Charban thinks ordinary speech, like we're doing, comes across as baby talk to them. Lieutenant Jamenson had the insight that Dancer messages to us in their original forms sound musical. Not like songs, exactly, but with a rhythm and cadence to the sounds. When we started replying with words cast in poetic forms, the Dancers began responding with clearer answers."

Dr. Cresida gazed at him for several seconds, her expression giving no clue to her thoughts. "Do you believe that songs will be a format the aliens would consider sophisticated?"

"Yes. We're trying some songs with them right now, but results are spotty." How much should he say? "The Dancers aren't being very communicative since we arrived here, so it's hard to tell how well or how poorly it's working."

"Would I be allowed to attempt my own format?"

"I don't see why not," Geary said. "If you've seen what Dr. Macadams is sending out, that's what not to do."

Cresida visibly hesitated. "I would much prefer sending the message myself."

"You want to come aboard *Dauntless*?" Having seen Jasmine Cresida's reactions the last time she was aboard the battle cruiser, in an environment that she equated with the death of her sister, the request surprised him. "That's fine."

"The . . . commanding officer of that vessel does not appear to be fond of me."

She wasn't fond of your attitude, Geary thought. But he kept that to himself. "Tanya Desjani was a close friend of your sister's. She's also professional enough not to let personal feelings impact her interactions with you."

"Then I have clearance to go to your ship?"

"Yes. Captain Desjani's ship. My flagship. Believe me, the distinction matters a great deal to the commanding officer of a ship."

The call with Cresida ended, Geary braced himself before calling Desjani on the bridge. "Captain," he began, to establish this as a fully formal communication, "I need to inform you of another visitor who will be coming aboard from *Boundless*."

Tanya eyed him with open suspicion. "Tell me the visitor is anyone but Jaylen's sister."

"The visitor is Jaylen's sister, Dr. Cresida."

Desjani inhaled slowly, her jaw tight. "There are moments when I wonder if I'm really dead and in hell. Why is she coming to my ship?"

"She needs to use the Dancer transmitter."

"Fine. Thank you, Admiral."

Knowing from that "fine" that he'd better end this conversation fast, Geary nodded and quickly ended the call.

GEARY decided to meet Dr. Cresida at the shuttle dock in order to minimize any interactions with crew members who might not appreciate her previous attitude. She was being gone over with extreme care by security personnel, who worked with grim efficiency that had only gotten more exhaustive since the murder of Inglis. "She's clean, sir," Senior Chief Tarrani reported.

Dr. Cresida followed Geary silently through the passageways of *Dauntless,* her expression unrevealing, only her eyes shifting about as she examined her surroundings. The sailors they passed gave her curious looks but none seemed to recognize her.

Just before they reached the compartment holding the Dancer communication device, Ensign Duck came waddling complacently down the passageway from the other direction, closely followed as usual by two of *Dauntless*'s Marines. Apparently this particular passageway was a favored walkway for the duck. A pair of sailors ahead of Geary saluted, grinning. "Good afternoon, Ensign Duck!"

"Ensign Duck?" Dr. Cresida said.

"It's a long story," Geary said.

Inside the compartment, General Charban, Lieutenant Iger, Lieutenant Jamenson, and John Senn stood up as Geary entered. "This is Dr. Cresida," he told them.

General Charban smiled in apparently genuine welcome. Even though his initial interactions with Dr. Cresida hadn't been jovial, she nonetheless was not part of, and was in many ways opposed to, Dr. Macadams's group. That alone redeemed Cresida in Charban's eyes. "If you have your questions already laid out, we can help you render them in the form the Dancers are most likely to respond to."

Dr. Cresida shook her head. "Thank you, but I believe my questions are already prepared properly."

Charban spread his hands, gave Geary a weary look, and then gestured to the device. "There's no one sending at the moment. Touch that to transmit."

Sitting down, Dr. Cresida looked over the device, humming as she did so and consulting her comm pad. Finally, she touched the transmit command.

A moment later she began singing, her voice soaring through the room as the others there stared in astonishment. Her words danced along, rendering phrases such as "normalized wave function" and "time-independent Schrödinger equation" into poetic sweeps of sound. Everyone watched, silent, until the song ended with an almost sad note.

Dr. Cresida touched the command to end transmission and sat looking at the device as if nothing special had happened.

"Oh my ancestors," John Senn said. "That was an aria. An unaccompanied aria."

Cresida spared him a glance. "That's correct."

"You wrote that?"

"I did. Have you studied music?"

"Yes," Senn said. "Just as a sideline."

"You're the history person," Cresida said.

"Yes, that's right."

"Interesting. How long until the Dancers respond?" she asked Charban.

"It's hard to predict," Charban replied. "Sometimes—"

He was interrupted by music coming from the transmitter, something that sounded like multiple flutes playing a polyphonic composition. "Please . . . wait for our reply . . . eldest one!"

The silence following that was broken by Lieutenant Iger. "*That's interesting.*"

"'Eldest one'?" Charban nodded toward Cresida. "I think they're impressed. The rest of us are going to have to up our game considerably now."

"It's not a game," Dr. Cresida said. "I asked some serious questions concerning theoretical physics."

"Of course you did," Charban said. "Well . . . I honestly don't know what to tell you as far as when or if we'll get an answer."

"I can wait," Dr. Cresida said, moving to a seat at the far end of the compartment where she quickly became absorbed in whatever was on her comm pad.

BY the time Geary got back to his stateroom there was a very high-priority message waiting from Dr. Macadams. Not particularly interested in hearing from Macadams, but concerned by the use of a message priority that was supposed to be employed only for critical emergencies, Geary called up the message.

It took only a moment of watching and listening to realize that Macadams had overheard Dr. Cresida's message to the Dancers and was considerably upset about it. Watching Macadams's frenzied motions, Geary found himself half hoping / half wondering whether Macadams would have a stroke. But even that wasn't worth listening to the entire message.

He hit the reply command. "Dr. Macadams, I will repeat again that my responsibilities include direct communications with the Dancers." Macadams himself refused to use the term Dancers, insisting despite all evidence to the contrary that the name offended them. "If your own attempts to communicate with the Dancers are having little result, I suggest that instead of blaming those having more success you might try learning from their experience and their example. I will also only warn you once that misuse of flash priority message precedence will result in you being banned from being able to employ that priority in the future. Do not use that precedence again except for a life-critical emergency. Geary, out."

◊

THE crew of *Dauntless* was used to the admiral walking through the passageways late in the evening. It helped him think, and let him occasionally interact with members of the crew under low-stress conditions. Having been vaulted from command of a single cruiser to command of a fleet of hundreds of ships, Geary had had a hard time adjusting to the knowledge that it was now impossible for him to personally know everyone under his command. But it was at least possible for him to know everyone aboard his flagship, so he was glad for the opportunity to do so. And if along the way he managed to think a bit, perhaps coming up with answers that had eluded him during busier periods of the ship's day, then so much the better.

Lately, though, since the murder of Inglis, he'd found himself feeling spooked if passing through an area without anyone else visible. He told himself he was overreacting, that whoever had killed Inglis could have already killed him if they wanted to, but nonetheless he found himself suddenly looking behind him as if that might reveal an invisible watcher.

At such times he wondered just how effective the defenses would be that Tanya Desjani had ordered her crew to build into his working uniform. Tanya had assured him that they'd trigger only if an actual attack were detected, but he still worried about them suddenly activating during a normal interaction with someone else.

As he walked down one nearly deserted passageway, Geary spotted Dr. Cresida in a break room. He stopped, seeing that she was slumped in a chair, eyes closed. Assuming that she would return to *Boundless* once she had sent her message to the Dancers, Geary hadn't thought to ensure she actually had. Apparently she'd been literally sincere when saying she intended to wait for the Dancer reply. "Dr. Cresida? Do you need a place to sleep?"

She sighed and opened one eye. "This *is* a place. I *was* asleep."

Geary shook his head as he walked to the nearest comm panel. "If you're going to remain aboard this ship, we need to get you a place to stay."

"'We'? Do you often talk like a royal?"

He glanced back at her, for some reason amused rather than aggravated. "'We' as in the sailors and Marines of the fleet."

Cresida sighed again. "I assure you that I did not expect nor do I require any special care."

"It's not about what you expect of us," Geary said. "It's about what we expect of ourselves. Duty officer? I need a stateroom bunk for Dr. Jasmine Cresida. Yes, now. She's in this break room with me. We'll wait here."

Cresida struggled upright in her chair, giving Geary a cross look. "Why are you rousting people so late in the ship's day?"

"It's my job," he said. "And it's their job to be rousted when something comes up. If you're asking why I happened to be here at this time, it's because sometimes I get restless and can't sleep. Walking through the ship helps me think, and lets me stay in touch with the crew and how they're doing. How are you doing?"

"I was recently awakened from slumber by an authoritarian individual who ignored my wishes to be left alone," Cresida said. "How are you doing?"

He decided to be open with her. "I'm wondering what the Dancers intend. Why they answer some of our questions and not others, and why they've communicated so little to us since we arrived here."

Instead of sniping at him again, Cresida gazed at the opposite bulkhead. "We know practically nothing about them. If they answer me, we might learn more."

"More physics?"

"More about *them*." Dr. Cresida shifted her eyes to look at Geary. "The quantum world is fundamentally different from what humans experience in the macro world that our senses have evolved to deal with. The only way we can seek to understand the quantum realm is by observations filtered through human senses and our ways of thinking.

That's why metaphors are often employed to try to make sense of quantum things that otherwise appear too strange. Schrödinger's cat is the most commonly known example. If the aliens answer my questions, the way they formulate those answers will tell us much about how they view the universe. If they also use metaphors, those metaphors will tell us something of how they understand things."

"That would be very important," Geary said, staring at Cresida in surprise.

"Of course it would. Hadn't you already thought of that?"

"No." He made a vague gesture around him. "I'm all too aware that there are many things I don't think of. That's why I try to surround myself with people who'll think of things that I don't." For some reason at that moment he recalled some of Victoria Rione's last advice to him. "And who will tell me those things even if I don't want to hear them."

Dr. Cresida smiled slightly. "I really don't want to like you. But sometimes you almost display admirable traits. When am I going to be allowed to go back to sleep?"

At that moment a lieutenant came hastening down the passageway. "Admiral," she said, "is there a Dr. . . . ?"

"Cresida," Geary said. "Lieutenant Amarin, this is Dr. Cresida."

"Hi, Doc! If you don't mind sharing a room, we've got a spare bunk."

Cresida stood up, sighing a third time. "Thank you." She followed Amarin without another word to Geary.

But that was all right. She'd given him some important things to think about.

THE next morning, Geary reviewed fleet status updates. Most things were unchanged, of course. Some ships had some systems go down due to part failures and provided estimated time of repair, which was always a concern but also a fact of life. And it was nothing like the problems the fleet had earlier endured when ships designed to last a couple of years had found themselves exceeding their planned life spans. Almost all of those ships had now had their primary systems overhauled and replaced.

On the other hand, disciplinary problems, mostly minor, were increasing in frequency, as always happened during periods of relative inactivity. Many of them involved sailors and Marines getting into scuffles. Like members of the same family, they'd unite fiercely against any outsider, but among themselves in the fleet Marines and sailors would sometimes squabble over the smallest things.

The longer they stayed in orbit here, waiting for something without any idea when it would happen and not even knowing what would happen, the worse morale would get.

That wasn't even taking into account the extra stress created by the Inglis incident. No one was supposed to have talked, but according to reports from other ships versions of the murder and Inglis's own actions were making the rounds of the fleet's gossip. The idea of an internal enemy, invisible and deadly, wasn't doing anything for anyone's peace of mind.

Tanya Desjani's arrival was a welcome distraction. "I understand yesterday's guest is staying."

"She's waiting for a reply from the Dancers," Geary said. "Dr. Cresida is like Jaylen that way, I think. Very work driven."

"Too bad she's not like Jaylen in other ways. I was going to check on the poor lieutenants who acquired her as a roommate."

"And you want me along to hear any horror stories firsthand."

Desjani spread her hands. "If there are problems I want the admiral to be aware of them."

"You're such a noble soul," Geary said, standing up and stretching. "All right. Let's go talk to Lieutenant Amarin."

Amarin was on duty in the engineering central control compartment, running maintenance checks on some of the equipment. She and the others in the compartment bounced to their feet when Desjani and Geary arrived. "At ease," Geary told everyone before focusing on Amarin. "I just wanted to check on how things went with Dr. Cresida last night."

"No problems, sir," Lieutenant Amarin said. "The doctor is a little . . . eccentric. But it's okay. She's nothing like Evil Esther. Right, Kari?"

"Ancestors, no!" Lieutenant Kari Ipjian agreed. "Nothing like Evil Esther."

"Do I know Evil Esther?" Geary murmured to Desjani.

"No," Desjani replied. "She was transferred off the ship a couple of months before you were found. There were some, um, personal issues involved. So, Lieutenant Amarin, you haven't had any issues with Dr. Cresida? Speak freely if you have."

"No, Captain. No issues," Amarin said. "She's one of those black magic doctors, right? Physics stuff? That's better than one of the medical docs. They sometimes get to talking shop and it's hard not to lose your lunch."

"I've been there," Desjani said dryly. "All right. Keep me informed if there are any problems."

"Disappointed?" Geary asked after they'd left the engineering compartment.

"Absolutely," Desjani said.

"I was going to go by the transmitter compartment and talk to Charban."

"I need to stop by there and make sure everything is fine," Desjani said. "Have there been any issues with that history guy?"

"History guy seems to be working out pretty well," Geary said. "It occurs to me that the more different perspectives we get on the Dancers the better."

"Things usually work that way," Desjani said. "Are you including Dr. Cresida in that?"

"Yes. She said some interesting things yesterday."

"I guess every black hole does have an event horizon," Desjani said.

"Ah. Here comes another one of my junior officers."

Geary turned to see Ensign Duck waddling majestically down the passageway, his usual two Marine escorts a few paces behind. Ensign Duck's walks had become routine by now, but everyone still got a kick out of them.

This walk appeared to be routine as well, until Ensign Duck was about two meters from where Geary and Desjani were standing. Ensign Duck suddenly stopped walking, flaring his wings and emitting a harsh, loud quack at the empty space before him.

"What the hell?" one of the Marines said. "He's never—"

Captain Desjani cut off the Marine's words as she produced a sidearm from beneath her uniform and emptied the charge into the vacant space before Ensign Duck.

ELEVEN

INSTEAD of hitting the bulkhead, the energy bolts slammed into something short of it, other energies flaring, portions of someone appearing as parts of their stealth suit failed.

Ensign Duck raced away from the fight, his two Marine escorts hurling themselves at the mysterious figure. The exchange of blows was too quick for Geary to follow, both Marines being knocked across the passageway.

But their attack had given Captain Desjani time to slam another charge into her weapon. "*Dauntless!*" she shouted. "To me!"

The figure in the stealth suit made a sharp gesture with one hand. Geary felt his arm hairs stand on end as his uniform's defenses sensed a threat and energized. The dart fired at him hit that invisible shield a centimeter short of his uniform, bouncing off.

Without waiting to see the results of their attack, the intruder turned to flee as Desjani emptied a second set of charges into them. Before they could get more than a few steps, the crew of *Dauntless* responded to their captain's call. Geary kicked the failed dart against the nearest bulkhead to keep it out of the way as sailors came racing down the passageway from both directions. The first sailors to reach the attacker were knocked aside as the Marines had been, but more and more sailors came, filling the passageway on both sides, crushing up against the attacker so that their arms and legs were pinned.

Masters-at-arms wove their way through the crowd, brandishing coil cuffs and shockers. So did Gunnery Sergeant Orvis, looking furious.

"Let 'em breathe," Captain Desjani ordered once the cuffs were in place on the wrists and ankles of the figure in the stealth suit. With sections of the suit's stealth capability shot out or damaged by the fight, the attacker seemed to be a partial three-dimensional jigsaw puzzle. As the sailors backed off, looking death at the person who'd invaded their ship, Desjani gestured to Orvis. "Get the stealth shut off."

Gunnery Sergeant Orvis pulled a device from his belt and slammed it into the attacker, who convulsed as a charge surged through the suit, overloading its circuits. As the intruder became fully visible, Orvis grabbed the mask covering the attacker's head, pulling it off to reveal a nondescript-looking man whose expression revealed nothing. "Get a picture," Orvis told the masters-at-arms.

"Send that photo to *Boundless*," Geary ordered. "There's a dart here that probably contains poison. I need it secured safely as evidence."

Some of the sailors had been crowding close to him, but now edged back, nervous gazes on the dart lying at the junction of the deck and a bulkhead.

"Get Dr. Nasr here now," Desjani ordered Senior Chief Tarrani, who had just arrived in a rush. "Chief Slonaker," she told the head master-at-arms, "I want that prisoner stripped to bare skin, I want every fiber of his suit gone over, I want every opening he's got checked, and I want him internally scanned so closely that if there's a stray molecule that shouldn't be there we'll find it."

"Yes, Captain," Chief Slonaker said. "We'll take him to the maximum-security brig cell."

"Hold on, please," Gunnery Sergeant Orvis said. "Hotch, Francis, status."

The two Marines who'd been escorting Ensign Duck and had first gone after the attacker both looked the worse for wear. Hotch, one side of her face rapidly purpling as a large bruise formed, was on her feet but holding one arm. "Got a break, Gunny."

Francis winced as he inhaled. "I've probably got some broken ribs, Gunny."

"We'll get them to sick bay!" some of the sailors offered, moving to help the injured Marines.

Orvis leaned close to the prisoner, his face a mask of demonic rage. But his voice remained steady, which somehow made it sound even more frightening. "You hurt some of my Marines. Give me a reason, and I'll show you what hurt is. You got it? Just give me a reason."

As Orvis and Chief Slonaker accompanied the masters-at-arms hauling the prisoner away, Captain Desjani held one arm high. "Well done, *Dauntless*! We'll splice the main brace tonight!"

Cheers echoed down the passageway at the promise of a booze ration with dinner.

"Do you think Orvis will rough him up?" Geary asked.

"Gunny Orvis?" Desjani said. "Not unless he gives the gunny a reason. Gunnery Sergeant Orvis is a professional. Oh, he'd love to have a reason to maul that guy, but you can be sure that Orvis made that threat at least partly to keep the guy from trying anything before he's locked up."

"How long have you been carrying a weapon?"

"Since a certain diplomatic reception." She pointed down the passageway. "The Dancer transmitter is in there."

"Yeah," Geary said. "That seems like an obvious target."

"That and you. When he was discovered he tried to kill you, so that must have been a backup instruction. Or didn't you notice?"

"I noticed," Geary said.

"This is where you thank me for having those automated defenses hidden in your working uniform," Desjani added.

"Thank you for having those automated defenses hidden in my working uniform." Geary looked in the direction the prisoner had been hauled. "He's not crew?"

"Nope. Definitely not."

"How'd he get aboard?"

"Don't know. Going to find out." With an approving wave to those sailors still in view, Desjani headed in the direction of the ship's brig where the cells were located.

He nearly followed, but decided to check on the alien transmitter room.

Only General Charban was present. He nodded in greeting. "I heard and saw part of it. You might want to take a seat."

"Why?" Geary asked, startled to realize as he sat down that his legs were wobbly.

"Someone just tried to kill you, and your brain is finally catching up with your reflexes." Charban smiled in a sad way. "I know. You're a veteran of a lot of battles. But you're not used to being targeted personally from close up. It's pretty nerve-racking once your brain has time to realize what happened."

"There were two assassination attempts on me at Unity," Geary said, feeling embarrassed to be having trouble handling this latest attack.

"You were in public, weren't you? Focused on presenting the right image after the attacks. But, here, you're in private. There's nothing to forestall your natural reactions."

"I guess you've been personally targeted more than I have," Geary said. "Ground forces is a different world." He breathed in and out slowly. "Still, I have been in fleet battles."

"Your first space battle was probably rough afterwards, though, right?" Charban asked.

Geary smiled slightly even though he felt nothing like humor at the memory. "My first battle was when I was in command of *Merlon* at Grendel. Afterwards was . . . about a century later when I was thawed out of survival sleep."

"That must have been very difficult," Charban said. "More so than I'd realized. All right now?"

"Pretty much, yeah." Geary looked about him. "Where are the others?"

"Lieutenant Iger rushed off to see what he could contribute to the investigation of the intruder. Lieutenant Jamenson had already taken Dr. Cresida and our historian to the ship's store to pick up some essential items they didn't have with them, so all three of them missed the fun." Charban looked around the compartment as well. "Interesting that the intruder was caught near here."

"I was thinking the same thing," Geary said.

"I was told this place has special security features to spot any bugs that tried to transmit what they overheard."

"That's right," Geary said. "Which makes it likely that any bugs planted in here were probably set to record, not transmit. Once picked up their data can be downloaded. When was the last time this compartment had a security sweep?"

"About two weeks ago," Charban said.

"I'm going to set up another as soon as possible. We need to know if someone was trying to find out what we were saying to the Dancers and what replies we received."

Charban made a face. "Which they could have easily determined simply by listening in on the transmitter in Macadams's hands." He brightened. "But Macadams won't allow anyone else near it. The buffoon actually helped us out by making our internal spy's job harder. Oh, the Dancers did finally give an answer to our questions about those two ships that seem to be those of yet another species. Would you like to hear all of it?"

"How long is all of it?" Geary asked.

"Three words. 'Ships are Taon.'"

"Three—?" Geary fought down an urge to say three words in reply to the Dancers, far-from-diplomatic words that would convey his frustration. "What does that even mean?"

"Technically," Charban said, looking weary again, "it might be an answer to the questions we posed. Who do the ships belong to? Are they representative of another intelligent species? And the Dancers replied, 'Ships are Taon.' Which would mean Taon is the name of the other species."

"A technically correct answer that tells us nothing but the name of the other species." Geary rubbed his forehead, feeling a headache coming on. "Are the Dancers trying to make us angry?"

General Charban drummed the fingers of one hand on the table near the transmitter. "If Senn's idea about what the Dancers are doing is right, and I think it makes a lot of sense that they'd be trying to herd us in the direction of their desired outcome, then my guess would be that our arrival caught the Dancers here flat-footed. They don't know what we're supposed to be told to achieve the desired herding, so they're telling us as little as possible while awaiting detailed guidance. That plan they spoke of needing, in other words."

"That sounds plausible." Geary stood up, gratified to feel his legs steady under him once more. "Unfortunately, it's just another guess."

"Guesses are all we have, Admiral."

He had to leave it at that, because Charban was absolutely right.

TANYA Desjani stood at the hatch to his stateroom. "Colonel Webb is trying to get a hold of you. Before you talk to him, I want to tell you that the probable source of our intruder was one of the routine fleet shuttle runs that have stopped at *Boundless* and then later on *Dauntless*."

"We're sure he came from *Boundless*?"

"Yes, sir, we are. He's part of the crew. Between him and that Lieutenant Commander George you told me about I'm starting to wonder how many of *Boundless*'s crew are secretly working for somebody else."

"I'm starting to wonder who did the security screens on that crew," Geary said. "All right. Let's see what Webb has to say."

Colonel Webb appeared on the display, looking happier than Geary had ever seen him before. "Our stealth spy is Maxwell Kaliphur, one of the section lead waitstaff on *Boundless*. That's the name he's been going under, anyway. It was a perfect cover. As long as he said he was delivering something to someone he could go just about anywhere on the ship. If no one could find him, he could say he'd been doing a delivery. And no one ever pays attention to mid-level waitstaff."

"Does Kaliphur have a roommate?"

"Unfortunately, no." Webb shook his head ruefully. "*Boundless* has so many staterooms a lot of the crew have single accommodations. A section lead on the waitstaff was the lowest-ranking member who could get a single room. We're searching his room now. So far, we've found nothing. I'm assuming he has a second location somewhere aboard where any compromising materials are safely hidden."

"We're still searching him and his stealth suit and other items he had with him," Geary said. "As far as I know, we haven't found anything that identifies who he's working for and why."

"But he did try to kill you when he was spotted?"

"Yes, he did." So simple and short an answer to such a question felt strange. "It turned out to be the same kind of nerve agent–loaded dart that killed Inglis."

"That doesn't mean he was the one who offed your sailor," Webb cautioned. "I can name three or four outfits off the top of my head who could've provided that kind of weapon."

Geary stared at Webb's image. "Are you saying there may be more spies running around in stealth suits in this fleet?"

"We can't rule it out, Admiral. I request full access to the suit Kaliphur was wearing and anything he was carrying."

"Granted," Geary said, not happy to realize that Webb's warning made sense. "Do you think catching Kaliphur means all of your people are off the hook?"

"I'm leaning that way. But I want to talk to this Kaliphur myself," Webb said. "A link to his cell will be good enough. And I'd like to send one of my sergeants to look him over in person and assist in his interrogation if you have no objection."

That last caused Geary to hesitate. "Colonel . . ."

Webb shook his head. "I'm not talking torture, Admiral. We're not stupid. I want real answers, not whatever reply that guy thinks will stop the pain. If Kaliphur has training against interrogation like my people have received, my sergeant might be able to spot that."

"In that case, please send your sergeant over," Geary said.

"One thing I'm very curious about, and I hope you can tell me. How'd you spot him?" Webb asked. "The preliminary data I've seen on that stealth suit is that it's a step beyond the latest official model. He was as close to invisible as any human can be. Are your ship's internal sensors that good?"

"One of our ensigns spotted him," Geary said.

"An *ensign*?"

"He's a duck."

"A duck." Colonel Webb actually laughed, a sound Geary had never expected to hear from him. "You've got a duck running security patrols?"

"I guess you could say that," Geary said.

"That turned out to be a smart move! All right, I'll send over Sergeant Tyminska. If there's anything to be learned from Kaliphur, she'll see it. Where'd you get your duck, by the way?"

"I'd have to ask the Marines who smuggled it aboard at Varandal."

"Why didn't I already guess that Marines were involved?" Webb smiled again. "I'm glad you came through this all right, Admiral."

"Me, too." The call ended, Geary looked at Desjani, who had listened silently. "Our boss-level Wendigo is happy. Should that reassure us or worry us?"

"Beats me," she said. "But we haven't actually caught him doing anything wrong. If Webb is playing both sides he's doing a really good job of it. Oh, one other thing. Those two ships that don't look like Dancer ships have left the Dancer orbital facility they docked at and are headed back toward the jump point they arrived at."

Geary nodded. "The Dancers say they're Taon."

"What's Taon? What does that mean?"

"Damned if I know. Charban thinks it might be the name of a new, different intelligent species."

"If so," Desjani said, "they're not very talkative. Maybe they'll contact us before they jump out of this star system."

THEY didn't.

The next day, Geary watched his display for the last twenty minutes before the new ships were estimated to jump. Whatever they'd done had already been done an hour and a half ago, but he wanted to be watching if and when a message finally came in from the Taon. But nothing did, the ships vanishing as they had entered jump space an hour and a half before.

Determined to try to accomplish something, he got up and headed for the brig.

Reaching the maximum-security cell holding Kaliphur, Geary was astonished to see Sergeant Tyminska from Colonel Webb's unit in close conversation with Colonel Rogero.

Rogero nodded in greeting. "Admiral, this is Sergeant Tyminska."

"I know. I'm a bit surprised to see you two discussing things."

"The sergeant appreciates that I am no longer working for the Syndicate."

"And appreciates that you've fought the Syndics, sir," Tyminska added. "And those enigmas. We got a look at your recordings of the action at Iwa."

This time Rogero inclined his head toward Tyminska in silent acknowledgment of her words. "The sergeant thinks your prisoner shows subtle signs of counter-interrogation training that differs a bit from what she and her companions have received."

"The prisoner's not saying anything, sir," Tyminska explained. "But it's how he's not saying anything. Tiny physical reactions, slight movements, body posture, that sort of thing."

"Since I know all too much about both Syndicate interrogations and their counter-interrogation training," Rogero explained, "the sergeant thought I might be able to offer some interpretation of my own." He smiled. "I also have considerable experience with assassins, of course."

"Have you two learned anything?" Geary asked, looking at a display showing the scene inside the cell. Kaliphur was lying on the bunk, his eyes closed, his face betraying no expression. Geary felt a twinge of anger at the sight of the attempted assassin apparently relaxing, but fought it down. Maybe anger was what Kaliphur was aiming for, because angry people made hasty decisions.

"He's not from a unit like mine," Sergeant Tyminska said, her gaze following Geary's to look at the prisoner on his bunk.

"We think he received his training from a nonmilitary source," Rogero added.

"His suit has nothing that could identify where it came from," Tyminska said. "None of his gear does. No surprises there. I viewed the ship's surveillance video of the fight where he was captured. He was using some advanced infighting moves, but nothing unique that I could use to identify where he learned it."

"It definitely didn't reflect Syndicate training," Rogero said.

"What about that nerve agent dart?" Geary asked. "Can you tell anything from that, and tell whether or not Kaliphur is the one who killed Inglis?"

Sergeant Tyminska grimaced. "No, sir, to both questions. That dart was made to not show anything about its origins, and it's similar enough to others of its type that someone else could have employed one that seemed identical."

None of that was surprising, but it was still disappointing. "Does that mean you consider it likely or just possible that there are more like Kaliphur concealed within the fleet?"

"In my opinion it's pretty certain there's another on *Boundless*," Tyminska said. "All of our luggage was scanned when we came aboard. So was all the cargo brought on. Those scans would've spotted that stealth suit. That means somebody else must have helped him get that suit aboard without it being seen by the security scans."

"I don't know your exact security situation on *Boundless*," Rogero said, "but with what I'm familiar with it wouldn't be impossible for one person to have smuggled the suit aboard. It would be very difficult, though. Anyone wanting to have a solid chance of success would have a helper to misdirect or blind the security scans when it came to that item."

"That's not the answer I wanted to hear," Geary said. "But if you both think it's the right answer I'll have to assume you're correct. What are the odds we'll learn anything from Kaliphur about a second spy, or about anything else?"

"Absolutely zero, sir, if you want my candid opinion," Sergeant Tyminska said.

"I agree," Rogero said.

Geary blew out an angry breath. "Do either of you have any recommendations about what I should do with him?"

"We're in war status," Sergeant Tyminska said. "You could order a field execution, sir. If he's dead, he can't create any more problems."

"That's really your only option," Rogero said. "Either keep him in this cell until you can hand him off to someone else, or terminate him."

Geary made a face. "It's true that if he's dead he's no longer a potential threat of any kind, but it's also true that as long as he's alive there's always a tiny chance we might learn something from him. If he has a co-spy somewhere in the fleet, would that person try to help him escape, or try to murder him so we couldn't get anything from him?"

Rogero shook his head. "He has no value. He's known to you. We're far from home. If he was broken out of his cell, he has no place to go, and would be a constant burden and danger to this hypothetical but likely co-spy."

Sergeant Tyminska nodded. "Yes, sir. I concur. If they do anything, they'll finish him off. Of course, if you have him executed first, they won't have to bother."

"I can't—" Geary stopped himself in mid-sentence. Because the truth was, out here beyond the borders of humanity, he had authority to unilaterally convict Kaliphur and order him executed. But he knew he'd be doing that only because it simplified things. And he couldn't order someone to die because he didn't want to deal with that person. "I understand."

Sergeant Tyminska frowned toward the cell. "If you're willing to risk it, sir, you could try leaking information that the prisoner was cooperating in some manner. That would be most likely to generate an attempt to murder him by any co-spy still free to operate."

"That might work," Colonel Rogero agreed. "But make it clear he hasn't said anything *yet*. Say he was negotiating to talk in exchange for an agreement to let him go when you get home. Something like that could motivate a quick try to silence him. You'd have to be subtle, though. Just spreading the word around would make it look like bait to lure someone out. It'd have to look like real leaks of information. Of course, if you do that, there's also the chance the co-spy would successfully murder Kaliphur just like that sailor who bought it."

"Got it." Geary thought about the ethics of risking Kaliphur's life in exchange for the possibility of luring another spy out of hiding. That seemed a lot more justifiable than executing Kaliphur just so Geary wouldn't have to worry about him anymore, especially when there was a chance any spy still free might attempt other assassinations. "Thank you for coming here, Sergeant. And thank you, Colonel, for assisting with trying to learn something from our prisoner."

"Admiral," Sergeant Tyminska said, "Colonel Webb requested that I bring the prisoner's stealth suit back with me so our unit can examine it."

Geary thought for a moment before nodding. "I'll authorize that, because I want anything you can tell us about how to adjust our ships' internal sensors to spot any weak points in that suit's stealth capabilities. And as long as it's clearly understood that the suit is being loaned to you. Ownership of it as evidence remains with the master-at-arms force aboard *Dauntless*."

"Understood, Admiral. I can't guarantee we'll find any exploitable weak points in the suit, but we'll do our best. May I make a personal request as well?"

"What's that?"

"Is there any chance I could see the duck?"

Somehow, humor could work its way into the strangest situations. "I think that can be arranged, Sergeant," Geary said. "Let's talk to Chief Master-at-Arms Slonaker about the suit, and about an escort to take you to see Ensign Duck."

That done, he sought out Tanya Desjani in her stateroom.

"I know how to spread false information in a way that makes it look real," she said. "Or rather, I know someone who knows how to do that." She touched her comm pad. "Bridge, notify Master Chief Gioninni that I need to see him right away."

"We'll need to tell the guards on the cell of the potential increased threat," Geary said. "How do we do that without one of them telling all of their friends?"

"We can't," Desjani said. "That information would be all over the fleet in a heartbeat. What we can do is order fairly frequent, random checks that keep them jumping, and occasional reminders that anyone trying to kill this prisoner the way Inglis was murdered might target the guards, too. We can also have the Marines on guard in full combat load-out, using the murder of Inglis as justification for the need for extra firepower and personal sensors."

"That's good," Geary said. "The Marines and the other guards will probably think it's an overreaction by the chain of command, but as long as they're on edge and well armed that should do the trick."

Desjani gave him an arch look. "How about posting Ensign Duck on guard?"

That actually made sense, he realized. Not so long ago he would've thought that posting a duck on sentry duty was a bad joke, but now it seemed like a smart thing to do. Except . . . "We can't keep the duck there around the clock. And if he is there all the time the co-spy might not try anything. It's too bad we couldn't have kept it secret that the duck spotted Kaliphur, but there were too many witnesses. How about random visits? Make it part of the duck's daily walk, but vary the time of the walk?"

"I will make it so," Desjani said. She looked over as Master Chief Gioninni arrived at her door. "If you'll pardon me, Admiral, I have some special tasking for the master chief."

"I have every confidence in Master Chief Gioninni," Geary said as he left, earning himself a pleased and slightly suspicious, slightly worried look from Gioninni.

HE had no idea if the plan would work. Or if the other spy would fall for the bait. Or how many other spies there might be in the fleet, either assigned by some part of the military or the government, or other human governments and militaries, or simply freelancer tools and fools like Inglis had been.

Nor did he know when the Dancers would either start giving them more and clearer answers or tell the Alliance fleet to go away because they didn't want a permanent human ambassador.

One of the military mantras that was probably thousands of years old complained about the need to "hurry up and wait." Having fought his way through to Dancer space, Geary had expected things to happen once he got there. Instead, the only things happening were inside his fleet, and so far they hadn't been good.

Inside his stateroom, Geary set to work tackling administrative paperwork, his least favorite task. If anything would distract him from other issues, it would be dealing with the strange turns of the fleet's regulations.

It was perhaps only to be expected for Lieutenant Iger to show up soon after he had begun, and for Iger to be wearing his "bearer of bad news" expression.

"Now what?" Geary asked.

"The security sweep of the alien-modified transmitter room found a bug," Lieutenant Iger said.

"That's unfortunately not a surprise. And it has nothing to trace its origins, right?"

"No, sir," Iger said. "The design is clearly Syndic in origin. It's an older design, about a decade old."

"Syndic? How could the Syndicate Worlds get a bug in there?"

Iger hesitated, looking more uncomfortable. "Admiral, we have two personnel aboard this ship who—"

"Kommodor Bradamont and Colonel Rogero?" Geary sighed and shook his head. "That doesn't make sense. In terms of people, former Captain Bradamont has an impeccable reputation."

Lieutenant Iger spoke stiffly. "I feel compelled to remind the admiral that during the war with the Syndicate Worlds, former Captain Bradamont was involved with a top-secret program which passed information to the Syndics."

"She was working for our intelligence agencies when she did that," Geary said. "Let me finish. While I don't know Colonel Rogero nearly as well, and he definitely has some leftover Syndic mindsets, he has struck me as an intelligent and capable officer. Do you agree that he'd be a challenging foe?"

"Yes, Admiral, I do," Iger said.

"Why would an intelligent and capable officer employ a bug that pointed straight back at him? Especially since he and Bradamont have been granted free access to that transmitter room. I'm having trouble with method and motive here."

Lieutenant Iger paused for several seconds. "It is difficult to explain," he finally admitted. "But we have the evidence."

"Evidence that creates more internal problems," Geary said. "There only seems to be one possible culprit, but he seems far too smart to have used a bug whose origin could be easily determined. Doesn't it seem far more likely that bug was planted by Kaliphur with an obvious origin aimed at misleading us if we found it?"

"Sir, we know the bug wasn't planted by Kaliphur, or whatever his real name is," Iger said. "All of the data recorded on it is from the last twenty-four hours. There's nothing earlier."

"Do you have an explanation for why this particular bug can be easily traced to a Syndic source, instead of having nothing that can identify where it came from as has been the case with every *other* bug we've been finding?"

"People can be sloppy, sir."

Geary shook his head. "Lieutenant, I don't want to shut you down. You've got reasons for what you're saying. But we know someone tried to set up Colonel Webb with alterations to his medical record that clearly pointed back to him. The bombs aimed at killing me during the diplomatic reception pointed back at Colonel Webb's unit. And now this bug that clearly points to Colonel Rogero. We have two categories of misdeeds. There's the stuff that contains evidence directly implicating someone, and then there are cases like Inglis and this Kaliphur where there's no evidence at all. We still haven't turned up anything about who gave Inglis his orders or provided that binary nerve agent, have we?"

"No, sir." Iger pressed his lips together. "Though it could be argued that in the case of Inglis, that evidence pointed back toward our own sailors. He was supposed to die along with Captain Bradamont and Colonel Rogero. That would make another case in which evidence pointed to a group to further internal dissension. In the only case where we have no evidence except that Kaliphur was a crew member on *Boundless*, he was clearly not expected or intended to be captured or detected."

"That's true." Geary looked sharply at Iger. "Are you agreeing with me about this?"

Iger grimaced. "Admiral, as you point out, we have a pattern. Espionage is clearly going on, but so is sabotage in a form designed to create internal problems. I was surprised at the obviousness of this latest bug, but even smart people make stupid mistakes at times."

"Myself included," Geary said. "I don't want you agreeing with me because I pushed back on Colonel Rogero's apparent guilt."

"I would not agree with you because of that, sir," Iger said, smiling briefly. "There is a consistent tactic being used. I nonetheless request permission to continue to monitor Colonel Rogero's movements and actions."

It was only reasonable, and Geary didn't doubt that Rogero fully expected the Alliance to be doing that, so he nodded. "Granted. Lieutenant, tell me if this is totally off the wall. We managed to capture Kaliphur because of an unexpected variable, that being the presence of Ensign Duck aboard this ship. Is there some other variable we can throw into the mix that might expose however many whoevers are messing with us?"

Iger lowered his head slightly in thought. "I don't know, Admiral. Request permission to discuss specifics of this with Lieutenant Jamenson. She has that unique ability to come up with unexpected conclusions."

"Once again, granted." It was like Iger to not have shared anything with his wife that she wasn't cleared for. "You might also want to discuss it with Master Chief Gioninni."

"The master chief?" Iger stared at Geary, aghast. "Him?"

"Lieutenant, if there is an expert on getting away with things that aren't supposed to be done, it's Master Chief Gioninni. If he knows how to hide his tracks, he might have some useful insights in how to spot someone else's tracks."

"I . . . suppose." Iger shook his head. "It won't look good back at fleet intelligence, though."

"It can be our secret," Geary said. "Or else I can give you written orders to discuss the matter with Gioninni. That'll ensure you're covered, and I'm certain that fleet intelligence already regards me as the loosest of loose cannons anyway."

"There has to be a written record of the disclosures," Iger said apologetically.

"Then you'll get the written orders to include with those," Geary said. "Are we good?"

"Yes, Admiral." But Iger hesitated before leaving. "Should Colonel Webb be briefed on this?"

Of course, was Geary's first thought. But then he thought about Webb's reactions to earlier problems. "Not yet. Let's see if we can develop some ideas about what to do before we brief Colonel Webb." That way he'd have something to push back with if Webb proposed any measures that seemed too extreme.

Once Lieutenant Iger had left, Geary turned back to the paperwork on his display, determined to get some of those dreary administrative tasks out of the way.

He had barely begun, his disgruntled gaze on his display, when he saw an alert appear.

Tabbing it, Geary saw that four Dancer ships had arrived at the hypernet gate.

It was probably nothing. Dancer ships had been coming and going without any change in activity concerning the Alliance fleet that was boring nonexistent holes in space in its orbit of this star. After a brief wish to his ancestors that the Dancers would stop stalling, Geary bent back to his work.

Only a few minutes later, another alert appeared. These four new Dancer ships had maneuvered immediately upon arriving at the hyper-net gate.

Maybe his ancestors had been listening. The new Dancer ships had maneuvered onto a vector to meet the Alliance fleet in its orbit.

TWELVE

A window popped open on his display, showing Tanya Desjani. "Did you see we have visitors on the way?"

"I did," Geary said. "Maybe the Dancer plan has finally gotten here."

Maybe it had. Within a couple of hours, messages began arriving from the Dancers. The one responding to Macadams's ever longer and more simplistic messages was brief yet at least laid out what the Dancers wanted. *Please speak clearly.* Anyone communicating with the Dancers from *Dauntless* could have told Macadams exactly what that meant, but of course Macadams would never ask them and he had stopped accepting messages from *Dauntless* unless they came from Geary himself, who could override any setting Macadams put on his communications.

Geary stopped by the alien-modified transmitter room as a more detailed reply arrived for Kommodor Bradamont and Colonel Rogero.

"Welcome here speakers

"For those different humans.

"Only wish speak one."

Rogero frowned down at the printout. "Does that mean what it sounds like?"

"It does sound like a brush-off," Charban said, looking unhappy. "As if they only want to talk with whoever is running this ship."

"They've personally encountered the admiral," Lieutenant Iger pointed out. "On Old Earth."

Bradamont shook her head, appearing stubborn rather than angry. "Admiral Geary cannot speak for Midway. President Iceni would never stand for it."

"Nor would General Drakon," Rogero agreed.

"We need to tell the Dancers that," Geary said to Charban. "As firmly as possible. Midway has to speak for itself. I have no right to speak for them."

Charban spread his hands. "We can try. I can't guarantee they'll listen."

Lieutenant Jamenson spoke up, sounding puzzled. "Why are they talking to the people on *Boundless* if they only want to speak with one?"

A moment's silence was broken by Bradamont. "Maybe they think *Boundless* is also being controlled by the admiral, that it's just him speaking from another place."

"Why would they think the admiral would be using 'baby talk' from *Boundless* when we know how to communicate better from *Dauntless*?" Charban asked.

"We don't know how they train their young or inexperienced," Bradamont said. "If it's a throw-them-in-to-sink-or-swim approach, they might assume *Boundless* is full of newbies learning how to talk right."

"Regardless," Colonel Rogero said, "the Dancers must understand that Midway will speak for itself."

"We can tell them that," Charban said, "but we can't make them understand. And if they choose to ignore our demands that they listen to you as well as ourselves, we won't be able to do anything about that, either." He still sounded a bit apologetic, but also defensive in the manner of someone who expected to be blamed for something they had no control over.

"We need to try," Geary said before Rogero and Bradamont could issue more protests. "Sooner or later, representatives of other human political associations, private companies, and who knows what will make it to Dancer space. The Dancers have to be ready to deal with all of them."

"Unless," Lieutenant Iger said in slow and cautious tones, "the Dancers choose not to deal with all of them. As General Charban says, we haven't had a lot of luck with asking the Dancers to do things."

"But we can try," Lieutenant Jamenson said. "Maybe attempt some new approaches? Different ways of saying it? Perhaps using the pattern idea?"

"A tapestry," John Senn added. "Didn't you say someone compared the Dancer vision of things to something like a tapestry that forms a picture? We could say that the threads of humanity form a tapestry but each thread remains unique and . . . is . . ."

"Able to decide where it fits in the picture?" Jamenson suggested.

"It can't hurt to try that argument," Charban said. "Admiral, do we need to clear this with the ambassador?"

"I'll let her know what's going on," Geary said. "But I don't expect any problems from that direction. Ambassador Rycerz has told me more than once that she was instructed not to take any actions that even implied the Alliance was trying to lean on or dominate Midway's government."

"Sir?" Lieutenant Jamenson said. "Why haven't we received more messages from the ambassador to forward to the Dancers?"

Privately, Geary thought the answer to that might be Ambassador Rycerz feeling temporarily discouraged and overwhelmed by the many obstacles set in place to hinder her task. "I don't know" was all he said, though. "I expect with the arrival of these new Dancer ships and how much they're communicating, the ambassador will want to send more messages soon."

"We'll get to work on the Midway issue," Charban said.

Bradamont glanced at Rogero. "Admiral, can we speak privately?"

That didn't sound good. He didn't want to rehash the matter of Midway's status among the Dancers when he couldn't do much about that. But he also owed Bradamont for her past service to the Alliance and her continued support of close ties. "Certainly."

The nearby high-security conference room wasn't occupied, so Geary led the way in there. "What can I do for you?"

He'd remained standing, hoping for a short conversation, and so did Bradamont and Rogero. "Admiral," Bradamont began, her words coming out heavy in the manner of arguments that the speaker knew those listening wouldn't want to hear, "if we come back with this situation unresolved, with the Dancers not wanting to talk to Midway's representatives, there will be suspicions among Midway's leaders that you somehow manipulated things to bring it about for your own reasons."

What? Rather than get angry, he was momentarily baffled. "How could I have done that?"

"You are Black Jack, sir."

"What does that have to do with it?"

Bradamont sighed heavily. "Admiral, President Iceni is absolutely certain that you are the cleverest political strategist in all of humanity."

"What?" He said it out loud this time as he sought to understand words that didn't make much sense. He'd heard similar things from Bradamont before, but that didn't make it any easier to grasp.

"General Drakon believes the same," Colonel Rogero said. "I've been impressed. You've outthought and outmaneuvered the Syndicate time and again, not just militarily but diplomatically."

"I . . ." At the moment, all he could think of was Victoria Rione disdainfully informing him what a terrible liar he was. And yet somehow the former Syndics at Midway thought he was a brilliant politician? "Captain . . . Kommodor Bradamont, you know full well that I'm a decent military commander. I've gotten lucky more times than I deserved. But my only political skill is knowing I should listen to the advice of people who are far more skilled at it than I am."

Bradamont glanced at Rogero. "Sir, I can tell you exactly what my husband is thinking at this moment. He's thinking that's precisely what a tricky, clever political strategist would say. You have to understand that everyone on Midway views you through the lens of their experiences in the Syndicate. That's how they interpret your words, your actions, and your successes."

Geary finally sat down, rubbing his forehead with one hand. He couldn't help noticing that Rogero didn't contradict Bradamont's statement. How could he respond? Rione had been right that he was a lousy liar. Maybe, then, he should try telling the truth. "When I took over command of the Alliance fleet at a very perilous moment," he finally said, "I knew I wasn't Black Jack. But I also knew I had to do my best, or everyone who trusted in me would die. That's still my motivation. I've been fortunate in the engagements I've commanded. I've been blessed with good, highly capable subordinates who gave me the support and advice I needed and then some. But when it comes to political games, I can't even pretend to be that person those at Midway are seeing. And if they're going to think my failure in a political endeavor is somehow deliberate and part of a strategy, I don't have any idea how to address that."

Colonel Rogero frowned in puzzlement. "Your actions, your decisions—"

"Colonel, anything that worked out right, including assigning Honore Bradamont to Midway, was suggested by Victoria Rione. She was my tricky, clever political muse. But she's gone, dead at Unity Alternate. All I've done since then is try to do what seemed like the right thing in each situation that's come up."

Bradamont gestured to Rogero and they both sat down opposite Geary. "But, Admiral," she said, "your actions since Rione's death, what we know of them, don't seem materially different from before she died."

"Perhaps," Rogero suggested, still appearing skeptical, "you learned the lessons this Rione could teach, and continue to apply them."

"That's a frightening thought," Geary muttered. "Please listen," he said in a louder voice. "I'm going to do everything I can to get the Dancers to acknowledge you and speak to you. If I can't get it done, it won't be for lack of sincere effort. I need, the Alliance needs, Midway and its, um, associated star systems to remain free. I have every reason to put every effort into getting you good relations with the Dancers."

"You want Midway to remain free," Bradamont repeated with a meaningful look at Rogero.

Rogero himself had the look of someone thinking things through. "You regard General Drakon and President Iceni as reliable partners?"

"Yes," Geary said. Did he mean that? Probably.

"Of course," Colonel Rogero said with the satisfaction of a person who'd come up with the right answer. "If you took over Midway, who would you replace them with who you could count on? It's to your advantage to continue the current arrangements as long as possible."

"Yes," Geary said, hoping he wasn't agreeing with something unsaid.

"Of course," Rogero repeated, smiling.

"Which means," Bradamont said, still watching Rogero cautiously, "that you have every reason to want the Dancers to support President Iceni and General Drakon as well."

"Yes," Geary said, feeling an instinct to continue saying as little as possible.

"Then our interests coincide," Colonel Rogero concluded.

"Yes." *I hope so, anyway.*

NOT six hours later, Geary was back in the same conference room, facing Ambassador Rycerz, whom he'd escorted there from *Dauntless*'s shuttle dock. "I imagine you want to talk about the replies the Dancers are finally sending," he said.

"First things first," Rycerz said, looking disconsolately at her mug of fleet coffee. "Captain Matson wants Lieutenant Commander George off of *Boundless*."

Geary, partway through a drink of his coffee, nearly choked on it. "How did the commanding officer of *Boundless* learn who George was?"

"I have every reason to believe that Colonel Webb leaked the information to Matson that Ship's Officer Joseph Paul was actually fleet intelligence officer Lieutenant Commander Christopher George," Rycerz said before finally risking a taste of her own coffee. "Yes, that's as bad as I remembered it."

"Why?" Geary asked, feeling glad that he'd told Iger not to brief Webb on the bug pointing to Rogero. "Why would Webb do that?"

Rycerz gave him a surprised look. "Isn't it obvious? You'd ordered George to cooperate with Webb, but George remains an element aboard *Boundless* who responds primarily to your orders, not to Webb's. Colonel Webb doesn't want George providing independent reports to you from *Boundless*."

Which meant Webb's displays of cooperation and good feelings were at least partly feigned rather than real. "Don't you have the final say in that?"

Rycerz's answering laugh was sharp and short. "You'd think so, wouldn't you? But, no surprise, it's a security issue. And a ship's issue. The way my orders were written, Colonel Webb has the authority on matters of security, and Captain Matson has the authority on ship's issues where *Boundless* is concerned. In this case, Matson is outraged, or making a good show of being outraged, that George joined the crew under an assumed identity."

"That's . . . understandable," Geary said. "About Captain Matson, I mean. But Lieutenant Commander George is helping to keep his ship safe. Now he is, anyway. If I speak to Matson I'm sure I can change his mind."

Rycerz shook her head. "Matson has already announced that George will be leaving the ship. Including revealing his true name to everyone on the ship."

"He . . ." Geary managed not to say what he'd been about to say, which would have been far from diplomatic.

"You may not have picked up on this much," Ambassador Rycerz said, "because from what I know of your life you haven't had much exposure to civilians these days, aside from members of the Senate, who are a special case. But there are those in the Alliance who have long been unhappy with the amount of authority the military wields over the civilian sector as a result of the long war. They've grown up with the military making a lot of decisions for them. And they don't like that. Captain Matson is a senior, civilian ship commander who has spent all of his life in space being told what he can and can't do by the military."

"I see." Geary sat back, trying to relax and think rather than let his anger speak for him. "You're saying he'll insist on his rights."

Rycerz nodded, trying another taste of her coffee. "Especially since this is a case of the military sneaking a spy onto his ship." She gave Geary a frank look. "Since George's real name and role are now known to everyone on *Boundless*, he's no longer of any use as a covert observer. I'd advise you to take him and give him something else useful to do."

It was good advice, he knew. But the situation still rankled. "That leaves Colonel Webb with exactly what he wanted."

"There's nothing either of us can do about that."

"Webb still doesn't trust me, does he?"

"Webb doesn't trust anybody." Rycerz paused. "Myself included, I think. I'd love to see whatever secret orders he has."

"There is so much wrong with this situation," Geary said, frustration replacing his earlier anger.

"I agree. And, as I told you before, I think it's deliberate. Someone, possibly numerous different someones, wants us to fail." Rycerz made a vague gesture with one hand. "Let's talk about the Dancers. Thank you for forwarding to me all of their replies so far. Without that, I'd be dependent on Dr. Macadams, who of course isn't forwarding anything. What's your impression of the messages we're getting since those new ships arrived?"

"They're saying a lot more," Geary said, "but with a few exceptions, like the messages concerning Midway's representatives, they don't seem to be *saying* much."

"My staff and I agree with you," Rycerz said, smiling for just a moment. "More words, not much more information. Have they finally responded to your request for access to one of their jump drives?"

"Not a word," Geary said. "General Charban has noticed that when the Dancers don't want to give us an answer, they simply don't. This looks like one of those cases."

"Have they asked for access to any of our technology?"

"Aside from duct tape?" Geary thought. "I don't think so. Although we can't be sure what the Dancers' software has told them about the transmitter we loaded it into. I think we need to assume that software has told them everything about the technology in the transmitter."

Rycerz took another tentative sip of her coffee. "I'm fairly certain that Colonel Webb, or some of his soldiers, have accessed the transmitter on *Boundless* that was loaded with the Dancer software. Not to send messages, but to covertly copy the software."

He took a long, slow breath to ensure his next words came out calmly. "Carrying around extra copies of that software is foolhardy. If Webb tries loading it in another transmitter, and hasn't adequately isolated that transmitter, that Dancer software could spread through every system in *Boundless* faster than we could react to it."

"What would it do?" Rycerz asked, speaking with almost unnerving calm.

"We have no idea," Geary said. "No one has wanted to risk it. We know the enigma quantum worms blinded our sensors to enigma ships and monitored our communications and movements. At Unity Alternate the Dancers demonstrated the ability to remotely activate and control uncrewed Alliance tugs and the systems aboard the captured Kick superbattleship. And that's without their software loaded into them. At least, we don't think it was. If the Dancers' software can modify itself to conform to our equipment, it might also be capable of hiding from every security system we've got."

Ambassador Rycerz nodded in the manner of someone who'd just heard their most terrible fears confirmed. "The worst case, then, is the Dancers gain control of every system aboard *Boundless*, and we don't even know it."

"That's correct." Geary waved in the general direction that *Boundless* lay relative to *Dauntless*. "I will be more than happy to inform Colonel Webb personally of how dangerous it would be to let that software loose."

Rycerz played with her cup for a moment before answering. "The worst case is actually that Webb may have already done so. I've managed to develop a couple of sources among Webb's soldiers who were seriously concerned about his actions during his witch hunt for spies among his own unit. They say Webb and his three skilled code monkeys were closeted for a while in one of their compartments, and finally came out looking uncharacteristically grim."

"Ancestors preserve us." Geary shook his head slowly. "Ambassador, if that's true, then the *actual* worst case is that the Dancer software has already used the fleet net to spread to every one of our ships and systems."

Ambassador Rycerz didn't move for a moment, then set her cup down with exaggerated care. "Can we purge it?"

"I'd have to ask my best code monkeys," Geary said. "Off the top of my head, I think that'd involve isolating all of our ships, wiping every system aboard them clean, and then reloading all the software. I'm not sure to what extent that's even possible, let alone how long it would take." He paused as another thought came to him. "But if the Dancer software has already infiltrated all of our systems, it'd likely be in the backup files as well. I need to talk to my people about this."

"If it did happen," Ambassador Rycerz said, "would that imply malign intent by the Dancers? Or would they regard it as a prudent measure to protect themselves?"

"It could be both," Geary said. "I'll repeat what I've said before, that the Dancers haven't ever demonstrated any hostility toward us, and in fact have actively aided us more than once. As upset as I'd be if the Dancer software had infiltrated all of our systems, I don't have grounds to think that was done for purposes of doing us harm. Not that I'm at all happy at the idea it might have happened."

Rycerz nodded, downing most of what was left of her coffee in one gulp. "I'm going to confront Webb about it, including your own assessment of the worst case, and see how he reacts. Hopefully he'll offer a convincing denial, and if he hasn't done anything stupid with that software yet, hearing your assessment will hopefully make him realize how dangerous it would be to play with that software." She set her cup down hard. "This would all be so much easier if the Dancers would just be open with us about what they want and answer our questions!"

"We're confronting so many unknowns that it's making us jumpy," Geary said. "The newly arrived Dancer ships are heading to join up with us. They seem to be sending the messages we've started getting. Maybe they're waiting until they're close enough that we can converse in real time to initiate more-detailed messages."

"I hope you're right about that." Rycerz sat back, looking about her at the mostly unadorned walls of the room. "What are they not telling us? That theory of your historian's seems plausible, but unless the goal of the Dancers is to make us bored and discouraged I can't figure out what it is they're trying to get us to do. Why did they help us at Unity Alternate?"

"Our guess at the time, and I still think it may be the best guess, is they wanted to avoid any danger from the Defender Fleet attacking them," Geary said, wondering when John Senn had become "his" historian. "The Dancers acted in their self-interest to avoid future problems from our AI-controlled ships running amok."

"Also plausible, but also a guess," Ambassador Rycerz said. "Is Dr. Cresida giving you much trouble?"

"None at all."

"Really? She doesn't like you, you know."

"I have noticed that," Geary said. "Have her fellow physicists on *Boundless* been having any luck with Dr. Macadams?"

"Not a bit," Rycerz said. "They have been using their access to sensors to try to spot and evaluate Dancer technology in any way we can detect. It hasn't produced much in the way of results, but it is building up a nice database, and it's keeping them busy and happy. At this point, I'm in favor of anything that keeps anyone I'm responsible for both busy and happy."

Geary nodded, but his mind was still at an earlier place in their conversation. "Do you trust Colonel Webb with your safety?"

"I have no alternative, Admiral." Rycerz absently took another drink of coffee, grimacing as the taste hit her. "I have no control over how he does his job. That reminds me, though." Rycerz eyed Geary. "Webb told me yesterday that he has received reliable information that you're close to striking a deal with that spy you caught."

"He did?" Hadn't Sergeant Tyminska briefed her commanding officer on the discussion about trying to lure a probable co-spy out of hiding? That felt like an odd oversight. Or had the rift between Colonel Webb and his soldiers also led to communication problems within the unit that hadn't been resolved? "He classified the information as reliable?"

"Yes. Not the usual rumor mill, he said, but moving along channels that caused him to assess the information as likely true."

Clearly Master Chief Gioninni was even better at misdirection than he'd let on. Which, with Colonel Webb choosing to leak information for his own reasons, made it all the more important not to tip off any co-spy that the story was made-up. "I'm not sure I can say anything about that."

Rycerz spread her hands. "Admiral, I hope you will share with me anything the spy tells you?"

"I guarantee it," Geary said. "Why did Webb tell you, though?"

"To make sure I asked you to share anything the spy tells you."

That made sense, and confirmed that Webb didn't trust Geary. "Speaking of the spy, has Captain Matson responded to my request to conduct an exhaustive search of *Boundless* for any other stealth suits or other unauthorized materials?"

"Captain Matson characterized the request as impractical," Rycerz said. "*Boundless* is carrying enough supplies to sustain us for years. That's an awful lot of things to try to search through. Staterooms were searched, but as Colonel Webb admitted to me, anyone following proper tradecraft wouldn't have such incriminating material hidden in their own stateroom."

The rest of the conversation didn't offer up any more answers. But it did, Geary thought, reassure both him and the ambassador that the two of them were sharing information and working together.

As soon as the shuttle carrying the ambassador left *Dauntless*, Geary called Lieutenant Iger. "Get your best software people and meet me in my stateroom. We might have a very big problem, and there might not be any way to know if it really exists."

That meeting proved to be as inconclusive and aggravating as most meetings seemed to be these days, because once again there were too many unknowns. Geary did authorize Lieutenant Iger to have his software experts check over the Dancer software in the transmitter for any possible indicators that could be used to spot it in other systems, even though they all knew earlier attempts to do that hadn't produced any results.

He'd barely finished that when Tanya Desjani stopped by, looking annoyed. "What's this about Lieutenant Commander George?"

"He has to leave *Boundless*," Geary said.

"I sympathize with his plight, but *Dauntless* is not a refugee camp for people fleeing *Boundless*," Desjani said. "I don't have an infinite supply of empty bunks. How many more new people am I supposed to take on?"

"Lieutenant Commander George is a fleet intelligence officer," Geary pointed out.

"We already have a fleet intelligence officer aboard this ship. If you bring Lieutenant Commander George aboard, Lieutenant Iger will be subordinate to him and have to start working for him while George becomes your primary intelligence officer."

He hadn't thought it through to that conclusion. Now that Desjani had expressed it, he knew he didn't like it. "That's a good point," Geary said. "I have a long-standing relationship with Iger. He knows what I need. And I think he's very good at what he does. But I can't leave George aboard *Boundless*."

"Admiral, *Dauntless* is one of a couple hundred some ships under your command here. Maybe another ship in the fleet would benefit from having a spare intelligence officer assigned?" Desjani suggested.

The answer to that seemed obvious. "*Tsunami*," Geary said. "General Carabali is aboard her, and Fleet Headquarters hasn't responded to my requests for additional support for Carabali."

"Do you think Lieutenant Commander George can properly support General Carabali?"

"Lieutenant Iger says George is good."

"Then why not give him to the Marines? It gets George out of our hair, gives him something useful to do, and gives the Marines one less fleet-support thing to complain about. He might even be able to help out Carabali. What's the matter?"

"I'm just surprised that we have a problem with a simple and good solution," Geary said.

"It's probably an anomaly," Desjani said. "We shouldn't expect it to happen again."

WHEN the shuttle carrying a somewhat forlorn-looking Lieutenant Commander George and his baggage arrived at the shuttle dock, Admiral Geary made sure to be there along with Lieutenant Iger. He had a suspicion that George was probably feeling like a failure at this point even though he'd done his job as well as anyone could have. "Welcome aboard *Dauntless*," Geary told George. "Let's go have a talk."

Once in his stateroom, Geary waved the intelligence officers to seats before sitting down across from them. Before he could speak, Lieutenant Commander George, who'd remained standing, launched into what was clearly a prepared speech.

"Admiral, I apologize for failing to carry out my duties properly. I don't know how my identity was compromised aboard *Boundless*, but take full responsibility for whatever happened."

Geary held up one hand to stop the speech. "I have a pretty good idea of how your identity was compromised, and it had nothing to do with any failure on your part. As far as I've been able to determine, you did your job well. Because of that, I have an assignment to offer you."

"Sir?" George, plainly expecting to be dressed down, appeared at a loss for words.

"For some time we've been trying to get an intelligence officer assigned to the fleet assault transport *Tsunami*," Geary said. "General Carabali, in charge of this fleet's Marine forces, needs that support. Lieutenant Iger tells me you know your job and could carry out this assignment well. If you haven't heard, the enigmas in particular pose a devastating threat against ground forces and Marines, so proper intelligence support for the Marines is vital."

Geary leaned forward a bit, trying to look as sincere as he was. "Lieutenant Iger has informed me that in some quarters of fleet intelligence, assignments to support Marines are regarded as a form of internal exile. I assure you that is not my intent here. I need good backup for General Carabali. Can you provide it?"

"Yes, sir!" Lieutenant Commander George said, looking baffled and grateful in equal measure. "Admiral, I screwed up on *Boundless*, but I'll do better on *Tsunami*."

Geary shook his head. "I also have reason to believe that you were set up to be spotted by Lieutenant Iger sooner or later in order to fuel distrust within this fleet. As far as this latest reveal, it was likely the work of someone who didn't trust you or me. Again, not your fault. You got caught in the middle both times. Can you tell me at this point whether your original assignment on *Boundless* involved anything other than observing and recording activity?"

This time George hesitated as he considered the question. "Sir, I think I'd be allowed to tell you that it did not involve anything else. Colonel Webb's soldiers searched everything I had, so they can affirm that they didn't find any equipment that would've allowed me to do any other mission than observe and record."

"All I need is your word on it," Geary said, thinking that it would have been nice if Colonel Webb had mentioned the results of that search to him. "Lieutenant Iger says you are worthy of my trust, and I fully trust Lieutenant Iger's judgment and knowledge. Not to rush you out the door, but since you don't have accommodations aboard *Dauntless* it'll probably be best to get you to *Tsunami* as soon as possible. However, before you leave I want to give you and Lieutenant Iger time to talk so he can brief you on anything he thinks you need to know about our current situation. Oh, Lieutenant Iger, make sure he also sees the alien-modified transmitter and meets General Charban."

"Yes, sir," Lieutenant Iger said. "Admiral, before I brief him, will there be any restrictions on what I can pass on to Lieutenant Commander George now that he's going to be on *Tsunami*? Subject to the security of the comm circuits, of course."

"Should there be restrictions?" Geary asked.

"No, sir, I don't think so."

"Then there aren't any." Geary pointed at Iger. "You know what I need. Keep telling me what I need to know, and make sure he"—he shifted his hand to point at George—"understands what I need and knows I won't blame him if he tells me something I'm not happy to hear. Questions? No? Then you have your orders."

ABOUT half an hour before the newly arrived Dancer ships reached Geary's fleet, another message came in from them, featuring multiple voices in a sort of strange harmony that was oddly entrancing to human listeners. "It's an answer to Dr. Cresida," General Charban said, studying the initial part of the translation. "There's something reassuring about knowing I don't understand this not because the Dancers are being vague or confusing but because it's really weird physics."

That message took a while, but immediately afterwards another came in.

"Follow us now please.

"Journey to new star by jump.

"Leaders/rulers/elders greet you there."

"Something is finally happening," Lieutenant Jamenson said, smiling. "That's an interesting multiple-word translation, isn't it? I wonder if the Dancers have one word for whoever is in charge that means all of those things?"

"Maybe we'll finally find out," Geary said. "I'm going to notify the ambassador, then the rest of the fleet. Once I've done that I'll call you to let the Dancers know we're ready to follow."

For better or worse, things were finally happening.

THIRTEEN

FOLLOWING the vectors of the four Dancer ships escorting them, it quickly became apparent that the destination was the hypernet gate. "I wonder where they're going to take us?" Desjani said. They were both on the bridge, watching their displays, even though aside from the fleet's movement in the path set out by the Dancers nothing was really happening that required their attention. "We still have no idea of how many star systems the Dancers control."

"I asked General Charban to ask the Dancers how long we'd be in their hypernet," Geary told her. "If they answer, that'll give us a rough idea of how far we're going."

It wasn't too surprising when the Dancers didn't answer over the next ten hours as they and the Alliance fleet approached the hypernet gate. They had sent two more melodious replies to Dr. Cresida, but otherwise seemed to have said all they wanted to for now.

However, once things started happening they kept happening, like an avalanche gathering mass as it tumbled down the side of a mountain.

Geary had been trying to get some sleep during the transit when a high-priority request came in from Captain Plant on *Warspite* requesting an immediate meeting at the highest security levels.

"Nanami Plant doesn't mess around," Tanya Desjani told him. "If she needs a meeting like that, there's a good reason."

"She wants only me in the meeting," Geary said.

"I'd assume there was a good reason for that, too."

Which is why he found himself once more in the highest-security conference room aboard *Dauntless*, wondering if he ought to decorate a compartment that felt like it was becoming a second stateroom for him given how much time he was spending in here lately.

The high-security links shook hands, green lights appearing to show everything was synced. A moment later Captain Plant's virtual image appeared, standing at parade rest. Every time he had seen her, Plant had looked (to Geary's eyes) like someone holding their cards close in a high-stakes game. This time was no different.

Next to Plant was Ensign Arwen Duellos, at rigid attention, her expression that of someone ready to face the worst.

"What's this about?" Geary said, trying not to let any concern appear in his voice. What could Roberto Duellos's daughter have done to merit this meeting?

Captain Plant spoke in a carefully professional voice, as if reporting routine events. "Ensign Duellos requested a personal counseling session with me. Based on what she told me, I judged it necessary to immediately contact you, Admiral." She glanced at Arwen Duellos. "Tell the Admiral."

Ensign Duellos's words came out in a rush, her voice quavering only slightly, her eyes fixed straight ahead of her. "I am compelled by honor and duty to report my involvement in actions aimed at subverting the command of this fleet."

He had thought nothing could surprise him anymore. But this . . . the new people he'd wanted an eye kept on. And Ensign Duellos had been one of those new people. But he'd never expected her to be part of anything improper. Roberto Duellos would be crushed.

Still, Geary told himself that he needed to focus on the most critical issues, not any personal ones. "What actions?" he asked. "Is there imminent danger to any ships or personnel?"

"No, sir! Not . . . to my knowledge," Arwen said. She licked her lips nervously before continuing. "It's possible. Longer term. I was told . . . lied to . . . that we were involved in an effort to ensure the safety of the Alliance. But when there was an attempt on the life of . . . your life, sir . . . I realized something was wrong with what I'd been told. And then instructions came down, for actions against . . ." Arwen Duellos struggled for words for a moment, anger appearing on her face. "Against my fellow officers on the *Warspite* and my commanding officer. And I knew I had to inform Captain Plant, and accept whatever consequences I deserved, because this wasn't about the safety of the Alliance. It couldn't be. Not if I was being asked to betray my own comrades in arms."

His heart sinking, Geary glanced at Captain Plant. She was watching him, knowing what he needed to ask, knowing he'd surely ask if this were any other officer. "Who is running this? Is Captain Duellos involved?"

"No, sir!" Arwen struggled for control. "Not in any way! I thought he would approve, but we were told not to contact anyone outside of our core group, our cell."

"Why did you think Captain Duellos would approve of your actions?" Geary asked, dreading to hear the answer.

"Because he's devoted his life to defending the Alliance!" Arwen grimaced. "But he's always told me that when things get bad, your comrades, your fellow officers and your sailors, they have to know they can depend on you. And . . . and this is against that. I know that now. My father will be . . . dishonored by my actions. Perhaps my death will—"

"You're dying?" Geary broke in, shocked by the words.

"I know the penalty for my actions," Ensign Duellos said, her voice breaking a bit. "I request an honorable execution by firing squad."

He hadn't gone there yet. Hadn't contemplated the consequences for Ensign Duellos. But she was correct that conspiring against the chain of command called for the death penalty.

A look at Captain Plant showed her registering mild disagreement. "I am convinced," Plant said, "that Ensign Duellos's actions have thus far been confined to communicating with co-conspirators."

"What specifically made you decide to come forward?" Geary asked Ensign Duellos.

"Two things, sir. One was when word came through the channels we'd been using asking for ideas on getting access to and silencing the agent held in the brig aboard *Dauntless*." Ensign Duellos revealed anger again, struggling to keep her voice under control. "That was when I realized I must have been involved in actions that included attempting . . . attempting . . . to murder the fleet's commander. Sir."

She inhaled deeply, composing herself. "The second thing . . . I was told action would be taken sometime after we arrived at the new Dancer star system. Something to prevent a peaceful outcome of the mission. Since my commanding officer was not part of the conspiracy, I would receive a package of malware disguised as a system update that would take control of *Warspite*'s fire control and weapons systems, as well as communications and maneuvering."

Arwen Duellos's eyes flashed, and for a moment she looked very much like her father when he was at his most determined. "I knew what my . . . what Captain Duellos would say about that. I would not do that, Admiral. I will not betray my shipmates. I will not betray my commanding officer. I will not betray my oath to the Alliance."

Captain Plant reached toward a control on her ship. Geary saw an alert appear to tell him that he and Plant were now on a private circuit, able to see and hear Ensign Duellos, but Duellos wouldn't be able to hear them and her sight of the others' faces would be blurred to hide

their words and expressions. "Admiral, I am confident that Ensign Duellos has been candid with me, and with you. She cannot provide much
more information, though. The cells the conspirators are using communicate using avatars, so she doesn't even know who her closest fellow conspirators are, let alone who's in charge of this. My own quick
analysis of the communications Ensign Duellos shared with me lead
me to believe this effort is concentrated among some of the newer personnel aboard *Warspite* and other battleships, and that whatever leadership exists is among senior battleship officers." Plant delivered that
bombshell with cool precision, her voice almost devoid of emotion.

Geary thought for a moment to take it all in. "Do you have any ideas
who those leaders might be?"

"Senior battleship officers," Plant repeated. "At least one captain."

"Who can I trust?"

"Me," Plant said, with a quick, fierce smile. "Captain Armus. There
is no steadier officer in the fleet. And, frankly, he wouldn't take that
kind of initiative."

Her words uncomfortably echoed those of Michael Geary. "Anyone
else?" Geary asked.

"Captain Casia on *Conqueror* is as solid as they come. And Hiyen
on *Reprisal* isn't Alliance at all, so he's unlikely to have been brought
into this or trusted by the conspirators. I do recommend that you speak
to Captain Geary aboard *Dreadnaught*," Plant said.

"You believe that she's involved in this?" Geary asked, trying to
numb his feelings.

"No, sir," Plant said, continuing as if unaware of the relief that
Geary himself couldn't conceal. "If she was, something would've already happened. Ensign Duellos's communications show a pattern of
slow movement toward action." Captain Plant grinned briefly. "Very in
keeping with battleships, which is one reason why I think those are the
officers behind this. A battle cruiser captain would've already done
something, leaping into action too early. Jane Geary has some of that
battle cruiser blood in her. And she's a Geary. I think it likely that who-

ever is behind this has sought her approval or involvement, though perhaps in ways she wouldn't recognize as such."

"They want a Geary to endorse their efforts," he said, once again remembering Michael's words. "Captain Burdock. Before he left, Captain Michael Geary told me that she seemed to be sounding him out."

"Burdock?" Plant frowned in thought. "That is very possible. She doesn't confide in many people, but everyone remembers how firm a backer she was of Admiral Bloch."

"What about Pelleas?" Michael had also mentioned him.

"Pelleas." Captain Plant smiled again, this time like someone reaching a conclusion to a long-term problem. "He's been taking the lead in discussions among us for the last few months. And he put on that show at Indras."

So, another strong maybe. "What do you recommend be done with Ensign Duellos?"

"I wish her to remain aboard *Warspite* with her current responsibilities," Plant said without hesitating. "She can tell us when this plot is ready to be triggered."

"The people behind it have already demonstrated their willingness to kill to keep their secrets," Geary said.

"Yes, sir," Captain Plant said.

Of course. Naturally. His only responsible course of action would be to cold-bloodedly put the life of the daughter of his best friend on the line. But did he have any alternative? "What's your best guess as to their intentions?"

"Once we're at the second Dancer system, one or two battleships will open fire on the Dancers. The other battleships and the battle cruisers will be neutralized by the malware. The intent will be to trigger hostilities and force the fleet to make a fighting withdrawal back to Alliance space." Plant squinted slightly as she thought. "That's how I'd carry out what I've seen so far, sir."

If that was what was planned, it was clever enough. Some of the Alliance ships attacking the Dancers, the other Alliance ships apparently watching passively, not interfering. The officers and crews of the battleships involved would follow orders from their captains that appeared to be legal. And afterwards Geary would be confronted with a disastrous situation involving the Dancers, as well as a command environment in which he had no idea which commanding officers and ships he could trust.

Assuming that malware didn't cause problems on *Dauntless* that removed Geary from the situation permanently, or another assassin didn't surface to strike at him.

"I concur with your assessment, Captain," Geary said. "See what more you can find out, staying as discreet as possible. We do not want to tip these people off before they show their hand. I will speak with Captain Armus and Captain Jane Geary. Now, please bring Ensign Duellos fully back into this conversation. I want her to hear your recommendation regarding her."

"Yes, sir." But Plant paused her hand in mid-motion toward her controls. "Sir, she's done her duty. And I have no doubt will now risk herself to atone. I believe that should mitigate against applying the most serious punishment to her."

"Noted," Geary said, because he couldn't commit to anything at this point.

Unsurprisingly, Arwen Duellos without hesitation agreed to fulfill the role of mole within the conspiracy. Cautioning her to be very careful not to reveal her change of heart, Geary reluctantly approved placing her at risk.

"If anyone asks what Ensign Duellos was meeting with me about," Captain Plant said, "I'll say she was expressing concern about the motives of the Dancers."

"Good." Once the virtual presences of Captain Plant and Ensign Duellos were gone, Geary indulged in several seconds of despair. Facing these problems again, after years of trying to fix a fleet nearly broken by a century of war. Why was he still trying?

He knew the answer, though. He couldn't break faith with those who trusted him. Not any more than Ensign Arwen Duellos could.

She'd be a fine officer someday. If she survived this.

GEARY stayed in the secure conference room as he called Jane Geary. Despite the lateness of the ship's day, he wasn't surprised that she responded immediately. "Captain Geary," he said, to establish clearly that this was a purely professional matter, "I need to know if anyone, especially any other battleship commanders, have approached you regarding . . ." What should he call it? "Disapproval of our current mission."

Jane paused before replying. "Do you mean like Captain Burdock did Michael before he left? He told me about that."

"Has Burdock talked to you?"

"No, sir." The firmness and sincerity of Jane's reply was a welcome relief. "But . . . Adam Pelleas seemed to be sounding me out while we were transiting through Lalotai. The usual complaints about the government, and then hints that a Geary should fix it." She sighed, looking aggravated. "The same things I've heard most of my life. Not very often these days, though. I told Pelleas a Geary was fixing it and asked whether he had problems with you. He backed off fast, and that was the end of it."

Pieces of the puzzle were falling into place. "Hang on while I get Captain Armus linked in."

Armus rarely displayed anger. When he got upset it wasn't so much the flash of an explosive as that of a volcano building slowly to eruption. But after Geary had explained what he'd learned, leaving out the identity of Arwen Duellos, Armus seemed very close to a catastrophic detonation. But he only said one word. "Unacceptable."

"When do you think they'll try attacking the Dancers?" Geary asked.

Captain Armus breathed in and out a few times like an engine strain-
ing to avoid overpressuring before answering. "Only when they're certain. They'll want to ensure they can hit and hopefully destroy some
Dancer ships so as to irreparably damage relations with that species."

Jane Geary nodded. "Yes. They won't want any chance of failure.
Keep us at sufficient distance from any Dancer ships, and they'll hold
off waiting for a better chance."

"Until we begin to depart for Alliance space again," Armus cautioned. "Then they'll take whatever shot they can."

They both sounded certain, but of course there wasn't any way to be
certain. "I don't want to risk leaving them room to maneuver, but I
can't make arrests without a lot more evidence than I currently have."

"You have to wait until they give you grounds," Jane Geary agreed.
"Black Jack acting in an apparently arbitrary way against potential ri-
vals would seem to justify a lot of the remaining concerns about you.
And it would seem far too much like how things had deteriorated before you assumed command of the fleet."

"I cannot disagree," Armus grumbled. "Pelleas has been showboating
a lot lately, trying to gain status against me. We will, very carefully, try to
determine which others of our fellow commanders might not be trust-
worthy. You should consider alerting the Marine detachments aboard
the battleships, though. It might be up to them to stop any traitors from
ordering actions that would dishonor us all and harm the Alliance."

"I'll consider that," Geary said. Armus's advice was wise, but the
more people tipped off, the more chance the leaders of the conspiracy
would hear.

THAT left only one person he had to tell. After all, if the worst happened
to him, Tanya Desjani would have to carry on to get the mission done
and deal with the conspirators.

She listened without interrupting until he was done. "Arrest
them now."

"I don't have grounds for that," Geary repeated to her. "I don't even know who they are, except for suspicion."

"You're in a combat zone, you're the fleet commander—"

"And I'm Black Jack." He shook his head firmly. "Everything I do has to be justifiable to the widest possible audience. Otherwise I'll do more damage to the Alliance than its worst enemies."

"Fine. At least it explains where the new, junior personnel have been getting their senior planning and directives from." Desjani looked off to the side. "What will you tell Roberto Duellos?"

"I can't tell him anything yet. You know that as well as I do."

She looked down, not saying anything else for a long moment. "I'm sorry. If something happens to Arwen, if she dies, Roberto will understand. He'll be proud of her for doing the right thing. But he'll never be able to forgive you. And even if she comes out all right, just knowing the risk she was exposed to, he may never forgive you."

"I know."

"But I honestly don't know anything else you could do. I hope Roberto Duellos understands that, too, as well as the fact that Arwen's choices got her into this position." She shook her head before finally looking back at him. "What about the ambassador? Are you going to tell Rycerz?"

"I can't," Geary said. "Rycerz herself told me that she can't trust any communications with *Boundless* to be secure. I have no way of safely getting word to Rycerz before we enter the Dancer hypernet."

"She's not going to be happy."

"This doesn't seem to be my day for making people happy," Geary said.

THE anticipated ten hours to rest a bit had collided with reality and turned into hour after hour of high-security meetings and hasty planning. On the one hand, there was relief in finally having at least a vague handle on who was behind so much of the internal sabotage in the fleet.

On the other, the stakes if Geary failed to handle this right (or even if he did handle it right but at a cost in lives) had gotten much higher.

As if there wasn't already enough to worry about, Colonel Webb called an hour out from reaching the Dancer hypernet gate. "The alien-modified transmitter on *Boundless* is disabled. No one knows why. It will receive, but not transmit." He gave Geary a challenging look, as if daring him to accuse Webb of involvement in that.

But one of the things Geary felt sure of was that Webb and his people didn't know enough about the Dancer software to monkey with it. "When was the last transmission possible?"

"A couple of hours ago. Macadams was sending a message and it just cut off. That's what he claims, anyway."

"How long a message?" Geary asked, remembering something that Ambassador Rycerz had told him.

"I don't know. The ambassador has commented that Macadams has been talking the ears off the Dancers. They do have ears, right?" Webb looked suddenly startled. "Do you think the Dancers cut him off?"

"I think it's a real possibility," Geary said. "The ambassador needs to get control of that transmitter before the Dancers get fed up and cut off the transmitter aboard *Dauntless*, too."

"She can't—" Webb halted in mid-sentence, a slow smile forming. "Unless it's a matter of security to the mission. If the way it's being employed risks provoking the Dancers . . ."

"I think it does. But what to do about it is the ambassador's call," Geary said, having gone as far as he wanted in urging that action.

"Not if it's a security issue, Admiral." Webb nodded to himself. "If Ambassador Rycerz doesn't know about it until after the fact, she can't be blamed back home no matter how Macadams complains. And I don't care whether he complains about me. This gives us the outcome we need. You have an amazing way of finding solutions, Admiral."

He hadn't actually been driving for that outcome, and didn't want Webb reading more into his words than he intended. "Colonel, I am not telling you to take the transmitter away from Macadams."

"Of course not," Webb said with a grin. "Because you can't. I'm separate from your command. This conversation never happened."

"You'll need to be cautious with that transmitter," Geary warned, deciding to partially change the subject. "We don't know how easily or widely that Dancer software can spread through other systems."

"So I understand," Webb said with a dismissive wave of one hand. "Not to worry, Admiral. I don't want primary responsibility for what anyone does with that transmitter as long as they're not, uh, provoking the Dancers. I'll let the ambassador take control of that and decide who gets access."

Maybe this would work out. Playing different sides against each other to give Ambassador Rycerz a chance to control things on *Boundless* bit by bit. It would be up to Rycerz to take full advantage of that, but from what Geary had seen of her the ambassador could play that game better than he could. She'd just lacked the right leverage up to now. It would also keep both her and Webb busy while Geary dealt with the conspiracy within the fleet. The last thing he wanted was Colonel Webb finding out about that and trying to intervene under his orders' vague umbrella of "security issues." "That's your call, Colonel."

Just before they reached the hypernet gate, the fleet's sensors spotted three more Taon ships that had arrived at one of the jump points five hours ago. "That's a different jump point than the last Taon ships used," Desjani observed. "Two of those big probable freighters, and one escort."

"It implies the Taon have free use of Dancer space for trade," Geary said. "Too bad they won't talk to us."

"If they sent a message as soon as they jumped into this star system and saw us, we still have time to see it," she said. "I'm not holding my breath waiting for it, though."

Sure enough, no message had come in from the new Taon ships before the Dancer escorts for Geary's fleet entered their hypernet, bringing the Alliance ships along with them on the way to an unknown destination.

Geary himself had sent a message to all of his ships. "The Dancers are friendly. Wherever we're going, we want to arrive there looking friendly as well. Shields at normal operating levels, no weapons charged, readiness condition at enhanced peacetime level." Even if there were Dancer ships near the exit of the hypernet gate when they arrived wherever they were going, any battleship captain planning trouble would have a lot of work to do powering up weapons before they could try to start a war with the Dancers. But since Ensign Duellos hadn't reported receiving the malware, that plot was clearly not intended to be sprung until later after the arrival of the human ships at the new star system. Until then, he had to act as if he suspected nothing of what Arwen Duellos had told him. "And, needless to say, we want to look our best."

Human ships couldn't match the graceful formations the Dancers managed with ease, so Geary had arranged the fleet for now in a sphere. It wasn't a good combat formation, but it looked good and was easy to maintain.

Just before entering the hypernet, the Dancers sent a short message to *Dauntless*.

"Ninety-eight of your hours," General Charban reported. "There's no explanation of what that pertains to."

"It must be how long we'll be in the Dancer hypernet," Geary explained.

"Ninety-eight hours?" Desjani said. "That means a moderate distance. Maybe forty to sixty light years?"

Which helped a little toward understanding how large a region the Dancers might control. But only a little. They might be on their way to the center of Dancer-owned space, or to the other edge of it.

THE hypernet differed from jump space in that whereas jump space was an ill-defined and ill-understood place but nonetheless a place, ships using the hypernet were (in the sense the universe understood it) nowhere at all when in the hypernet. Geary had been told the hypernet made use of quantum mechanics phenomena such as entanglement and tunneling, but beyond that the explanations went into places his mind had trouble following. He was sure that Dr. Cresida could explain it, but was also sure that Jasmine Cresida would begrudge the time spent trying to make him understand. He didn't really need to understand how it worked, anyway. What mattered was the hypernet did work, and he knew how to make it work if his ship had a key for the hypernet they wanted to use. *Dauntless* carried keys for both the Alliance and the Syndicate Worlds hypernets (or for what was left of the Syndic hypernet anyway), but not for the Dancer net. The Dancers of course had keys for their own hypernet, which was why they'd had to be present to bring the human ships along.

What he did know with certainty was that ships in the hypernet were totally isolated from each other while in transit, meaning he had no way of furthering any investigations into what Ensign Duellos had revealed. Or any means of knowing whether Ensign Duellos's actions had been discovered by other conspirators aboard *Warspite*, and whether she was in great danger as a result.

Unable to work at those critical matters, and with no means for external interruptions to distract him from them, he did his best to focus on getting some of the dreaded administrative paperwork done.

And to ensure he knew the current state of the fleet. A century ago he'd learned how difficult it could be as a commanding officer to stay informed of everything important on a single ship. Now that he had hundreds of ships under his command, that problem had been multiplied a few hundred times over.

And he now had a special reason to check the status of his battleships, especially Captain Pelleas's *Gallant* and Captain Burdock's *Encroach*. He studied their updates in vain for any hint of hard proof of their involvement in a conspiracy to start a war with the Dancers. And for any problems that might inhibit their ability to act on their plans. But both *Gallant* and *Encroach* were in outstanding condition. As Michael Geary had said, Pelleas and Burdock were models for what the Alliance sought in battleship captains.

Not that he had problems on any of the rest of the ships. Fuel status was still excellent despite the fuel cells used to reach Dancer space. Reserve fuel cells on the auxiliaries had been used to replenish all of the ships, and the auxiliaries had used the enforced wait to manufacture more cells from the materials they carried.

Food stockpiles were also good. The auxiliaries couldn't manufacture new food (though fleet rumor held that the horrible Danaka Yoruk ration bars were in fact compressed leftovers from toxic manufacturing processes) but the ships had brought along enough to last a while yet before food became a concern. Spare-part inventories were good, and while a variety of ships had a variety of the inevitable equipment problems, nothing critical was broken on any of them.

Morale had improved once the fleet got moving in the wake of the Dancer ships taking them to the hypernet gate. Disciplinary problems had fallen off almost immediately, though they never went away. General Carabali reported that she'd sentenced one of her Marines to hard labor and bread and water in the brig of *Mistral* after he was convicted of assault, battery, and theft. Most incidents weren't that bad, but like bad coffee the occasional bad egg was a fact of life in the fleet.

Balancing that were commendations and promotions recommended for individuals who'd done particularly well during the engagement with the enigmas. Confirming those was a part of his job that Geary always enjoyed.

But always in the back of his mind were dreadful premonitions of him informing his best friend, Captain Roberto Duellos, that Duellos's daughter had died as a result of Geary's own decisions.

Nearly four days of work nearly eliminated his backlog, but instead of basking in the glow of accomplishment Geary no longer had much to distract him. Maybe he'd spend an hour or so pretending to try to relax before the fleet left the Dancer hypernet.

His stateroom display chimed urgently.

"We need to have a meeting," General Charban said. "Before we leave the hypernet. It's very important."

Apparently the living stars had granted his unspoken prayer for another distraction.

Since there were only a couple of hours remaining, Geary quickly called the meeting in the secure conference room. He brought along Captain Tanya Desjani, wanting her perspective on whatever Charban needed to discuss so urgently.

Also in the room were Lieutenant Iger, Lieutenant Jamenson, John Senn the historian, and Dr. Cresida. Desjani, unhappy at being called away so soon before her ship left the hypernet, was doing her best to ignore Cresida's presence, while the doctor herself seemed absorbed in something she was reading.

"General?" Geary prompted. "We're pressed for time. What's so important?"

Charban gestured toward the physicist. "Dr. Cresida has been able to develop a major insight into the ways the Dancers think."

Cresida finally looked up. "It's a theory. Consistent with what evidence we have, but not proven by any means."

"Nonetheless," Charban said, "I think the admiral needs to hear it before we leave the hypernet and can communicate with the Dancers again."

"Keep in mind that I'm still formulating this," Cresida said, tapping her comm pad. "To summarize, I believe the Dancers may view the universe in purely mechanistic terms."

"What does that mean?" Geary asked.

"It means they reject uncertainty." Dr. Cresida paused, her head tilting to one side slightly as she thought. "Have you ever heard the dice quote? A long time ago, a physicist and mathematician named Einstein rejected the concepts of quantum mechanics by saying that the governing power of the universe does not play at dice. Einstein had formulated what we still call relativity, which postulates a universe in which everything is predictable, everything physical can be known, and every outcome can be exactly calculated. Describe any set of conditions, and what happens next can be predicted with absolute, mathematical precision."

"All right," Geary said. "But isn't quantum mechanics about things being unpredictable?"

"That's correct," Dr. Cresida said, looking mildly surprised that Geary knew that. "The universe of quantum mechanics is different. It is full of uncertainties and probabilities. There are some things we cannot know. All we can do is calculate the chances of certain things happening. Einstein rejected that, but could never disprove any of it, for the simple reason that quantum mechanics experimentally works. Unfortunately for physicists, so does Einstein's relativity. Both work, yet they are incompatible with each other. In all of the years since, we've been unable to reconcile those two different universes. We, that is humans, have dealt with that by using whichever is appropriate in any given situation."

Geary nodded again, more cautiously. "Are you saying the Dancers approach it differently?"

"I am saying," Dr. Cresida replied with more taps on her comm pad, "that their responses to my questions about quantum mechanics indicate to me that the Dancers have philosophically followed completely in Einstein's footsteps. If I read their interpretations and metaphors correctly, they have wedged the square peg of quantum mechanics into the round hole of relativity by rendering the uncertainties and probabilities into absolute factors."

This time Geary frowned, seeing the same expression on Desjani's face. "Didn't you say that relativity and quantum mechanics are different? But the Dancers see them as the same? How can they do that?"

Dr. Cresida let out a long-suffering sigh. "Admiral, they do that in the same way that humans can and have done that many times in the past regarding other matters. They interpret their observations in terms that match their model of how things work."

"But how do they do that?" Desjani asked, sounding not hostile but curious. "Aren't physical facts . . . facts?"

That brought another heavy sigh out of Dr. Cresida. "Everything can be interpreted. Everything *must* be interpreted. What we see, what we observe, what we understand, is all filtered through our senses and our minds. If we believe a certain model is true, we find ways to make our observations fit that. In ancient times it was believed that everything in the universe revolved around Old Earth. The ancient scientists were not fools, and they had access to detailed astronomical observations. But they firmly believed in their model and they made the observations fit that model. The model got more and more complicated, but they could make it work even though it was absolutely wrong."

"And that's what the Dancers are doing with quantum mechanics?" Geary asked. "They're seeing it in absolute, predictable terms?"

"Yes." Dr. Cresida looked down at her work. "This remains a theory, but I believe the Dancers are not consciously seeing it in those terms. Based on how they tried to explain their thinking to me, I think it may be the only way they *can* see it."

"Born engineers," Desjani said. "They see the universe in terms of known factors."

"Essentially," Dr. Cresida said.

"But what impact does that have on their interactions with us?" Geary said.

"Don't you get it, Admiral?" Charban said, pointing to first John Senn and then Dr. Cresida. "Our resident historian has postulated that the Dancers are pursuing a concrete goal, a precise outcome, and therefore the Dancers may be trying to position us to achieve that outcome. If they believe the universe does not contain uncertainties, then wouldn't it follow that they believe that our actions can also be precisely calculated, and the exact actions necessary to lead us to do what they want can also be precisely worked out?"

John Senn spoke up, his voice apologetic. "One thing I'm trying to grasp is that from an historical perspective theories always run into obstacles. And this particular one . . . well, they're going to be wrong, aren't they? If the Dancers are calculating exact outcomes in situations that don't allow for exact outcomes, won't they run into cases where the predicted outcome doesn't match their calculations?"

"Of course they will," Dr. Cresida said, smiling thinly. "Of course they have. I can see evidence of that in their explanations to me. But it appears to me that they resolve that in the same manner that humans would. If the outcome does not match the calculation, then the model is not the problem. The calculation was in error. Redo the calculation to match the actual outcome, and the model remains valid."

"That's frightening," Desjani said.

"That is how humans have often done things," Dr. Cresida said in the tone of a teacher speaking to an uncomprehending student. "We have only the two examples of humanity and the Dancers at this point in this regard, but it implies the possibility that any intelligent species deals with the universe by rationalizing it in terms of how their minds must see it."

"And humans are more willing to accept the idea of chaos and uncertainties than a species that are born engineers?" Geary asked. "Lieutenant Jamenson, you're very good at discerning patterns in things. Have you had a chance to compare your thinking about this with Dr. Cresida?"

Lieutenant Jamenson nodded. "General Charban suggested I go over it with the doctor. There are a lot of concepts that go beyond my knowledge of physics, but I had the same sense of it that she does. The Dancers are postulating a universe in which everything works just so."

"I've been thinking about our experiences in the last star system," Charban said. "The days when the Dancers offered no answers or minimal answers to everything we asked. Then some new ships showed up and we suddenly got more answers. Suppose our arrival at that star system was not just unexpected, but unpredicted? And the local Dancers didn't know what exact things were supposed to be said to us to nudge us in the proper direction to achieve the desired outcome? Not just general things, but exact, precise things. They couldn't wing it. They had to wait until other ships arrived with those detailed instructions. The 'plan' they said they needed."

"I see." Geary looked over at Desjani, who was frowning but also nodding in agreement. "It would explain a lot. The Dancers often seem to expect that we'll understand or react in a certain way to what seem to us to be vague statements. But if they've been watching humanity for a long time as we believe, how could they think that humans are predictable, either as individuals or in groups? How could they possibly make us fit their model?"

To his surprise, it was Desjani who answered, looking unhappy at her own words. "If Victoria Rione was here, she'd be telling us that people are predictable. That's what she did, Admiral. Everything she said and did was designed to push people in the directions she wanted. And right up to the end she was prepared to deal with what she saw as likely, predictable outcomes."

"Not everything," Geary said, remembering Rione's anguish when it was discovered that her husband was still alive and her actions could have been construed as betraying him. "But, in general, there's a lot of truth there."

"Outside observers can see things those on the inside don't see," Charban said. "To the Dancers, we may seem predictable enough."

"We may seem predictable to the enigmas as well," Lieutenant Iger said, finally speaking up. "We think the leaking of hypernet technology to the Alliance and the Syndicate Worlds was done by the enigmas because they expected that once we learned what powerful weapons the gates were we'd use them to annihilate each other."

"That was unfortunately a reasonable prediction for them to make," General Charban said. "I would've guessed that was what we'd do."

"We would have," Desjani said. "If not for Jaylen Cresida working out a way to disarm the gates, and if not for leadership," she added, glancing at Geary, "who rejected the use of the gates as weapons."

"Two unpredictable factors," Charban agreed.

"Two *unpredicted* factors," Dr. Cresida said firmly. She'd stiffened a little when Desjani mentioned her dead sister, but otherwise hadn't reacted. "Add them into the calculations after the fact, and the method still appears valid."

"Like building something," Lieutenant Iger said. "If you put together a transmitter, and it doesn't work, that means you made a mistake building it. It doesn't mean transmitters can't work."

"That's how engineers would see it," Charban agreed.

Geary sat back, resting his chin on one fist as he thought. "If this is right, it reinforces the idea that the Dancers think they know exactly what they're doing to reach their goal. To complete the pattern they desire. But we still don't know what that goal is, and we don't know what specific things they are planning to get us to do what they need. Not knowing what they want means we might react to their prodding in a way they haven't predicted and don't expect. A way that might be disastrous."

The others around the table nodded. "We *have* to find out more of what their goal is," Charban said. "But the one thing they've made clear is that they won't tell us that."

"It would change the outcome," Lieutenant Jamenson said. "Knowing that would alter our actions."

"But," Geary said, "they inadvertently told us some important things when they answered Dr. Cresida's questions. Maybe if we ask more questions about things that aren't about the Dancers' goals, that aren't specifically about them as a species, they'll tell us more that indirectly helps us understand them and what they want."

"That is a surprisingly good suggestion," Dr. Cresida said.

"You're welcome," Geary said. "Your contributions have been invaluable, Doctor. We owe you a great deal for a major insight into how the Dancers think."

"It's still a theory," Dr. Cresida said. "Umm . . . you're welcome."

"Do you have any suggestions for what to do next?" Charban asked her.

"The most important thing to do would probably involve a fatal accident involving Dr. Macadams," Cresida said. "He's a rigid, ideological roadblock to progress in dealing with the Dancers."

"A fatal accident?" Geary asked, too surprised to look shocked.

"Hasn't that option occurred to you?"

"I admit that it has a few times, but I'm a little surprised to hear it coming from you."

"I am experienced in the field of academics," Dr. Cresida said. "Competition among professors can be brutal. Are you saying you couldn't arrange it?"

"Well . . ."

"I'm joking," Dr. Cresida said with another tiny smile.

"Joking or not," Geary said, "I have reason to believe Dr. Macadams has already encountered some difficulties of his own. He may not be as big a roadblock anymore."

"He's not dead, though?" General Charban asked, sounding disappointed.

"Probably not," Geary said. "Dr. Cresida, will you continue to work with the others here on trying to understand the Dancers?" She wasn't, strictly speaking, under his command. He couldn't order her to do anything unless it pertained to the safety of others.

To his relief, Dr. Cresida nodded.

"This problem intrigues me," she said. "I am willing to work with my colleagues to try to develop more questions aimed at gaining indirect knowledge of the Dancers."

"Colleagues?" John Senn grinned. "I'm not used to hearing that word. Am I really a colleague?"

"Yes," Cresida said. "Even though you are but an historian. 'A friend should bear their friend's infirmities.'"

Lieutenant Jamenson gazed at her in astonishment. "You're quoting Shakespeare?"

"'I contain multitudes,'" Dr. Cresida said, her expression totally serious.

With time closing down to when they'd leave the hypernet, Geary and Desjani left the others to continue the discussion. As they walked down the passageway Tanya suddenly spoke up, her voice wistful. "There were times in there where Dr. Cresida felt more like her sister, Jaylen. She's a lot easier to like when that happens."

"I never had a chance to get to know Jaylen Cresida all that well," Geary said.

"It's your loss, believe me. Jaylen was interested in *everything*. And when you were around her that sort of rubbed off a bit, and you found yourself looking up stuff like indigenous peoples' mythologies back on Old Earth. I wonder what she and Dr. Cresida were like as girls. They probably sat around discussing Shakespeare and . . . what was that guy's name . . . Einstein." Desjani looked back toward the conference room. "How do you suppose she figured out that bit about the Dancers? Because it's great. I freely admit that. But how is it she can understand intelligent aliens better than our experts?"

"Maybe because she's not an expert," Geary said, giving a sidelong look at one portion of bulkhead as they passed. The spots damaged by Desjani's shots at the intruder in a stealth suit had all been repaired, leaving no sign of the event. Ensign Duellos had said she'd had no advance knowledge that an assassin would target him. He desperately wanted to believe that. "I admit to wondering how humanity had developed experts on intelligent aliens when we just confirmed their existence a few years ago. But Dr. Cresida wasn't trained in that, so she came into this without any preconceived theories, or models, she might say. All she wanted was the Dancers' answers to some questions in quantum mechanics. But she was well-rounded enough to spot a lot more in the answers than the Dancers may have intended."

"She was right about Macadams, too," Desjani conceded. "I'm glad you think he's being sidelined, and I'd love to hear what you did to bring that about. Please don't claim you know nothing about it. But since he's still a threat in being I'm sure you won't have any trouble finding volunteers if you want to bring about that fatal accident for him."

"Very funny. As soon as we leave the hypernet I need to talk to Ambassador Rycerz about this."

"Good idea," Desjani said, nodding to Master Chief Gioninni as he came down the passageway before putting two fingers to her eyes and pointing them at the master chief. Gioninni affected an expression of affronted innocence as he passed them. "Ambassador Rycerz will probably enthusiastically endorse the fatal accident idea for Macadams."

"Tanya . . ."

"Yes, Admiral. I'll make sure comms is ready to link you to *Boundless* on a secure circuit as soon as we drop out of jump. Oh, Master Chief!"

Gioninni turned and snapped a brisk salute. "Yes, Captain?"

"If you wanted to hide something and you had your choice of any type of ship in the fleet to hide it on, which type would you pick?"

"Captain!" Master Chief Gioninni feigned bafflement at the question. "Why would I—?"

"Just assume you want to, Master Chief," Desjani said. "What type of ship?"

"A battleship, of course," Gioninni said. "Really big. Lots of compartments, lots of storage. Speaking purely theoretically, you understand, Captain."

"I do," Desjani said. "Thank you, Master Chief." As a relieved

Gioninni continued on his way, she looked at Geary. "We've been telling everybody to search *Boundless*."

"Which is also big and full of compartments and storage," Geary said. "It never occurred to us to search any of the battleships." He shook his head. "But I don't know how to do that without tipping off the wrong people."

"No," Desjani conceded. "Anything . . . inappropriate . . . would be hidden from a routine inspection. But, like you said, it never occurred to us that we might be wrong to focus on *Boundless*." She paused, frowning. "And that makes me wonder about one other thing." Desjani glanced backward again toward the compartment holding the alien-modified transmitter. "When Dr. Cresida said the Dancers saw the universe in a way that was wrong, she said they might not have any choice. That they saw it in the way they had to see it."

"Right," Geary said. "And?"

"That implies we do the same thing. Like with *Boundless* and our battleships. What is it humans have to see when we look at the universe, things that other species might look at and wonder how we could get it so wrong? And just like humans can see and accept quantum uncertainty where the Dancers can't, what might the Dancers be seeing that we're not?"

He inhaled sharply as the implications hit him. "That's a very good and a very disturbing question. I wonder why Dr. Cresida didn't think of it?"

"I think she did," Desjani said. "But she avoided bringing it up because saying that might have made us defensively question her other ideas. Dr. Cresida might not seem like she understands people, but when it comes to getting them to think, she knows what she's doing." Tanya's lips twisted in a self-mocking smile. "Maybe that's also what sentient species do. We learn how to get other members of our species to do things we want."

"That's not something I was ever very good at," Geary said.

"Is that what you think?" She shook her head, still smiling. "At least you know how to listen to those better at it than you, then."

◊

AN hour later the fleet left the Dancer hypernet. Unlike leaving jump, which temporarily scrambled human brains, leaving the hypernet was not simply painless but impossible to feel. One moment the fleet's displays showed literally nothing outside the ships, and the next the stars flared brightly all around.

"Wherever they took us looks big," Desjani commented, her eyes on her display.

Geary nodded wordlessly as he also watched data rapidly appearing. The first thing he took note of was how many Dancer ships were near the hypernet gate and thus near his fleet. He'd have to pay particular attention from now on to any Dancers within weapons range of any of his battleships. But the closest Dancer ships were the four that had escorted them here through the Dancer hypernet, and those were already accelerating onto a new vector, fortuitously opening the distance between themselves and the human ships.

The second thing was something usually far down the priority list when arriving in a new star system, which was checking the status updates pouring in from his own ships to show any internal events or changes during the transit. To his relief, *Warspite* reported no significant events. Ensign Duellos was still all right.

Reassured on both of those counts, Geary turned his attention to this star system. The information being compiled by the fleet's sensors supported the hope that this would be an important Dancer-controlled star system. The hypernet gate they'd arrived at was, as usual for such gates, positioned a good distance from the star, four and a half light hours out in this case. Twelve planets, two of them habitable, though one was at extremes for humanlike life-forms, and hundreds of orbiting facilities ranging from city-sized to smaller factories and even smaller single-use habitats. Hundreds of ships wove their ways between worlds and orbiting facilities, or were moving from or toward the three jump points the star system held.

There was too little known about the Dancers to be able to extrapolate a firm number from all of that, but the fleet's systems offered up a guess. "Population at least five billion," Geary said. "If this isn't the Dancers' capital, it's something close to that in importance. Ambassador Rycerz must be very happy." Reminded by that, he touched his controls to send the ambassador the summary he'd thrown together of what Dr. Cresida had suggested about how the Dancers thought.

He still hadn't decided how, or how much, he'd tell the ambassador about the conspiracy within the fleet.

An alert sounded as the sensors keyed on something unexpected. A different group of spaceships was coming into view of the fleet from where it was orbiting one of the star system's gas giant worlds. "Taon?"

"Looks like it," Desjani said. "Six of them. All of them the smaller ones about the size of our light cruisers."

"Should we try to send them a message again?" Geary asked, speaking as much to himself as to Desjani.

"Isn't that the ambassador's call, Admiral?"

"It is."

A call from General Charban came in. "Admiral, the Dancer ships with us have sent us a message requesting that we follow them in-system."

"Tell them we'll be happy to do so," Geary said, relieved to hear that the fleet wouldn't again be stuck in a distant orbit while the Dancers decided what to do with them. "As soon as they steady on a vector, we'll match it."

Shortly thereafter, Geary ordered the fleet to turn "starboard" toward the star, and slightly "up" toward the plane in which the planet's stars orbited. The Dancers were leading them on a vector that formed a broad arc swooping through the star system until it intersected in its orbit the Dancer-inhabited planet seven and a half light minutes from the star. The Dancer ships escorting them continued moving at point zero eight light speed, so Geary kept his ships at that velocity as well, not trying to close the distance opened by the Dancers' earlier maneuvers. No one should notice or comment on that since protocol for being escorted by alien spacecraft hadn't exactly been firmed up yet.

"On this vector it will be fifty-seven hours until we reach the planet," Lieutenant Castries reported.

Roughly two and a half days. Two and a half days to wonder when and how the conspirators would act. And to wonder how many Dancer ships would be passing near whatever orbit the four escorting ships led Geary's fleet to.

With nothing left to do on the bridge, Geary headed for his stateroom. To his surprise, Desjani followed. It wasn't like her to leave the bridge so soon after arriving in a new star system. "What's happening?"

"Nothing, yet," she said. "I hate giving the other guy the initiative. Waiting to see what they'll do."

"Me, too," Geary said. "But what else can we do?"

"I talked to someone about that," Desjani said. She looked behind her.

Kommodor Bradamont had also been on the bridge of *Dauntless* for the arrival here, and now was following Geary and Desjani at a discreet distance. "You told her?" Geary said, surprised. "Why didn't you ask me first?"

"I used my initiative while you were busy with other things," Desjani said.

Frowning, unhappy at having Bradamont brought into this without his approval beforehand, Geary led the way into his stateroom.

Before he could say anything, Desjani nodded to Bradamont. "Tell him, Honore."

"First of all, Admiral," Bradamont said, "thank you for trusting me with this information. I'm glad that you realize I am still loyal to the best interests of the Alliance."

Geary managed not to shoot a glare at Desjani for not letting him know that Bradamont thought he'd agreed to this. "This is a very difficult situation," he finally said.

"I think I can help," Kommodor Bradamont said.

Mentally climbing down off his high horse, Geary gestured to a seat. "Please do so."

He and Bradamont sat facing each other, while Tanya Desjani chose to remain standing. "I guess this does feel like something from a drama about Syndics," Geary said.

"More than you realize," Bradamont replied. "Unless the Alliance fleet has changed a great deal since I left it, odds are your errant battleship commanders are a minority among the battleships. So unless they plan to martyr themselves as part of starting a war with the Dancers, they'll want to have plausible cover for their actions and a means to not just neutralize the other battleships but to bring in with them commanders who would not knowingly commit actions contrary to your orders."

"Knowingly?" Geary asked, keying on that word.

"I was told all about certain things I needed to watch for when I was given command within Midway's forces. The Syndicate has a long-standing problem with what they call False Face Operations. When someone wants to discredit another Syndicate officer or leader, or manufacture evidence to use against someone, they'll create false orders or other documents, including videos created to apparently show that person giving the false orders." Bradamont paused. "This malware that's going to be employed. I think, based on similar situations among the Syndicate that I was briefed on, that it will only be employed against those ships believed likely to not follow the false orders. *Dreadnaught*, for example. Or *Colossus*. And *Dauntless*, of course, to silence you during that critical time after the false orders are sent. The hope will be that enough other ships will fall for the false orders and help carry them out."

"Giving the people who started it cover among the ones who acted because they thought the orders were real," Desjani said.

"Exactly," Bradamont said. "But you don't have to wait for them to decide it's time to act. You can set up things so it looks like the perfect time for them to act, when in fact you're trying to trigger their actions at the time of your choosing." She smiled. "Hideki . . . excuse me, Colonel Rogero told me of a time when General Drakon suspected he was about to be set up by a False Face Op. He staged an accident that supposedly incapacitated him, and when the saboteurs set off the False Face he was there monitoring everything, able to immediately counteract the fake orders, and nail those who'd sought to take him out."

Geary nodded, frowning again, this time in thought. "How would we set up that bait in this case?"

Kommodor Bradamont rubbed the back of her neck as she considered the question. "You'd have to arrange some means of plausibly being out of contact for a while, and you'd have to set it up well in advance. These are battleship captains. They're not going to jump quickly on a momentary advantage. They have to have plenty of advance notice so they can decide to act and put their plans in motion."

Desjani laughed. "Sure. All we have to do is set it up so the admiral will apparently be out of contact with the fleet for a while, and make it look like we planned for that to happen well in advance."

"I never said it'd be easy," Bradamont said. "Someone already tried to kill him, though. Maybe say another assassin hurt him badly . . . ?"

Geary shook his head. "That might generate a lot of additional problems. And if all of the assassins have come from the same source, they'd know they hadn't done it and might be extra suspicious. Nonetheless, I'm grateful for your warning and your advice. If anything else occurs to you, please contact me."

"Yes, sir." Bradamont stood up, but hesitated. "Am I authorized to share this information with Colonel Rogero?"

Geary considered that before shaking his head again. "Not yet."

"I understand." She paused once more. "I'm pretty certain that his advice would be to make use of whoever your source is to set up the bait. Feed the source misinformation to pass on."

"That sounds risky for the source," Geary said.

"It would be. You'd have to be willing to sacrifice the source." She must have seen the reaction Geary wasn't able to completely hide. "I understand that might be a hard decision to make."

After Bradamont had left, Geary sat gazing at one wall. *This would be a lot easier if the source were someone other than Arwen Duellos*, he thought. Then winced internally at the thought that he'd more willingly risk the life of someone else, as if they counted for less than she did even though they'd also be someone's daughter or son, perhaps someone's spouse, or someone's mother or father. Yet he had to admit that's exactly how he felt even as he sought reasons not to make such an awful choice. "The conspirators probably wouldn't believe anything Ensign Duellos told them. They'd wonder how a junior officer would be privy to such information."

Tanya Desjani spoke slowly. "It would be plausible if Ensign Duellos heard the information from her father. It would be plausible that you'd tell Captain Duellos something like that, though we'd have to urge him to share it with his daughter without saying why and . . ." She broke off, grimacing. "I hate myself for even thinking of that."

"I didn't hear it," Geary said. As if in punishment for his lie, an urgent alert sounded on his room's comm panel. "A message from Captain Plant on *Warspite*." As he reached for the command to accept the message, his mind quickly came up with a dozen horrible reasons why *Warspite* would be sending him a special high-security message.

Tanya waited, her posture tense, as the image of Captain Plant appeared. "Admiral, I have information I thought you should receive as soon as possible," Plant began in a manner that didn't carry any hint of tragic news. "First off, I had the opportunity for a couple of more counseling sessions with Ensign Duellos. I confirmed to my satisfaction that she was indeed lured into the conspiracy by appeals to her patriotism and claims that the conspirators were actually working under the table for you. That explains why she came to me when she realized the conspiracy was in reality aimed at you."

Plant gestured to one side. "Ensign Duellos gave me access to the comms being used by the conspirators. The message feeds are hidden in routine fleet network traffic. Supposedly, Ensign Duellos is one of six in a covert cell, of which nine cells exist aboard *Warspite*."

"You'd think she'd be more upset to hear that," Desjani said. "More than seventy sailors on her ship engaged in subversion?"

Plant's composure did seem strange, but her next words explained the oddity.

"I had my most trusted and skilled code monkey aboard *Warspite* go over Ensign Duellos's information," Plant said. "All of those in it are represented by avatars, and it is the opinion of that expert that the great majority of the avatars do not in fact represent real people. They bear signs of being fronts for artificial intelligence programs mimicking human responses. In my expert's assessment, only perhaps seven of the avatars at most are fronts for real personnel aboard *Warspite*. It's certainly possible that on other ships that aren't as well-run as *Warspite* there's a higher percentage of real lower-level conspirators, but on my ship at least it is very likely the leaders are misleading their own followers about the popularity of and support for their efforts.

"Ensign Duellos will notify us the moment she receives the malware, and is aware of the danger she is currently facing if her cooperation with fleet authorities is discovered. I will await further instructions. To the honor of our ancestors. Plant, out."

Desjani let out a short laugh, sounding relieved. "Trust Plant to put in a dig against ships that aren't as well-run as her ship. This is good news. The senior personnel involved can still cause a lot of damage, but they don't have the sort of widespread backup among the crews that we feared."

"It looks like that," Geary said, rubbing his eyes as he took in the information. "But she may well be right that ships like Burdock's *Encroach* have more real conspirators in the crew. We can't be complacent." Something else occurred to him, causing his jaw to tighten. "Plant wasn't able to identify who the real sailors involved in this aboard her ship are. Which means Arwen Duellos could still be targeted by any of them."

"Or another assassin in a stealth suit who came from a different ship," Desjani said. "How can we set up a bait situation without making Ensign Duellos part of the bait and therefore one of the targets?"

"Let's hope we can figure that out."

AMBASSADOR Rycerz called about an hour after the arrival at the new star system, looking calm and conspiratorial. "It's all looking good, Admiral. I wanted to ensure you knew that I now control the Dancer-modified transmitter aboard *Boundless*."

Geary had taken the call in his stateroom, hoping that he'd figure out a means to tell Rycerz about the latest development. "Did something happen to Dr. Macadams?" he asked, hoping that he was projecting surprise about that.

"Dr. Macadams is confined to his stateroom," Ambassador Rycerz said, smiling. "By order of Colonel Webb on grounds of security matters. Sadly, I cannot overrule Colonel Webb on security matters."

"That's a shame," Geary said.

"The majority of Dr. Macadams's staff are willing to work under different supervision," Rycerz continued. "But they need lessons and examples of how to communicate with the Dancers in ways that are actually effective. I'm requesting permission for them to speak directly with General Charban and his staff."

"I gladly grant permission for that," Geary said. "General Charban has wanted to discuss those matters with Macadams's people for some time. He'll be happy to finally be able to pass on some of his information. Speaking of which, I'm assuming you reviewed the message about the way the Dancers think that I sent you on arrival here?"

"Yes." Ambassador Rycerz looked vaguely unhappy. "It might be useful, but it's only speculation."

"I thought it was a very important insight," Geary said, taken aback by the ambassador's lack of enthusiasm.

"Speculation," Rycerz repeated. "Dr. Cresida is a brilliant physicist.

She's not a behavioral scientist. There are big differences between how the universe works and how people work."

"Physicists are people, too," Geary said. "And I believe that Dr. Cresida has not confined her interests to one field."

"Perhaps." Ambassador Rycerz offered a smile that seemed aimed more at mollifying Geary's feelings than expressing any agreement. "For now, let's focus on what we can learn about communicating better with the Dancers. I'll be in touch. Please route any future communications with the Dancers through me."

Unhappy to have had a hopeful insight discounted, he decided to try another tack. "I'd like to try contacting the Taon ships in this star system," Geary said.

Rycerz shook her head. "Not yet. We need to concentrate on the Dancers. We can look into the Taon after we've gotten things running with the Dancers. That's my mission, and my priority."

Increasingly unhappy with this conversation, Geary decided to shift topics again. "I need to speak with you about other matters."

"We are speaking," the ambassador said.

"These are matters requiring the highest security," Geary said. "In light of concerns about communications, I thought another in-person meeting aboard *Dauntless* would be wise."

Rycerz pursed her lips, then shook her head. "I don't think it would be wise for me to leave *Boundless* at such a critical juncture of our negotiations with the Dancers," she said, apparently deliberately echoing Geary's words.

"Then I'll find another means to get the information to you," Geary said. He sat glaring at his display after the ambassador's image had vanished. Her position much more secure, the ambassador was asserting her authority again.

Not wanting to put off the inevitable, he called Charban. "I have good news and bad news, General."

"Oh, how about the good news for a change?" Charban replied.

"Dr. Macadams no longer controls the transmitter on *Boundless*.

Members of his former staff should be contacting you directly for advice on communicating effectively with the Dancers."

"That is good," Charban said, visibly surprised. "It's great. What's the bad news?"

"Now that she controls the transmitter, Ambassador Rycerz wants all communications with the Dancers routed through her."

Charban nodded, smiling crookedly. "That didn't take long, did it? We're no longer necessary except to pass on what we know and get out of the way. What if the Dancers don't want to deal exclusively with *Boundless*? Am I supposed to ignore any messages sent to us here on *Dauntless*?"

"No," Geary said. "We'll prepare replies to any messages sent specifically to us, and forward them to *Boundless* with the provision that unless otherwise directed we will transmit them ourselves."

"I love that 'unless otherwise directed' thing," Charban said. "It keeps things from being ignored or bureaucratically bottled up. All right. We have our orders. Thank you, Admiral."

"Thank *you*, General." Whatever else happened, he wasn't going to let General Charban be sidelined.

THE ambassador had expressed her wishes to Geary about communicating with the Taon ships, but five hours later Geary learned that the Taon had their own ideas in that area.

"I think you want to be on the bridge," Tanya Desjani said. "We have a message coming in from an unknown source. It conforms to the video formats used by the Dancers, so we can view it, and appears to originate from near the gas giant closest to the star. That gas giant is where the Taon are," she added. "I can forward it to you in your stateroom if you prefer."

"Hold on until I get to the bridge," Geary said. He moved quickly, but not so quickly that sailors observing him would think anything was wrong or danger threatened. In fact, things were wrong and danger did threaten, but from within the fleet. He didn't want word going around that he believed the Taon were a danger, because as far as he knew they weren't.

Yet.

Once on the bridge and in the fleet command seat, he nodded to Desjani. "All right, Captain," Geary said, bracing himself for the worst (open hostility) and hoping for the best (friendly overtures) from the Taon. "Accept the message."

FOURTEEN

A window opened on his display as well as on Desjani's, revealing a brief burst of pixelization before steadying into an image.

Instead of numerous beings on a large bridge or control deck, he saw an image of a creature seated alone in what seemed to be a small compartment whose walls were lined with controls and displays. The creature gave the impression of being broadly built, the head seeming to rest almost directly on the shoulders, numerous bony ridges and protrusions marking the head. Two bony ridges coming down a short distance from the jaws might mark vestiges of what were originally neck-protecting shields. The skin had a gray cast to it, and any hair must be too fine to be apparent.

But the arrangement of sensory organs was familiar enough, with large eyes on top, a fluttering flap of skin revealing the triple slit of a nose beneath the eyes, and on the bottom a wide mouth currently open in a broad oval showing no teeth.

"Dr. Shwartz once told me," Geary said, "that the nearly universal arrangement of organs we see is because it just makes sense. A creature wants eyes set as high as possible, able to view what's being eaten and to avoid being eaten, and without risk of anything from the mouth or nose falling into them. The smelling organ should be near the mouth, and since scent rises placing it just above the mouth works best. And of course the mouth lowest down so whatever falls out won't hinder the other organs."

"I guess something that evolved in really low gravity might look different," Desjani said, gazing without visible emotion at the image on her own display. "Any idea what they're waiting for?"

"No. I wonder what their language sounds like?"

Almost as if having waited for that prompt, the image began speaking, the words they heard coming with perhaps a second's delay after mouth movements that didn't match the human language sounds. "Happy welcome, human."

"They have a translator for our language?" Geary said, astounded. "Can we tell what their real language sounds like?"

"All that's coming through on audio is words in our language," the comms watch reported.

The new alien was still speaking, the understandable words still coming out of sync with the mouth movements so it looked like a badly dubbed video. "Taon happy meet human. Welcome."

"Is Taon that one's name, or the name of their species?" Desjani wondered.

The answer came on the heels of her question as the alien kept speaking. "Lokaa of Taon. Leader. Come Taon star. Bring all ships. Come Taon."

"What?" Geary said, once again surprised.

"Taon welcome human! Be friend. Come Taon. Bring all ships!"

Lokaa made a pursing motion with their lips. Moments later the transmission ended.

Desjani shook her head, looking baffled. "Hi," she said, "we just met and I love you. Please bring your big fleet of warships to one of our star systems. Are they serious?"

Geary rested his cheek against one fist as he gazed at his own display. "Apparently. They know enough of our language to have programmed a translator, so they must know something about humanity."

"Maybe, but if they do, that's my point," Desjani insisted. "If they know anything about people, why would they invite a big fleet of us armed with lots of weapons to their star system? They must know how dangerous we can be, and they don't know whether we're Syndics, or Alliance, or from Old Earth, or even from those Shield of Sol idiots who settled stars past Old Earth toward the edge of the galaxy."

"I think this is where Victoria Rione would be saying they must want something from us."

"And this is where I'd do what I rarely did and agree with her." Desjani raised an eyebrow at him. "You don't think the ambassador will jump feetfirst into this, do you?"

"I'll have to ask her," Geary said. "But she didn't want to deal with the Taon instead of focusing totally on the Dancers. Is that secure channel to the ambassador still set up?"

"Set up and ready to go, Admiral. But you might want to talk to her in your stateroom."

Remembering his last talk with the ambassador, Geary had no trouble realizing the wisdom of that suggestion. He went back to his stateroom, sat down, took a moment to center himself, and then called.

Ambassador Rycerz answered quickly, appearing slightly annoyed. "I assume this is about the communication from the Taon. They're certainly enthusiastic, aren't they?"

"Very enthusiastic," Geary said.

"Why did they message us this time? Had you already sent them a message before you asked me?"

He paused before answering to make sure he didn't sound annoyed himself at the question. "Ambassador, it would have been physically impossible for a message from me to reach the Taon and for them to send a reply in the time that has passed since we arrived in this star system. That would require a minimum turnaround of six and a half hours from our current location."

"I see. That's right." Rycerz looked like she'd tasted something sour. "We're finally in a position to make real progress with the Dancers. I don't need this distraction."

"This is a new intelligent species," Geary said. "One that seems to be happy to see us. I wouldn't call that a distraction so much as an opportunity."

"Admiral, my job here is to establish firm relations with the Dancers." Rycerz grimaced, running one hand through her hair. "I am not authorized to do anything else. I *can't* go to Taon space. My instructions are clear that I am to go to Dancer space and *stay there*."

"That doesn't mean we can't talk to them here," Geary said.

"Talk to them." Rycerz shook her head. "How can they speak our language?"

"I don't know."

"How will they respond if we reject their invitation? We know nothing about them or their customs. For all we know, that level of fervent welcome is expected in their culture and anything less would be insulting. They might regard a rejection as even more insulting!"

"How are you going to respond?" Geary asked, dumping it all in her lap rather than saying "I don't know" again.

Rycerz sat back, spreading her hands in the age-old gesture of helplessness. "My orders do not permit me to take *Boundless* to Taon. I am required to reach Dancer space and stay in Dancer space, if they permit that, until relieved by a subsequent diplomatic mission."

"*Boundless* is not the only Alliance ship here," Geary said. "Why couldn't some of our other ships go to Taon?" He made a face himself as his own words hit home. "It would be risky, since we know nothing about the Taon except that they have peaceful relations with the Dancers."

Rycerz gave him a flat look. "And risky because I can't go, so you'd be the one making the initial contact with this species."

"Is that such a bad thing?" he asked, feeling once again on the defensive.

"I'm not . . ." Rycerz sighed heavily, slumping a bit. "Admiral, first contact is a very delicate matter. There are a tremendous number of things that can go wrong."

Once again, his sense of humor came to Geary's rescue. "Ambassador, it wasn't so long ago that I and this fleet were being sent into alien space specifically to establish contact with the enigmas and anyone else we found."

"So far relations with the enigmas aren't an endorsement for that decision. And the other species, the . . ."

"The Kicks," Geary said. "If our first contact with the Kicks had been a diplomatic mission, they'd have died before they could escape. I will remind you that we also established relations with the Dancers and managed to do that successfully enough that they aided us at both Midway and at Unity Alternate."

Rycerz gazed at him for a long moment before nodding. "Fair enough, Admiral. Fair enough. How do you believe we should respond to the Taon? Before you answer, I think we need to be careful about rejecting their invitation."

He had to take a few seconds to think about that. "You, and *Boundless*, have to stay here. I wouldn't want you to be left unprotected as of yet since the Dancers haven't agreed to let *Boundless* remain, or even offered any guarantees of safety for you. And, frankly, since we know so little of the Taon, any ships sent in response to the Taon invitation would be at risk of not returning. If the Dancers end up rejecting our request to establish an embassy, you would need a strong escort for *Boundless* back through enigma space."

"This Lokaa invited all of your ships," Rycerz pointed out.

"But we already know that's impossible," Geary said.

"Then instead of rejecting the invitation outright and possibly causing a serious incident, why not send only a portion of your fleet?"

"I can't—" He couldn't trust the security on this line, so he couldn't tell her that he couldn't run such a risk given the threat within the fleet from the conspirators. But at the same time he faced that dilemma, he heard Bradamont's voice in his memory. *You'd have to arrange some means of plausibly being out of contact for a while, and you'd have to set it up well in advance.*

Did he dare take such a risk? It would give the conspirators an apparently perfect opportunity, what should be irresistible bait, but he wouldn't be present to ensure they were stopped. Could he trust whoever was left here to handle such a critical matter? "I need to discuss this with my senior ship commanders."

"Let me know what you decide," the ambassador said, clearly happy to dump a matter outside of her assigned mission back into Geary's lap.

All right, then. This was his ball to run with. "In the meantime, we can ask the Taon for more information about themselves," Geary added. "And we can ask the Dancers for more information about the Taon. That is, if I am permitted to." It wasn't just a matter of getting a dig in, but also stretching whatever boundaries the ambassador was trying to establish on his ability to talk directly to the Dancers.

"Just send your proposed message through me," Rycerz said, looking pained. "Didn't the Dancers already tell us something about the Taon?"

"Yes," Geary said. "At the last star system the Dancer reply to our questions about the Taon was answered with 'Ships are Taon.' That's it."

"Oh, yes." Rycerz closed her eyes as if the words were inciting a headache. "Which means everything if you know what Taon are, and nothing if you don't. Still, they're here in Dancer-controlled space. They apparently conducted some trade activity at the last star system we were in. That tells us something."

"It tells us they're able to get along with the Dancers," Geary said. "Whether that means they can get along with us as well remains to be seen."

AN hour later, Geary found himself once more in the fleet conference room, but this time only the fleet's senior captains were present in virtual form, along with General Carabali, Colonel Rogero, and Kommodor Bradamont. Geary had just replayed the message from Lokaa of Taon for them. "All right. I need advice, suggestions, insight. Go."

Captain Jane Geary, her chin resting on one hand, shook her head. "This sets off so many alarms. Like, 'Hi, we just met, we're friends, come visit with all of your warships.' Really?"

"That was my reaction," Desjani said.

"That sort of . . . effusive behavior might be normal among them," Captain Badaya pointed out. "It might be regarded as simply polite."

"That was Ambassador Rycerz's reaction," Geary said. "And it may be true. But we have no way of knowing."

"I wouldn't want my daughter spending any time with a human male who acted like that on their first encounter," Captain Duellos said. He paused for just a moment before continuing, as if he had noticed the reaction his words created in Geary. "But this is an alien of a new and unknown species. We don't know what normal is for them."

"It is a nice change," Badaya said. "I mean, thus far two out of three alien species we've contacted have simply wanted to kill us. The third might be friends. Maybe the fourth, these Taon, might be as well."

"When did you become so trusting?" Captain Desjani wondered.

"I'm just saying it's a nice change of pace not to be threatened with death on first contact."

Captain Armus snorted. "I must agree with Captain Badaya as far as it goes. The question is whether the Taon are sincere."

"Admiral, are you seriously considering the invitation?" Jane Geary asked.

Geary shook his head. "Not in terms of all of our ships. *Boundless* has to remain here. Since we have to face the possibility that the Taon invitation is a trap, and any ships sent in response may not return, we need to leave enough ships with *Boundless* to get her and themselves home if necessary."

Captain Smythe sighed theatrically before taking a drink of what was supposedly only coffee. Since Smythe was only present in virtual form and could get away with drinking anything he wanted to, Geary suspected it might be something stronger than even fleet coffee. "Admiral, normally I'd be advising to bring at least half of the auxiliaries. However, I sense considerable unease among the rest of your officers regarding this invitation. If there's concern that you might need to hastily depart Taon space, you might not want auxiliaries slowing you down."

"There's wisdom in that," Captain Duellos said.

"What about your Marines and their transports?" Geary asked General Carabali.

Carabali made a face as she gazed at the image of Lokaa of Taon. "Depending on what the Dancers tell us, I can't see what possible use a large force of Marines would be to you. And the transports would slow you down somewhat. Not as badly as the auxiliaries, but they would slow you down."

Captain Armus shook his head, his voice a low rumble that perfectly matched the battleship he commanded. "If you leave that much behind, the auxiliaries and the transports, then you need to leave at least one division of battleships as well to protect them." He looked at Geary, making it clear the idea of leaving behind a single division of battleships concerned him.

"If we're thinking we might have to make a quick exit from Taon space," Duellos said, "why bring any battleships? They're unmatched in a fight, but we won't be wanting a battle, will we?"

Why bring any battleships? Duellos had, without any coaching, suggested exactly what Geary had been thinking. He nodded toward an alarmed-looking Captain Armus to let him know not to object.

"If it's a trap," Captain Hiyen of the battleship *Reprisal* said, "it must be assumed it was well prepared. I agree that any force sent in response to this invitation would want the maximum possible speed and maneuverability."

"You wouldn't insist on being included to represent the Callas Republic?" Geary asked.

Hiyen shook his head, frowning. "Like Ambassador Rycerz, my orders pertain to the Dancers. Otherwise I am supposed to employ my ship as ordered by you, sir."

Captain Duellos's hand moved as he worked with something on the table in front of him aboard the battle cruiser *Inspire*. "All of the battle cruisers, I'd suggest. As well as half of the light cruisers and half of the destroyers."

"You think we should leave all of the heavy cruisers here?" Geary asked.

"Do you want to plan for a battle, or for an escape, Admiral? I think," Duellos added, with a wave toward Captain Hiyen, "that my fellow captains are right that any trap would be designed to overwhelm any force we brought with us."

"Which means planning for an escape," Desjani said.

The sudden appearance of General Charban's virtual presence drew attention to him. "The Dancers may be aware of the message sent to us by the Taon. We just received something from them about the Taon."

"More information?" Geary said, feeling hopeful.

"Not . . . exactly." Charban paused, looking at a transcript he was holding.

"Taon are Taon,

"Taon are always Taon,

"Must remember this."

After a moment of silence, Tanya Desjani spoke. "Is that supposed to tell us anything?"

"It says Taon are Taon," General Charban replied with a hapless shrug.

Armus glowered at nothing in particular. "What are they saying with such vague things? Does it mean there's something we have to learn that they can't tell us? That we have to figure it out for ourselves?"

Captain Badaya leaned back, his eyes on the overhead. "I had a math teacher like that once. 'You have to work it out for yourselves,' she'd say. And I'd say, 'If I could work it out for myself, then I wouldn't need to be in this class in the first place, now would I?'"

"Everyone," Geary said as others laughed at Badaya's remark, "we have a theory that the Dancers may have a very precise goal in mind in terms of what they want from us. But in order to get us to that goal, they have to avoid telling us what to do." He explained more of Dr. Cresida's theory, the others listening intently.

"Who came up with this?" Captain Jane Geary asked.

"Dr. Cresida," Geary said.

"Jaylen's sister?"

"Yes."

"That's good enough for me," Duellos said, inspiring a chorus of agreement from the others that was a testament to how admired Jaylen Cresida still was within the fleet. "But do these very specific Dancer goals have anything to do with the Taon? Has Dr. Cresida looked at their message yet?"

Geary looked to Charban, who nodded.

"She read it in the same manner as someone watching a shipwreck," Charban said. "I asked her opinion afterwards and her reply was that she had insufficient information."

"Why don't we simply ask the Dancers whether we should go?" Badaya said. "I hate to be blunt, but why not be direct about it? Should we go? Is it dangerous? If the Dancers have some very specific goal they're aiming for they have to give us a clearer answer."

"*You* hate to be blunt?" Desjani said, giving him a level gaze. "Captain Badaya is right, though, Admiral. Let's not dance around this. Let's give the Dancers a direct question and see if they answer."

"That sounds like a good idea," Geary said. "General, please draft a message for the Dancers making sure they know that the Taon have invited us to bring our entire fleet to their territory. We want to know if the Dancers believe we should go. We have to know whether the Dancers believe that accepting the Taon invitation would involve danger to us."

"I will do so," Charban said. "Since this pertains to the fleet's security, I assume it can be sent directly?"

Geary took a moment to think about that. Charban was right that he could invoke the safety-of-the-fleet issue to insist on the right to continue communicating with the Dancers directly. But he wasn't ready to force the ambassador's hand. "Let me see it first."

"We should ask them about the Taon technology," Captain Armus added. "That translator of theirs. What we hear through it sounds sort of primitive, but they put it together without any actual human input. That's impressive in a way we need to take note of. Could we have done that with an alien language?"

"He's right," Duellos said. "If that translator is any guide the Taon may well be more technologically advanced than we are."

"Either that," Kommodor Bradamont said, "or they know a lot more about us than we know about them."

That brought about a long moment of silence, finally broken by Captain Jane Geary. "That could put a different spin on their motivation for the invite, wouldn't it?"

"Especially," Bradamont said, "if, like the enigmas, the Taon knowledge of and experience with humans is based on dealing with the Syndicate."

"Then it would definitely be a trap," Duellos said.

"It would certainly make it more likely," Bradamont said.

"Honore," Badaya said to Bradamont, "did the people at Midway have any knowledge that these Taon existed?"

"No," she said.

"Would they have told you?"

Bradamont's eyebrows went up and her mouth opened. Everyone watched, anticipating an explosion, except for Badaya, who seemed as oblivious as usual.

But Bradamont visibly calmed herself before replying. "Captain, I *am* one of the people at Midway. President Iceni would have told me if there was even a hint of another intelligent, space-faring species just beyond enigma space."

Colonel Rogero rubbed his chin. "I have been trying to remember anything in Syndicate records that might indicate any contact with the Taon. I don't recall anything, even in the files kept by the snakes. There were secret annexes covering the disastrous encounters with the enigmas, but nothing about any other species."

Armus gave Rogero a questioning look. "Why didn't the Syndics try probing more beyond their borders?"

"Because the enigmas were an invisible enemy who had already pushed the Syndicate out of two star systems, wiping out the human populations there," Rogero explained, "and repelling or destroying every Syndicate attempt to learn more. They seemed to be all-knowing, and impossible to defeat. That was, we now know, because of the quantum-coded worms they had placed in our sensor systems that blinded our ships to their presence and allowed the enigmas to know exactly what we were doing as soon as we did it. And, of course, there was the war with the Alliance, which consumed the attention and resources of the Syndicate."

"Colonel Rogero, Kommodor Bradamont, if we accept the Taon invitation," Geary said, "I'd be commanding whichever force went, and *Dauntless* would be part of that force." He made a small hand gesture to Captain Armus to prevent another startled reaction. "I don't know what your orders are from Midway regarding this situation, Kommodor. Are you like the ambassador and tied to Dancer space? Or would you want to be along when we went to Taon space?"

"We'd want to be along with you," Bradamont said without hesitating. "These species are far, far from home for the Alliance. They're on Midway's doorstep. Even the Taon. We need to know as much as we can, and if peaceful relations are established we need to ensure Midway is also covered."

"Fair enough," Geary said. "Are you all in agreement that we should leave the battleships, the Marines, and the auxiliaries here with *Boundless*?"

"I think there are other matters we need to discuss before agreeing on that," Captain Armus said.

"Those matters are part of this plan," Geary said.

"Are they?" Armus nodded slowly. "All right, then. If *all* factors have been taken into account."

"I want to modify my earlier advice," General Carabali said. "You might need some Marines. The Marine detachments on the battle cruisers are pretty small. I think we should reinforce those detachments to give you some better capability. And, in the same light, your standard fleet shuttles on the battle cruisers can handle lifts and drop-offs okay. But maybe it would be a good idea to swap some of them for stealth-configured shuttles."

"How many stealth shuttles do we have?" Geary asked. "Four, right?"

"Yes, with the Marine scouts," Carabali said. "I'd recommend taking two of the stealth-configured shuttles. That would give you some extra capability if you needed it, but leave some with us if we ran into trouble that required them."

"We'll swap them out with the regular shuttles on *Dauntless* and *Inspire*," Geary said. "I want everyone preparing for this operation even though we still have to wait on agreement from the Taon. Ambassador Rycerz wants to focus exclusively on the Dancers in accordance with her instructions. She's delegated dealing with Lokaa to me. That means the Taon are our problem. We don't know what their technology is like, we don't know how sincere their expressed friendliness is, we don't know whether this invitation to visit is a trap or not. But the potential benefits of establishing peaceful contact with another species are so large that we can't afford to pass up this opportunity. If the Taon are hostile, the sooner we learn it the better. If we go in to Taon space, it will be with our eyes open and our defenses ready."

"We have to learn more about them," Kommodor Bradamont said. "Whether they're dangerous or peaceful or somewhere between those things, we need to learn as much as we can. I'm saying that not as a representative of Midway, but as a representative of humanity as a whole."

No one disagreed, at least not openly, so Geary nodded to everyone. "Thank you. We're going to do this right." He had already made some adjustments to the meeting software, so that when Captain Smythe's and Captain Hiyen's virtual presences vanished, everyone else remained, the others looking at Geary in surprise. "Kommodor, Colonel, could you please allow this meeting to continue without you?"

"Certainly," Bradamont said, gesturing to Rogero.

As soon as they, too, had left the secure conference room, Geary looked at the others. "There's a critical matter of which some of you are already aware. The rest of you need to know of it." He quickly summarized what was known of the conspiracy, as Captains Duellos and Badaya and General Carabali listened with increasing concern.

"And you trust the source of this information?" Captain Badaya asked when Geary had finished.

"Yes," Geary said. "I don't want to reveal who the source is, but regard their information as absolutely reliable."

"Admiral," General Carabali said, her brow furrowed with worry, "you have a reputation for unconventional tactics, but . . . why leave the battleships when you go to the Taon if you're concerned some of their commanding officers are disloyal and plotting to start a war with the Dancers?"

"Because at this time the plotters have the initiative," Geary said. "They can decide when and where to act, without much if any warning. I want to give them a perfect opportunity to act, and have them know that opportunity is coming."

Captain Armus nodded, smiling. "I understand now. Captain Pelleas and Captain Burdock, and any others in league with them, will regard the admiral's departure as also being proof their plot is not suspected. They will be emboldened to act. And we will be ready, knowing they will choose that time."

"*You* will be ready," Geary said. "Captain Armus, I want you to know that I decided on this plan knowing that you would be in command in my absence."

As Captain Armus appeared to swell visibly with pride at the compliment, General Carabali nodded, her eyes hooded in thought. "The Marine detachments on the battleships will have to be ready to act. *Colossus* and *Dreadnaught* are definitely not a danger. Are there any others we can be sure of?"

"*Reprisal*," Tanya Desjani said. "They wouldn't let a commander from the Callas Republic in on this."

"And *Warspite*," Geary said. "Captain Plant is definitely loyal."

"I think also Captain Casia on *Conquerer*," Jane Geary said, "as well as Captain Cordoba on *Glorious*."

"That's six out of twenty battleships," Carabali noted. "We really can't be surer of how many others are in league with Pelleas and Burdock?"

"We can't ask them," Desjani said. "I'm certain that a lot more than six are dependable."

"Yes," Geary said. "That's why we think the plotters will use a fake order to lure in more ships. Those captains would believe they were following a real order, while the plotters could claim to have been fooled as well and be just as innocent of deliberate wrongdoing. Some other ships, such as *Warspite*, are supposed to be crippled by malware to prevent them from intervening. But we'll be ready for all that. Before I leave, I'll record orders telling everyone in the fleet not to fire on Dancer ships under any circumstances. Our source will be given a copy of the malware, but instead of planting it in their ship's systems will provide it to their commanding officer. By the time the plotters try to activate the malware our code monkeys should've worked out a counter for it. They'll broadcast their fake order from me, Captain Armus will see who responds immediately, and broadcast my real orders. Any commanding officer who does not respond to my real orders will be relieved of command by the Marine detachment aboard their ship."

"And the conspiracy will be thoroughly dismantled," Desjani said.

"I'd hoped the fleet was past these kinds of things," Carabali said, shaking her head.

"Not yet," Geary said. "The institutional damage caused by a century-long war isn't so easily put aside. But we will get past them someday, because the Alliance can count on officers such as all of you. I'll provide more detailed planning for all of you before I leave this star system."

"And bait the trap," Captain Armus said.

After the meeting ended and the virtual forms of most of the remaining participants vanished or left, Jane Geary and Roberto Duellos lingered. "When this goes down," Jane said, "no one is going to have any question about whether the other Gearys stand with Captain Armus."

"I never doubted that," Geary said. "Thank you, Captain."

Jane grinned and saluted before her virtual presence vanished.

That left Geary and Tanya Desjani alone with the virtual presence of Captain Duellos.

"Admiral," Duellos began, his voice carefully controlled, "you had a reaction when I mentioned Ensign Duellos earlier. Can you tell me whether she is in any particular danger as a result of this conspiracy? Perhaps because I'm seen as such a strong supporter of you?"

Geary looked at Desjani, who gazed back in a way that made it clear she wasn't going to try to influence his decision. Duellos had given him a perfect out for admitting to special peril for his daughter without disclosing her role in everything.

But he could not betray Duellos that way.

Geary sat down again, gesturing to Duellos to do the same. "It's more complicated than that."

"Does my daughter know who this source is?" Duellos asked, staying on his feet. "Is that why she is in danger?"

"Your daughter is the source," Geary said.

Roberto Duellos frowned in puzzlement. "You said the source was part of—" He stopped speaking, his face stricken. "Why?"

"They played on her patriotism," Desjani said, "pretending this was about supporting the Alliance, and the admiral. When she realized

what it was really about, she went to Captain Plant and disclosed everything."

"I see." Duellos seemed to have aged twenty years in a moment of
time. "Conspiring . . . against lawful authority . . . during combat operations."

"Which calls for the death penalty," Geary said, knowing why Duellos had said that. "Except in exceptional circumstances."

"You cannot play favorites, Admiral."

"This has nothing to do with playing favorites," Geary insisted,
standing up as well to emphasize his words. "If your daughter had been
caught being part of such a conspiracy, it would've been almost impossible to justify not ordering such a penalty. But she came forward. She
gave us the break we needed, the information we'd been looking for,
and if we successfully foil this conspiracy as we plan to it will be thanks
to her. *Those* are exceptional circumstances, Captain Duellos."

Duellos closed his eyes, breathing slowly, before finally looking at
Geary again. "How does Captain Plant feel about that?"

"She's been broadly hinting that Ensign Duellos deserves special
consideration for her contributions to taking down this conspiracy,"
Geary said.

Duellos sagged as if his muscles could no longer hold him. He finally sat, carefully, as if afraid of falling. "Plant and I have never been
close. And her reputation as the hardest captain in the fleet will work
against any claim of favoritism."

"Excuse me?" Tanya Desjani leaned in toward Duellos. "Who did
you say is the hardest captain in the fleet?"

"Plant is the *second*-hardest captain," Duellos said, managing to
muster a slight smile that quickly vanished. "This conspiracy . . . they
tried to kill the admiral."

"That's right," Geary said.

"Your daughter's life is in danger," Desjani said. "Not from the fleet.
From the same conspirators who killed that sailor and tried to kill the

admiral. If they learn that Ensign Duellos is telling us everything she knows . . ."

"They'll kill her." Captain Duellos sat silent and unmoving for several seconds. "Why can't we take her with us? Transfer her to any battle cruiser—"

"Ensign Duellos will let Captain Plant, and through her Captain Armus, know the moment she gets that malware," Geary said. "And turn it over to them. It's critical that she carries that out."

"Anything we do to protect her," Desjani said, "will focus attention on her. You know that, Roberto."

"Yes," Duellos said, sounding as if he was in pain. "As I know that Arwen must earn a pardon for her serious mistake in getting involved in this. The living stars demand great efforts to make up for great errors. But . . . she's my girl."

"Captain Plant will see that she's protected," Geary said, regretting the need to delegate that task to Plant rather than seeing to it himself. Didn't he owe that to Duellos? "Nothing can happen until the moment the plotters move. Then, the moment they realize their malware has been compromised, Ensign Duellos will be surrounded by a solid wall of Marines."

Duellos nodded, his movements still those of an old man. "It's hard to let go. I know she's already her own person. I'd hoped I taught her well about the dangers and the rights and wrongs of this universe, but . . ."

"She's doing the right thing," Geary said.

Another nod. "Ensigns make mistakes. It's what they do. I didn't expect a mistake quite this large."

Desjani spoke again. "She's making it right. She decided that on her own. She seems to be a lot like her father."

"I hope she's wiser than her father has ever been." Duellos nodded a third time, standing with careful movements. "I do understand why you couldn't tell me before this. Her best protection was keeping as few as possible aware. It's going to be hard saying goodbye to her before we jump for the Taon star, saying goodbye without letting on that anything unusual is happening. Thank you for informing me now, Admiral. I know you had every professional right to avoid doing so."

"Professionals look out for their people," Geary said. "Do you want to stay here? I can work out justifications for leaving the First Battle Cruiser Division here as backup for the battleships."

"No," Duellos said, his voice firm and his posture straightening. "My daughter has made a serious error, and is working on her own to make it right. She is her own person. I'm very worried about what might happen to her, but I should not create a situation in which it appears I might have been directing her." He glanced at Desjani. "Besides which, you might well need my battle cruisers at that Taon star. Professionals get the job done. In this, too, I have to be the role model my daughter deserves. Despite how hard that will be."

When Duellos had also departed, Geary looked at Tanya. "This discussion about responsibilities to a child reminded me of my great-nephew Michael never mentioning having children. But Jane Geary told me once that her brother Michael had three children, and when I asked Michael about that before he left it was . . . awkward."

Tanya shook her head. "I already told you that's something you need to ask Jane about."

"Do you know the answer? Why is this a mystery?"

"It's not a mystery. It's a tragedy. Ask Jane."

The last thing he wanted to spend time on right now was a personal matter, but he knew if he didn't follow up it would distract his every thought. With an exasperated grunt, Geary sat down and called Captain Jane Geary again.

When her virtual presence reappeared in the conference room, Jane gave him a curious look. "Is this about Captain Duellos? Did you tell him who the source was?"

"We told him who the source was," Geary said. "But this isn't about that. It's a personal matter. A family matter. You told me once that Michael had three children."

"Oh." Jane made a face and rubbed her forehead. She sat down in the matching conference room aboard *Dreadnaught*, appearing to sit opposite Geary. "I shouldn't have said anything."

"He did have children? What happened to them?"

Her expression twisted. "I've told you about how being a Geary, the Geary curse, impacted me and Michael, but you never experienced it. You never lived it."

Jane's voice didn't sound accusing, but he still felt defensive. "I've been living with the Black Jack nonsense for a while now."

"It's not nonsense!" Jane said, her voice sharp. "A lot of our family died because of it. Call it a curse. Because that's what it is. You've met Michael again. You know how he feels about the Geary legacy." Jane shook her head, looking down at the palm of one of her hands as if a message were written there. "We tried to live our lives. I never tried to start a family of my own, though. I wouldn't put them through that. Michael and I made a vow to end the Geary line with us so no other kids would have to grow up with that fate dominating their every moment."

She sighed. "But, Michael . . . hell, he fell in love. A wonderful girl, he said. And realized he wanted kids. Convinced himself they could be okay if their last names weren't Geary and they lived on an out-of-the-way planet in an out-of-the-way star system and they never learned who they were related to. But then Kahoku died. Some sort of accident. Michael was out on a campaign. What public records existed there used a false identity for him. None of Kahoku's family had ever met him. So when the local authorities asked the fleet to notify Kahoku's husband the answer came back that no such officer existed, and every-one concluded that Michael had been one of those sailors with a wife and family on more than one planet. Michael told me by the time he heard about Kahoku his kids had already been taken in by part of her family. And that's how he left it, so they'd never suffer from the Geary curse."

Jane looked at Geary. "So there's your answer. Yes, Michael has children. But they have no idea who he is, and he hasn't been in contact with them since before Kahoku died."

Geary stared at her, stunned. "But . . . but now . . . why couldn't he . . ."

"Because he knows the real you." Jane smiled in a slow, sad sort of way. "If you'd been the boogeyman Michael and I grew up thinking you were, maybe he'd be okay tracking them down now. But he knows you. No, you're not Black Jack. You're the guy who finally won the war and ended the slaughter. You're the guy who's held the fleet together and reminded us all that we serve the Alliance and the Alliance serves the people of the Alliance. You're the guy who finally found aliens. Michael is more afraid now that if those kids learn who they are they'll *want* to be like you, they'll go off into space, and maybe never come home, not because they have to anymore, but because they'll want to be like you."

As Geary wrestled with his feelings and his thoughts, Tanya spoke up.

"Like Roberto Duellos and his daughter," Desjani said.

Close to a minute passed in silence while Geary tried to sort out this news. "What should I do?" he finally asked.

"Great-uncle," Jane Geary said, "with all due respect, it's not your decision to make."

"But don't those kids . . ." They weren't kids now, were they? Teens. The eldest a young adult from what Jane had once told him. "Don't they have a right to know who their ancestors are? To make their own decisions about this?"

"I don't know the answer to that," Jane said. "I do know if you seek out those children on your own Michael will never forgive you. Get his approval first or let it go."

"I was taught," Tanya said, "that our ancestors always know. Even if we lose track of them, they always know who we are. Your ancestors are surely looking out for Michael's children."

Jane nodded. "If they're meant to know who they are, it'll happen. Checking their DNA against the fleet databases will give them that answer if they seek it."

Not knowing what else to say, Geary nodded back to Jane. "Thank you for letting me know. When we get back to Alliance space I'll talk to Michael."

"Don't assume he'll want to talk to you about it." Jane stood up. "And don't worry about this conspiracy, Admiral. You're baiting a trap that Captain Armus, Captain Plant, General Carabali, and I will all bring down hard. We'll make every effort to protect Ensign Duellos when that happens."

"I know," Geary said. "I also know her safety isn't guaranteed. You need a contingency plan if the conspirators figure out she's turned on them and . . ." It was very hard to think about, let alone say. "Attempt to silence her before she can turn the malware over to Captain Plant."

"We'll be prepared if that happens," Jane said. "But, as you say, no guarantees."

IT came as a welcome relief that the Taon didn't wait on a reply from the humans, sending another invitation that came in while the Alliance fleet was still short of reaching the Dancer planet. The six Taon ships had broken orbit about the gas giant and were heading for the same planet.

Lokaa spoke with the same enthusiasm as before. "Welcome human! Come Taon! Be friend! Bring all ships!"

Ambassador Rycerz, who now that she had control of the transmitter on *Boundless* had indeed been personally going over every message intended for the Dancers and looked just as worn-out as expected from that, gave Geary an aggravated wave-off when he asked for approval to reply. "Take care of it."

He called Charban first. "Do you know if our direct questions to the Dancers about the Taon have been sent from *Boundless* yet?"

Charban shook his head, his expression carefully unrevealing. "No, they have not."

If Rycerz wanted him to handle this, she had to let him handle it. "Send them from our transmitter," he told Charban. Then he sent the ambassador a message informing her that he'd sent the Dancers some messages dealing with fleet safety and security issues.

That still left replying to the Taon message.

Geary sent his reply from his stateroom, trying to look friendly but also a little reserved. How that would appear to a Taon he had no idea. "This is Admiral Geary of the Alliance fleet. We are happy to have made contact with your species and are honored to have received your invitation. Our primary purpose here is to meet with representatives of the species which controls this star system. For this reason, we have to discuss the matter with that species before we commit for some of our ships to visit Taon. Please be patient as we work to resolve this problem. To the honor of our ancestors. Geary, out."

He'd considered also saying some variation on "we come here in peace" but considering he was sending his message from a warship that was among hundreds of other warships, those particular words had felt too awkward.

The Alliance ships were close enough to the Taon ships by now that the reply took only a couple of hours. "Welcome human Geary. Some ships? How many? Wish visit Taon. Bring many."

"Lokaa still likes us a whole lot," Desjani observed. "No reply from the Dancers yet?"

"No," Geary said. Now that he wanted to go to the Taon star as part of the plan to trip up the conspiracy within the fleet, he had to avoid seeming too eager to go. But he also still had to worry about what the Dancers might tell him about the Taon. A warning from the Dancers would trip up the entire plan. "If our guesses are right, the Dancers should be trying to nudge us in one direction or another."

"The lack of replies might be the nudges," Desjani said. "What do Charban and his colleagues think?"

"I guess I should find out."

As it turned out, Charban and his "staff" had just had breakfast and were bouncing around ideas when Geary arrived. "I need some advice on the Taon and the Dancers," he said.

"Taon are Taon," Dr. Cresida said, not looking up from her comm pad.

"The Dancers haven't answered our questions," General Charban said. "And we know basically nothing about the Taon."

"We know they're not like the Kicks," Lieutenant Jamenson said. "They can coexist with another species. At least one other. I keep looking for evidence of lots of species mingling," she admitted. "Like those stories of galactic civilizations with different species working together in them."

"We haven't seen that evidence," Lieutenant Iger said, half apologetically. "But then, from our available observation regions we'd have a lot of trouble spotting individuals on the planets."

"Historically," Senn said, "on Old Earth, when new groups came to a new land, they'd settle in separate areas of cities. If possible, they'd build houses and other structures that matched their traditional architecture. That still happens when a large group of settlers from a planet that's been inhabited longer goes to a new planet."

"Have we seen that kind of thing in any of the Dancer cities?" Geary said.

Lieutenant Iger called up some images and reports, studying them. "No, Admiral. We haven't. The Dancer cities and towns that we've been able to observe all reflect roughly the same layouts and building designs, allowing for changes in styles over time."

"Does that mean even when a different species like the Taon are freely traveling through their space, the Dancers and other species don't want them settling on their worlds?" Charban asked, appearing unhappy at the possibility.

"Absence of evidence is not evidence of absence," Dr. Cresida murmured, not bothering to look up from her comm pad.

"Yes!" John Senn said, pointing at her. "Dr. Cresida has it. That quote has been around in various forms for a long time. I've used it myself. Because it's true. We haven't seen it yet. That doesn't mean it's not out there. Whatever it is."

"But why is there an absence of evidence?" Geary asked.

Lieutenant Iger answered, looking as if he'd just realized what he was saying. "We've only seen a few Dancer-controlled star systems. Maybe we were brought to this one because it lacked such evidence."

"Which would mean the Dancers don't want us interacting with or having knowledge of other species yet?" Charban asked. "But then why did we see the Taon ships in the last star system? Oh. Because the Dancers didn't know we were going to be there. The Taon ships could have already been in jump when we arrived at the Dancer star."

"Are you suggesting the Taon ships at the last star system never communicated with us because the Dancers didn't want them to?" Geary asked. "But now . . . but now," he continued as the thought hit him, "the Dancers have had time to figure things out and told the Taon they could speak to us."

"Either that," Lieutenant Iger said in a cautious voice, "or this Lokaa is powerful enough that he doesn't have to listen to the Dancers' wishes when it comes to talking to us."

"We just keep going around in circles," Lieutenant Jamenson complained. "We don't know enough to reach any conclusions."

"We can't tell you anything remotely definitive," General Charban said. "We lack enough information. Barring a sudden change in Dancer communication that showers us with hard data, I would suggest that this has to be a gut decision, not one based on firm information. It comes down to this, Admiral. Do we listen to our hopes or to our fears?"

Put that way, Geary instantly knew his answer. "We listen to our fears to the extent that we take reasonable precautions. But we let our hope decide." He couldn't tell these others, except Lieutenant Iger, who had already been secretly briefed, the other reason why he was reaching this decision. "Unless things change, we're going to go to Taon."

He still waited several hours before replying to Lokaa, hoping against all experience that the Dancers would be more forthcoming. When they weren't, Geary called Ambassador Rycerz, who didn't reply. Leaving her a message about his intentions, he then composed his answer to the invitation. "Greetings to Lokaa of Taon. This is Admiral Geary. We wish to accept your invitation to visit Taon, but we must leave many ships at this star. Our plan is to bring one hundred of our ships. Is this number acceptable to you? To the honor of our ancestors. Geary, out."

One hundred ships. The even total had been a coincidence, the product of bringing all eleven battle cruisers, twenty-five of the light cruisers in five squadrons, and sixty-four destroyers in eight squadrons. It seemed both far too many warships for a peaceful visit, and far too few for the first visit to an alien species of unknown intentions and capabilities.

With the human fleet and Lokaa's ships converging toward the same planet, the reply this time took only a little more than an hour. "One hundred. Understand one hundred. Also human Geary? Come now?"

To Geary's surprise, Ambassador Rycerz finally called to urge him to accept the invitation to go to Taon space now. "It will show the Taon our sincerity," Rycerz said, "and allow me to concentrate on relations with the Dancers, who are becoming much more communicative, without any crosscurrents or cross communications."

Crosscurrents or cross communications. Rycerz's attitude wasn't so surprising after all. She had realized that sending Geary to Taon would eliminate the presence of a second Dancer-modified transmitter, and a source that the Dancers had often preferred to communicate with. He'd already gotten her where she needed to go in Dancer space, so why not get the admiral out of her hair? That was understandable, given all of the obstacles faced to get to this point, and how many factors had conspired to prevent getting to where Rycerz could finally do her job. But, still, it rankled a bit. "Thanks," Geary muttered after the call ended.

He knew he should inform the ambassador about the conspiracy. He could hide behind technicalities in interpreting his orders and say this was purely a security matter, though. His sense of duty nagged at him to inform Rycerz anyway, but he couldn't see any way to do that without a substantial risk that Colonel Webb would hear of it and launch one of his heavy-handed attempts to deal with the matter. And if Webb did that it wouldn't only put at serious risk Geary's plan to trap the conspirators into revealing themselves, it would also put at serious risk the life of Ensign Arwen Duellos. And that was only the danger from Webb. Rycerz herself had cautioned that she couldn't trust anyone aboard *Boundless*, and didn't trust even secure communications.

It wasn't hard to imagine what advice Victoria Rione would be giving him right now. Most likely she'd give him a scornful look and demand to know why he was even asking the question when it was obvious he shouldn't risk informing Rycerz. And he had no doubt that this, too, would be one of those rare occasions when Tanya Desjani agreed with Rione's advice.

Ambassador Rycerz would likely be extremely angry when she found out. But he had to live with her only until the Dancers accepted the diplomatic mission aboard *Boundless*. He'd have to live with himself a lot longer than that. Which meant he wouldn't add additional risks to those Roberto Duellos's daughter was already facing. Especially when that would also risk what seemed the best plan for exposing the leaders of the conspiracy within the fleet.

Having decided that, he called his fleet. "All units in the Alliance fleet, this is Admiral Geary. In accordance with earlier instructions I sent out, Task Force Alpha will form immediately under my command for transit to Taon space. The remainder of the fleet will be under the command of Captain Armus, and will stay in this star system to protect *Boundless*.

"We can't be certain of what awaits us in Taon space. But the only way to learn is to go there, and be ready for anything that happens, just as our ancestors did when they left Old Earth for the stars that became our homes. To the honor of our ancestors, Geary, out."

At least, he hoped they'd be ready for anything that happened, both here and in Taon space.

FIFTEEN

COMING out of jump was always tense because of the brief period of disorientation. It was especially so when not knowing what to expect to happen during those moments of mental fog. Geary waited them out with grim resolve, relieved when he realized that no alarms were sounding to warn of nearby dangers. At least accepting the Taon invitation hadn't resulted in an immediate ambush.

As his mind cleared, he focused on his display, where the sensors on *Dauntless* and the rest of the ships in Task Force Alpha were automatically processing and displaying everything they could detect within the star system. For the first time in days he had something to focus on besides worrying about what lay ahead and what might be happening back at the Dancer star system.

In terms of a solar system, this one was fairly average. Geary felt a pang of disappointment at that, having hoped for something spectacular like vast artificial structures filling the space around the star.

Instead, seven of the worlds orbiting the slightly reddish star were large enough to qualify as planets, three of them gas giants, the closest to the star thirty light minutes from it, the farthest more than two light hours from the star. A passably habitable but probably cold world orbited ten light minutes from the star, with three more planets close enough to the star to be too hot for human life. Apparently that was too hot for Taon as well, given that the only habitats visible on any of those worlds were only town-sized and sealed against the outside environment.

There were enough orbital facilities to give it the feel of a star system that had been inhabited for a while. Which didn't match the scattered small cities visible on the settled world. They seemed too few and too small for a star system that had been occupied for a long period.

The star system had only one other jump point, and no hypernet gate.

Two other things drew his attention. One was what the fleet's systems characterized as a "moderate-to-high" level of craters pockmarking the surface of the inhabited world, and the other was the fairly large Taon fleet orbiting near that world.

He didn't like what he was seeing. "How does this look to you?" Geary asked.

Tanya Desjani, studying her display, which was still updating as the fleet's sensors gathered and displayed information, shook her head. "Scattered small cities. Lots of recent cratering visible on the inhabited world. Quite a bit of wreckage orbiting the star. This looks like a fought-over star system to me."

"Can we get an estimate on how recent the largest craters are on that planet?" Geary asked.

"Not a good one, sir," Lieutenant Castries said. "We have planetary atmosphere obscuring our view, and we don't know anything about the planet's climate to estimate how long it would take to erode craters. The fleet's systems are estimating the age of the newest craters at ten years or less."

"Ten years or less." Geary shook his head in a way that mimicked Desjani. "Meaning they could be very recent, or the legacy of a war concluded a decade ago."

"This doesn't feel like a star system that's been at peace for ten years," Desjani said. "Why are there ninety Taon warships here?"

"If this is the Taon capital star system, they've been beaten on badly," Geary said. "But I'm not seeing the wreckage of any large cities on that planet. It feels more like a border star system during a war. Are we just seeing it that way because of our own experiences with star systems like that?"

"We're seeing it that way because it looks like that," Desjani said. "Are you wondering why our buddy Lokaa didn't mention that we were heading for a war zone?"

"Yes, I am."

As if summoned by their name, a call from Lokaa popped into view on Geary's display. The Taon ships escorting them from Dancer space were only a few light seconds ahead of the human formation.

Accepting the message, he saw Lokaa with their mouth in the usual oval-shaped "smile."

"Welcome!" Lokaa said. "Welcome Taon star! Happy safe arrival! Follow!"

"The Taon ships in company with us are altering vector," Lieutenant Castries reported.

Geary forced a smile he didn't feel as he replied to Lokaa. "We are also happy to have arrived safely. Is this star system dangerous? Is there war here?"

"War here? Past. History. Human safe in ships of war. Follow!"

"I'm not reassured," Desjani said.

Neither was Geary. But . . . "I can't ruin our chances at peaceful relations with another species just because we've got a bad feeling about this. If the Taon have recently concluded a war, it might explain their eagerness to be friends with us. They'd want whatever help we could provide to their war-ravaged worlds and economy. As soon as the Taon ships steady out, we'll follow their vector."

"How close are we going to get to that Taon fleet?" she asked with a raised eyebrow. "They're all about the same size, but there are ninety of them."

"That's interesting, isn't it?" Geary said. "Every ship about the same size, a little larger than one of our light cruisers. Nothing bigger, nothing smaller. We won't go closer than one light minute to that fleet. We'll see if Lokaa tries to bring us closer than that."

He hesitated, wondering if he should risk the next step. But exhausting his officers and sailors by keeping them at alert for days on end wouldn't do anything good for their ability to respond quickly to emergencies. "All units in Task Force Alpha, this is Admiral Geary. Stand down from Readiness Condition Two. Maintain enhanced readiness consistent with allowing sufficient rest for your crews. We may yet need them at their best at short notice. Geary, out."

It quickly became apparent that the Taon ships were leading them to intercept the primary inhabited planet in its orbit. Before reaching the jump point in the Dancer-controlled star system that they'd left, the Taon ships had slowed to point zero five light speed. The Alliance ships had matched that, wondering if the Taon jump drives couldn't handle a faster velocity when entering jump. Now that they'd arrived the Taon ships maintained the same velocity. Traveling at the relatively sedate (for warships) velocity of point zero five light speed, the Alliance task force and their Taon escort would require more than three days to reach the planet.

"Those ninety Taon ships are orbiting five light minutes from the planet we're heading for," Desjani commented. "If they stay out there, we shouldn't have too much to worry about."

There were other matters to concern them, though.

"Everything's encrypted," Lieutenant Iger reported within a few hours of their arrival in the star system. "Every transmission we can pick up across the spectrum is encrypted."

"That's odd," Geary said. Even during the war, human star systems had been filled with many unencrypted transmissions. News reports, entertainment, personal communications, and others. "Is there any chance we can break the encryption?"

"We have no baseline," Iger said. "We don't know their language, or their conventions for transmissions, or anything else. We'll try, but I'm not confident we'll achieve anything."

"What about observing their cities and orbital facilities? Have we seen anything that tells us important information?"

"We haven't determined much yet." Iger paused. "Though Shamrock, excuse me, sir, Lieutenant Jamenson, noted that none of the cities we can see on the inhabited world are located on the coasts of seas or lakes."

"None of them?" As common as various forms of flight and space-flight had become, oceans were still widely used on human planets to move commerce between continents.

"There are port facilities on the coasts in various places," Iger added, "but there's nothing near them except what are probably mass transit tracks leading to the nearest cities."

"That might make them sort of the opposite of the enigmas," Geary said. What little they'd been able to see of enigma cities had revealed that they straddled coasts and oceans, part of the cities in the water and part on land. "That and the avowed friendliness and invitation to visit instead of death threats if we didn't leave immediately."

Lieutenant Iger nodded, but he didn't seem happy about it. "Yes, Admiral. If it's all true."

"Believe me, Lieutenant, we're all skeptical." That was easy to say, but Geary also knew he had a responsibility to make friends with the Taon if possible, or at least avoid making them enemies.

And that would require taking more risks that he'd really prefer not having to take.

THE time spent transiting to the planet proved to be remarkably un-eventful for what was supposed to be a first-contact experience. Lokaa didn't send more messages. Occasionally a few Taon ships would arrive or depart from the other jump point the star system boasted. Most of those ships coming and going were the large ones the humans had decided must be freighters or passenger ships or perhaps both. But it was impossible to miss that every large ship had at least one smaller warship escorting it.

The numbers of Taon warships in their large fleet near the inhabited world fluctuated a bit with the comings and goings, but never went below one hundred.

"Their total numbers always add up to multiples of six," Lieutenant Jamenson observed. "Lokaa's group of ships was six in number."

"Add that to our list of things we need to try to understand," General Charban said, rubbing the bridge of his nose as if that would help him think. "Really, Admiral, can't you keep us to one baffling alien species at a time?"

"Does Lokaa have six fingers?" Geary asked. He'd come down to the transmitter room where Charban's homegrown experts were still gathering, hoping they might have seen something significant.

"Lokaa has four fingers, or rather three fingers and what looks like a finger-thumb," Jamenson said.

"So this makes no sense at all," Geary said.

"Welcome to the universe, Admiral," Dr. Cresida said without looking up from her comm pad.

BY the time the Alliance task force neared the planet, their crews were well rested but restless. "There are few things more stress inducing than expecting something to happen that keeps not happening," Captain Duellos commented to Geary during a brief meeting in his stateroom that had kept mostly to professional topics. "Or knowing something may have already happened, and not knowing how it came out."

"Knowing when they'll act should help protect her," Geary said, being careful with his words even in his stateroom where no one should be able to overhear.

"Which is why I didn't protest the plan," Duellos said, his face taking on additional years of age as he spoke. "But it is hard. It is very hard." He sighed. "Why do we never get used to this? During the war, depending on how far distant someone was, it might take a year for word of a particular death to reach you. At a minimum, it would be a few months. The only times you knew what had happened when it happened was when you were in that same star system." He paused. "And even then if you were a few light hours distant you'd only learn the worst when you finally saw it. Oh, my friend must've died an hour ago when that ship exploded."

Duellos gave Geary a glance. "There are those who claim they have received such news the moment it happened, even if the loss of a close friend, or a family member, took place hundreds of light years distant. They say they felt it instantly, only to have the pain confirmed months later."

"I've heard such things," Geary said. It was very hard to think of anything else to say. "Do you believe that can happen?"

Duellos shrugged. "I believe I don't know enough to know. Maybe it does happen sometimes. Maybe it doesn't. Your grand-niece Jane always said she was certain her brother Michael was still alive because she had never felt him die. Here's what I do know. When you have a child, the entire universe changes in that moment. It never returns to what it was before. They don't warn you about that. Tantrums, diseases, puberty, you can find lots of advice for dealing with those. But they never warn you how everything changes. It's . . . wonderful, and it's also the source of many sleepless nights, and worries for them every day of what is left of your life.

"And, after years and years in which they are your responsibility, they leave. You no longer get to decide for them." He gave Geary a rueful smile. "Even though you still worry just as much. I confess I'll be relieved to return to that Dancer star system, and yet also dreading that moment for what I might learn."

"Some of the best people in the fleet are watching over her," Geary said, feeling that his words were woefully inadequate.

"That means a great deal," Duellos said. "Not so long ago her fate would have rested in the hands of commanders like the late Captain Falco or Admiral Atropa. I do sleep better knowing that Armus, Jane Geary, and Plant have their eyes on her. Of course, right now they're wondering what's happening to us."

"We're not dead yet," Geary said. "Beyond that, we're waiting, too."

GEARY had tried occasional messages to Lokaa, which were invariably answered with the Taon smile and assurances that the human were welcome.

Finally, when the fleet was only ten light minutes from the planet, Lokaa sent a more substantive message. "Go here. Safe. Good orbit."

The accompanying diagram did indeed show the Alliance task force in orbit about the planet. But it was low orbit, only a couple of thousand kilometers from the surface.

"Maybe they're trying to show that they trust us near one of their inhabited planets," General Charban suggested. He and the other alien communicators still hadn't had any luck figuring out anything about the Taon. "Am I correct that this fleet from that orbit could bombard that planet lifeless before the other Taon ships could do anything about it?"

"You're very likely correct," Geary said. "We don't know what the Taon combat capabilities are, but they'd have to act remarkably fast to stop us if we unleashed a bombardment."

"It's not a low enough orbit to create too much danger from whatever anti-orbital defenses they have hidden on the planet's surface," Captain Desjani conceded. "It's actually at the high end of low orbit. I'm not thrilled with it, but I can't honestly say it poses too great a danger to us."

Forty-two hours after arriving in the star system, the Alliance fleet assumed a low orbit about the Taon-inhabited planet.

And waited.

"We are literally just going around in circles waiting for the Taon to do something," Desjani complained two days later.

"I've sent messages to Lokaa asking about meetings, in person or virtual," Geary reminded her. "You've seen their replies."

"Yeah. 'Hi, friends! Safe! Not worry!' Well, I'm worrying," she grumbled.

They were in Geary's stateroom, along with Kommodor Bradamont and Colonel Rogero, having an impromptu meeting. "Does what the Taon are doing make any sense from a Midway perspective?" Geary asked Rogero and Bradamont.

"No," Rogero said. "Not if the goal is to establish relationships. That requires meetings, even if you don't like whoever you have to meet with."

"It does make sense if their goal is to keep us here," Bradamont said. "But why? It's not like the Taon could be launching a sneak attack on the rest of the fleet in Dancer space while we're tied up here."

"If we've read the Dancers at all right," Geary said, leaning back with a sigh, "they would defend their star system, and the rest of our fleet, from such an attack. I wouldn't want to find out the hard way what kind of defenses the Dancers have against that kind of danger."

"Are we waiting for somebody again?" Desjani asked. "Just like at the first Dancer star system? But there's been no sign of any courier ships rushing about to send word that we're here to some high boss at another Taon star. I do *not* like the way that Taon fleet keeps edging closer and closer. It looks like ships just moving around in their formation, or coming and going, but they always end up closer to this planet. They started out five light minutes from us. Now they're just over three light minutes away."

"They must realize we can see that happening," Bradamont said. "Are they waiting for us to object?"

"I did," Geary said. "Lokaa said everything was fine."

"We're not learning anything about them," Desjani said. "I don't know what they think they're learning about us. Maybe how far they can push us before we say goodbye and leave?"

Geary was searching for an answer, and failing to find one, when another message came in.

Lokaa had their oval "smile" on and the usual effusive attitude. "Human welcome. Come planet! Come surface. Relax. Fun. Special place. Safe. One-third crews good. Come now!"

"They want us to send our crews to the surface for rest and recreation?" Desjani said in disbelief.

"Up to one-third of our crews at any one time," Bradamont added. "Is this a way for them to learn how large our crews are?"

"We need a senior ship commanders meeting," Geary said.

Less than half an hour later he was in the conference room along with Desjani, Bradamont, Rogero, and General Charban, who had been picked up along the way. Seated in virtual form along the table were Captain Duellos and Captain Badaya. Geary had known how his forces had been worn down in battles, how many battle cruisers had been lost, but only now when he realized these were all of the senior officers present did that finally sneak past his emotional barriers to hit him.

"They want us to send up to one-third of our total crews on liberty on the surface at any one time," Duellos repeated as if unable to believe what he had heard.

"That would be popular with the crews," Captain Badaya said. He didn't seem to entirely approve of the idea of doing something on that basis. "But that would leave us with one-third of our crews away from our ships and subject to whatever the Taon want to do. Hostages. A lot of them. And enough of the crews gone that our ships' fighting ability will be compromised. That's what I'm seeing."

"For once," Captain Desjani said, "I'm in full agreement with Captain Badaya. We still know so little about the Taon."

"Where are they talking about our sailors visiting?" Duellos asked. "That would make a difference, wouldn't it? If they were in the middle of a Taon city it could make that city hostage to us if anything went wrong."

"A special place that is safe," Captain Desjani said. "That's how they identified it."

"That could be the description of a prison," Badaya said.

"I'm leaning toward agreement with your officers," General Charban said. "Except that this would offer a tremendous opportunity to see and interact with the Taon face-to-face for those who went to the surface. An invaluable opportunity that we might not be offered again."

"If it's a trap they'll offer again," Badaya said.

"I'm not comfortable with this," Geary said. "But General Charban is right. If this means face-to-face meetings with the Taon we have to consider it."

"One-third of our crews on the surface?" Desjani demanded. "At the mercy of the Taon who we know so little about?"

"No. Not one-third. That's far too many."

"Offer less," Kommodor Bradamont suggested. "Bargain with them. Say we'll send a few down to see how things are, and if all goes well maybe we'll send more."

"I could accept that," Duellos said.

"How many is a few, and which few?" Badaya asked skeptically.

"Which few should be Marines," Duellos said. "Who better to stress test a liberty site? And if things do go to hell, the Marines will be better suited to fighting their way out than our sailors would be."

"That's amazingly cynical," Desjani said, grinning. "Should we inflict Marines on liberty on the Taon, though?"

"It's practical! We have the two stealth shuttles," Captain Duellos pointed out. "If they keep their stealth capabilities unused until needed, they could offer an escape means even if things get hot. Use the reinforced Marine detachments aboard *Dauntless* and *Inspire* to select some volunteers, then send down a total of thirty or forty Marines in those two shuttles."

"Unless they're sleeping on the shuttles they'd need to be able to get to the shuttles to escape," Badaya pointed out. "If the Taon want to double-cross us, they're not going to let anyone on the ground just dance their way onto the shuttles to leave."

"Sending down fully armed Marines might trigger just the problem we want to avoid," General Charban warned. "We can't make our liberty party look like an assault team."

"We'll tell them that's how we always do things!" Badaya insisted. "Our Marines take their weapons with them on liberty."

"Just thinking about Marines with weapons on liberty scares the hell out of me," Desjani said.

Geary nodded emphatically. "It does seem like a great way to start a war with the Taon. If we do this, we want a chance of a peaceful outcome. But I also want those Marines to have an escape option if worst comes to worst."

The following silent pause was broken by General Charban. "A Trojan horse. You need a Trojan horse."

"How does hiding all of the Marines inside the shuttles help us figure out a way for them to go on liberty on the surface?" Desjani asked.

"You don't hide all of them," Charban said. "Say twenty Marines to a shuttle? Send five of them with a full combat load-out. Those five stay hidden and sealed in the shuttle. As far as the Taon know, they're not there. But if the Marines on liberty suddenly need strong backup, the armed Marines on the shuttles come out and give them the cover they need to get to the shuttles."

"That's not a bad idea," Duellos said. "Why did you pick five out of the twenty on each shuttle?"

"Your shuttles are similar to the ones the ground forces use," Charban said. "They're not made for long-term habitation, but you can do it for several days with five people. More than that and you might end up with life-support problems."

"I hear the voice of experience speaking," Duellos said.

"Yes," Charban said, memories flitting across his face. "Ten of us were sealed inside a shuttle for nine days after an emergency landing. I don't recommend it."

Desjani turned to Geary. "We need to talk to Gunnery Sergeant Orvis. He'll be the one in charge of *Dauntless*'s Marine liberty party."

"Who's the commander of your Marine detachment?" Geary said to Duellos.

"Sergeant Barnwell," Duellos said. "She's been with *Inspire* for years. She's a solid performer."

"We'll bring Orvis and Barnwell in on this," Geary said. "Get their opinions before we go any further with the plan. If they agree it's doable, with acceptable risk, we'll proceed."

"Admiral," Colonel Rogero said. "May I request a place among the, um, liberty party?"

Kommodor Bradamont bit her lip, but said nothing.

"That's not a bad idea," Badaya said, not noticing Bradamont's reaction. "You're experienced with Syndic practices. If the Taon try anything sneaky you'd be better at spotting it than our own people."

"Colonel Rogero might well see things our Marines wouldn't notice," Desjani agreed with visible reluctance.

Bradamont, having recovered her poise, spoke in a controlled voice. "Colonel Rogero is also a field-grade officer with extensive combat and command experience. If things go bad on the surface he could be very valuable to the Marines."

"Will our Marines take orders from him, though?" Duellos asked.

"He's got a good reputation with them because of the combat records from Iwa," Geary said. "I admit it would be a comfort to me to know someone of Colonel Rogero's caliber was on the surface with our Marines. But are you both certain that Midway would approve of you running that risk?"

"Yes, Admiral," Rogero said.

"Yes, Admiral," Bradamont agreed, no longer betraying any personal feelings about the idea.

"Then let's run with this plan," Geary ordered. "We *have* to learn more about the Taon, and this may be our best opportunity."

Gunnery Sergeant Orvis and Sergeant Barnwell, after conferring over the idea, both gave it a thumbs-up and began selecting which five of each of their detachments would form the Trojan horse force. No one wanted to be part of that group since those five from each ship would end up confined inside their shuttles while their fellow Marines enjoyed whatever pleasures the Taon offered.

After some debate, it was decided the shuttle pilots would also remain concealed aboard their birds, staying hidden along with the five Marines who had "volunteered" for the assignment.

The stealth shuttle pilots were less than thrilled with that decision. But, being Marines themselves, they also ended up volunteering to do it.

There was another volunteer as well, when Geary stopped by the Dancer-modified transmitter room to discuss what the Marines should be told to look for.

In the midst of the discussion Lieutenant Iger hesitated, not looking at Lieutenant Jamenson, then spoke up. "Admiral, I should be part of the group sent down to the surface. The opportunities for collection of information require my presence."

Jamenson inhaled sharply, clenching into a fist the hand visible above the table, but said nothing. She also avoided looking at Iger.

There were a lot of situations where making one person happy meant making another unhappy. In this case, though, the danger posed by going to the surface made the decision not very difficult. "Thank you for volunteering, Lieutenant Iger," Geary said. "But I can't permit that. You know too many Alliance secrets to risk having you in the custody of a species that is still unknown to us in too many vital ways. I want you in contact with the Marines on the surface, but I want any collection you do to be from this ship."

"Yes, sir," Iger said, crestfallen. "I understand."

Lieutenant Jamenson shot Geary a grateful look, but he avoided meeting her eyes. Because he knew that if the circumstances had been different he might have accepted Iger's offer regardless of the danger.

But one more member had to be added to the "liberty party."

"There are things only a medical doctor will see, will understand," Dr. Nasr said gravely. "It is vital that a doctor accompany the landing group. Especially considering that we have no way of knowing what sort of environmental factors we might encounter."

Geary wanted to reject this offer as well. But he couldn't. "That is true, Doctor. Hopefully you won't encounter any environmental danger that our medicine can't handle. I'll look forward to whatever you can learn about the Taon. However, I hope you'll be careful. I value your support and insight. Make sure you get back to the ship alive and well."

Nasr smiled. "I will do my best, Admiral. It is the duty of doctors to go where they are needed."

And so the size of the group to be sent down to the surface grew to forty-four; forty Marines of which only thirty would leave the two shuttles, two pilots who would also remain in the shuttles, Colonel Rogero, and Dr. Nasr. "I want you all back safely," Geary told the part of the group leaving from *Dauntless*. "Have fun if you can. The Taon say it's a fun place, but we don't know what Taon consider fun. Stay out of trouble. Do *not* knowingly provoke any problems with the Taon. You're planned to stay down there for ten days. If there are difficulties, we'll get you out of there. Gunny Orvis, get going."

"Yes, Admiral," Gunnery Sergeant Orvis said with a salute sharp enough to cut a steak. Most of the Marines wore dress uniforms and carried small bags with changes of clothing and personal necessities. They also all had cameras with sound pickups embedded in the collars of their uniforms so if necessary they could relay events on the surface back to the ship. But five of the Marines bulked larger in their battle armor. They wouldn't have to wear it the entire time they were in the shuttle, but Orvis had wanted them ready when the group landed.

Colonel Rogero also wore a dress uniform. He was speaking softly to Kommodor Bradamont, who was nodding, her stoic expression that of countless others through human history who had sent someone off to possible danger.

Dr. Nasr had already had a brief talk with the medical personnel staying behind on *Dauntless*, and seemed eager to leave.

As they watched the shuttle ramp seal and the shuttle rise to depart, General Charban spoke to Geary. "Someday their names may be in all of the histories."

"If they are, hopefully they'll be listed among great explorers, and not among famous last stands," Geary said.

ON their way down to the surface, the two shuttles were met by an escort of six Taon aerospace aircraft. Physics in atmosphere being the same on this planet as on other planets, the Taon aerospace craft outwardly bore a lot of resemblance to human craft of the same type. But their propulsion method appeared to be both very efficient and very powerful as the six smaller Taon craft wove their way about the shuttles and guided them down.

The destination proved not to be one of the small cities, or even a town, but an isolated cluster of buildings about a hundred kilometers from the nearest population center.

"I guess that's just prudent on the part of the Taon," Charban remarked. "They don't really know anything about us, either."

"Like Badaya said, it looks like a prison," Desjani grumbled suspiciously.

THERE were nearly continuous brief updates from the liberty party over the next two days as they settled in to their accommodations and dealt with the group of Taon who were introduced as people who worked there. Late on the second day after arriving on the planet, the leaders of the liberty party called Geary from one of the shuttles for a more detailed briefing. Dr. Nasr, Colonel Rogero, Sergeant Barnwell, and Gunny Orvis were crammed into the front of one of the shuttles, the shapes of the five hidden Marines, their empty combat armor, and the shuttle pilot visible behind them.

"We're assuming the Taon are intercepting our collar cam signals," Orvis explained. "We wanted to use the more secure communications on the shuttle to give you a more detailed and candid report than we're comfortable saying on the cams."

"My impression from your earlier, brief updates is that things are okay but not great," Geary said.

"Nothing too bad has happened yet," Sergeant Barnwell said. "We are isolated here, that's for sure."

"If this was a human facility, we'd consider it a resort," Colonel Rogero said. "We're on the shore of a lake, surrounded by forest. We saw coming in to land that there aren't any nearby towns, and the buildings here pretty much match a resort layout."

"Maybe a kids' resort," Barnwell said. "Or a boot camp. There are a few individual rooms, and a lot of big rooms with lots of beds in them. Also large dining rooms. That sort of thing."

"It's definitely not a boot camp," Orvis said. "Too nice for that. The rooms have been pretty much stripped, though. No art, only absolutely vital furnishings, that kind of thing."

"There are multiple places in each room where electronics such as displays may have been mounted," Rogero said. "But there's nothing left except bare walls."

"What about toilet facilities?" Geary asked. "Are those still there? Surely those will tell us something about Taon anatomy."

Dr. Nasr shook his head. "Toilet facilities are all basically waste deposit and waste removal devices. They don't vary much in design across human cultures except in the degree of elaboration and comfort. The Taon facilities are larger and sturdier, but aren't dramatically different from human facilities. I didn't expect them to be."

"Everything left is hands-free," Orvis added. "No touch required to flush or get water or whatever."

This time Nasr nodded. "Yes. Handles might have offered some more clues to Taon anatomy. Hand strength. Things like that. Maybe the handles were removed, or maybe the Taon always use hands-free controls for such things."

"How about interacting with the Taon down there?" Geary asked. "Are they talking with you? Sharing anything?"

"Oh, they're talking," Sergeant Barnwell said, rolling her eyes. "Asking us stuff, asking us for stuff . . ."

"What are they asking for?"

"The Taon requested DNA samples from all of us," Dr. Nasr said. "Allegedly to ensure no food or drink they offer would be hazardous to us, and that none of their materials would trigger reactions in us. We have politely declined every request, instead offering the Taon samples of our rations so they know what is safe for us."

"But they keep asking," Orvis grumbled.

"The Taon seem to be very interested in the differences between our males and females," Rogero said.

Dr. Nasr winced. "They asked many of the Marines to strip so they could see their outer anatomy."

Gunny Orvis grinned. "Lucky for us, the Taon didn't know that you usually need to feed a Marine several beers before asking them to strip for you."

"And even then they'd probably wallop you one," Barnwell added wryly.

"Are the Taon there all male?" Geary said.

"They're all the same something, I think," Orvis said. "Admiral, they might all be female. Or something else. None of them have removed any clothes, even their tops. But they all look the same in terms of the, uh, physical characteristics we can see."

"That's not a sure guide," Dr. Nasr cautioned. "The vast majority of species we've encountered on different planets do show at least minor external physical differences between sexes. Those that have sexes, that is. But some do not. And some species shift between sexes at different phases of their lives. All we can say here is that externally all of the Taon we've seen appear to be the same."

"There are individual differences," Rogero said. "The exact shapes of those bony ridges on their faces vary in minor ways."

"Like human noses," Orvis agreed. "We can tell some of them apart. That's helped us get a count. We think there's about forty Taon here. That many have shown themselves, that is. There could be a few thousand staying quiet in the woods beyond the buildings. They're bigger than we thought, Admiral. You've seen that. The short ones are a bit more than two meters. And they're wide to match."

"From the way they walk," Dr. Nasr said, "their pelvises must be sturdy, but less flexible as a result."

"Heavy-duty frames," Barnwell agreed. "I wouldn't want to wrestle any of these Taon."

"They have not acted hostile," Dr. Nasr interjected. "They are . . . pushy, by human standards. But that is all we have seen."

"None of them have tried to kill us yet," Colonel Rogero agreed.

Gunny Orvis nodded. "Which is kind of a big thing compared to the enigmas and the Kicks. They're not answering any of our questions, though."

"No, they're not," Nasr admitted. "Every question I ask of them is met with it being turned back on me. How many star systems do Taon live in? How many do humans live in? Can I speak with one of your doctors, the ones who heal the sick or injured? Our doctors are busy healing the sick and injured, and will speak with you when they have time. May I examine a Taon? May we examine a human? I've been able to learn nothing."

"We've discussed making a bargain," Rogero suggested. "We'll show you one of ours if you show us one of yours. But none of us wanted to do that without clearing it with you."

Geary didn't entirely like that idea, but they were here to learn. "We can't expect them to share information with us if we won't with them. Doctor, see if they'll agree to let you conduct an external exam of one of the Taon in exchange for us agreeing to let them conduct an external exam of one of our people. If that goes well we can see about swapping information about internal physiology."

"I will try," Dr. Nasr said, looking pleased.

"I did discover one thing," Colonel Rogero said. "I asked a Taon how they'd known enough of our language to put together their translation devices before we ever met them. The Taon told me, 'Trade eight-legs.'" Rogero paused. "That disclosure may have displeased that Taon's superiors. I haven't seen that particular Taon around since that time. What he told me sounds like the Dancers traded some knowledge of our language to the Taon. I realized that such information about other species may be a very valuable trade item in the Great Galactic Bazaar if such a thing exists. Which made me wonder whether the reason the Dancers have shared so little about themselves with us is because they're waiting for us to make an offer. What are we going to give them in exchange for the information about themselves, or other intelligent species, that they give us?"

Geary sat back, feeling stunned. "That's . . . certainly possible. I can't recall anything the Dancers have sent along those lines. Maybe the trade negotiations are supposed to be carried out in a very subtle way that we've missed. No, wait, when the Dancers wanted duct tape, they asked for it. We had to figure out what they wanted, but they straight-out asked for it."

"Nonetheless, I think you, and Midway, need to consider the possibility," Rogero said.

"I think you're right. I'll talk to General Charban about it. What's your gut feeling about the situation down there?"

Rogero paused again for a few seconds before replying. "The Taon act friendly enough. But we're isolated. And when I see the Taon with us here something in me thinks I'm looking at ground combat soldiers. That's just an impression, but it keeps coming back to me. The ways they move as individuals and in groups, the ways they seem to be conversing among themselves, the ways they watch us. Groups of six, by the way. They really seem to prefer that number."

Orvis nodded. "You know, there might be thirty-six Taon watching us. Forty is just a guess. But I agree it feels a bit like having friendly prison guards watching you. Like one of those minimum-security places that rich people get sent to instead of the tough jails."

"I would not go so far," Dr. Nasr objected. "I do agree they watch us, but isn't that what humans would do if aliens were visiting one of our planets? It is perilous to judge the motives of a different species by whether or not their actions seem to resemble certain human behaviors."

"That's a reasonable argument," Geary said. "Is there any clue why they like six so much?"

"Nothing about them shows six of anything," Sergeant Barnwell said. "Nothing we can see, anyway."

"Humans," Dr. Nasr offered, "have always seen three as a special number, one with special powers and importance."

"Any idea why, Doc?" Barnwell asked.

"No."

Colonel Rogero smiled. "If we don't know why we have a special affinity for three it doesn't help us understand why the Taon like six."

"I haven't seen much in the way of diversions on the collar cams," Geary said. "What are they offering in the way of entertainment for you?"

"That's a funny thing," Gunnery Sergeant Orvis said. "There aren't any swimming pools. At least, none outdoors, and none in any of the buildings we've been in. There are docks extending into the lake, with some really heavy-duty railings along the sides, but no sign the shore has ever been used by swimmers."

"I am thinking the Taon may have denser bodies than humans," Dr. Nasr said. "We see a lot of bony ridges on the exterior, and their build is very stout by human standards. They may have more bone and larger bones than comparable humans would. If so, staying afloat in water would be more difficult for them."

"They probably wouldn't think fighting to avoid drowning was much fun," Orvis agreed. "I did try asking about swimming in the lake and the Taon didn't understand. Since we don't know what might be lurking under those waters, I haven't let any of our Marines go in. They're not happy about it, because other than the swimming pools we don't have, all we've got are running tracks, and open fields to run in, and long hallways to run down."

Colonel Rogero shook his head, looking puzzled. "I expected the Taon to have more materials available here. Lots of different items that would allow them to see how we interacted with those items. Even the sort of things you see in tests for children to determine abilities. But there's basically nothing. I don't know what they hope to learn about us from this."

"It may," Dr. Nasr said cautiously, "reflect an emphasis on how individuals interact with each other, rather than how they interact with objects. Perhaps the Taon are primarily interested in how humans act together. By giving us little to do individually, the lack of diversions requires us to deal with each other almost constantly."

"That's possible," Geary said. "I should let you know that things are more tense up here. The Taon fleet sped up their moving around and getting closer until they're less than one light minute from us now. Projecting their movement shows them heading to assume high orbit above our fleet within the next day or so."

"Is that as bad as it sounds to a ground fighter?" Rogero asked, concerned.

"It's not good. It will put us in a very vulnerable position. I'm trying to decide whether to move the fleet, but doing that would leave you all cut off from quick recovery if anything requires you to leave fast."

"Is that why the Taon wanted some of us on the ground?" Sergeant Barnwell asked, her eyes narrowed in thought. "So you couldn't move out of where you are?"

"That's likely," Geary said. "If the Taon intent is to force us away from where we can support you, they're going to be disappointed."

"It sounds like we need to be ready to get out of here fast, though," Gunny Orvis said.

"Yes," Geary said.

The call over, he looked at Desjani, who was standing nearby in his stateroom and had listened and watched. "What's your assessment on this?"

"Admiral, we need to get them back up here now and get away from this planet before they pin us in lower orbit," she said without hesitating.

"Noted," Geary said, rubbing his eyes. "Captain Desjani, are you saying that you couldn't come up with a way for the fleet to outmaneuver and outthink the Taon so we can safely leave this orbit even after they reach high orbit above us?"

Desjani glared at him. "No, sir, I am not saying that. Whatever mess you get us into, I can get us out of."

"I have every confidence in you," Geary said.

HE had only a day and a half longer to wonder if he ought to recover the liberty party and move the fleet before his hand was forced.

Geary had barely reached the bridge of *Dauntless* in response to urgent alarms when reports started coming in.

"Sir, a lot of new ships have arrived at the other jump point." Lieutenant Yuon squinted at his display as new information cascaded onto it. "Sixty-six of them."

"Are they more Taon?" Desjani asked, gazing at her own display, her face hard. "They're not enigmas or Dancers."

"Our systems are giving them a tentative identification as Taon," Yuon said. "There are some small differences in the exteriors even though the basic designs are similar to the Taon ships we've seen so far."

Desjani shook her head. "How would you compare a Syndic battle cruiser to an Alliance battle cruiser, Lieutenant?"

Yuon's expression grew worried. "Differences in the exteriors even though the basic designs are similar, Captain."

"Yeah." Desjani looked over at Geary. "This stinks."

"The shields on the new arrivals appear to be set much stronger than that we've seen on Taon ships prior to this," Lieutenant Castries said. "And . . . Captain, the Taon ships near us are increasing their shield settings. We're also picking up indications that sensors indicate may be weapons charging."

"This stinks," Geary agreed.

"Incoming message from the Taon," the communications watch announced.

Geary saw a virtual window pop open on his display, showing the image of Lokaa.

"Lokaa of Taon speaks to human friend! Enemy here! Will friend fight beside Taon?"

SIXTEEN

"SO, it was a trap," Geary said. "But not the one we expected. They want us to get involved on their side in what looks like a war between different factions of their species."

Desjani frowned heavily as she made rapid touches on her display. "Admiral, once we get out of this low orbit trap, getting out of this star system won't be easy if the new Taon try to intercept us before we reach the jump point we arrived at. We are leaving, right?"

"Damn right we are. But we have to figure out how to get our people on the surface into the shuttles and pick up the shuttles on the way without getting Taon suspicions up."

"Tell the Taon if we're going into a fight we need all of our people with us," Desjani said. "How can they object to that?"

"If they do, it wouldn't say much for their intentions," Geary said. He touched his comm controls to call the leaders of the group on the surface. He wasn't going to give the Taon a heads-up that his people were leaving, so he used the code phrase they'd agreed on for an emergency departure. "Liberty party, this is Admiral Geary. Muster a working party on the double. Over."

The reply came quickly. "This is Sergeant Barnwell. Understand muster a working party on the double, Admiral. It's late night where we are on the surface. Hopefully that will minimize any bystanders. Out."

"Here's a suggested vector to pick up the shuttles," Desjani said. "You do want the whole task force moving as one, right?"

"Yes. I don't want any ships separated from the rest." He studied the plan that Tanya had sent to his display. The entire Alliance task force would slide beneath the Taon ships in higher orbit, skimming just above atmosphere as they moved to intercept the two shuttles that would be rising to meet them. "How about after we pick up the shuttles?"

"I think we need two options, Admiral. One, if the Taon are just watching and not raising a fuss, and another if the Taon decide to chase us."

"That second option will depend on exactly what the Taon do," Geary said, rubbing his lower face with one hand. "Can you be ready to throw a vector together on the spur of the moment?"

She actually looked offended. "Is Betelgeuse a variable red supergiant star?"

"Last I looked," Geary said. It was past time to get his ships ready. Since Lokaa had called on the humans to aid in their fight, getting prepared for battle shouldn't raise any concerns among the Taon even though the "enemy" was light hours away. "All units in Task Force Alpha, this is Admiral Geary. Come to Readiness Condition One. I say again, come to Readiness Condition One."

As the general quarters alarm sounded aboard *Dauntless*, the same way the same alarm would be sounding on every one of the one hundred Alliance ships here, Geary turned back to his display. "All right. Let's see how our Marines are doing." The images from the collar cams were fuzzy. Were the Taon on the ground trying to jam them?

His message should have alerted the Trojan horse Marines in the shuttles as well. The more powerful communications from the shuttles and the Marines in them hadn't been impacted by whatever was hindering images from the collar cams. When he called up views from their battle armor he saw almost all of those Marines were ready to go.

While linked in that way, he could hear their communications as well. "Corporal Maya!" Gunnery Sergeant Orvis called over bursts of static. "You apes ready?"

"Ready to roll, Gunny," Maya responded, her voice tinged with excitement. "You've got a lot of noise on your circuit. What's holding you up?"

"We had to pop some locks to get everyone out. Expect to be on our way to you in thirty seconds."

"Thirty seconds," Corporal Maya repeated.

The shuttles had landed in a large open area bordered on three sides by three-story buildings and on the fourth by the lake, with plenty of room for passage between and past the structures. The human visitors had all been placed in the center building, facing the shuttles and beyond them the lake.

Geary saw the alerts on the corporal's armor heads-up display at the same time that Maya did. "Gunny, we got movement," she called. "Looks like some Taon running out into the open from one of the side buildings."

"Are they armed?" Orvis demanded.

"Sensors are giving me an ambiguous read, Gunny. The Taon hand weapons may not show up right to our scans. I think they are carrying."

"Stay in the shuttle until I give you the go-ahead. If they start shooting, don't wait for orders, just come out hot. Got it?"

"Got it, Gunny," Corporal Maya said. "Charge and load, Marines," she ordered her small force.

Geary clenched a fist so tightly it hurt. Should he be telling the Marines not to shoot? But Orvis had already ordered his support force not to engage unless the Taon started shooting. *I need to let the commander on the scene decide this.*

One of the shuttle display screens lit up as a Marine activated it, showing the outside in enhanced vision, two lines of Taon running out onto the landing field. The Taon moved in a slightly cumbersome manner, but quickly, reminding Geary of images he'd seen of Old Earth rhinos and hippos on the charge. The paths of the Taon made it clear they intended blocking the unarmed Marines who were spilling out of the building where their rooms were. "Gunnery Sergeant Orvis, Sergeant Barnwell, talk to me," Geary ordered. "Do you have Colonel Rogero and Dr. Nasr?"

"We've got both, Admiral," Sergeant Barnwell reported, her words coming out quickly as she moved. "They tried to lock us in, Admiral. We had to blow several locks with some concealed gear we had along just in case. I don't know what tipped the Taon off, but they knew we'd be leaving before we did."

"They might have done it as soon as they asked for our help against their enemies," Geary said. "I'd prefer to get this done without any dead or injured Taon. Don't open fire unless you absolutely have to. But you're on scene. You make the call if you have to do that." He knew Gunnery Sergeant Orvis was steady in a crisis, Sergeant Barnwell's record showed her having the same reliability, and backing them up was Colonel Rogero.

"Got it, Admiral," Orvis said over more bursts of static. "Only if we absolutely have to. I don't know how well you can see the view from our cams. We're facing a double line of Taon blocking our way to the shuttles." He raised his voice to shout to the Taon. "We've been recalled to our ships. We have to leave now."

"Not safe," one of the Taon called back. "Not safe to leave. Stay."

"We have orders to leave," Sergeant Barnwell shouted. "We cannot stay. We have to follow orders."

"Not safe," the Taon repeated. "Must stay."

Corporal Maya's voice came on the circuit. "Gunny, I'm picking up energy signatures. I think the Taon are charging weapons."

"Damn," Orvis muttered. "We must leave," he shouted to the Taon. "Move aside!"

"Not safe. Must stay."

"That's it. Pop the Trojan horses," Orvis ordered.

On his view through Corporal Maya's armor, Geary saw the big shuttle ramp drop and the five Marines come down it. He knew the same would be happening on the shuttle from *Inspire*.

"We must leave," Sergeant Barnwell shouted. "Move aside."

The Taon were shifting about, some looking back at the ten fully armored Marines who'd emerged from the shuttles, and others keeping their eyes and possibly their aim on the unarmed group of Marines to their front.

"Advance," Orvis ordered the Marines with him. "Slow step, keep it steady." With Orvis and Barnwell in the lead keeping the unarmed Marines moving at a slow pace, the liberty party began walking in a rough column toward the lines of Taon.

"How's it going down there?" Desjani asked him. "Why haven't they lifted yet?"

"The Taon don't want them to leave," Geary said.

"Hostages. Man, I hate it when Badaya is right," Desjani grumbled.

"Gunny, we got lots of movement showing off to the west!" Corporal Maya called. "I think they've got a butt-load of friends coming!"

"Advance your team," Orvis told her. "No weapons. Just use your armors' bulk. Clear us a path even if you have to shoulder the Taon aside."

"Advance, aye," Maya said. "Stay on me," she ordered the others. "Nobody shoot."

As the Marines in battle armor advanced on their rear, the double lines of Taon wavered. Even if all of them were armed, a fight between unprotected Taon and armored Marines would be one-sided. And while the Taon were physically more imposing than humans, they were not as large and powerful as the humans in battle armor.

The Taon slowly gave way, backing, as the armored Marines moved until they'd forced open a lane in the Taon lines. "Pick it up!" Sergeant Barnwell ordered as she and Orvis broke into a trot. "If anyone lags I'll let the Taon keep you for a souvenir!" The unarmed Marines dashed between the Taon, splitting into two columns once past and heading for the two shuttles.

The Taon watched without moving, their weapons still lowered.

As the Marines ran up the ramps into the shuttles, the armored Marines backed toward them, keeping their eyes and weapons on the Taon as more alerts popped up. "There's at least a hundred more coming around that building!" a shuttle pilot shouted. "No, two hundred! Let's get out of here!"

"Give me a count!" Orvis ordered as the Marines hastily strapped in and the shuttle ramps raised and sealed.

"We're one short! Where's Francis?"

"Sergeant Barnwell!" Orvis called. "We're short one. Have you got Private Francis?"

"Wait. Yeah. He got on the wrong bird."

"Francis, you idiot! Have you got a full count of yours, Barb?"

"I've got a full count," Sergeant Barnwell confirmed.

Through Maya's armor, Geary could see Gunnery Sergeant Orvis looking around the shuttle interior. "Colonel Rogero? Got you. Doc? That's everyone. Let's lift!"

"We've detected the shuttles leaving the surface," Desjani reported. "They're both rising fast."

"Let's go get them," Geary said. "All units in Task Force Alpha, accelerate to point zero zero five light speed, match movements to *Dauntless*." This close to a planet, normal deep space maneuvering commands were too clumsy, and velocities in any appreciable fraction of the speed of light were very dangerous.

As the Alliance ships accelerated at what, for them, was a very sedate pace, Lieutenant Yuon called out. "Captain! We've spotted some probable Taon aerospace craft rising from bases west and south of the shuttles. Performance profiles match those of warbirds."

"That's our guys' cue to go stealth," Desjani said. A moment later the two shuttles suddenly vanished from the displays as they activated all of their concealment capabilities.

Hearing something behind him, Geary turned to see Kommodor Bradamont strapping into the observer seat at the back of the bridge. "Colonel Rogero is aboard our shuttle," he told her. "No shots have been fired."

Bradamont nodded, looking and sounding calm. She had to be worried about Rogero, but she'd been in a lot of dangerous situations before this one. "This is where we find out how effective Alliance stealth technology is against Taon sensors."

"Yes," Geary said, because there really wasn't anything else to say.

"Six minutes to rendezvous with the shuttles," Lieutenant Castries said. "We've got movement from the Taon ships in higher orbit. They appear to be maneuvering to keep us blocked in lower orbit."

"Captain Desjani," Geary said, "I need a vector from where we pick up the shuttles to the jump point at maximum fleet acceleration, one that avoids coming close enough to either the Taon ships above us or to the new Taon to risk an engagement with them."

He gazed at the message window, trying to decide whether to respond to Lokaa again. Lying about his intentions felt wrong, putting him on the same moral plane as Lokaa's attempt to force the Alliance into fighting on their side. But he didn't want to tip Lokaa off that the human fleet definitely wouldn't be taking part in this battle. Lokaa might have more surprises up their sleeve.

It wouldn't hurt to make Lokaa think this was going their way, though.

Triggering the message function to the Taon, he spoke calmly. "This is Admiral Geary to Lokaa. My ships are moving to pick up our shuttles prior to any fighting in this star system. I request you advise the purpose of your ships' movements."

They were still three minutes from recovering the shuttles when Lokaa's image appeared on Geary's display. "Human friend not need recover shuttles. Safe with Taon. Advise your battle plan."

Geary decided now was a time to be truthful, because otherwise he'd have to outright lie. "We do not want a battle."

Did Lokaa's expression indicate surprise or some other emotion? "Human not want war? Human in ship for war. Human have lots of ships for war."

"To defend our people," Geary said. "We had to cross the space of a species we call the enigmas to reach the space controlled by those you call the eight-legs. We do not want a battle."

"So human say," Lokaa commented. A moment later their image disappeared.

"That translator of theirs is getting better at a pretty quick rate," Geary commented. "I wish we had any idea at all what types of weapons the Taon have, how good they are, and how well their ships can maneuver at maximum."

"Maybe we'll find out soon," Desjani muttered as she worked the maneuvering problem. "I'm having to use assumptions about their acceleration and maneuvering capabilities on this vector workup. But you also need to think about how this is going to look like we're running away."

Which was a problem in a fleet that still subscribed to a mantra developed during the long and bloody war with the Syndics that the fleet never retreated. Geary touched his fleet command comm circuit. "All units in Task Force Alpha. We've been set up by the Taon, who want us to get involved in their war by forcing us to engage these newly arrived warships. I have no intention of losing human lives in a war being fought between two factions we know nothing about. We fight on our terms for causes we choose. After recovering the shuttles which were on the planet's surface I intend repositioning the task force to return to the jump point that will bring us back to Dancer space. We will attempt to avoid engaging any of the Taon ships in order to prevent any claim that we did intervene in the battle that's about to take place in this star system. Stand by for high-stress maneuvering orders. Geary, out."

"The shuttles should be thirty seconds out from recovery," Lieutenant Yuon reported. "We have twenty Taon probable warbirds conducting search patterns in the upper reaches of the planet's atmosphere."

Geary studied the movements of the alien warbirds. "They're in the right general area. Either that's based on estimating the vectors of the shuttles, or they're picking up some indications of the shuttles but can't localize them." He touched the command circuit. "Lieutenant Commander Cady, maneuver the Sixth Destroyer Squadron to block any of those Taon warbirds from trying to continue their search for our shuttles past the atmosphere."

"The Sixth is on it, Admiral!"

Like the Taon on the ground, the warbirds dropped away as the Alliance destroyers roared into lower orbits that challenged the Taon to respond.

A couple of seconds before reaching *Dauntless* and *Inspire*, the two shuttles deactivated their stealth, abruptly appearing on sensors just as they approached the shuttle docks on both battle cruisers. The shuttle pilots came in with more finesse and a little less speed than nonstealth pilots used, but still had their birds grounded safely very quickly. The shuttle dock crew on *Dauntless* jumped into action, securing the bird without waiting for anyone to disembark.

"Dock reports shuttle secure," Lieutenant Castries said.

"*Inspire* reports her shuttle is secure," the comm watch added.

"Here's my best guess," Desjani said as Geary's display lit up with the arc of the proposed vector.

His gaze went from the arc to the Taon ships in higher orbit. "They're already moving to block that vector."

"It's too obvious," Desjani said.

"Then let's do something not obvious. We're stuck in lower orbit at the moment, so . . ." He grinned, though the smile felt too tight with tension. "Let's stay there. Let's whip the fleet around this planet far enough we can slingshot off the other side on a new vector."

"What, like some ancient spaceship?" Desjani smiled as well. "No, that's not obvious. Let's see how well the Taon can keep up with this."

"All units," Geary sent, "match movements of *Dauntless*. We're going to loop closely around the planet before accelerating away. Sixth

Destroyer Squadron, return to your places in the formation." Ending the message, he nodded to Desjani. "Take us around, Captain."

"With pleasure, Admiral." Her hands moved over the maneuvering controls while Desjani gazed intently on her display where the planet, their altitude above its surface, and the levels of atmospheric density were portrayed. Despite their apparently streamlined shapes done for engineering and defensive reasons, the Alliance ships weren't designed for use in dense atmosphere. If they accelerated all out in such an environment their shields would fail almost instantly and the resistance the air created would incinerate the ships.

And in any case staying above the planet in a lower orbit required limiting the velocity of the ships. Desjani accelerated *Dauntless* carefully, at a small fraction of her capability, using thrusters to cant the battle cruiser's nose "down" toward the planet to compensate for the tendency of an object moving faster to rise to a higher orbit. With the Taon ships above them, the Alliance ships couldn't rise far without appearing to threaten the alien force.

Usually in space, higher velocities were effectively invisible to humans. Whether you were going one thousand kilometers per hour or ten thousand kilometers per hour, the view outside was the same, though at one hundred thousand kilometers per hour relativity was kicking in enough to distort the outside views a bit.

But here they were only a couple of thousand kilometers from the planet beneath them, providing a clear reference as the Alliance ships spun around the globe. It was breathtaking, and a little dizzying.

The Taon ships trying to block the Alliance task force were caught unprepared by the move, belatedly accelerating to match the movements of the human ships, but thrown off again when the human ships continued on around the planet rather than breaking quickly for open space.

"We're going to have the opening we need," Desjani said.

"Take whatever vector looks good," Geary ordered. "We'll work out the path to the jump point once we're clear of the planet."

Another message from Lokaa came in. Humans hadn't had any luck translating emotions amid the bony ridges on the Taon faces, but Lokaa's mouth formed a straight line instead of the open oval that was apparently a Taon smile. "Where go human friend? Wish match movement. Fight enemy. Fight battle."

Even in the midst of everything else going on, Geary noticed for the first time that the Taon translator kept getting better but still didn't seem to have any grasp of personal pronouns. Did that offer a clue to how the Taon thought? If so, he couldn't waste time worrying about that now.

"We do not want to fight this battle," Geary told Lokaa.

"Why not? Why not fight? Human have ship for war."

He decided to be fully candid. "Humans fight for reasons. For causes. For what we think is right. We do not know your cause. We do not know your enemy. We do not want to kill or destroy those we know nothing of."

It was easy to imagine Victoria Rione, or even General Charban, giving him a sardonic look in response to those statements. He'd told Lokaa what humans liked to believe about themselves. What they aspired to, but often failed at. But if he was going to give Lokaa a reason, he preferred offering an aspiration to confessing to human failures.

After a long moment, Lokaa spoke again. "So human say." A moment later that message ended as well.

What exactly was going on with the Taon? Geary wondered. But he kept that doubt inside. There was enough worry around without him letting the fleet know he was uncertain about what was happening.

"Here we go," Desjani announced as *Dauntless* and the rest of the Alliance ships went past three-quarters of an orbit, the Taon ships commanded by Lokaa trying to catch up but open space ahead. She punched her thruster controls, pitching *Dauntless*'s bow toward the stars.

It was time to get out of here.

"All units in Task Force Alpha, this is Admiral Geary. Immediate execute accelerate to point two light speed at maximum sustained acceleration. I say again, immediate execute accelerate to point two light speed at maximum sustained acceleration. Continue to conform to *Dauntless*'s vector. Geary, out."

He felt the force of the acceleration pinning him to his seat as the battle cruiser's main propulsion lit off at full power, hurling *Dauntless* away from the planet. All around her, the rest of the Alliance ships were doing the same, leaping outward at a rate of acceleration that caused the inertial dampers to whine in protest and set off stress warning alarms on every ship.

"I love this."

Tanya Desjani had spoken in a low voice, but he'd heard her. Geary turned his head carefully against the g-forces pressing on him, seeing her gazing at her display with a fierce smile. "I hate to break up this moment between you and your ship, Captain, but the destroyers won't be able to match this acceleration for long."

"I'll be easing up the acceleration a bit in thirty seconds," Desjani said. "I wanted to get off to a quick start."

"And put on a display for the benefit of the Taon."

"That, too." She was watching her display still, a wary look replacing her earlier joy. "In a moment we're going to see if they can match our acceleration."

Or exceed it, Geary thought. If that happened, he'd face some hard choices fairly soon.

The Taon ships near the planet had been caught off guard again, but were now scrambling to re-form as they accelerated after the Alliance warships.

Something about their movement bothered Geary, but it took a moment to realize what it was. "They're matching us."

"In acceleration, you mean?" Desjani nodded, studying her display. Her initial calm acceptance of his words faded into a worried frown. "They're accelerating at the exact same rate we are."

"Yes. What are the odds they'd have exactly the same capability as us?"

"Pretty slim," Desjani said. "That implies they're holding back, not accelerating as hard as they could. But why? And why are they lining up to chase us instead of heading to intercept that enemy fleet that showed up? I thought those were Lokaa's enemies. Why would they leave their planet uncovered while they chase us?"

With Lokaa's fleet staying at a fixed distance astern of the Alliance ships, the situation didn't look too complicated. The Alliance task force was accelerating on a vector for the same jump point they'd arrived at, aiming to return to Dancer space. At point two light speed, they could cover the two light hours to that jump point in about twenty hours, but time required to accelerate, and then brake their velocity to point one light to enter jump, meant it would require more like twenty-three hours.

Off the port bows of the Alliance ships was the new Taon fleet, the enemies that Lokaa had referred to. Those ships had come in at a jump point two point six light hours from the star, and after arriving had quickly accelerated onto a vector aimed at intercepting in its orbit the planet that the Alliance task force and Lokaa's Taon fleet had been at. If the new ships held to that vector, they wouldn't come anywhere near the Alliance ships. And there was no reason to expect them to change their vector.

But since those warships were still close to two light hours from the current position of the Alliance fleet, that information was two hours old.

"As of now, it looks like we've got a clean shot out of here," Desjani said.

Geary scowled at his display, mistrusting that good fortune and still trying to understand Lokaa's motives. "The new Taon fleet. Call it the enemy Taon fleet. What happens if they alter vector to intercept Lokaa's Taon when they see Lokaa's ships are chasing us?"

Desjani ran one hand over her display, her fingers moving rapidly as she made some swift calculations. "They'd catch Lokaa's ships about twenty light minutes short of the jump point. If their acceleration and maneuvering capability is roughly equal to ours."

"How close would the enemy Taon get to us if that happens?"

"A minimum of ten light seconds."

Geary felt his jaw tighten. "That's too close for comfort."

"It's way outside of weapons' range," Desjani pointed out. "Unless . . . you're not thinking about helping Lokaa, are you?"

"I don't see how we can do that and stay neutral in whatever war is going on here," Geary said. "We don't need another war with another alien species. Especially after . . ." He let his voice trail off, not wanting to go down that road.

"Permission to speak freely, Admiral."

He gave her an exasperated look. "You know you always have that."

She turned to look at him, her expression intense. "Admiral, you may be justly worried about getting us involved in another war, about what people would say if Black Jack found yet another alien race and promptly started fighting them. But I urge you not to make decisions on the basis of what people might say. All we can do is try to take the right actions based on our best estimates of what is going on and what is in the best interests of this task force and of the Alliance. But, whatever your decisions are, they shouldn't be made because of worries about what some people might say. You've never done that. I advise you not to start."

"Thank you, Captain," Geary said. "That's good advice."

"In another hour and a half, we'll see what the enemy Taon fleet did when it saw Lokaa's Taon come chasing after us, and then we'll have a better idea of what we need to do differently, or if we should just get out of this star system as fast as our ships can get us to that jump point. But there's no reason to believe at this time that we'll have to jump into the middle of someone else's war instead of jumping away from this star system."

An hour and a half later, they had a reason.

"The enemy Taon force altered vector when they saw us," Lieutenant Yuon began. "They're . . . what?"

"Lieutenant?" Desjani prompted sharply.

"They . . . they altered vector to intercept us short of the jump point, Captain!"

"To intercept *us*? Not Lokaa's Taon?" Desjani glared at her display, looking for errors in the estimate that weren't there. "They are. Why in hell would they be trying to intercept us?"

"Maybe they'll adjust their vector when they see . . ." Geary shook his head in disbelief. "They stayed steady. They should have seen our exact vector by that time, as well as the exact vector of Lokaa's Taon. But they're on a clean intercept aimed at us."

"They'll hit us twenty light minutes short of the jump point," Desjani said. "We— What's Lokaa doing?"

"The Taon ships astern of us are accelerating," Lieutenant Castries said. "At the current rate they will be within estimated weapons range in five hours."

"This is a setup!" Desjani said. "Admiral, Lokaa and this new force aren't enemies. They're going to hit us together."

"No," Geary said, earning himself a disbelieving look from Desjani. "Captain, if that was Lokaa's intent, why wouldn't they be aiming to get within range of us at the same time as the enemy Taon force intercepted us? Why close the range hours before that time and make two separate, uncoordinated attacks?"

She glowered at him, then at her display. "That's true. Why would Lokaa have set up a perfect double attack and then blow it? But what *is* Lokaa doing?"

"I guess I should ask," Geary said. He called on the circuit Lokaa had always used, and received an almost immediate response. "Friend Lokaa," Geary said, "why are you pursuing my ships? We only wish to leave this star system in peace."

"Human think odds bad?" Lokaa asked, the translated voice sounding strangely flat.

It seemed curiously like a taunt, one schoolchild trying to egg on another.

"It has nothing to do with the odds," Geary said. "If we joined in with you against those you call your enemies the odds would be very good. We do not wish to fight in a war being fought for reasons we don't know. We do not wish a battle here."

"Battle come. Will human in ships of war fight?"

"We do not wish to fight," Geary said. "We will defend ourselves if necessary, but only if necessary."

"So human say." With that, Lokaa ended the call.

NORMALLY space actions allowed more time to relax the crews before a battle. But in this case, with possibly only five hours until Lokaa's ships would be within firing range, and possibly less time than that if the Taon had superior weaponry, there wasn't much time available for standing down the crews. "All units stand down from combat readiness to ensure that your crews are fed," Geary ordered. "Get them what rest you can. Alertness meds are authorized. All units should be ready to return to full combat readiness in four hours." Maybe that was too early, but if the Taon had any more surprises up their sleeves he wanted to be ready.

Dr. Nasr came by the bridge to administer "up" patches to everyone to maintain alertness as their continuous time on duty went over the maximums allowed. Nasr paused by Geary as he slapped a med patch on his arm. "The Taon on the surface did not seem hostile to me," he said.

"How many lives do I risk on that judgment, Doctor?" Geary asked in a low voice.

Nasr took a moment to reply. "I judged the Kicks based on what I saw of them. I am doing the same with the Taon."

"Thank you, Doctor." As much as he respected Dr. Nasr, and his judgment, that seemed to Geary to be a very slim reed on which to decide the fate of a hundred ships and their crews.

Unable to focus on anything else, he stayed on the bridge, eating ration bars and grateful that their taste wasn't really registering on him.

Desjani sat in her command seat next to his, her eyes on her display. Probably knowing he wasn't in the mood to talk, or possibly not knowing of anything to say that would help him decide what to do, she remained silent.

At the four-hour point all of his ships reported their full readiness for a battle he didn't want to fight.

He tried another message. "Lokaa, your behavior is threatening to us. We feel endangered by the approach of your ships of war. I request that you maintain your distance from my ships to avoid any possibility of inadvertent exchange of fire."

Lokaa's arms shifted in what might have been a Taon shrug. "Why human friend talk of exchanging fire? Human said did not want to fight."

"We don't know what you intend," Geary said.

"Friend trust friend." With that, Lokaa ended the message.

"The Taon ships commanded by Lokaa will be within estimated range in thirty minutes," Lieutenant Castries reported.

There seemed only one good option at this point: giving Lokaa an ultimatum. How should he phrase it?

General Charban chose this of all times to call.

Geary was moving to deny the call when he took a moment to think about it. Charban knew what kind of pressures he was facing at this moment. Charban had been in tough command situations. If he was calling, it must be for a good reason.

Geary tapped the accept tab, angry at himself and at Charban.

Charban spoke quickly, without any greeting. "Admiral, I see the Taon force tailing us is closing the distance. Are you thinking of establishing a red line that they must not cross?"

"Yes. That's exactly what I'm thinking of doing. I can't let them get too close and do nothing."

"And what will you do if the Taon cross that red line?"

Geary hesitated. "I'll decide when that happens, based on the total situation."

"Admiral, as a former combat commander to a current combat commander, I urge you in the strongest possible terms not to set out a red line the Taon must not cross unless you have already decided what you will do if they cross it."

What kind of advice was that? Geary almost ended the call, but paused once more to think. Charban knew his advice wouldn't be welcomed, but he was giving it anyway. "Why?"

"Because once you declare a red line, you *have* made a decision," Charban said. "A decision that if and when the Taon cross that line you will only have two options. Either open fire, and turn this confrontation into a hot war, or back down and do nothing, which will make you look weak and perhaps encourage the Taon to attack. You'll have to do one of those two things. Are you ready to decide which one?"

"No," Geary said.

"Will you be if and when the Taon cross whatever line you've established?"

"Probably not. I hate having my choices limited, and I don't like giving an opponent the power to force specific actions on me." Geary paused to think again. "What's my better option, General?"

"If you look at the actions of the Taon up to this point," Charban said, "they could be said to constitute a series of trust games. Will the humans accept the invitation? Will they bring a substantial number of ships into an unknown situation? Will they agree to go into low orbit about a Taon planet? Will they accept the local Taon fleet getting closer and closer and ending up in high orbit? Will they accept the invitation to send some of their people down to the planet? Will they open fire in order to evacuate those people?"

"You're saying this might be another trust game by the Taon? Closing on my forces like a pursuing enemy trying to get within range of their weapons?"

"I am saying," Charban insisted, "that we don't know what they intend this time, but every prior time they have not opened fire on us. We were pretty well trapped while in low orbit with them in high orbit above us. Am I correct in that?"

"If they'd chosen a surprise attack on us under those circumstances, it would have been a difficult situation," Geary admitted.

"If the Taon don't want war, maybe they want to test whether we really want war," Charban said. "Will we do the stereotypically military thing and start blazing away when things get difficult or scary? Can we be trusted to trust them? Or, if the Taon do want war, why haven't they already hit us when we were in a disadvantageous position? Or perhaps their laws or their culture may demand that the other side has to fire the first shot, and they're pushing to cause us to do that. Either way, we don't want to shoot. And I say that as a man who lost far too many soldiers in ground actions against clever opponents, and knows that sometimes there is no alternative to firepower discreetly applied."

"I will carefully consider your arguments," Geary said, his mind swirling with contradictory possible courses of action.

"I can't ask for more than that. Thank you, Admiral."

"No, thank you, General."

Geary ended the call, staring glumly at his display. "Captain Desjani, what would've happened at the planet if the Taon had launched a surprise attack on us before we left orbit?"

"You mean when they were two light seconds away in higher orbit?" She shook her head, her eyes still on her display. "You know the answer to that. Unless their weapons are far inferior to ours, we would've been cut to pieces."

"If they want to attack us, why didn't they do it then?"

"You're asking me to explain how these Taon think?" She gave him a sidelong glare. "Isn't that why we're here? To figure out how they think? Maybe they didn't want a lot of debris from destroyed Alliance ships falling on their planet. Maybe they were celebrating a holiday when surprise attacks are prohibited. Maybe their commander lost their nerve. Maybe they sacrificed whatever a Taon goat is and didn't like the looks of its entrails. I don't know, sir!"

Lokaa's ships continued approaching steadily closer.

Geary knew he had plenty of justification to open fire. Warning shots, at least.

Rione had often urged him to look at things from different angles. What would be the different angle here?

That Lokaa had given him plenty of justification to open fire.

That by this slow, steady approach, Lokaa was effectively giving Geary every opportunity to open fire.

"I can't judge a Taon by human thinking," Geary said out loud. "But that's all I've got to work with."

Desjani glanced at him. "Should we lock our fire control systems on targets?"

"No." Geary checked his display. A control there gave him, the fleet commander, control over all of the fleet's weapons, allowing him to give permission to them to fire, or forbid it.

He made sure the control was set to red.

"You're denying our ships the ability to fire even in self-defense?" Desjani asked, her voice very carefully modulated.

"Yes."

SEVENTEEN

THERE was a long pause, Captain Desjani's eyes on her display. "I know you've thought this through," Tanya Desjani finally said in a very low voice. "Let me know what you need from me."

"You just gave me what I needed," Geary said.

He watched, and waited.

"Five minutes until Taon ships reach maximum estimated weapons range," Lieutenant Castries reported, unable to resist a curious and anxious glance at Geary.

"Very well," Captain Desjani said, sounding totally unworried.

Geary nodded to signify that he'd heard.

"Admiral?" Kommodor Bradamont said.

He looked behind him, seeing her in the observer seat at the back of the bridge. Colonel Rogero had come up at some point, still looking slightly disheveled after his adventure returning to the ship, and was standing beside her. "Yes?"

"Sir, what do you think the Taon are doing? This looks aggressive."

"It does," Geary said. "I think, though, that the Taon are trying to figure out just how aggressive we are."

Bradamont didn't argue the point, instead nodding in understanding and speaking to Rogero in a quiet voice.

"It's a little scary," Geary muttered to Desjani, "that people trust me so much."

"They trust you for a reason," she murmured in reply. "You earned it."

He really, really hoped he wasn't making as big a mistake as anyone could make.

"Taon ships astern are within estimated maximum weapons range," Lieutenant Castries reported.

"And still coming on at the same pace," Desjani said.

Geary nodded silently again, thinking that Lokaa's ships had just passed the red line he would've established for them, and realizing how right Charban had been. Because if he had faced only those two options right now, he wouldn't have wanted to take either one of them.

Lokaa's ships kept closing the distance, now well within any possible weapons range.

Captain Badaya called in. "Admiral? What's our plan here?"

"You need to talk to them," Desjani told Geary.

"I'm going to inform the entire task force," Geary told Badaya, then shifted to talk to every ship. "All units, this is Admiral Geary. Lokaa has not demonstrated hostile intent. I believe they are progressing toward our formation in order to engage the enemy Taon force which is on intercept with us. We will not engage Lokaa's Taon force, which has had ample opportunity before this to attack us if they so desired. I want every unit focused on dealing with the enemy Taon force if necessary. Geary, out."

Badaya came on again. "Admiral, are you certain of this?"

Hell, no. "Yes."

Desjani was speaking to someone else on her display. Finishing, she glanced at Geary. "That was Roberto Duellos. He's concerned. I told him not to be."

"I really hope I don't make a liar of you," Geary muttered too low for anyone but her to hear.

It got harder to look calm and decisive as Lokaa's ships kept coming.

The Alliance task force was still in the "nonthreatening" sphere formation, as usual a three-dimensional lattice of ships. The Taon ships coming in behind had been in a lozenge shape, a rectangular box, but as they reached the edge of the Alliance formation, the Taon split into groups of six that proceeded slowly among the Alliance ships.

"I have never seen anything like this," Desjani said, staring at her display as the Taon ships slowly edged in all about the inside of the Alliance formation. "This is insane."

"What are they doing?" Kommodor Bradamont asked, sounding as aghast as Desjani was.

Geary knew what she was really asking, what everyone in this task force was probably asking at this moment, was "What are we doing?"

He clenched his fist, determined not to let his growing unease cause him to release weapons control. For better or worse, he'd committed the Alliance ships to this course of action.

The Taon ships began finally slowing their acceleration as the last of them slid in among the Alliance formation, slowing until they all exactly matched the vectors of the Alliance ships.

If a fight started now, with the two forces intermingled and relative velocity and movement at zero, it would be a bloodbath. Even if they managed to return fire and seriously hurt Lokaa's fleet, the Alliance task force would be massacred.

A clamor of messages started coming in for him. Ship captains, urgently requesting release of weapons control. Urgently asking to take action before it was too late.

But Geary kept wondering why the Taon would want their own ships in such a vulnerable position before they started shooting. He breathed in and out a couple of times, calming himself, running differing arguments through his mind.

Reaching for his controls, he activated the fleet command circuit to respond to everyone at once. "All units in Task Force Alpha, this is

Admiral Geary. I am retaining central control of weapons on every ship. No one is authorized to fire. Geary, out."

Desjani gave him a despairing look, before nodding and shifting to grim resolve. "Got your back, Admiral."

"I know."

The last word had barely left his mouth when Lokaa's Taon ships opened fire.

IT was one of those moments in which time seemed to slow to a crawl, everything happening very slowly even though part of Geary's mind knew it was an illusion. The strident cries of alarms on *Dauntless* nearly drowned out the gasps of shock and fear from members of the crew.

Geary, knowing it was already too late, blaming himself, hating himself for being responsible for the deaths of so many lives entrusted to him, reached for the weapons-free authorization command with what felt like glacial slowness. By the time he could reach it, *Dauntless* would be riddled by shots.

Desjani began to snarl in defiance of the death that seemed inevitable, her own hands reaching for her firing controls.

But Geary stopped his hand's motion as he realized something was missing.

Where were the warnings of hits? The announcements of damage? *Dauntless* hadn't shaken as her shields took hits. And the Taon had only fired a single salvo, not following up with more shots.

Tanya Desjani had noticed, too. "How could they have missed?" she demanded. "Zero relative speed. Close enough to hit us with a spitball. And they *missed*?"

"I'm not seeing a single damage report from any ship in the task force," Geary said, scanning his display. "All units, this is Admiral Geary. Any unit that took a hit to its shields or hull report immediately."

Silence answered him.

"Captain," Lieutenant Yuon said, his voice a bit shaky, "the Taon employed directed energy weapons. There weren't any registered hits, but . . . either their weapons are much weaker than ours, or they were fired on a low-power setting such as we use for hell lance training."

"That was a *test*?" Desjani growled, her face a mask of anger. "They scared the hell out of us because they wanted to see what we'd do?"

"Apparently," Geary said, his mind still catching up to the fact that he wasn't dead. That no one was dead.

"How incredibly *stupid* was that? If we'd been poised to shoot, someone's finger would've twitched on the controls and right now we'd be bashing each other to pieces at short range!"

"I guess they learned that we weren't poised to shoot," Geary said, trying to slow his breathing as stress hormones belatedly raced through his body.

"It's still *stupid!*" Desjani got her own breathing under control. "I'm torn between a desire to unload every weapon I've got at them for doing that, and admiration for how much guts it took for them to risk that move."

Geary saw a message coming in from Lokaa and tapped accept.

The Taon looked out at Geary with an attitude that somehow no longer conveyed effusive welcome, but rather measured judgment. "Human is human. Human words truth. Lokaa see true human friend. Other Taon enemy. Lokaa fight. Human return to eight-legs."

"Why are the other Taon *our* enemy?" Geary asked, still too rattled to yell at Lokaa for taking such an incredible risk to see if the humans had been honest when saying they did not want a fight.

"Enemy Taon enemy humans, enemy any not Taon," Lokaa explained. "Want Taon space only Taon."

"Xenophobes," Desjani said. "A political faction that hates aliens. That's why they turned to intercept us. That's why Lokaa knew they'd do that."

"We understand," Geary told Lokaa. "We are leaving. But we remain friends to Taon who seek friends."

"Understand. May have fight anyway before jump." Lokaa's mouth formed the oval that seemed to correspond to a human smile. "Peace between this Taon and human."

"Peace to you," Geary said. "To the honor of our ancestors."

"Wait," Desjani demanded as Lokaa's image vanished, "are they the good guys now?"

"Looks like it," Geary said. "But we're not out of the woods yet."

"The enemy Taon are ten minutes from intercept," Desjani said, pointing at her display.

"The Taon ships among our formation are accelerating again," Lieutenant Castries called out. "Fast. They're going to clear our formation within two seconds at their current rate."

"They're moving to intercept the enemy force before it reaches us," Geary said.

"The shields of the Taon ships near us are increasing in strength," Lieutenant Castries added, her voice taking on an element of disbelief. "They are stabilizing at approximately thirty percent higher than our maximums. Across the board, thirty percent higher than our maximum shield strengths."

"I wonder how they manage that?" Geary murmured, his mind on what might have happened if he had tried to engage the Taon in combat.

"They can outaccelerate us and they have better shields," Desjani said, her expression grim. "I've got a bad feeling about how their weapons stack up next to ours."

"Can we get out of this without engaging the other Taon?" Geary asked, studying his display.

"No," Desjani said, eyes narrowed as she studied options. "Not if the other Taon force can accelerate like Lokaa's. Not even if Lokaa's ships engage them. We'll need to outmaneuver them. Lieutenant Yuon! Have the combat systems mark all of Lokaa's Taon ships with green markers and all of the xenophobe Taon ships with red."

"You're right, Captain," Geary said as he studied his own display, watching the movements of Lokaa's ships, the xenophobe Taon, and the

Alliance task force. The xenophobe ships were above and off the port bows of the Alliance ships, staying steady on that relative bearing as they closed on an intercept. "We can't avoid a serious exchange of fire even if we dodge."

"That depends on how we dodge," she said, her entire focus intent on her display. "We've got six minutes left before intercept. What are the enemy Taon going to expect us to do? All they've seen us do so far is head for the jump point, so they know that's where we want to go."

"They've seen us accelerate away from other Taon," Geary said. "They know we want to reach that jump point. So . . ."

"They'll expect us to either accelerate or try to blow past them at this velocity," Desjani finished. She glanced at him. "Sounds like we need to either swing wide or brake."

"Or both."

Lokaa's ships were leaping forward, clearing the human formation and angling to hit the oncoming xenophobe Taon before they could reach the human ships. As they closed to intercept, the xenophobe Taon formation also disintegrated into six-ship groups. Geary gazed at his display in disbelief at the swarm of small formations interweaving, totally different from the large formations that humans used. "This isn't our kind of fight."

"Maneuvering recommendation on the way," Desjani said.

Geary gave it a quick once-over before forwarding it to every ship in the fleet. "All units in Task Force Alpha, this is Admiral Geary. Immediate execute come starboard one five zero degrees, up zero two zero degrees, brake velocity to point one light at maximum sustainable rate."

It was long past time to drop the inefficient sphere formation as well. "All units in Task Force Alpha, immediate execute, assume Formation Tango. I say again, assume Formation Tango."

Worked out beforehand, Formation Tango had the outer human ships collapsing in toward the center of the formation to form a bulging ovoid with one wide side facing the oncoming attackers, the Alliance battle cruisers forming three centers of firepower in the center and out toward either side, the light cruisers and destroyers lined up around them.

More alerts were sounding on the human ships as the swarm of six-ship xenophobe Taon formations blew through Lokaa's swarm only to find the human ships swinging out, up, and braking hard. Aiming for where the human ships would have been if they'd kept on the same vector, the fifty-five surviving xenophobe ships found themselves too far ahead and below the vector the Alliance task force was bending onto.

Too far away for short-range weapons, the xenophobe Taon unleashed a volley of missiles aimed at the Alliance warships.

"Damn those things are fast," Desjani gasped as the Taon missiles leaped toward the human ships.

"We can't dodge or outmaneuver them," Geary said. "All units, continue braking and pivot bows to engage oncoming missiles."

With the main drives pointed in another direction, the human ships began curving at a shallower angle from their former vector, still slowing as the Taon missiles rapidly closed the gap.

"Release weapons control," Desjani said as if to herself.

Cursing his absentmindedness, Geary punched the control to let all of his ships fire on local control. "I'm an idiot sometimes."

"You read Lokaa right," she said. "Those missiles are coming in very fast and aiming for where we'll be at our current rate of deceleration."

"Got it." Geary watched the Taon missiles, knowing he had to call this maneuver right. "All units in Task Force Alpha, immediate execute, cease braking velocity."

Without their main drives slowing them, the human ships kept moving faster than the missiles had aimed for. The flock of missiles, moving too fast to adjust vector in time, swept across the back of the human task force. Every human ship, their bows pointed aft, unleashed hell lance particle beams as the missiles swung about to make another approach on the human ships.

Only about a dozen missiles survived the hell lance barrage, getting close enough for the nearest Alliance warships to unleash grapeshot at them, the shotgun blasts of metal ball bearings impossible for the last missiles to evade.

"Those xenophobe guys shot first," Desjani said.

"I noticed," he said.

"I just wanted to be sure."

Geary was already watching the xenophobe Taon force coming around on a variety of vectors to engage the human ships. They were spread across space along the same vector the Alliance ships would need to reach the jump point, and accelerating toward the Alliance ships at the same impressive rate that Lokaa's ships could achieve. "All units in Task Force Alpha, immediate execute, come port zero four zero, come down zero one zero, accelerate to point one five light speed."

The Alliance ships swung their bows to point toward the jump point again, their main propulsion kicking in to hurl them toward the oncoming xenophobe Taon.

"The battle cruisers are going to accelerate faster than the rest of our ships," Desjani said. "Are we leading the charge?"

"We are," Geary said. "All battle cruisers of the First, Second, and Third Divisions. Concentrate your fire to clear out the xenophobe Taon ships closest to our vector as we go through them."

Lokaa's ships were charging back into the xenophobe ships as the Alliance task force tore through both, the human ships hurling shots at the xenophobe ships. Geary felt *Dauntless* jolt from hits as the Alliance ships raced through into open space.

"They were coming at us at better than point one light," Desjani said. "We were also above point one, so combined relative engagement speed was well above point two light."

He knew why she was pointing that out. At velocities higher than point two light, human fire control systems had trouble scoring hits in the tiny fractions of seconds in which other ships were within range.

As a result, the human fire hadn't knocked out any xenophobe ships, though it had badly damaged a few.

But this was one area in which the Taon didn't seem much better than humans. They hadn't scored many hits on the Alliance ships, either.

But they had managed a number of hits using Taon directed energy weapons more powerful than human hell lances.

"Light cruisers *Croice* and *Pommel* took two hits that penetrated their shields," Lieutenant Yuon reported. "The xenophobe Taon concentrated fire on *Daring* and *Formidable*, but neither ship suffered major damage. All ships retain full propulsion and maneuverability."

"That jump point is coming up, Admiral," Desjani said. "We need to get back to point one light before we get to it or we'll have to come around again."

"Give me the maneuver, Captain Desjani!"

"Here."

"Beautiful," Geary said, taking in the maneuver in a glance. "All units in Task Force Alpha, immediate execute come port zero zero four degrees, come down zero zero one degrees, brake to point one light at ninety-two percent main propulsion."

The xenophobe Taon, their numbers now down to forty-eight after tangling once more with Lokaa's ships, were whipping about to come at the Alliance formation again. The Alliance ships had their bows pointed at the oncoming xenophobes as their main propulsion slowed them at just the right rate.

"Those Taon ships are tough," Bradamont said. "They're taking a lot of hits and keep coming."

"It's a good thing our friend Lokaa is helping us out," Geary said.

"I wonder just how far the effective range is on those Taon energy weapons?" Desjani said as the xenophobe Taon ships raced to catch the human ships before they reached the jump point. "What do you think, Lieutenant Yuon?"

Yuon, startled, took a moment to reply. "I think we're going to be really close to finding out, Captain."

"Me, too," Desjani said. "Ensure forward shields are at maximum."

"Thirty seconds to the jump point," Lieutenant Castries said.

Geary saw an alert on his display as the destroyer *Bolo* took a hit from the closest xenophobe Taon ship as all of the enemy warships strained to get close enough to reengage the humans. *Bolo*, also hit during the fight with the enigmas, would be getting a reputation as a hard-luck ship.

"All units in Task Force Alpha," Geary sent, "initiate jump when we reach the jump point."

Two seconds later, as the xenophobe Taon unleashed a final barrage of shots, the jump drives lit up and the human fleet entered jump space back toward the last Dancer star system.

Desjani let out a long breath. "So, did we avoid starting another war or not?"

"I think maybe we did," Geary said. "But if those xenophobes would've gone after us regardless, I think maybe we made a very powerful friend."

"Do you think the xenos will chase us through jump?"

"Into Dancer space?" Geary said. "If they do, I think the Dancers will be very unhappy with them."

"That'd be fun to watch," Desjani said. "But the xeno Taon will probably be too smart to try that."

"Probably," Geary said.

IT seemed odd that returning to Dancer space had the feel of returning home, but that was how the crew seemed to take it now that the human ships were safe in jump space.

They didn't know what only a few people with this task force did, that back in Dancer space an attempt had likely already been made to undermine Geary's command and create hostilities with the Dancers.

Geary stopped by the cell where Kaliphur was still confined, and still revealing nothing. "Whatever you were supposed to accomplish isn't happening," Geary told him. "You're on the losing side. If you were smart, you'd talk."

He wasn't surprised when Kaliphur said nothing.

Chief Master-at-Arms Slonaker, seeing him, reported that no other sailors had been identified as having possibly been sympathizers or assistants to Inglis in his murder attempt. "Inglis claimed he didn't know any of the others," Slonaker said. "Maybe there weren't any others, just whoever was pulling Inglis's strings."

Geary would have liked to believe that, but knew he couldn't afford to. It was consistent with what had been learned of the conspirator cells aboard *Warspite*, though. Maybe there were only one or two other low-ranking cell members still left aboard *Dauntless*. Had Inglis gotten his orders from someone aboard this ship, or had they come from someone like Captain Pelleas or Captain Burdock as was apparently the case with Kaliphur? But there was no way of confirming such guesses as of yet. Hopefully when they reached Dancer space Captain Armus would have the answers.

It was fairly late in the ship's day after the long engagement escaping from the Taon star system. Geary, restless, worried about what was happening or had happened back in Dancer space, and with the alertness drugs not quite worn off, roamed the passageways of *Dauntless*, trying not to look concerned, talking to those members of the crew still up or those on watch.

"I thought we were dead for sure, Admiral," one petty officer admitted.

Me, too, Geary thought. But he laughed along with the sailors, because being alive was something worth being happy about.

Finding himself near the compartment holding the alien transmitter, Geary headed that way with a vague desire to speak with General Charban.

But with communications with the Dancers impossible while in jump space, the only person there at this hour was Dr. Cresida, absorbed as usual in some work she was doing on her comm pad.

He was about to leave, but hesitated.

That got her attention. Dr. Cresida looked up, appearing only mildly annoyed. "Do you need something?"

"I was wondering if I could ask you a question," Geary said.

"I don't see how I can stop you."

Taking that as a less-than-enthusiastic yes, Geary sat down. "Something's been bothering me about the discussions we've had on the Dancers. If you're right, from what we know their approach to quantum mechanics is wrong, which means their way of viewing the universe is at least partly wrong."

Dr. Cresida shrugged. "It would be more accurate to say that from our perspective their perspective on quantum mechanics is wrong."

"That's what's bothering me," Geary said. "If they're wrong, from our perspective, does that automatically mean we're right?"

"Not at all." Cresida scrunched her face up as she sought the right words. "We, humanity, are trying to understand how the universe works. Our knowledge of that remains imperfect. We have sets of rules, some of which contradict each other, that we can use. But for centuries we've sought a simple, clean theory that ties it all together, that will reconcile the contradictions. We haven't found it yet, meaning we're still missing something fundamental. There are those arguing that perhaps no such thing exists, that the universe is made up of a hodgepodge of different systems coexisting alongside each other, and the complex fundamental truth is that different rules exist for different aspects of the universe. Others, myself included, believe that a simple fundamental theory exists, but we haven't yet been able to see it because of the limitations of human perceptions. That doesn't mean we won't someday perceive it. At the least, I believe it would be a mistake to stop looking. But I can't yet prove my argument. Neither can those who believe differently."

Her words, the interplay of complex and simple, reminded him of something. "Someone once wrote that everything in war is simple, but all of the simple things are complicated."

That at least startled her. "That's an interesting insight into many things."

"Am I correct that you're implying that even though the Dancers' approach to quantum mechanics seems wrong to us, it might actually be right?"

"Yes." Dr. Cresida waited for a reaction of denial that Geary didn't provide. "It's not impossible that the Dancers are actually seeing deeper than we are, discerning some fundamental level of the quantum world in which the probabilities and uncertainties are resolved. I lack enough information to make such a call." Cresida paused, then shrugged again. "We do our best, Admiral, to find the underlying truth despite our own limitations. That's all we can do. Seeing how the Dancers view 'reality' can hopefully teach us something about how we view 'reality.' That's the best answer I can offer you."

"I see," Geary said, thinking about her words.

"Do you?"

"Yes." He stood up. "Thank you, Doctor. I guess what you said applies to everything humans do. We do our best, despite our own limitations."

"Perhaps."

"Why didn't you explain these things during the meeting?"

Dr. Cresida shook her head. "Because they carry the weight of the possibility that an alien species can see things, understand things, that humans can't. That would not be welcome news. You're probably not used to being the bearer of bad news, Admiral, but it is rarely welcomed."

He didn't know why he didn't get angry at her words. Maybe because they reflected such a fundamental misunderstanding. "Doctor, every time someone under my command has died, I have had to be the bearer of bad news to their families and loved ones. It is a very painful but important part of my responsibilities to those I command. I assure you that I fully appreciate the ache that comes with delivering bad news, because I have had to deliver far too much of it to far too many people."

Having said that, Geary turned to go, but stopped when Dr. Cresida spoke again in a voice that held an almost painful level of emotional control.

"How did my sister die, Admiral?"

He turned back to face her. "I sent a letter to the family with the details."

"I refused to read it," Dr. Cresida said. "It wasn't something I could face. But I want to know."

"We were at Varandal, trying to catch and defeat a Syndicate flotilla. The enigmas had caused the Syndic hypernet gate at Kalixa to destructively collapse, destroying almost everything in the star system, wanting the Syndics to blame the Alliance for the act. The Syndics had sent a retaliatory force to collapse the gate at Varandal, which could have set off a tit-for-tat cycle of revenge that would've wiped out both the Alliance and the Syndicate Worlds.

"We had to stop them before that happened. I formed all of the fleet's surviving battle cruisers, including this one, into a formation and charged to intercept the Syndics. We managed to catch them and engage them short of the hypernet gate, but we were facing bad odds. On one of the firing passes, the Syndics concentrated their fire on your sister's ship. *Furious* took too many hits in an instant's time, collapsing her shields and triggering a power core overload."

He stopped speaking, watching Dr. Cresida, who was now gazing fixedly at the far bulkhead. "An instant," she finally said. "Did . . . she know? Did she see it coming?"

"No," Geary said. "It happened too fast. No one saw it coming. We saw the aftermath. We'd already broadcast the instructions she'd developed on how to modify hypernet gates to prevent them from collapsing destructively. Your sister, Jaylen, gave her life to make sure that wouldn't happen again, not at Varandal, and not at any other star system, anywhere."

He waited, but Dr. Jasmine Cresida said nothing else, her eyes looking fixedly at the bulkhead.

He wondered what she was seeing.

Turning again, Geary left.

EIGHTEEN

AND so they returned to Dancer space.

Geary stared at his display as it updated, searching for any sign of what had happened while they were gone.

The rest of the fleet under the command of Captain Armus was in the same orbit and the same formation, all of the battleships sailing through space without any outward signs of trouble having occurred.

Did that mean nothing had happened? That the conspirators hadn't bitten on the bait offered them, and the danger remained unresolved? Had Ensign Duellos's disclosures been spotted by the conspirators, with terrible results for her? Or had the attempt been made and squashed? Though that last outcome didn't guarantee that Ensign Duellos had survived the showdown.

The fleet was orbiting one and a half light hours from this jump point. It would require three hours for the light showing the arrival of Geary's task force to reach Armus and his reply to reach Geary.

Three hours could be an incredibly long time.

With no grounds for delaying the inevitable, Geary sent out his report to Ambassador Rycerz to explain the battle damage visible on some of his ships. He wondered whether the outcome with the Taon would be described by others as successful first contact or as hostilities with a new species.

The first message *Dauntless* received after arrival didn't come from either Captain Armus or Ambassador Rycerz, though.

"The Dancers want to know what happened," General Charban told Geary, not bothering to hide his astonishment. "They're asking us. Their message came from one of the ships about twenty light minutes from the jump point that we arrived at. I'm trying to think how we can summarize everything in the way Dancers prefer communications. It will take a while."

"Why not send them right away a copy of the last conversation I had with Lokaa?" Geary said. "That's sort of the executive summary, isn't it? We worked things out with Lokaa, and had to escape from the xenophobe Taon."

Lieutenant Jamenson shook her head, her bright green hair flashing in the light of *Dauntless*'s "morning" interior illumination. "Not all Taon are Taon. We need to take the Dancers to task on that."

"How do you think the ambassador will react to what happened?" Charban asked Geary.

He shrugged. "We still don't know what happened here while we were gone." Of those present, only Lieutenant Iger knew the real significance of that statement. "As for what we went through in that Taon star system, I don't really care what the official reaction is. Retirement back on Glenlyon is looking real good this morning."

"I don't think the Alliance is done with you, Admiral," Lieutenant Jamenson said.

AS could be expected from Captain Armus, his report showed up exactly three hours and two minutes after the return of Geary's task force.

"Admiral, I'm attaching a detailed time line," Armus said, his expression impossible to read. "To summarize, four days after your departure Ensign Duellos aboard *Warspite* was given a package of malware to covertly insert into her ship's communications, fire control, weapons, and maneuvering control systems. She immediately passed the package to Captain Plant. The malware was swiftly analyzed and a protective patch sent out to all ships under the guise of a routine maintenance upgrade.

"Five days after your departure, a message was broadcast to this fleet purporting to be orders from you to engage the nearest Dancer ships, allegedly in retaliation for Dancer attempts to sabotage the fleet's systems. Simultaneously, malware packages aboard *Colossus*, *Dreadnaught*, *Conqueror*, and *Guardian* attempted to activate and disable the ships. As planned, those ships and *Warspite* all simulated being disabled. Captain Pelleas aboard *Gallant* broadcast that he was assuming command since *Colossus* and *Dreadnaught* had been disabled by a Dancer attack, directing the remaining battleships to independently move to engage the nearest Dancer ships. Pelleas was immediately seconded by Captain Burdock on *Encroach*, as well as by Commander Cui on *Magnificent*."

Captain Armus smiled slightly. "At that point, *Colossus*, *Dreadnaught*, *Conqueror*, *Guardian*, and *Warspite* ceased pretending to be disabled. I broadcast your command, recorded before you left, not to attack any Dancer ships, and informed all ships that I remained in command. I ordered all ships to remain in formation, and in the cases of *Gallant*, *Encroach*, and *Magnificent* ordered those three ships to return to their places in formation since they had all begun moving. After a slight delay, Captain Pelleas and Commander Cui acknowledged the order, claiming to have been fooled by the false order. Since Captain Burdock did not acknowledge the order, and *Encroach* continued to maneuver away from the formation, the Marine detachment aboard *Encroach* was ordered to immediately relieve by force of arms Captain Burdock from command of the ship. Since the attempted mutiny we have unraveled the cells aboard several warships, which proved to be mostly AI-driven false fronts and only a few real sailors, just as Captain

Plant suspected. A total of twenty-five personnel are under arrest, mostly junior sailors in addition to Captains Pelleas and Burdock and Commander Cui."

Armus's expression shifted to a frown. "Unfortunately, regarding Ensign Duellos—"

Geary felt something tight grab at his guts.

"Approximately twenty minutes after the attempted mutiny, word was passed through informal communication channels in the fleet that Ensign Duellos had been part of the conspiracy. Captain Plant and I believe some of the actual conspirators had belatedly discovered Duellos's part in foiling their actions and were seeking to have loyal personnel attack her in vigilante actions."

Armus paused, looking uncomfortable, while Geary waited with dread for the rest.

"I . . . took it upon myself," Captain Armus said, "to tell all ships that Ensign Duellos from her position within the conspiracy had provided the information needed to thwart it. This seemed the best way to protect her and prevent any other vigilante actions within the fleet by loyal personnel outraged by what they were hearing about the conspiracy. I subsequently learned that my words have been widely interpreted to mean that Ensign Duellos had joined the conspiracy under orders so as to assist in its detection and elimination. Ensign Duellos remains under guard but has not been physically threatened. An exhaustive search of *Encroach* uncovered another stealth suit matching that taken from the attempted assassin aboard *Dauntless*. No other suits were found and we believe that threat within the fleet has been neutralized."

Arwen Duellos was all right? Armus's discomfort had been over reporting his own use of initiative? Geary heard himself laughing while Desjani watched him with concern that shifted to relief.

"Ambassador Rycerz," Armus continued, "was told by me that there is no threat to her or *Boundless*, but has demanded a full report explaining what happened. I have informed her that I am working with all due deliberation on such a report.

"I have the honor to report that the conspiracy has been decapitated, if not eliminated, and this portion of the fleet remains ready and willing to carry out all lawful orders. I relinquish command of this force to you, though I will remain in local command until your task force rejoins us.

"To the honor of our ancestors. Armus, out."

"All is well," Geary told Desjani. He would have to let the rest of the ships in the task force that had gone to the Taon star system know what had happened here, but one particular person needed to be informed as quickly as possible. Geary entered a command to forward Armus's report to Captain Duellos on *Inspire*, adding a brief note at the beginning—*She's all right.*

Ambassador Rycerz's initial reaction wasn't received by Geary until his task force was less than one light hour from rejoining *Boundless*. The ambassador appeared to be reserved, clearly withholding judgment on what she had heard thus far. "While very glad to know you have brought all of your ships back safely," she said, "I am unclear as to whether we've acquired a new, friendly relationship with this Lokaa, exactly who Lokaa is, and whether the so-called xenophobe Taon are a threat outside of Taon-controlled space.

"I've also been made aware of events within your fleet here while you were gone that may have imperiled this mission," Rycerz added. "I expect a full report on those events, a report I have already requested and have yet to receive."

Not himself having any answers to the questions about the Taon, and recognizing the wisdom behind Armus's decision to slow-walk the report to Rycerz on the conspiracy, Geary decided to wait to discuss those things further with the ambassador until their ships were close enough for a real-time conversation.

Captain Duellos called in, looking much better than he had been. "All's well that ends, as they say. I've heard from some others in the fleet, congratulating me on my daughter's bravery, and I've heard from Arwen. She's upset to be cast as a hero when she considers herself as sharing in the blame. Arwen is still expecting to be charged for her earlier role in the conspiracy."

"She won't be," Geary said. "If I did that it would undercut Captain Armus by making it appear he was either fooled or deliberately lied about Ensign Duellos's role in shutting down the conspiracy. Neither of those things are true. What's important is that she didn't participate in any actions against the chain of command, and she risked her life to correct her mistake when she realized it. I consider the books balanced."

Duellos sighed with relief. "I am grateful to hear that."

"She's not out of danger," Geary said. "It's unlikely that we've caught everyone involved in it, and a revenge attack on her remains a real possibility. When we rejoin the fleet, I've asked Colonel Rogero and Kommodor Bradamont to speak with your daughter about precautions against assassination attempts."

There was still the matter of deciding what to do with Captain Pelleas, Captain Burdock, Commander Cui, and the others being held with them under arrest aboard *Tsunami*. Pelleas in particular had been well regarded in the fleet, so his fate would require careful thought. A firing squad was legally justified, but aside from other factors Pelleas, Burdock, and Cui had all served well during the war. There were times when legality and justice were not the same thing. Lieutenant Commander George was speaking with all of the prisoners who would talk. Whatever came of those talks might help decide what to do with each of the conspirators.

He expected some difficult conversations with Rycerz when the task force rejoined the rest of the fleet and *Boundless*, but *Dauntless* was still fifteen light minutes from *Boundless* when another message came in from the ambassador. She appeared both delighted and surprised, her words spilling out with unusual quickness. "Admiral, there's been a breakthrough. The Dancers have accepted our offer to establish *Boundless* here as an embassy ship. And they want to talk about formalizing their relationship with the Alliance. Their message said something about Lokaa's words. That seems to have made a difference to the Dancers. Do you know what the Dancers meant?"

Rycerz paused to inhale slowly. "There's something else. The Dancers sent us a star chart. I'm attaching it to this message. It's . . . a lot to absorb. We'll speak more on it later. Rycerz, out."

He called Desjani down to his stateroom before opening the attachment.

Over the table in his stateroom, a three-dimensional star chart covering a very wide swath of this arm of the galaxy appeared.

"That's the Alliance," Desjani said, pointing to the stars off to one side on the chart. "And that would be the Syndics, or what used to be all Syndic-controlled space. And that's where the Rift Federation is, next to the Callas Republic. This whole region must be human-occupied space. Doesn't look that big on this kind of scale, does it?"

"There's Sol," Geary said. "Old Earth's star." He looked around the borders of human-occupied space. "That would be the enigmas. And there are the other Kick stars the Dancers told us about."

"All of this is Dancer space?" Desjani said, running her hand through the stars. "Jack, this chart is priceless," she added, so overwhelmed that she used his first name in a professional setting. "People back in the Alliance are going to go nuts when they see this."

"Maybe it's not all good news," Geary said, his eyes on other groupings of stars. "This would be Taon space, I guess. But who is it who controls these stars across the Rift from the federation?"

"They've got plenty of stars under their control, whoever they are," Desjani said. "I guess we know now why none of the robotic probes sent across the Rift ever came back. And look here, this grouping. They're separated from human space by these stars that are farther apart than usual, but they control a lot of territory." She stepped back, eyeing the chart in its entirety. "You know what? Looking at this, it almost seems like humanity is surrounded. We didn't know it because of the distribution of stars that kept us from going in certain directions, but there are others everywhere."

Geary nodded slowly. "There are. The Dancers don't seem to know much about the regions on the other side of Sol, where planets were settled by those Shield of Sol fools. Humanity may still have room to expand that way. But everywhere else, we're facing potential trouble."

"Is this chart just knowledge," Captain Tanya Desjani said, "or is it a warning?"

Admiral John Geary shook his head. "I guess that's the next thing we have to find out."

ACKNOWLEDGMENTS

I remain indebted to my agent, Joshua Bilmes, for his ever-inspired suggestions and assistance, and to my editor, Anne Sowards, for her support and editing. Thanks also to Robert Chase, Kelly Dwyer, Carolyn Ives Gilman, Simcha Kuritzky, Michael LaViolette, Bud Sparhawk, Mary Thompson, and Constance A. Warner for their suggestions, comments, and recommendations.